NEMESIS

NEMESIS

ANNA BANKS

SQUARE
FISH

FEIWEL AND FRIENDS

NEW YORK

SQUARE
FISH

An imprint of Macmillan Publishing Group, LLC
175 Fifth Avenue, New York, NY 10010
fiercereads.com

Square Fish and the Square Fish logo are trademarks of Macmillan and
are used by Feiwel and Friends under license from Macmillan.

Our books may be purchased in bulk for promotional, educational, or business use.
Please contact your local bookseller or the Macmillan Corporate and Premium
Sales Department at (800) 221-7945 ext. 5442 or by e-mail at
MacmillanSpecialMarkets@macmillan.com.

Library of Congress Cataloging-in-Publication Data
Names: Banks, Anna, author.
Title: Nemesis / Anna Banks.
Description: New York : Feiwel and Friends, 2016. | Summary: "A futuristic
 fantasy in which the fate of the world's energy source is in the hands of a
 prince and princess who are rivals"—Provided by publisher.
Identifiers: LCCN 2015042553 (print) | LCCN 2016021198 (ebook) |
 ISBN 978-1-250-12969-7 (paperback)   ISBN 978-1-250-10609-4 (ebook)
Subjects: | CYAC: Fantasy. | BISAC: JUVENILE FICTION / Love & Romance. |
 JUVENILE FICTION / Science Fiction.
Classification: LCC PZ7.B2256 Nem 2016 (print) | LCC PZ7.B2256 (ebook) |
 DDC [Fic]—dc23
LC record available at https://lccn.loc.gov/2015042553

Book design by Anna Booth

Square Fish logo designed by Filomena Tuosto

Originally published in the United States by Feiwel and Friends

First Square Fish edition, 2017

1 3 5 7 9 10 8 6 4 2

LEXILE: 890L

For Maia, my most beloved person in the whole world,
and my favorite manuscript thief.

1

SEPORA

IF I WERE NOT SUCH A COWARD, I WOULD HURL myself from Nuna's back and plummet to the Underneath below. I would fall with purpose, headfirst on the rockiest part of the land. From this height, it would be painless. It would be swift.

It would prevent war.

But I am spineless, and so I urge my Serpen, Nuna, to fly higher and higher above the morning fog and mountaintops, which float against the sunrise and cast shadows like dark clouds onto the Underneath. Ah, the Underneath, that forbidden bit of land perched just beneath our mountains—mountains that are claimed by individual families or larger clans of families related in some way. Rope ladders sway in the wind all the way down, disappearing into the tall grass in places. If I weren't fleeing my home kingdom of Serubel, I'd be caught up in the beauty of it all, so high, scraping at what feels like the ceiling of the sky and looking down upon the monotony of the life I used to live, running through the grasses, throwing rocks into the River Nefari from the safety of Nuna's back, trampling over the undulating rope bridges connecting each of our mountains.

Yes, any other day, this would be a precious outing, a reprieve from Forging spectorium. Any other day, I would enjoy the freedom of flight, the time with Nuna, the endless possibilities of the morning.

But today will be the last of many things, and I mourn the loss of them already.

My thoughts wander again to far below us, far beneath the early mist and the waterfalls cascading into the River Nefari, to where my body should be sprawled, bloodied and lifeless and mauled. Yet, I tighten my hold on Nuna.

Saints of Serubel, but I am gutless.

Mother would have me believe otherwise: that it takes far more courage to hide, to live a life among the Baseborn class, who live in the poorest corner of our enemy kingdom Theoria. That the living conditions are rough, and the general mood of its residents even rougher. Those Serubelans who live there are not slaves anymore; stark poverty is what keeps them under Theorian control. If they could afford to, they would return to their homeland. If they could afford to, they would become citizens of Serubel again.

But I do not have that freedom. I can never return.

Not as long as Father wants to conquer the kingdoms. Not as long as I have what he needs to do so.

Nuna squirms beneath me as tears slip down my cheeks; she knows my feelings as well as I've come to know hers. She's beautiful, Nuna, even if she is a Defender. Most Defender Serpens are ugly, and not only because of their rugged training scars, but also because they are the color of the green mucus that seeps from noses when someone catches cold. Their spiked tails and thick underbellies resemble calluses instead of the glistening, pearly scales of other Serpens of different uses, and their facial features seem naturally arranged to be fierce, all arched brows and mouths set in an almost humanlike scowl.

But to me, Nuna could never be ugly, perhaps because I've handled her for ten years already, since a time before the weight of my body entrenched a natural saddle along her neck, just behind her head. Grandfather always said that time grew things, like trees and children and affection. Perhaps because of the time I've spent with her, my affection covers over Nuna's flaws. Oh, but it wasn't always so. When I was barely waist-high to my father, he announced that the entire royal family would ride Defenders henceforth to ensure our protection. I remember that day well, even though my understanding of the way of things was only proportionate to my age. I knew the people of Serubel were upset, and I knew it had been Father's doing. Father's decree had come as a shock—a king who felt he needed the protection of a Defender was concerning, especially after a fragile Trade Treaty between Serubel and Theoria had just been penned. It was a cold treaty, but one promising peace—and so why would His Majesty need a Defender Serpen all of a sudden? It put our people at unease, to say the least. But no one in the kingdom could have been more shocked than me, a quiet six-year-old princess, scared of Serpens in general and morbidly terrified of Defenders in particular. Politics were matters for the adults, but riding Defender Serpens was a most pressing concern for a child.

Still, Nuna struck me as different almost from the beginning. Her green coloring runs a bit deeper than the other Defenders', like fern leaves darkened by morning mist, and though she has the necessary scars from training to protect her royal rider, I had seen to it that the wounds were cared for and healed properly, so they are not as pronounced as the other Defenders'.

And when she sees me, I'd swear on the snowy caps of Serubel that she smiles.

Absently, I pet her head now as I spy the edge of the kingdom on the horizon. Where the grassy, rolling fields of Serubel end, that is where the Theorian desert begins. No, that is not entirely true. The kingdoms technically do not border each other; there is the Valley of the Tenantless that sweeps between the kingdoms, a vast, desolate dust bowl full of thickets and thorns and nothing of value and so uninviting and void that neither kingdom will lay claim to it. No one knows why this phenomenon occurs, where the bowl comes from, or what keeps it so bereft of life. Why the lush green grass of Serubel gives way to sand, then shriveling plants and prickly thorn bushes. Even the most intelligent of the Theorian scholars cannot solve the puzzle. And so the phenomenon is subject to rumors of a curse. Looking down upon the Tenantless from the safety of Nuna's back, I could convince myself of a true curse. But curse or no, I have to cross the valley to get to the Theorian desert—which, in my opinion, might be considered cursed itself.

Who would choose to live in such a dry, desolate place, I wouldn't know.

Perhaps it's fitting that I should flee to an afflicted, bleak kingdom. That if I should live, it will be among the Baseborn class of Theoria. That each day I should break my back for my portion of food and shelter and that I should become a slave to my own hunger and thirst.

Yes, it's fitting, and I want that for myself. I want that for myself more than I want an eternity in the cold recesses of the prison cell my father reserved for me. I want it more than the worry that he will soon grow tired of my resistance and perhaps trade my cell in favor of torturing me into Forging precious spectorium. I would rather hide in desolation and poverty, whether it be in the Baseborn Quarters or the Tenantless, than be the cause of thousands of deaths in all the five kingdoms.

And saints forgive me, I would rather hide than end my own life.

Nuna recognizes the boundary ahead of us—all Serpens are trained to halt at the sight of it—and she begins to slow, her three pairs of wings catching the wind instead of moving it. I coo into the small orifice that is her ear and bid her to land just before the grass fades into outstretched sand, the first of the overgrown thorn bushes standing guard in front of the rest of the valley.

Nuna cannot come any farther than this. If my father were to search for me, Nuna would be easily spotted, as I'd have to travel by air rather than by foot; she is much too big to navigate the thistles on the ground. Alone, though, I could hide among the thistles themselves, carefully of course, and from above be indiscernible and by ground be imperceptible.

It is the worst way to travel the valley, yet the best possible chance for escape. And so I dismount Nuna at the edge of the bushes.

According to my map, the kingdom of Theoria dwarfs the other kingdoms in size, though it's mostly desert and the population tends to accumulate in Anyar, where the River Nefari widens and cuts straight through. I'll follow the river to this capital city. I'll do as my mother says and I'll embrace this new life. She wants the best for me, Mother. But she also wants the best for Serubel.

And what is best for Serubel is that I never return.

I come around to face Nuna and rub her nose, which causes her tail to whip about in pleasure. Serpens have only wings, no hands or feet or hooves or claws. No limbs to scratch an itch or to self-groom—which makes them especially grateful for a good rubbing down. They enjoy being petted, bathed, touched. Serpens may look formidable, especially Defenders, but with their riders—their bonded riders, that is—they are as gentle as butterflies on a breeze.

And I will miss my Nuna.

I nuzzle the tip of her scaly nose with mine, which would be a ridiculous sight to see, I'm sure. Father would not approve. Even Mother might roll her eyes. And Aldon, my tutor, would sigh and mutter to himself, "Princess Sepora, a lost cause of a princess who treats her Defender as a pet." A pet that is longer than fifteen lengths of me, her head alone three times the size of my body—and so nuzzling really is a delicate matter indeed. But I need this one last comfort, this one last gift of affection from her, before I begin my journey.

She holds very still, careful not to open her mouth and expose her sickle-sharp teeth. I've had many stitches because of her accidental overexcitement, and while I usually do stay away from her mouth, this is a special occasion. "This is good-bye, my lovely friend," I whisper.

The words feel like a bite to my tongue, sharp and painful. Nuna nuzzles back, squirming to get as close to me as possible, slipping on the velvety sleekness of the undisturbed soft sand and losing traction. I step away from her. This is not good-bye for Nuna. She has no idea this will be the last time we see each other. She knows something is amiss, for I've never taken her this close to the border before. But she probably assumes I'll mount her soon, and we'll fly away together.

With my hands, I give her the signal to return to her holding on the far end of the mountains where all the Serpens are corralled. No one must know she's been out this morning. No one must know Mother flew her to my cell to aid me in my escape.

Nuna is not happy with my command and protests with a high-pitched squeal. She's leery of the boundary still, as she should be. I shake my head at her, firmly, and make the signal again. Another tear streaks all the way down to my throat when she slithers backward, away from me. She watches me then, blinking once, as if to give me time to change my mind.

I gesture again for her to go.

I watch after her for a long time as she glissades through the air, leaving me behind. I watch until I can't see her any longer. Then I turn toward the Tenantless. Toward my new life. And I take the first step.

2

TARIK

TARIK MAKES HIS WAY TO HIS FATHER'S BED-
chamber in the farthest wing of the palace, the tension building
with each barefoot step. Behind him, Patra pads along quietly, stealth-
ily, the way only a feline could, pausing to stretch and let out an
enormous, soundless yawn that brings the muscles in her back taut,
the golden sheen of her coat glistening in the candlelight. Despite
Patra's great size, Tarik suspects if his giant cat had the notion, she
could sneak up on the wind. He waits for her yawn to subside, his lips
curling up in a grin.

"You didn't have to come with me," he tells her, and she responds
by nudging his palm with her nose, leaning down to do so as it
were, since her head nearly reaches the height of his shoulder. Even
though it's late in the evening and Rashidi's messenger had put
her on alert, she purrs at his side, recognizing that they are going to
visit Tarik's father—something they've done together since he was
a boy.

They walk past the towering marble columns and the layered
stone fountains illuminated with small pyramids of spectorium and,

finally, the rows of guards on either side of them leading up to his father's door, swords and shields at the ready. *They can protect my father from any outside intruder,* Tarik thinks bitterly. *But they cannot protect him from the thing inside him, asking him for his life day after day.* Not even the Healers at the Lyceum can figure out what is killing the king of Theoria. Even they, of the Favored Ones, are powerless against this new illness.

The two soldiers standing at the great wooden barrier pull the ornate handles and open it wide for their prince and his feline companion, the hinges creaking loud enough to wake the statues in the massive garden outside.

His father's magnificent bed is at the end of the cavernous room, and it takes Tarik and Patra several more moments to reach it. Taking the steps up to the bed quietly, Tarik motions for Patra to stay behind. She obeys, spilling out onto the floor and resting lazily on her side as she watches him. Rashidi, his father's most trusted adviser, sits on the edge of the bed holding the king's hand. Tarik does not like this rare show of affection from Rashidi, does not want to consider what it must mean for his father's health.

"The Falcon Prince has arrived, my king," Rashidi whispers.

Tarik shakes his head, taking a place next to Rashidi. He cannot recall a single time his father has ever actually called him the Falcon Prince, not since he gave him the title when Tarik was but seven years. "You see into matters with the eyes of a falcon," he'd said. "Knowing discernment when others allow room for ignorance." The name had caught on in the palace and then throughout Theoria, and though he doesn't feel deserving, he could never admit such a thing to a father who had been so proud.

"Let him sleep," Tarik says, absorbing that the great King Knosi, in his weakened state, now takes up so little of the bed.

"I would, my prince, but he has summoned you for a reason," Rashidi says softly.

"The reason can wait until morning," Tarik says, already knowing what the old adviser will say. He doubts his father summoned him at all but rather it was Rashidi's need for tradition, for formalities that brings him to the bedchamber this night. Tarik cannot imagine, though, that his father will even wake, much less speak the decree making his firstborn son the new king of Theoria.

"I'm afraid it cannot, Highness."

"Please, Rashidi. I will never get used to you calling me Highness and meaning it." As the royal family's closest friend, Rashidi had had the displeasure of knowing Tarik when he was a boy. A very rambunctious boy.

The old man laughs. "Perhaps you are not a Lingot after all, my prince. Surely you would know my insincerity."

Tarik snorts. Rashidi wants to convince him that he doesn't mean *Highness*, that he is not officially acknowledging him as a ruler of Theoria. But as Rashidi said, Tarik is a Lingot. He can distinguish a truth from a lie, and right now, Rashidi is telling the truth. He is indeed calling him Highness. And he does indeed mean it.

"My father will recover from this," Tarik says, recognizing the lie in his own voice. Rashidi does not have to be a Lingot to notice.

"No," Rashidi says. "The Healers do not think him to live through the night."

"The Healers have been wrong before." Haven't they? Tarik is not sure.

Rashidi sighs. It is full of pity, Tarik can tell. Sometimes he wishes he didn't have the ability to deduce so much—even from body language. Rashidi is always composed, but tonight, there is an almost imperceptible slump to his shoulders. Rashidi feels defeated. Tarik swallows hard.

"Your father has requested that if he ceases to breathe this night, we will not summon the Healers. You understand what this means, Highness."

"I'm not ready, Rashidi." Not ready to lose his father. Not ready to rule as king of Theoria. At eighteen years old, he has been groomed all his life for kingship. But that was supposed to be in an official ceremony whereby his father would relinquish power to his firstborn heir—an heir that would be at least thirty years old by then, if circumstances permitted. Eighteen years or thirty years makes no difference to Tarik. A lifetime of preparation is not enough to make one ready to oversee an entire kingdom of living, breathing people who depend on the decisions he makes. The risks he takes.

The risks he doesn't take.

"What your mind does not yet know, your heart will make up for," Rashidi insists. "You prove you have the wisdom to rule by admitting that you are not ready to do so. The people love you. Let them support you."

Tarik mulls over Rashidi's words and finds them to be true. The adviser believes the people of Theoria do love their prince, and Rashidi is confident in his ability to act as king. It's reassuring, if only a little, that Rashidi is so steadfast. He is, after all, an advocate of the people first and foremost and adviser to his king second.

"The people do not know me," Tarik feels obligated to say. The people know a boy who takes after his mother. A skilled Lingot. A dutiful son. But they do not know his ability to rule as king. How could they?

Rashidi waves in dismissal. "I well know you, boy. I speak for the people. You'll not disappoint." The truth, or at least what Rashidi sincerely believes to be true.

Tarik places a hand on the linen next to his father's legs and leans on it for support. The king's breaths come in shallow, wheezing whispers, and Tarik is sure it does not help that the air is so hot and so very dry. A trickle of blood seeps from his nose, and Rashidi dabs at it with a damp cloth. The bleeding from his ears and mouth has lessened, but Tarik suspects it's because his father doesn't have much blood left to give.

Rashidi is right. It will not be long now. "What will I tell Sethos?" Tarik whispers. His younger brother, Sethos, just turned fifteen years and is, by far, the most precious object of their father's affections. A son after his father, Sethos is. King Knosi was a great warrior, and so Sethos will be. And so Sethos already is. He studies his craft at the Lyceum with the other Majai Favored Ones. His tutors are pleased with his progress. Father is pleased with his progress. Father will not like missing out on his youngest son.

It is time Tarik summoned Sethos home. He will want to be present when their father dies. It has been difficult enough keeping him away this long. But Father had insisted he continue on at the Lyceum. Father never imagined this sickness would progress so quickly.

Rashidi bows his head. "I will call for him, Highness." A slight pause. Then, "Will you tell the people what took him?"

On this Tarik is torn. It is something he's given a great deal of thought to, and guiltily so. For if he was worried what he would tell the people, he was more certain than he cared to admit of his father's death. All he really knew, though, was that he could not shrug the thought from his shoulders.

"I fear it will cause a panic," he says finally. After all, the kingdom sees his father as the epitome of strength and power, as they should their pharaoh. They may reason that if King Knosi can perish from such a disease, they cannot protect themselves from it. Yet, is that not the truth? If the illness has such far-reaching fingers, surely no one is safe. "On the other hand, if I don't tell them, I fear they won't give this the proper attention it deserves. They will carry on their lives as if he perished from some common illness. What if this new sickness spreads?" His father had just returned from the southern kingdom of Wachuk to negotiate the continued mining of turquoise there. It would be an easy thing to make the people assume he'd contracted something from that place. Wachuk's methods of medicine are primitive at best, and disease is rife there, a fact well-known among the citizens of Theoria.

But the Healers have ruled out any foreign infection. His father has something new, something they've never seen before. Still, if he instructs them, they will speak nothing of it.

"The people need not give it attention so much as the Healers do," Rashidi says. "It would be unwise to circulate news of a plague that our Healers do not have under control just yet."

Just yet. "And if the people begin to present symptoms?" They'd only had a handful of cases and all had been inside the palace walls, easy enough to contain. Easy enough, that is, until his father contracted it. Tarik remembers the day his father suffered his first nosebleed. The king had waved it off, dismissed it as if it were a soldier or a servant, as if such a thing could be controlled with a command. "It's nothing but an inconvenience," he'd said. "Fetch my Healer at once and tell him to put a stop to it." It had taken the Healer two frustrating hours to stop the bleeding. That night, his father had awakened with blood pooling in his ears. From that point on, he'd grown fatigued but refused food to help his energy because he could do nothing but wretch up even the smallest of bread crumbs. Within a week, a sturdy beast of a man who'd personally trained his own guard had wilted into something that resembled a weed with bones.

Tarik swallows.

"By then, the Healers will have found the cure. They always do, Highness."

But it doesn't sit well with him. Hiding something from his people, especially something so lethal, does not seem like the best way to begin his reign as their new king. Not to mention, the Lingots will know something is amiss. There are always ways to bend truths, but they will sense deception coming from the palace. And what message will that send?

"What else do you require from me this evening, Highness?" Rashidi seems aware he is not going to convince Tarik of anything at this moment. He is often shrewd in that way, to know when his usefulness has met its threshold and when to excuse himself. It is obvious now that King Knosi will not be waking up again to do the formal bidding of his most loyal adviser.

Tarik sighs in resignation. "A miracle."

Rashidi leaves him then, alone with his thoughts and worries. Alone with his father for the last time.

3

SEPORA

THE THORNS PULL AND TEAR AT MY SERVANTS' dress (Mother had known it wouldn't do to escape dressed as royalty) as I make my way through the Valley of the Tenantless. The path is beaten enough for me to conclude that something roams these parts, though not often, because the tracks are just holes puncturing the sand in some places. No, this trail hasn't been used in quite some time. Which is neither here nor there; if I came across trouble, I could defend myself. Mother gave me a dagger and a sword, and I've been trained in all the delicacies of fighting off a man. In fact, all Serubelan women are trained to wield a sword at the age of thirteen. Aldon says the other kingdoms think it barbarous to expect our females to fight, but Father insists it's a Serubelan tradition, and one that he'll not do away with, in view of the unsturdy times. I suppose if I could protect myself against a man, I could protect myself against a dumb beast that has no sense of what my next move will be. Besides, I'm not so concerned with staying on the trail as I am with keeping alongside the River Nefari. I could find Theoria without a map, just keeping that river to my right at all times.

The trail simply makes it easier to navigate the thistles until I hit desert, until I hit the boundary of Theoria.

Theoria. I've been wandering through the Tenantless thinking of my new home, trying to imagine all the things Aldon, my tutor, tried to instill in me during our history lessons. It goes something like this, I think:

Untold ages ago, the Serubelan king at the time and his highest councillor had a falling out. The councillor (whose name survived generation after generation of being written in the copyist's scrolls, only to elude my own limited memory at the moment) broke away from his king and led nearly one third of the Serubelan people beyond the Valley of the Tenantless and into the desert. He set out to prove that even under the harsh living conditions, he and his followers, who named themselves Theorians because of their willingness to try many theories on how to execute efficient rulership, could still provide citizens with a kingdom superior to Serubel in every way. Many of the great thinkers of Serubel joined the high councillor, including none other than the princess of Serubel. Indeed, she actually married the high councillor—oh yes, Vokor was his name—and remained at his side while he established his kingdom. But the bliss of marriage and rulership did not last long; she died within months of becoming his wife.

When the king of Serubel caught wind of the demise of his daughter, he blamed Vokor for tickling her ear and persuading her to leave the safety of her home. The king immediately set out for the desert in pursuit of war with Vokor. But somehow Vokor's fledgling army prevailed; rumor holds that he used unscrupulous trickery and dark magic to win. Aldon, who is not given to belief in magic or trickery, suspects that Vokor simply was expecting the king, and having been on the war council, knew the king's most likely moves and countered them with vigor. Vokor captured nearly one half of the Serubelan army and immediately pronounced them slaves, setting them to work on the great pyramids of the city of Anyar and beyond. (It is said that Vokor believed his precious Healers could find a cure for death, and so he made pyramids and kept the dead there, including his beloved princess, until one day they could rise again. As of my last history lesson with Aldon, that had not yet occurred.)

The defeat left a bitter taste in the mouths of my Serubelan ancestors, and Serubel has considered Theoria its enemy ever since. Though the actual fighting had come to an end, and trading eventually did open up again, it was with a cold and polite unease that we've traded spectorium for the splendor of Theoria's riches. It was even rumored that King Knosi had released the Serubelan slaves and invited them to return to Serubel, and while Aldon believes it to be true, my father is vehement that the decree, too, was some sort of trickery, because why else would slaves remain in Theoria instead of returning to their home kingdom?

It's a question I intend to answer, as it is to the Baseborn Quarters I flee now, where the freed ancestors of the Serubelan slaves live and work and die. Slaves to their lot in life, Aldon suspects, instead of to any master.

It is not lost on me that I do not have to live as my brethren in Theoria. I am a Forger of spectorium, the last Forger, and I could produce enough of this valuable element to make me very rich in that kingdom. But with wealth comes more than fine clothing and nicely appointed chariots; with it comes attention and even scrutiny. And under scrutiny, my ability becomes a danger to all.

Aldon used to say that my Forging makes me powerful. Perhaps that is true, but in light of the circumstances, it is nothing more than a lonely burden. No one can know that I alone possess the capacity to Forge. In fact, no one can know that a mere person possesses the capacity to Forge at all; the world must continue to think spectorium is mined from deep caverns in the Underneath in a secret location in Serubel.

And as I am the last Forger, no one can share with me the responsibility of keeping spectorium safe from those with ill intentions. I'm a Forger of spectorium. And I have become its last protector.

Soon, trading for spectorium will come to a halt. Father will run out of it without me there to make it for him. Leaving will stop the war, but it will also stop the trading. How will Serubel survive without trading? But how will Serubel survive if I stay and Forge enough for a mighty war? My father is ravenous with the need for power; he would stop at nothing to get what he wants. Theoria would be razed, its citizens bowing at his feet. And who knows if the war would stop there? Perhaps Father would extend his power to all the five kingdoms. People would die. Father would kill them, and I would give him the means to.

And so I continue on with my escape.

Churning the history lesson over and over in my head, I kneel to the ground. The Tenantless sun beats down upon me while I dig a hole in the sand with my bare hands. It has been mere hours since I last Forged and though I still have many more hours before I'll become faint and weak with the power building up inside me, I want to expel as much as possible while I'm alone in the valley and can hide my gift. Besides, stopping to Forge and bury the evidence is a good excuse to rest. The heat is more taxing than I'd supposed it would be, especially in the long, modest servants' attire Mother had given me, and I've not even stepped foot upon the Theorian desert. Sweat trickles from my temples, down my throat, down my back. If the Theorians are as clever as their reputation, they'd have picked a more hospitable place to live. If it gets much hotter, I will think them foolish indeed.

Father always did say they were too proud to admit folly. Perhaps Father was right about some things.

The increasing heat is enough to make me miss my Serubel even more. The cool mountains and faces of rocks devoured by vines full of wild orchids and broom brush and campion flowers so vivid in color they could be made of spectorium itself. The smell of the ravines; the air gravid with the aroma of a blossoming spring. I miss running across the rope bridges swinging precariously between the mountains, the fleeting sensation of flying when my feet lift from the safety of the boards. What could there be in uppity Theoria, among their sophisticated machines and complicated inventions, that is more beautiful than a simple, vibrant gully? For the smartest kingdom among us, they seem to overlook a great deal in the wake of their search for knowledge.

I dismiss the thought of Theoria and its haughty ways as I summon the liquid element deep inside me and direct it toward my palms. The spectorium seeps out in beads, as sweat on a forehead, building and collecting in a pool in my hand, an accumulation of all the colors in a rainbow with the indiscernible colors in between, glowing brilliant white and metallic at the same time. It feels refreshing to release, a cool rush of energy that opens my pores and slides out as though I were a faucet at the well. Because spectorium attracts spectorium, it amasses the static energy it creates, allowing it to float between my hands. I spin it into a ball and poke at it, trying to decide if I will just deposit it into the ground or if I shall make something. Before I know it, I'm structuring a figurine of Nuna in flight. I stretch and smooth the runny spectorium before it solidifies. With my thumbs, I press and prod the element into a replica no longer than my arm.

The wings are the most difficult to shape and I make them as thin as possible, blowing on them to cool quickly.

She really is beautiful, my miniature glowing Nuna. I decide to keep her, this small statue, to bring her with me on my journey. It goes against Mother's instructions and really, against my better judgment, but as soon as I set the eyes, I know she can be a substitute companion for me. I place her aside in the sand to cool as I expel more liquid spectorium into the small, deep pit I've dug. In the Tenantless heat, the puddle takes longer to cool, but gradually it begins to congeal at the bottom and solidify fully as I fill the trench with bright molten energy.

Energy that I must hide from the world for the rest of my life.

Yet, I cannot be entirely sorry for it. There was a time when spectorium was not understood, and the kingdoms survived without it. Serubel, because of the shelter and defense that our mountains naturally provide. Theoria, because of its advances in science and numbers and architecture. Hemut, because of brief moments of ingenuity and scads of time and experience gathered in the aptitude of simple survival in a land covered in ice. Wachuk, because of a primitive nature requiring only the barest of necessities, and because of its citizens' peaceable beliefs. And Pelusia, because of the ocean at its fingertips, which carries with it fish and trade by sea to the Foreign Kingdoms. I rarely count Pelusia as part of our five kingdoms, because it is so far north and it chooses to seclude itself entirely from the rest of us. Even when spectorium became recognized as a source of great power, Pelusia never bothered to trade for it.

All the kingdoms survived before spectorium, I remind myself. They will all survive again.

After the element has completely solidified, I cover the hole and spread around the remaining dirt, taking care to walk on it, leaving footprints in the direction I'll be heading. The blustering desert wind will soon smooth over any evidence that the area had been disturbed at all, making ripples in the sand like natural steps ascending toward a peak. I take a sip from my water jug and consult my map of Theoria once more, hoping perhaps this time something will have changed, that I'll be closer to Anyar than I'd originally thought. But if I'm still in the Valley of the Tenantless, I have much, much farther to go. For a brief moment, I am homesick, for I'm closer to the comfort of my castle and Nuna than I am to my new home in the Baseborn Quarters of Theoria.

But the only comfort I can take now is that I'm no longer within my father's reach. As Mother said, he'll never suspect that I've headed in the direction of Theoria, his greatest nemesis, the kingdom that fuels his hate. He'll never think to look for me in the Baseborn Quarters, where the freed slaves of the old war still reside. And he'll never suspect that Mother helped. To my father, Mother is a waif, a servant with a title. She does as she's told. No, Mother would not defy Father. I'd be a fool to think that she helped me flee out of some sort of maternal affection; the fate of Serubel is her concern. Father will think I've flung myself into the Nefari far below my cell, which opened over a steep cliff. Father will think me dead.

Oh, if only he hadn't been so greedy. If only he'd been content with his own kingdom instead of conquering others. If only he'd been reasonable. Then I would not be on this wretched journey to begin with.

4

TARIK

TARIK GRIPS THE LEDGE OF THE ROYAL CHARIOT and looks up at the small gathering of clouds overhead. They'll not actually erupt into rain, he knows, for it never rains in Theoria, but even the skies seem to acknowledge the kingdom's great loss in the death of King Knosi.

Beside him, Sethos stands stiff, his jaw locked. It has been a long time since his brother was required to wear the ceremonial gold and silver body paint of the royal family. In fact, it was at their mother's funeral that he last wore it, and being only a boy, he'd smudged it before even leaving the palace for the procession to the pyramids. "You are sure you called in only the best embalmers?" Sethos whispers. The horses meet a bump in the pathway, and Sethos is forced to grip the ledge, too.

Tarik fixes his gaze on the elaborate gold-plated cart ahead of them. The cart that bears the king's body to its final destination in the Canyon of Royals. "He will be well preserved for many years," Tarik says softly, knowing his brother needs reassurance but unsure of how much he'll actually accept. "Surely long enough to find the cure for death."

Sethos nods, as though this is what he'd been truly meaning to ask. If anyone in the five kingdoms could undo death, their Healers could. No other realm has come even close to the advanced knowledge of the healing sciences that the Lyceum has gathered over the centuries. And as soon as his father drew his last breath, Tarik had already doubled the resources designated to the Lyceum to perform its research—all the resources he could divert from the living, that is.

But this new illness has left the walls of the palace and now creeps through the Superior class, Rashidi reports. Some perish sooner than the King had; some last a few days longer. All suffer greatly. All waste away, losing blood and vitality before their families' eyes.

Yet, it does not appear contagious; the servants attending their masters and those closest to the sick are not falling ill.

"Curious," Tarik says more to himself than to Sethos.

His brother looks at him sideways; to be having a conversation during the funeral procession would be disrespectful. Tarik bows his head against the hypocrisy—his brother had, after all, spoken not a minute before—careful to keep the rest of his thoughts to himself. Sethos's body language seems to beg for privacy and silence. He is not taking the death of their father well; he would not appreciate an accounting of symptoms their father suffered before he died, and how some in the kingdom seem to be immune.

Tarik himself has not had time to mourn. In the days since King Knosi's passing, he's been rushed to session after session of council gatherings. His coronation ceremony was a hurried, informal affair to which the public—and surrounding kingdoms—had not been invited.

If it had not been for Rashidi, Tarik is certain he would have buckled under the pressure.

Rashidi continues to disagree. "You were born a ruler," he insisted. Something else Rashidi sincerely believes. But Tarik has not had time to correct his father's—and now his—closest adviser. He has not had time to take in a decent meal, either. A fact that his stomach reminds him of now—and loudly.

Sethos cuts him a look as if he'd done it on purpose, as if somehow the people gathered along the procession road could hear it above their wails and weeping as the chariot passes by.

He sighs. Sethos relieves anxiety through combat. He always has, and he's probably looking for a reason to start a brawl with his brother, king or not. Tarik knows if his brother can make it through one public appearance without causing a scandal, he will count himself fortunate. Sethos's moods have the tendency to swing as if on a hinge, and he can go from brooding to elated within moments—and brooding nearly always means a display of temper. It's his only flaw, as far as Tarik can tell, but a crippling one at times. Even his tutors complain of it. But their father never kept Sethos on a leash. And neither will Tarik. No matter how many moans and groans he hears from the council.

He will allow his brother to mourn in his own way—as long as his now-clenched fist does not make it to Tarik's jaw on this day.

5

SEPORA

I'M NOT OF THE TRAVELING SORT, I DECIDE AS I stop for the second time in as many hours to rub my aching feet. My calves burn with the task of digging my feet out of the sand with each heavy step. I haven't eaten in three days. I would trade enough spectorium to build one of the legendary Theorian pyramids for a single apple or a sliver of smoked meat. I'm out of water again, too, which means I'll have to brave the banks of the River Nefari to refill my jug.

The river is a fickle snake of water, widening in places and thinning in others, flowing straight for a day or two, only to become a winding stream, with strong visible currents lapping at the surface. Sometimes the water runs brown and muddy, and sometimes it changes to a deep red. I get drinking water only when it runs clear, and not just because it tends to taste better.

River Nefari is home to the Parani—evil, finned creatures with webbed hands and humanlike faces and a craving for the flesh of a man. I've never actually seen one, but I've heard stories about them and they are the stuff of nightmares.

In Serubel, parents warn children of the river by telling the tale of Ragan, the boy who was dared to swim in the river alone. While his taunting friends watched from shore, he made his way across the stream, taking care not to splash too much for fear he would alert the Parani to his presence. Even so, right before he reached the other side, he disappeared from the surface as if snatched under. Within minutes, two Parani sprang toward the bank where the other children stood screaming, and with one steady hoist, they tossed the full skeleton of Ragan at them, the bones clattering at their feet. The only flesh left was the skin keeping the hair attached to the skull.

It's with this in mind that I head toward the river with my jug, feeling fearful yet silly and superstitious all at the same time. Steps away from where the water meets shore, I glance around me and unsheathe my sword. If a Parani wants to surprise me, well then, I'll surprise it, too. With sword in one hand and jug in the other, I take the last few steps toward the river, squatting to refill my jug. The water is warm and not unpleasant, and it takes all my willpower not to drink it as soon as I've collected enough to gulp down. Uneasily, I keep my eyes on the river flowing past me, looking for shadowy figures below the surface or splashes of movement above it.

I see nothing. For several timeless moments, I stay and watch the waves and the current and the water separating me from the opposite embankment. Fear ebbs away from me as if caught up in the flow of the river. The story of Ragan simply could not be true. It would take more than a few moments to separate a boy from his flesh, and if the Parani were so predatory then why hadn't anyone else ever been eaten? Certainly not because all children obeyed their parents and stayed away from the river henceforth. I knew a servant boy who would exercise the Defenders and come back from the Underneath with hair as wet as a mop and sopping clothes to match. I told Aldon once about the boy and Aldon had said that sometimes young men get the ideas of bravery and stupidity horribly mixed up. But he didn't deny that the boy swam the Nefari when he went to the Underneath.

The Nefari is clear here, and the bed of it is full of round pebbles with small aquatic plants that look like weeds sprouting in between them. A bath would be nice. I've no soap, but mud would do for scraping most of the dust from me, and my hair might be more manageable if it were wet. It's in sore need of rebraiding as well.

I could keep my sword with me and be watchful. I could be quiet as a cloud. And I could be clean.

I set down my leather satchel and place my water jug next to it. Bathing nude is risky. Aside from the obvious exposure to unexpected strangers, it makes for a sloppy getaway in the unlikely case of a Parani attack. If, of course, I make it out alive, which, if I'm to believe the tale of Ragan, is also highly unlikely. And, well, my clothes need a thorough rinsing if truth be told, and if I do it now, they'll have time to dry before it gets cold. The Theorian desert is a flat, parched, unforgiving adversary during the day but at night is when it becomes truly miserable. At night is when the crawling and slithering and flying creatures come out, and the air is so cold you can see your breath in the moonlight.

Despite all of this, I convince myself that a bath is a good idea. Not only a good idea, but an absolute necessity. The only things I remove are my tattered, worn servants' shoes. Shoes that were meant for padding around the castle floors and across bridges and perhaps into the Serpen stables, but were never intended to walk for days across the Tenantless or traverse across a scalding desert whose tiny grains embed themselves into my feet, in between my toes, rubbing the skin there red and raw.

At first the water stings the blisters that gnaw on my heels, and I gingerly scrub the sand out of the open welts. I breathe a sigh of relief as the pain begins to subside and my feet become used to being unrestrained. The pebbles feel smooth and inviting and before long I'm completely submerged, basking in the way my body feels weightless instead of encumbered by the terrible burden of my own flesh and limbs I've been dragging around for days.

Slowly, I dig a hole underneath the pebbles and get to the muddy riverbed, scooping up a handful of the rough silt. I tackle my face first, scrubbing it violently until I'm sure it will shine in the midday sun. Next I scour my arms and legs and neck, careful not to get mud inside my clothing. Rinsing is a thorough affair, and I spend more time doing it than I do actually cleaning myself. My servant dress is lavender linen, and the stains easily disintegrate from it in the warm water with some wringing and twisting.

Feeling pleased and refreshed, I untangle my braid and begin to sort it out into something more manageable. Just as I tie the end back in place, an immense dunking sort of splash, a mere Serpen-length away, startles me from my vanity. A bit of terror steals through me as I imagine a large fin making just that size ring of ripples swelling outward ahead of me. It was something big. It was something that isn't *there* anymore, something that could be *here* now. Part of me wants to tear out of the river as fast as I can, to put distance between myself and the ripples. The other part knows that would be a mistake. That the clamoring sounds of escape would only attract attention to myself.

But so will the sound of me trembling in the water, of my teeth chattering in fear, of my throat closing around a whimper of desperation to flee. These are things I cannot keep quiet, these are things that no longer fall under my control and so if I'm to be loud, I'll be loud while retreating to the safety of the riverbank. Making no further attempt to keep quiet, I leave my sword abandoned in the water—oh why had I put it down in the first place?—and sludge toward shore and—

Run directly into the largest man I've ever seen. My head doesn't even reach his shoulders. Where the water hits my waist, it hits him at the groin. With the sun shining behind him, I can only make out his gigantic silhouette. But I do recognize when he raises a fist above him. And I wait for the blow.

6

TARIK

SETHOS HOISTS HIMSELF UP ON THE BALCONY rail and settles against the column at his back. He pops a grape into his mouth and gives Tarik an expression sweet enough to match the fruit. It is an odd feeling, to be entertaining his brother in the king's day chambers—a place Sethos had never been allowed. This is where decisions are made, wars are planned, peace is negotiated. It is not a place for boys. At least, it hadn't been a few weeks ago.

"You know what would help with all this tension," Sethos says after a while.

"I hadn't noticed any tension," Tarik says absently, moving some scrolls aside to review more of them on the table at which he sits. No wonder Father was always busy, even taking scrolls to his bed in the evenings.

"You may be able to discern a lie, brother, but you certainly cannot tell one. Anyhow, I was thinking how much stress would be relieved after a visit to your new harem."

"It's Father's harem, and there is nothing new about it."

"It's your harem now, Tarik."

A harem. Out of all the responsibilities and obligations Tarik inherited, his brother is most concerned with a harem. A harem full of beautiful women with beautiful mouths to feed: a burden in its own right, as far as Tarik is concerned. "You're too young to be visiting a harem, even if I could change the law to allow it." But the law is, and always has been, that the king is the only man who may look upon the royal harem. The king, and eunuchs. When Tarik asked to dissolve it and send the women on their way, Rashidi had laughed. Apparently when one is king, one must keep a harem as a matter of prestige.

"Rashidi says you haven't even visited. It's your duty to inspect your own harem," Sethos says, pouting a bit.

"I don't want to speak of duties just now. Or harems."

"You've always been the odd child."

"And you've always been the obnoxious one."

Sethos grins. "A boy after his father."

"That couldn't be more true." Their father wasn't known for his discretion and was delighted when he'd found that Sethos had the same temperament. It was an easy relationship between them.

With Tarik and his father, not so much. It wasn't that the king wanted his heir to be more like his second born; he recognized their differences and accepted them. But Tarik had always gotten the distinct impression that he was not all that he could be to his father, even in his own way. Rashidi says it was because Tarik is so much like his mother that he was a painful reminder of her death to King Knosi. His mother had been a Lingot and was very useful to his father at court. She had trained Tarik when his Favor was first discovered, but after she died three years after giving birth to Sethos, his education had been turned over to the Lyceum. The king was proud of Tarik, he'd said as much and Tarik could discern he spoke the truth. But there was always the impression he could be doing more.

That he could *be* more. And he's not sure he disagrees.

"Did you hear that the princess of Serubel fell to her death? What was her name? Magar, was it?" Sethos asks.

Tarik nods. "Rashidi informed me." A terrible accident, he'd heard. Somehow she'd fallen off her flying beast and down to the Underneath; the River Nefari apparently ran close by as she'd evidently been swept away by the current. As far as Tarik had heard, they never recovered the body. She probably became a royal meal to the Parani lurking there, is what the rumors say, and Tarik is obliged to agree with them.

Rashidi had made him send a caravan of condolence gifts, even though the Serubelan king had failed to acknowledge the death of King Knosi. "We are not the barbarians," Rashidi had reminded him. Not that Tarik was set against sending condolences, but an entire caravan for a princess he'd never even met? The fact was, most people had never met her. Most thought her a recluse or a snob. Though she met with a tragic end, Tarik can't help but be more interested in the fallout of the catastrophe. Since the princess's death, the Serubelan king has not traded out his spectorium—and Theoria relies on spectorium for many things, including the research of the Healers.

"She was supposed to be beautiful," Sethos is saying, daydreaming at the sky. "Rumor has it that her beauty is why her father never allowed her outside the kingdom. That he planned to marry her to the king of Hemut, and so he hid her away from company and such."

Tarik analyzes the rumor, turning it over in his mind. Sometimes he can discern the truth from secondhand information, but not always. It usually depends on how much the person relaying the message believes it. And Sethos wants to believe it badly. Tarik shakes his head. "I believe she was beautiful. But I don't think he kept her to himself for that reason."

This makes Sethos curious. He sits straighter and pops another grape in his mouth. "What do you think it could be?"

"Perhaps she was ill-mannered. Or irretrievably stupid."

Sethos bursts out laughing, startling some birds on the balcony behind him. Tarik is grateful for the sound. His brother has not been himself of late. "Not everyone can be as smart as you," Sethos says.

"If I had a daughter who was irretrievably stupid, I would hide her from the world, too."

"I doubt you're capable of producing a stupid daughter. But while we're talking about heirs, have you plans to marry anytime soon?"

Tarik nearly snarls. He's barely managing the kingship and now he's expected to manage a wife? "Are you truly not capable of talking about anything other than women?"

"Is there something more interesting than women? Someday, brother, a woman will knock the breath out of you at the sight of her, and you'll know why the rest of us think of little else."

Tarik highly doubts that, but arguing about women is a waste of time with Sethos. "The matters of the kingdom might interest you."

Sethos rolls his eyes. "I am a fighter. I'll leave the politics up to you."

"This illness is something that affects us both, Sethos."

His brother leans back and contemplates. Their father just died from what the citizens are now calling the Quiet Plague. Tarik knows he takes that seriously, at least. "Curious that it doesn't touch the Baseborn class, isn't it?" Sethos says. "Perhaps it comes from some food not available to them, something too expensive for their table. Or perhaps the Serubelans themselves are immune."

"The Healers are looking into both of your theories, actually. Neither has been ruled out. For now, we have no answers."

"The people won't blame you, you know. For the plague, I mean."

For not being a Lingot, Sethos is perceptive at times. It was exactly what Tarik was thinking. That if he doesn't find a cure for the plague, the people will leave Theoria. They'll feel safer elsewhere, that their king cannot protect them. And everything will fall apart. Everything his father worked so hard to keep together. Everything his ancestors had worked so hard to build and establish. Could it really all end with one bad king?

Tarik thinks of all his history lessons of the barbaric kingdom of Serubel. Long ago, its succession of terrible kings led to the creation of the four surrounding kingdoms. Of course, Theoria had been the first to leave, when the king's high councillor Vokor—now recognized to be one of the Favored Ones, probably a Lingot—fled the king and formed his own government in the safety of the empty if somewhat harsh desert. After the Princess Ailan died and Vokor went to war with Serubel, other sects began to break away from that once great kingdom. Wachuk became an encampment for refugees who had taken asylum in the trees just south of Theoria. After the blood and loss they experienced in the Great War, they preferred to live a spiritual existence, worshipping fire as their god and keeping pillars of fire burning day and night as sacrifice. They even stopped communicating with words, insisting that actions speak volumes over words, which could carry deceit in them. To this day, they continue to speak in hand signals and primitive clicks of the tongue.

Too, Pelusia was formed after the Great War. The haughty Serubelan king had rewarded his highest general for his excellency on the battlefield and had given him the coastal area of Pelusia, a vast land stretching along the coast of the immense northern ocean. Though Pelusia keeps to itself mostly, it has always had a relatively friendly rapport with Serubel. Princess Magar's mother had been from Pelusia, if Tarik is not mistaken. Pelusia is known for its people's skills in building ships and other seafaring structures, and prefers to trade mostly with foreign lands across the ocean, though its fish-preserving factories produce much of the food consumed by Serubel.

And, of course, there had been the ice kingdom of Hemut, which started out as a family wanting to improve their quality of living, having survived under the king of Serubel's oppressive thumb far too long. That particular king, Tarik believes, was called the Cracked King. He starved his people on purpose and regularly fed them to the Scaldlings—his favored flame-breathing Serpens—as entertainment. The sizable Hemut clan saw an opportunity that other citizens either failed to see or were not brave enough to attempt, in making the ice lands a place of holiday for the other kingdoms. Their success was limited at first, and many perished from the harsh conditions of the icy terrain, but eventually they made the unclaimed icy territory their own. Many merchants from the surrounding kingdoms eventually chose to take up living in that icy paradise rather than return home in favor of the wealth bestowed upon them from visitors there for a good time.

In fact, Theoria's own Superior class ventures out to the kingdom of Hemut regularly for rest and entertainment when the summer heat proves too scorching for them. They pay for their retreats with spectorium, which helps keep the inner caves of Hemut warm and cozy.

And what will happen when there is no more spectorium for the Superiors to trade?

"If the Superiors aren't happy," Tarik says more to himself than to Sethos, "or if they perceive a threat, they'll leave, taking their resources—and our economy—with them. And I will be powerless to stop it. It's bad enough that the price of spectorium has soared since Serubel is not trading it anymore. Only the Superiors can afford it now, and they grumble about paying the higher prices."

Sethos snorts. "What *don't* the Superiors grumble about?"

Tarik sighs. "That is a short list, brother."

Sethos hops down from the balcony and stretches. He's grown much in his years at the Lyceum; even at fifteen, his body resembles that of a man rather than that of a boy. "I need to return to my Majai mentors. I miss my daily victories. And you're as boring as ever."

"I'm as busy as ever, you mean."

Sethos shrugs as he strides toward the chamber door. "Reconsider allowing me to attend to the harem's needs, won't you?"

"Give your tutors my highest regards, Sethos."

7

SEPORA

T HE HISTORY OF SPECTORIUM WAS NEVER WRIT-
ten down, for fear the secret would fall into the wrong hands.
The story of it has been handed down through the generations of
Forgers (the gift skips a generation at a time) and is a verbal tale—a
rite of passage as it were—to the poor soul inheriting the ability from
a predecessor. And so it goes something like this, according to my
grandfather:

A few hundred years ago, after the five kingdoms had split and
gone their respective ways, a royal Serubelan toddler, a boy child, was
found in his bed covered in glowing liquid. His nursemaid cleaned
him up and reported the incident, but her tale was too wild for the
king and queen to comprehend, and so they dismissed her and hired
another woman in her stead. The very next night, the same occurrence happened, only it wasn't discovered until the mother queen
found her child stuck to the bedding by a worrisome glowing rock
that illuminated the entire room more than hundreds of candles. The
mother queen took their child to the king, who knew just exactly

what to do. (Reports are that it had to be carefully chiseled away from his tiny body.)

In a private caravan, the three of them and a few guards set upon a journey, traveling past the Valley of the Tenantless, into the sands of The Dismals, and finally into the city of Anyar. There they sought the help of the Lyceum of Favored Ones, the most creative and educated men and women of all the five kingdoms. The King of Serubel consulted with the brilliant minds about the rock they chiseled from their baby boy. (It is of import to note here that the king used the utmost discretion, never revealing to the Favored Ones where exactly the glowing rock had come from for fear his son would be considered cursed, an abomination, and unsuitable for the kingship. Why else would it come to enslave the child while he slept?) Almost immediately, the Favored Ones proclaimed it the newest living element and named it spectorium, for it glowed the entire spectrum of the rainbow. Not only did they request to keep this spectorium the Serubelans had brought, but they requested more of it. But the king was too confused to offer them any help.

After the king and his family returned home from Theoria, the king set upon watching his son very closely. All night, he would sit in his room and try to keep awake, trying to ward off whatever curse might come in the night and illuminate the room, effectively welding the baby to his silken sheets. It was on one of those nights that he realized that his son was not being attacked by a curse or a spirit, but his son was making the spectorium himself! It oozed from the child's palms as he slept, drying in a crust and glowing as white as the sun at midday.

The king was not so relieved that he had forgotten the pleas from the Favored Ones to obtain more of the glorious spectorium, and so the king began to spend more and more time with his son, watching his affliction, and learning how to teach his son to control it.

That is how the first Forger came to be.

I think of that story now as I float in and out of lucidity, trying to ascertain whether I have leaked out my precious spectorium during unconsciousness.

The first thing I notice when I fully come to is that the night is closing in, moving across The Dismals like a silent phantom. The next is that my hands are bound behind my back and that I'm sitting upright. Then, that my left eye won't open—and it hurts immensely. After a few moments, flashes of memory stir in my mind. The river. The splashing. The large man whose body blocked the sun. His fist rising in the air.

Nothing else. And to my relief, I feel faint and dizzy; a sure sign I have not Forged during my blackout.

My retrospections fade and the world comes into focus. The man from the river has built a fire and he sits across from me, watching me with a smug grin. In the glow of the flames, I see what his looming shadow didn't reveal before: This man is uniquely ugly. My tutor, Aldon, used to tell me that there is beauty in everything, that things that are outwardly ugly could be appreciated as interesting. But this poor man is just hopelessly hideous. Every feature of his face bears at least one considerable flaw. He's missing two top teeth and the ones left intact on the bottom appear intermittently black, which I hope for his sake are just shadows cast by the firelight. His eyes droop as though the skin of his cheeks is melting, and one eye appears as though it gazes in the opposite direction of the other just the slightest bit. His nose is bulbous, and even from here I can see the cavernous pores embedded in it and the dirt that takes up residence in them.

From his dress, he's clearly Theorian; he wears only a white linen wraparound skirt—a shendyt is what it's called—which does nothing to complement his rather extended and rather hairy belly.

It does not slip my notice that his shendyt—and my own clothing—is dry. Hours must have passed since we were in the Nefari. I'm now grateful that I spent all that time needlessly Forging in the Tenantless so that my body did not have the urge to dispense with it while I slept here against this boulder. I'm also thankful that I'm dry, since my attire would most assuredly be transparent when wet. But I'll not allow myself to blush at that; there are far more important things that warrant my horror at the moment than the thought of transparent clothing.

As it is, in Serubel, this man's attire would be required to cover him from neck to ankle, and as such his middle would not appear so prominent. Of course, in Serubel, we have the heights of the mountains to keep us cool; Theorians have only the desert sun. No wonder they dress so scantily. Even now, I feel sweat sliding down my back and plastering my hair to my neck like clinging vines. A servants' attire is especially modest, and here, modest is sweltering.

The man watches me while I watch him, and there is an air of expectation hovering between us. Still, it startles me when he speaks, perhaps because it sounds like a barking of words. "I've never seen eyes like yours before." His voice is deep, gruff, and moves the lump on his throat considerably when he talks.

Of course he's never seen eyes like mine before. I'm the only Forger left. The only person in the five kingdoms with silver eyes, because of the spectorium built up inside me. He must have gotten a good look at them in the river—right before he pummeled one of them with his fist. "What do you want?" I say, dismayed to find that my lip is also busted and that I openly wince when it stretches around the words.

My captor grimaces. "A thousand apologies, mistress. Sometimes I forget how big my hands are. My purpose was only to disarm you."

"I wasn't armed." Or had he been watching me long enough to know I had discarded my sword? Again, I won't blush. I do not have the luxury of being remorseful at the moment. I need to focus my energy on the sole task of escaping.

"Well, I wasn't sure, so."

I sit up straighter against the large boulder to which I'm propped up. "So then, since I wasn't armed, why did you tie me up?"

The man nods, appearing eager to converse. I get the sense that he's better with his big hands than he is with his brain. His eyes hold a sort of vacancy in them, at least in the soft firelight. "You're our prisoner. Rolan said we could get a month's worth of food if we traded you at the Bazaar." So, there are at least two of them. This brute, and one named Rolan. And Rolan is apparently thinking for the both of them. I'd wager Rolan wouldn't want him talking to me right now. I'd also wager that Rolan didn't count on me waking up before he returned.

The man adds some parched brush to the fire and appears delighted when it begins to sizzle; a childish look of wonder overtakes his expression. The burning foliage stings my nose, and it reminds me that I'm unfamiliar with most of the plants here in Theoria. That I'm unfamiliar with almost everything here in Theoria—except what I've learned from mere history scrolls.

"The . . . the Bazaar?" I ask. We have what we call the Square in Serubel. That's where all our trading is done. Row after row of booths set up with goods to barter. I've never heard it referred to as a bazaar, though. An inkling of hope wells up inside me. I could be closer to Anyar than I thought. Surely the capital city of Theoria would have a square like Serubel. Surely this bazaar is it. "Is the Bazaar in Theoria? Is it in Anyar?"

"Of course it is. What a silly question to ask."

I try not to take exception to that. Father always said only a fool argues with a fool. I feel a certain amount of relief in the fact that this pair of bandits apparently does not know who I am. And that apparently they're traveling in the very direction in which I want to go. This could either be disastrous or advantageous. Only time will tell which. "Who will you trade me to?"

He shrugs. "Rolan says because of your beauty and those peculiar eyes, you'll likely go to a wealthy trader who needs a new someone to warm his bed. It wouldn't be so bad, that, the life of a ladylove." But he won't lift his eyes to mine anymore.

I'm not sure which infuriates me more: the idea that I'm to be traded as a goat or a sheep would be, or that I'm to warm the bed of a complete stranger who is not—and likely never will be—my husband. Such things do not happen in Serubel. And I will not allow it to happen to me. But I need to keep him talking. "And have you ever been a ladylove?" I all but spit.

He scowls. If I weren't bound, and if I weren't at his and this vagabond Rolan's mercy, I might laugh at his pitiable density. "Of course I've not been a ladylove. Can you only ask silly questions?" He shakes his head. "A beautiful woman with no sense at all."

"Well, certainly you wouldn't speak of how well it is to be one without having been one yourself." Or a goat. Or a sheep. What is this Theoria that women are held in such low regard?

From his grimace, he doesn't appear to fancy my reasoning. "I hadn't thought of that."

I should move this along, I know. I could easily Forge a small spectorium blade, cut my way free, and run. For all his strength and size, this man is surely too big to be nimble on his feet. I've a good chance at escaping, if I do it before this Rolan fellow gets back.

But it would be risky, Forging spectorium in front of another person. If he and Rolan witnessed me do it, if they knew what I was capable of, they would never stop looking for me. Rumors would spread about my existence, about the girl with the silver eyes. There would be no hiding, not in any kingdom, not even in the Baseborn Quarters of Theoria.

And the embarrassing truth is, I haven't spoken aloud in days and I've been a bit lonely and since this man doesn't appear to want to hurt me—at least, not more than he already has—I suppose I could wait it out a bit longer until a better opportunity presents itself. My satchel and shoes are not far from me, lying in the sand a few arm's lengths away, but perhaps too far to snatch up before I flee. Empty as it is, I still need the jug inside the satchel to collect water, else I'll merely escape to my eventual death. And my shoes, for all the tight fit they are, will keep my feet from crisping on the hot sand.

What's more, I don't know where Rolan actually is—or if he could chase me down on foot. No, I mustn't run. Not now. Maybe in a few hours when night has completely fallen. The moon is already out and bright at that, bidding farewell to the sinking sun. I could navigate the desert by a moon such as this, as long as I can find the river swiftly enough. Toiling about in The Dismals is a deadly game I'd rather not play.

But suddenly I'm overcome with an idea. "My name is Sepora," I tell him. "What's yours?" Of course, I should have come up with a false name, one that no one will recognize. But only those closest to me know me by my middle name of Sepora, and as far as anyone of importance is concerned, Princess Magar has most likely fallen to her death. Besides, Sepora is a common enough name in Serubel. Hopefully it still exists among the freed slaves in Theoria.

The man has the good sense to at least consider not giving his name, but in the end, his idiocy wins. "Name's Chut."

"It's a pleasure to meet you, Chut."

"You don't mean that; I can tell." And he seems put out by it.

"You hit me, Chut."

He appears flustered, crossing his arms tightly. "I apologized for that. A thousand times, in fact. Don't you remember?"

"Yes, that's true. Perhaps we could be friends, then?"

He snorts. "Why would I want to make friends with someone's bed warmer?" There is no malice in his voice. He says it as though I've asked if he'd like a chalice of curdy milk.

"I'm not anyone's bed warmer just yet," I say, trying to keep the bite out of the words. "And you may not have to trade me after all, Chut."

"How's that, mistress?"

"I have something to trade myself. It's in my satchel. If you bring it to me, I'll show you."

"Already investigated that in case you had any valuables. We've got your little Serpen, Mistress Sepora, and we thank you for that. Other than the statue, all we found was a water jug."

And what did I expect? Of course they'd gone through it. If they would steal a person, they would certainly steal a person's things. But all is not lost. "Ah, but you've missed something in the satchel, Chut. Bring it here and I'll show you."

But Chut looks doubtful. "Looked in it myself, Mistress Sepora."

I lift my chin. "If you don't bring it here, I can't show you. Only I know the trick, the secret pocket in the bag." Saints of Serubel, how hard can it be to sweet talk an imbecile? Perhaps I've more pull than I'm using. After all, he's said he thinks me beautiful. Couldn't beauty be a resource?

I smile at him and his face softens instantly. It's an odd thing, to conjure up power with a mere smile. "Please, Chut? I wouldn't want you to miss out on what I have just because you didn't know about the compartment."

Chut is already nodding as he hoists himself from his spot across the fire. I arrange my expression into one I hope portrays excitement as he retrieves the satchel and walks it to me, trekking sizable holes in the sand in his wake.

I look up at him. "I can't show you unless you untie me." When I see that he's hesitant, I smile at him again, this time wider. "Chut, have I tried to escape? I did not simply wake up and decide to run, did I? And aside from that, we both know you're stronger than me. You could easily tie me back up if I try anything." I say it as though he were silly for not knowing that.

Clearly, Chut doesn't care to appear silly. He's probably been made to feel silly all his life. What's more, he seems satisfied with this line of reasoning. He has a purity about him that I don't enjoy blemishing. He's simply in the wrong business to be this trusting, and it's not lost on me that I'm about to teach him a hard lesson. "All right, then," he says.

I turn to the side, allowing him access to my bindings. I'm surprised at how gently he unties them and I decide then to forgive him for my swollen eye. Chut follows orders. It's obvious that he's easily persuaded to do the bidding of others.

I open the flap of the satchel and reach inside, pretending to dig around for the nothing that is in there. Chut leans closer, an innocent curiosity drawing his straggly eyebrows together. All the while, I Forge a ball of spectorium in the satchel, a ball big enough, worth enough, so as to secure my release. I have to hunch over the opening, so he can't spy the glow emanating from inside. It's heavy, almost too heavy for me to hold with one hand. After it cools, I peer up at Chut, fixing my face into what I hope looks something like delight. "I found it," I announce happily.

He squats down on his haunches, waiting for me to pull his reward from the leather bag. I gingerly extract it, slowly enough that he can see the light of it before the actual ball. When I present it to him, his eyes go round as the moon above us. He accepts it, and swallows. "You had more spectorium hidden in there? Where did you get it?"

"I'm from Serubel." I can't see the point in hiding that particular fact. "I've brought it along with me to trade for food. But Chut, it's yours if you just let me go."

He frowns. "I'll have to ask Rolan, Mistress Sepora. He'll want to know about this. And how would I know what's worth more, you or the spectorium?"

Precisely what I did not want to hear. I do my best to pout, pushing my lips out—split open though they may be—so that they feel unnaturally plump. It occurs to me that seducing a man was not something Aldon ever intended to teach me. And why would he? Father would have been the one seducing my suitor, choosing someone he could easily control in order to keep our bloodlines secure. But until that time came, I was far too busy Forging for him to worry about inconsequential things such as finding a husband and having a family of my own. I wonder how Mother felt about that. I wonder if Mother ever had to purse her lips, the way I'm doing so now, to get what she wanted.

"This is enough spectorium to trade for three months' worth of food at the Squa—the Bazaar, don't you think?" I've no idea what this spectorium will fetch, but at the moment I'd trade it for food myself. My stomach growls, as if in encouragement.

"Well now, mistress, it looks to be plenty valuable to me, but I've no experience with trading spectorium, you see. And if it's all the same to you, we'll wait to see what Rolan thinks of it." Before I can protest, Chut grabs my arm, yanking it behind my back and securing the rope, binding me even tighter than before. He moves much quicker than I'd expected, which makes me second-guess my original plan to run. He's fast with his hands, but is he fast on his feet as well? If he had to give chase, would he overtake me after all?

Gently, Chut props me up against the rock again and straightens out my skirt. He returns to his place across the fire, cradling the spectorium in both hands as delicately as one would handle an uncooked egg. Inexplicably, I appreciate watching him inspect the ball, turning it over and over in his hands and waving it in front of his face to see the light move. I wonder where Chut comes from. Obviously Theorian, but why did he decide to become a thief and a kidnapper? I wonder if he decided it at all. Sometimes our fates are handed to us. Sometimes there is no deciding for ourselves. I, especially, can appreciate that.

I hope that my escape doesn't require me to hurt Chut.

"What have you got there?" a voice calls from just outside the reach of the fire's light.

"The Mistress Sepora is trading us a ball of spectorium to let her go on her way," Chut calls toward the voice.

After a few moments, a tall, thin man appears at the edge of the firelight. He shares many of Chut's features, though his are not so horrifically pronounced; they could be related. Brothers, even. Thrown over his shoulder is an enormous fish that appears too heavy for a lanky man such as himself to be carrying. In his other hand he carries a pair of dead snakes. The size of the knife tucked into his belt is enough to make me shiver.

So. This is Rolan. The thinker.

"What have you got there, Rolan?" Chut perks up, eyeing the fin hanging across the man's chest.

Rolan laughs, smugness engulfing his expression as he swings around to show the other half of the fish. Chut and I gasp when we see not a fish, but a face. A blue, slimy face with round black eyes set in hollowed cheeks, a mouth with large lips gagged with some sort of leaved vine pulled tightly so that its mouth stretches open a bit. A head with a pointed ridge protruding at the top, which looks like a tiny mountain range running from the forehead down the creature's back. Arms, bound. And the hands. Webbed hands splayed out and bound together at the wrists.

A Parani.

Rolan has captured a Parani. And a live one at that.

8

TARIK

NOW TARIK KNOWS WHY HIS FATHER ALWAYS complained of how small his throne was. Having the same large build as his brother and father, Tarik has difficulty getting comfortable in the cramped, unaccommodating seat. Of course, it has a high, elaborately decorated marble back and lion heads for armrests—which Rashidi has had commissioned to change to falcon heads—but the seat itself is narrow and hard. Still, having a throne that engulfs the king would look much less intimidating to visitors and foreign emissaries, which would be completely unacceptable.

And so Tarik tries to keep from squirming in the marble chair as best he can. Perhaps he could manage better if the ornamental gold paint he must wear on his entire body were not so stifling. Each of his pores on his face, his shoulders, his arms, legs, and back—they all seem to absorb the stuff, which requires his attendants to give him many touch-ups at intervals throughout the day. Then, too, there is the enormous, jewel-encrusted golden headdress he must wear, which towers over him like an extra appendage.

Why a king must appear as a golden statue, he is not sure. It's nearly impossible not to feel ridiculous and a bit pretentious in this meddlesome attire. Do other kings make such a show of holding domestic court? He makes a note to ask Rashidi, though the old adviser will likely say something to the effect of "Theoria is unlike all other kingdoms" or something else as traditional and unbudging.

Rashidi announces the next caller. "Cy, a Healer of the Lyceum of Favored Ones."

Tarik perks up. He is not often visited by Healers outside of his council sessions in his day chambers; he hopes this could be news in the wake of the monotony of silence he's received from the Lyceum. The Quiet Plague has begun to trickle into the Middling class and all the Healers have done so far is found a way to at least stifle the bleeding—sometimes. But squelching the bleeding does little more than make the affair of dying a little less horrific. Hopefully, the Healer here today is not attending over a mere mundane dispute with another citizen.

After being introduced, Cy the Healer makes his way nervously to the center of the throne room and kneels before Tarik, bowing his head deeply, his chin nearly touching his chest. Tarik wants to tell him to get on with it, to stand up already, but Rashidi would likely pass away directly if he were to shun tradition so openly.

As it is, Tarik calls on him the moment it's appropriate to do so. "You may stand, Cy the Healer. What do you ask of me, friend?" Cy is young, very young. Possibly thirteen years, maybe twelve at that. Addressing him as friend seems to put the juvenile Healer at ease.

"My king," Cy says, "I must speak to you in private. I know it is not the way of things, but the matter is urgent."

Tarik can feel the tension and disapproval radiating off of Rashidi, who stands next to him in rapt attention. "That would be unwise,

Highness," Rashidi whispers, bristling with unrest. "You must not show favoritism at court."

Tarik considers, watching Cy, assessing his body language. Cy has an urgent message, is what he concludes. Or at least, a message that Cy himself considers urgent. Tarik glances up at Rashidi, who is trying very hard to convey his displeasure without coming right out and expressing it again. Tarik smiles, and Rashidi sighs in resignation.

"I have much respect for Healers, young Cy," Tarik says. "How old are you, exactly?"

Cy lifts his chin. "I'm but thirteen years, Highness. But sometimes age is not a limit, as you yourself may understand."

Clever. And brave. If anything, Tarik is amused by Cy, which is more than he can say for any of the other callers this morning. They've offered nothing but disputes over trades at the market, debates over the proper dowry for engagements, and bickering over land boundaries. A private meeting with a young Healer surely guarantees an interesting end to a tedious day. "Guards, please escort him to my day chambers, and I will meet with him shortly after court."

"Thank you, my king," Cy says, bowing even as he's being led away.

The rest of the afternoon drags on as Tarik becomes more and more curious about Cy the young Healer. At his age, he couldn't be close to completing his term at the Lyceum, and even if he were, only the top mentors from the Lyceum ever visit the king with pressing matters. The fact that an apprentice Healer has come to him has him nearly spilling out of his tiny throne.

There are so many small, repetitive matters to handle, from the settlement of a merchant dispute over chicken theft, to an accusation of adultery from a relatively wealthy Superior, and ending with an emissary from the ice kingdom of Hemut, who extends an invitation for a visit from King Ankor and his daughter—which will probably be a poorly disguised proposal of marriage between himself and the Princess Tulle. The latter turns his stomach, especially since Rashidi perked up when it was time for the emissary to be announced. First Sethos and now Rashidi, all pressing upon him to marry. As if he doesn't have plenty of problems already, all of which seem to be presented at court. Not that some cases aren't interesting, but do they *all* require the attention of the king? Tarik decides to consult with Rashidi about this after the session has adjourned. Surely a council could be appointed to handle such mundane matters so he can attend to the more compelling cases. In fact, all of today's petitions seem to pale in comparison to the fact that a thirteen-year-old Healer had the courage to request a private meeting with him.

After court, it's late in the day and time for his evening meal, but once again, Tarik finds a matter more pressing than food. Down the corridors, he keeps a pace too fast for Rashidi and must slow down several times for the adviser to stay in stride with him.

"Perhaps we could move your private day chamber closer to the throne room, Highness," Rashidi says dryly. "If you intend to entertain many more juveniles."

"You're not the least bit interested in what he has to say?"

"He's breaking tradition by presenting in court, Highness. Whatever could be so important that he would fail to advise his tutors of it?"

"Let's find out, shall we?" Tarik says, entering the double doors of his chamber. He motions for the guards to shut them. After he and Rashidi have settled in their seats, Tarik leans across the marble table, facing Cy, and folds his hands upon it.

Cy swallows, allowing Tarik to see that he's both nervous and excited.

"My adviser Rashidi is joining us," Tarik informs the boy. "And Rashidi is wondering why such a Healer of thirteen years would be presenting in court instead of one of the Masters of the Favored Ones."

"My king, I *am* a Master," Cy says. And as astonishing as it is, Cy is telling the truth. One does not normally reach Master level until age seventeen at the earliest. Cy must be rather brilliant. And by his expression, rather humble.

"One so young?" Rashidi says. Then recognition falls upon his face. "Ah, but I've heard of this one."

"It's true, then," Tarik says to himself more than the old man. "So, an eighteen-year-old king and a thirteen-year-old Master Healer have convened to a meeting. Tell me why that is, Cy."

Cy takes a deep breath, one that Tarik gets the sense he will use thoroughly. "As you know, my king, a plague has stricken the Superior class and makes its way through the Middlings. I believe it will not be long before it pervades all the classes; the rumors that it doesn't touch the Baseborn are preposterous, I assure you. And I'd like to try some experiments that the other Masters consider . . . unconventional."

Tarik nods for him to continue, his pulse picking up. Not only news of the plague but also finally an offering of help. It's more than he'd hoped for this day.

"You see, the plague strikes healthy and fragile alike. The healthy, of course, have a better chance of fighting it and surviving."

"Have there been survivors, then?" If so, he has not been informed of it.

Cy licks his lips. "No. But it is my assumption, of course, that the healthy would stand a better chance. Oh, my apologies, Highness,

I've forgotten to offer condolences for your father, the Warrior King. The kingdom has suffered an immense loss with his passing."

Tarik feels his body tense. "Yes, it has, Cy. Thank you. As you were saying?"

"Yes, my king. As I was saying. It strikes strong and weak. And by weak, I do not just mean old." Tarik nearly bursts out laughing when Cy glances at Rashidi. "What I mean is, even young ones who would normally be healthy, but whose bodies are not as resistant to certain illnesses, are more likely to die from this plague. As I said, my solution is unconventional. The other Masters have insisted that I obtain your permission before taking such a . . . unique approach in finding the cure. They have refused to support me in this request."

So far, everything Cy says is what he believes to be true. "And what approach would that be, Cy?"

The boy Master Healer sits up in his seat and leans forward as if to tell a secret. "I mean to inject the sick with spectorium, Highness."

Tarik feels his mouth fall slightly ajar. "*Inject* them? Why?" And how exactly, is what he also wants to ask. But Cy must be made to feel comfortable. He must offer his explanation in his own time, Tarik senses.

At this, Cy sucks in a breath. "Spectorium, as you know, is a source of great power. I believe the weak ones would benefit from such power in their bloodstream. That their bodies would use it to heal, rather than allow the plague to overtake them."

"Injecting spectorium into a person would kill them," Rashidi says, affronted. "No one would possibly allow that."

Cy shakes his head. "I would need volunteers, of course. But I've injected rats with liquefied spectorium, rats infected with a severe stomach pestilence. They lived, Highness, where their untreated counterparts died within days." How he could inject the element into a living thing is beyond Tarik. Spectorium must be superheated to melt it down to liquid form; surely it would burn the patient from the inside out. However, once again, Cy tells the truth. He must have found a humane way to do it—or at least, Tarik hopes he did.

"Rats are not people," Rashidi admonishes. Clearly the aged adviser agrees with the Masters in that this is not a conventional treatment.

Perhaps we've been too conventional all this time.

"No, they are certainly not," Cy concedes. "But by my calculations, this plague could wipe out the entire kingdom in a little over two years. It will spread through Anyar first, then it will make its way to the outer cities and, of course, to other kingdoms, if it hasn't already. I think administering spectorium to a few volunteers is worth the effort, Highness. Otherwise, disaster is on our horizon."

Tarik leans back and contemplates. It worked on rats, but with a completely different illness. Could it really work on people with the Quiet Plague? Will the people take his request for volunteers seriously? It's much for a new king to ask. It's much for anyone to ask. Which is probably why Cy requested a private meeting.

"We've a problem, Cy," Rashidi says, less agitated. Perhaps he sees the urgency of the matter as well. "Spectorium is no longer available to us. The Serubelan king has gone mad after the loss of his daughter—though I think we can agree judging from history it was only a matter of time—and refuses to trade it."

A rumor, Tarik detects. And one that is not true. "The king has his reasons for not trading," he says, "but mourning the loss of his daughter is not one."

Rashidi slumps his shoulders. "I was hoping it was, Highness.

We've already sent out runners to deliver our condolences, but I had thought to make more of an effort to comfort him. Perhaps he would have come around."

Tarik nods at his adviser, but this is not the time to speak of such things. Rashidi seems to realize this all at once. He clears his throat and folds his hands in his lap, looking back at Cy. "Well then, young Cy, how do you propose we call for volunteers without causing a panic? Obviously the other Masters—who are older and more experienced than you—disagree with your theory."

"We won't call for volunteers," Tarik says decisively. Both men look at him in surprise.

"Highness?" Rashidi says. "We cannot force such a thing on the people. It would start a riot."

"You misunderstand me," Tarik says. He turns his attention back to Cy. "The other Masters are right not to accept your theory. You've only tested it on rats. When you come to me again, Cy, you'll need to bring me more evidence. Test every sick thing you stumble upon—except people. Then we will talk more."

"But Highness, how will I procure the spectorium? By your own words, there will be a shortage of it very soon."

Tarik scratches the back of his neck. He cannot force the king of Serubel to trade his spectorium. Though if Sethos had his way, he'd be marching an army to Serubel to do just that. His brother has grown short of temper of late. Perhaps Tarik should send him to the harem after all. He would recoil at the thought of using the palace's spectorium instead of demanding it from the Serubelan king himself. Just like their father likely would, though the peace treaty they signed long ago, when Sethos and Tarik were just children, forbids it.

No, he cannot force the king. He can only encourage him.

Still, Cy is right; if the Serubelans don't open up trade soon, there will be a kingdom-wide shortage of it. His gaze rests on Rashidi. "Call a council session first thing tomorrow morning. If the Lyceum—if Cy—needs spectorium, we will give him all we can spare."

"We use it frugally as it is, Highness."

Rashidi is right; they do. Except for the pyramids—which are built completely from spectorium. But Tarik is not about to tear down their ancient monuments to the dead. Especially since only the newest ones may be used—the spectorium in the older pyramids has long died out. And asking the wealthy to give up a portion of theirs would cause too much concern. "We'll start here. The palace will have to spare some of its own. Check the fountains. Replace the spectorium lighting the halls with candles. All the lighting, in fact."

"Who shall I assemble for the council session, my king?" Rashidi says, eyes wide.

"Everyone," he responds, standing. He knows his adviser is surprised by his bold action, but perhaps boldness is what is needed in this instance. "Our scholars need to prepare for the coming shortage. We need to develop new ways of producing power. We've been dependent on the Serubelans and their spectorium for far too long."

9

SEPORA

SEEMING TO FORGET HIS BALL OF SPECTORIUM, Chut takes a few steps toward Rolan, eyes bloated in wonder. "A Parani?" he whispers. "Are we going to trade that in the Bazaar, too?"

I've never seen a Parani before. I've seen drawings and paintings of them, and heard tales such as that of Ragan, which emphasize how very vicious the creatures are. Vicious, and essentially uncatchable. Weapons are near useless against their skin, which acts as a flexible netting, rejecting the points of spears and arrows without serious puncture. It is said that Serpens are the only natural predator of a Parani and that they enjoy the taste of their flesh. As the stories go, Serpens can spy them from the sky and swoop down upon them, snatching them from the water and eating them alive. Aldon used to say that the difference between an arrow or a spear and the blade-like teeth of a Serpen is the amount of pressure a Serpen can apply with its jaw. That Parani skin is puncture *resistant*, but not infallible. How Aldon knows this, I'm not sure. In my seventeen years in Serubel,

I've not heard of a single Serpen feasting on the flesh of a Parani. To me, it sounds like fabrications contrived by Serubelan mothers meant for embellishing the tenacity of the Serpens to calm what might otherwise be an unreasonable fear of the Parani. The very fear that the story of Ragan continues to instill in each generation.

The only other way to kill a Parani is to remove it from the water and let it suffocate on land. Supposedly that takes the space of two sunsets to happen, for they can breathe our air for a time but the water sustains their lives.

Reconciling the stories of such savage beasts to the creature trembling in Rolan's arms as he sets it down by the fire is quite impossible. Its skin does not appear so elastic to me as to be impenetrable. And so far, it has done nothing to lash out or attack its captor.

All it does is quiver uncontrollably.

"Trade it?" Rolan laughs. "I was under the impression you were hungry, friend. Nay, we're going to eat her. Keeping her alive long enough to trade wouldn't be worth the trouble. Besides all of that, do you know of any shortages of Parani in Anyar?"

Her. Somehow Rolan knows this Parani is a female. And she looks young—or at least, not as big as the Parani in the drawings and paintings Father keeps in the great hall. Perhaps those are all of males, and the females are smaller in comparison. Or perhaps all of them are exaggerated fantasies of someone's imagination. Perhaps no one in Serubel really knows what a Parani truly looks like. Or likely, they're all as unimpressive as this, and care had to be taken to make them more fearsome.

It's difficult to say, because most Serubelans never ventured to the Underneath, much less to the River Nefari; if they wanted to swim, they could do so in the fresh, natural pools of rainwater among our floating mountains. Apparently Theorians have much more knowledge of the creatures than we do, the Nefari being the pulse that keeps their kingdom alive.

"I've never eaten Parani before," Chut says, disappointed. "What if I don't care for it?"

Rolan looks Chut up and down, deliberately stopping when his eyes reach Chut's belly. "Seems to me you care to eat, period. You'll enjoy Parani, I'm certain." Rolan turns to me. "What about you, *Mistress* Sepora," he says with amusement. "Have you ever feasted on fire-roasted Parani?"

I behold the small creature staring back at me with eyes full of panic. Does she understand what they're saying? Does she understand that they mean to eat her? Surely not. Though intelligent enough to be afraid, she has a feral look about her. The same look a Serpen would have if captured in the wild.

I meet Rolan's eyes. "Of course I've eaten Parani. It's a delicacy in Serubel." A lie. And a rather transparent one at that. Still, saving this creature's life is worth a small lie. Declaring it a staple is also a good way to tell whether these two have ventured into my kingdom. If they had, they would know how full of rubbish I am.

"Is that so?" Rolan says, even more amused. "Do tell us, mistress, how does it taste?"

"Rancid," I say, feigning disgust. "Especially the females."

"What do you suggest we do with this rancid beast, then?"

I shrug. "I'm sure I couldn't care. But if you were in Serubel and weren't going to eat it, you'd be expected to throw it back."

Rolan laughs. "Fortunate that I'm not in Serubel, then. Aside from all that, I've heard it's a wretched place." I try not to take offense, try to focus on the fact that Rolan has obviously never been to Serubel—and what's more, he would not know whether the place was wretched. If he saw the greens and blues and purples of the mountains, he would surely know how wretched a place his precious Theoria really is.

Or perhaps he wouldn't. Theorians are known for their imperial pride.

He scratches his cheek and turns back to his companion. "Chut, what has the mistress here given you? Let me see that."

Chut pounds his way to Rolan, and the two scrutinize the spectorium ball as though it were an animal they've never seen before. Could that be possible? Could there exist someone who has never even seen spectorium up close and in person? Of course not. Not Theorians, anyway. The very pyramids of Theoria are made from spectorium; they know what it is. Theoria is Serubel's most eager trading partner for spectorium. Theoria is the reason I labored day and eve to Forge it.

I can tell that Chut is relaying our transaction to his friend. Rolan's head snaps up, and his eyes narrow as he looks at me.

It's time to see how much of a thinker Rolan really is.

The shorter man strides toward me where I lean against the rock and squats before me. "Chut here says you've requested to trade your spectorium for your release."

"That's correct."

"Where did you get the spectorium?"

"I told you I'm from Serubel. That's where all the spectorium is."

"We checked your satchel, mistress. There was nothing but the Serpen figurine in it when Chut here came across you in the river. Nothing." Rolan is no longer entertained. Everything about him feels hostile. This could go badly.

"As I told Chut, it was in a secret compartment. You must have missed it." I can Forge a blade and kill him if I need to. I'm surprised at how quickly this thought forms in my mind. I'm not going to kill anyone. The whole point of this journey was to *save* lives.

Rolan wipes a hand down his face. Then uses the back of the same hand to strike me hard across the cheek. Searing pain resonates through me. The force of the blow knocks me on my side, and I take a bit of sand into my mouth. It stings the already open cut on my lip. Gruffly, he uses the crook of my arm to pull me upright. Grabbing my chin, he rubs his thumb along my bottom lip, taking care to touch my wound. "Stories amuse me," he says. "Lies do not."

I glance at Chut, who's looking on intently, fidgeting with the ball in his hand. A pity. Chut, the gentle one, doesn't have the sense of a worm. If he did, he would stop this madness. Rolan, the thinker, has the mercy of a Scaldling. I get the feeling that he craves this sort of cruelty. In the growing dark, the blacks of his eyes seem to get bigger.

Without warning, he seizes my throat, squeezing it between his long fingers, fingers that seem to have been made for just this thing. "Hidden compartments have their place," he growls. "Good on you for having one. But that . . ." He nods toward Chut holding the glowing ball. "The weight of that alone would be difficult for you to carry, let alone any other supplies. We would have felt a burden like that when we handled it, mistress."

He's right, of course. It would weigh me down and the heaviness would be noticeable to anyone. It was different when I was trying to convince Chut. I'd thought I could barter for my release and be gone before Rolan returned. But that is not the way things turned out.

Perhaps instead of lying, I should say nothing. Nothing is what I have left, after all. The truth is not possible to tell and several different versions of a story will make me appear less trustworthy. I should stick to the one and be done with it.

I feel his fingers loosen their hold. "Be a good little chit and tell me." When he loosens his grip even more, I'm finally able to take a sustaining breath.

"I did," I gasp.

His grip tightens again. Would I have to kill him then? *Could* I kill him? And what would I do about Chut?

"Do you know what a Lingot is, mistress?"

Saints of Serubel, how does he expect me to answer, clutching me so tightly? I think hard, as hard as Rolan squeezes me. The word strikes nothing but air in my mind. Aldon never taught me about a Lingot. The darkness I see now has nothing to do with the setting sun. Slowly, I shake my head.

"What were you doing in the river to begin with?"

"Bathing," I force out.

Rolan shoves me away, and I crack my head on the boulder behind me. The horizon seems to tilt. The fire dances in three different places instead of the one pit that contained it mere moments before. Vomit. I'm going to vomit. I will, and I'll do it all over Rolan's smug face.

All three of them.

"She doesn't even know what a Lingot is." He snorts. "But you do know how dangerous the River Nefari is, don't you? You Serubelans have your superstitions about it, do you not?" He shakes his head. "To think, I could have lost such a magnificent spoil to a carnivorous beast such as that." Rolan nods toward the Parani, who now holds very still as she watches us. There is an understanding in her eyes that I missed before. How I could have thought her a simple animal I'm not sure. The corners of her mouth tug down, and I wonder if it's because of the gag or if she's actually grimacing. She must discern what is happening here. At the very least, she discerns that she and I are in the same predicament. Is she concerned for my safety as I am for hers?

Or has Rolan brained me on this blasted rock?

Rolan stands. "Anyhow, where are my manners? I thank you for the gift, Mistress Sepora. It was very thoughtful, and though I believe none of your lies, we'll gladly accept this offering."

Gift? Offering? "And my release?"

He laughs into the night sky. "We have decided to decline your request. Now sit quietly while Chut brings you some snake to eat."

So there will be no trading for my release. Of course there won't. And even if there were, I couldn't leave now.

Not when *she* needs my help.

10

TARIK

TARIK ABSENTLY SCRATCHES PATRA'S HEAD AS he listens to his advisers and royal scholars fight among themselves. Patra leans in for a fuller caress, pushing her ears back and nudging his palm with her nose. He chastises her with a look, but only halfheartedly because he'd much rather be coddling his giant cat than listening to these nobles bicker. Calling an assembly together to discuss alternative methods of creating power had seemed, in theory, to be a good idea. Now that he has his entire council and collection of the kingdom's brightest thinkers gathered in the same room, it seems the only true power everyone is concerned with appears to be each individual's superiority over his or her peer.

"Steam power has long been determined impractical," says one of his best tutors of the sciences at the Lyceum. She crosses her arms at one of his royal advisers. "It takes more power to create the steam than the steam gives off itself."

The man beside her huffs, adjusting his long blue robes in an apparent attempt at nonchalance. "Yes, well, it's not nearly as ineffectual as the water power you're suggesting. We've already diverted the River Nefari to water the crops in the eastern part of the kingdom. To divert any more would have a dire effect on the fishing trade. How would you like to explain the shortage of fish to the Middling fishermen, who depend on their day's catch to feed their children?"

She scowls. "And when we run out of power completely? What would you have me tell them then?"

Tarik pinches the bridge of his nose. More than fifty of Theoria's finest minds convened in this great throne room and all they can do is bicker. He wonders what his father would say, what his father would do. One thing he's certain of—his father would never allow things to get out of hand as he has done today. Advisers speaking out of turn, and none of them addressing Tarik himself, as is the custom at assemblies such as this. He must put an end to it.

"Enough," he roars, louder than he'd intended. The council members and the tutors and the engineers all desist with their squabbling. Some appear ashamed at having been chastised; others appear shocked. Even Rashidi, who stands beside the royal throne, seems surprised. *Get used to it*, he wants to tell them all. *I am not going to allow my father's kingdom to fall prey to chaos.* "All we have determined today is what is *not* working," he says. "Tell me, what are the other kingdoms doing? And I swear if any of you speak out of turn again I'll have you escorted to the Half Bridge." A lie. A few of those present are Lingots, and they can discern the deception, but most in attendance pay grave attention to their young king.

At first, none will raise their hands. At long last, though, someone finally does. It's the woman scholar who'd stolen the floor moments earlier. She's older, with gray-tinged wisps of hair peeking out of her stately golden headdress, symbolizing her premium rank at the Lyceum. "Your Highness, if I may?"

He nods to her. "Please."

"The information we've gathered suggests that the other kingdoms are simply going without power or using fire. Trade with Wachuk for their lumber has increased, as you can imagine. But as you know, Highness, Theoria strives for a higher standard of living than that for our citizens. To go without power would mean—"

Rashidi snorts. "His Majesty is well aware of the severity of the circumstances, Mistress Raja. Is there anyone at all here today who can offer a solution, rather than reiterate—and therefore exacerbate—the problem?"

This time, the assembly falls as quiet as usually Patra does before she springs to attack.

"What of Pelusia?" Tarik says. "What are the reports coming from there?" The northern kingdom of Pelusia is rarely spoken of. Located on the edge of the vast ocean, some say the land there is cursed. Others that the inhabitants are mad, even resorting to cannibalism to survive. What it all tells Tarik is that no one really knows—and that Pelusia seems perfectly content with that.

"There are no reports from Pelusia, Highness," Rashidi says. "They are of a solitary assortment, I'm afraid. They never traded for spectorium in the first place."

He'll speak to Rashidi in private for pointing out the obvious in front of an entire assembly, as if he didn't already know that Pelusia was estranged from the rest of the kingdoms. "Yes, but what sort of power do they use, then?"

At this Rashidi seems confounded. "It's not known, Highness. We've not had communication with that kingdom in decades. They are much too bonded with Serubel for us to form a trusted alliance."

Tarik shakes his head. "Then we must reach out to them. Select a representative and send a caravan to the king. Let us see how the

Pelusians have managed to survive without the convenience of spectorium. We shouldn't assume anything that hasn't been ascertained by one of our trusted ambassadors." He leans on his elbow, gently pushing Patra's imploring head away from his lap. "And since we cannot seem to find a way to manage without spectorium, we should be endeavoring to regain possession of it. Send a richly appointed caravan to Serubel as well. Let's see what it will take for King Eron to trade."

"It may well be more than we have," Rashidi mutters for Tarik's ears only.

"We'll reconvene this assembly when we've heard from our ambassadors. Until then, keep working on the solution, not the problem. I find it rather unamusing that the brightest stars in the kingdom have come up with nothing but creative ways to insult one another."

As his most educated subjects file out of the throne room, Tarik turns to Rashidi. "I am not impressed with my collection of intellectuals."

"You were very wise to put an end to their petty quibbling."

"And what of my idea to send caravans to the outer kingdoms?"

Rashidi sighs. "It is better to do something than nothing, Highness. What have you in mind to trade the Serubelan king?"

"If this plague persists? Anything he wants."

11

SEPORA

CHUT TAKES ANOTHER BITE OF SNAKE AS IF out of habit, as if it were his duty to take bite after bite of a thing he despises. He'd complained already that he hated snake, that he'd much rather try the Parani. But Rolan wouldn't hear of it. "Parani must dry out first, before you can eat them," he'd explained. "Gives their fins more of a flaky texture that you'll adore. Give it a day or two, my friend. Then we'll dine like the Falcon King himself." The Falcon King? The last I'd heard, he was the Falcon Prince. Had his father, the Warrior King Knosi, turned the reins over to him at such a young age? Why would he do such a thing? In Serubel, only death moves the crown of royalty. I can't help but think how grave a mistake it would be to entrust the kingdom of Theoria to a mere boy king—especially with all the plans my father has for it.

Chut sighs. "Move that Parani closer to the fire. That ought to dry her out faster." The first astute observation I've seen him make.

Even Rolan is surprised, chuckling around a yawn. "You know, you're quite brilliant when you're hungry." He lies down on his fur mat, tucking his arm under his head as a pillow. "Move her closer if you wish."

"It's my survival instinct," Chut says proudly, tapping his finger to his forehead. He stands and walks to where the Parani is bound and bent on her side in awkward angles. I've watched her deteriorate all evening. If she is to survive, I must help her soon. Even now, she pants, her breaths coming in quick short rushes.

Chut grabs her fin and drags her unceremoniously to the fire's edge. Anyone would be hot sitting that close to the flames. By now the fire is a bulking thing that licks high at the night sky. From where I sit, I see the heat radiate from it like the hot stoves in the kitchens of my castle back home. The Parani tries to roll away, loosing an eerie, high-pitched squeal.

Chut seizes her again and drags her back. "Should she still be this feisty, you think, Rolan?"

"You nearly threw her into the fire," Rolan says, appearing bored. "I suppose anyone would show some feistiness in that case."

Chut purses his lips. "I'll dig a pit here so she can't roll away." Chut really is brilliant when he's hungry. He sets to kicking at the sand, moving enough of it to form a small trench just deep enough to fit the Parani.

She'll cook in there; I know it. I thought I had a day—or at least, the rest of the evening—to work this through in my mind, what I would do. What I was willing to risk. As Chut digs that pit, I realize that is no longer the case. It must be soon. I'll lose the comfort of daylight, yet gain the advantage of the cloak of night.

Rolan yawns again. He is smart enough to keep a watch—and keep awake during his shift—yet selfish enough to have Chut take the first one. After all that Chut has eaten, I'm hoping he'll fall asleep within an hour of Rolan.

During that hour, I will have much to think about. I will have to reassess my current goals.

In the beginning, walking to Theoria and blending into the Base-born population seemed simple enough. My most pressing concern had been food and water on my journey. I had known there was the risk of meeting someone along my way—and that that someone could be unfriendly. But having those risks become reality seemed unlikely at the start of my journey. More so after all the time I spent without encountering a single soul in the Tenantless. Perhaps I've been naive.

Now, I have no food or water, I've met someone unfriendly, and I've decided to rescue a potentially dangerous creature from captivity. Mother would not approve. Mother would tell me that risking myself and my identity by rescuing an animal is a selfish goal and that I'm not thinking for the greater good. And she would be right, of course.

But it's of no use to ponder over what Mother would say. I'm going to save this Parani because . . . well, because of the way she's looking at me right now. Eyes full of pain and helplessness. Her skin seems to be having a reaction to the proximity of the heat; from here, I see slivers of steam rise up from where she lies. I don't want to see this happen. I don't want to watch her die. I don't want to watch her cook.

Yet, I'm hesitant.

It's as though Mother's words are chains keeping me here, urging me to sleep and let things lie as they are. Yet, why should I want to please *her*? A waif who left me to my own devices and worse—to my father's devices. Never once did she stand up for me against him. Never once did she stop him from beating me. Now I should be the one to pay for that negligence? How is that fair? *She* should be the one tied up here, contemplating her next move.

Fortunately for the Parani, she isn't.

And fortunately for me, Chut has already dozed off.

It will be a relief to Forge even a small blade. I've not Forged nearly enough lately aside from my "gift" to Chut and Rolan; my veins feel full of spectorium, my body faint of power. Up until this point in my journey, Forging had been simple enough. I'd either dig a hole and Forge, or sometimes I'd even Forge small orbs and throw them in the deep part of the river to pass the time as I walked, watching them sizzle at the surface and sink to the riverbed below. Perhaps secretly I was hoping to attract the attention of a Parani, to see one for myself.

Perhaps I was a dolt.

Now I ache with the need to Forge. And if I don't do it soon, I'll not have the strength I'll need to save this creature. My grandfather had been the last Forger until I was born. A Forger's purpose, Grandfather always said, is to Forge, not to become a vessel for unspent spectorium. It's not what we're meant for, he'd said. We're meant to share it with others. To let such power build up inside us is selfish, and therefore it's fitting that it makes us ill and weak.

With that thought in mind, I urge the spectorium to my palms, releasing it slowly, letting it seep into my hands and solidify, clasping it between my fingers to make it flat and hopefully sharp. I press my back closer to the boulder behind me, in case the glow of my Forging can be seen from the fireside where Rolan and Chut sleep.

It's only a small relief, this knife I've Forged. My body screams to release more spectorium, to dispel it and gain blessed energy back. Perhaps when I've freed the Parani, I'll still have enough time to Forge more and somehow hide it before my captors awaken. The longer I can hide my ability from them, the better. After all, it's safer for me to travel with them to Anyar than to do so alone. They'll likely feed me on the way, I'm sure, just as they did tonight; even Rolan would agree

I would be of no use to them if I were to perish, and the wealthy merchant they're hoping for won't be interested in a malnourished companion for his bed. They'll fetch more for me at the Bazaar if I'm in good health. At least, that's what I'll tell them.

Because truly, they'll fetch nothing for me. As soon as we reach the Bazaar, I'll escape. I'll escape, and I'll melt into the Baseborn Quarters. These two goons shall never see me again.

After the blade cools in my hands, I use it as a saw, cutting through small layers of rope at a time. The awkward angle hurts, and I must stop often else my wrists begin to ache. The process is long and strenuous; the blade is not nearly as sharp as I thought it would be, but I saw back and forth consistently and with enough pressure so that the threads of the rope snap one by one. Every now and again Chut startles awake. His eyes dart to me first, then the Parani, and satisfied that we're still here and bound, he allows himself the luxury of drifting off again.

Finally, I cut through one of the layers of rope. I push and stretch my fingertips to determine how many layers I have left, how many times they looped the rope around my wrists when they bound me. I count four more layers still intact. This will take much more time, between Chut's moments of clarity and my dull blade. I wonder how long Chut's shift is. Rolan is sure to stay awake during his, and all will be lost.

The Parani will surely die, and I will not be able to tear my eyes away from it.

Hastened by the thought of entering Theoria with the weight of a death about my shoulders, I work faster as the night grows colder and I begin to shiver. The Parani is no longer watching me, just whimpering in her pit as more steam floats into the night air.

After what feels like an eternity, I cut through the last of the rope.

My hands pop apart and I long to rub the ache from my wrists, but time is too precious for that. I dig a small but deep hole and press the knife into it, covering it over and stepping on it to hide the mound; there is simply no time for cutting more rope with a dull blade. Quickly, I Forge another, sharper one to unbind the Parani. I tuck it behind my back and approach her cautiously.

To my horror, she begins to whimper louder. Chut stirs, coughing away a snore. Rolan shows no outward response. I wait several moments, mere feet away from them, watching them sleep. If an insect were to land on their noses or the wind whip their hair in just the right way or the chill of the air get just a touch colder, they could both wake up. They could wake and see me standing here with a spectorium blade, ready to release their next meal.

I should listen to my mother. She is a survivor. She doesn't let inconvenient things such as emotions get in her way. She completes the tasks set before her and complains of nothing. My mother will live a long, subservient life. And who am I to judge? Who am I to want something more for myself than subservience? I should return to my rock and sleep, covering my ears as the Parani's whimpers grow louder throughout the night as they surely will while she dries completely out. While she dies. They'll see I've managed to escape my ropes but that I didn't leave altogether. It will gain their trust. It will make traveling to Anyar easier.

Yes, that's what I'll do.

I turn away from her and take the first few steps back to my boulder. But she cries again. A hopeless, defeated cry that sounds as though she is giving up the way I am.

I cannot do this.

Whipping around, I press a finger to my lips, sure that she won't understand to be quiet and more than surprised when she actually ceases to fuss. I squat next to her and begin slicing the ropes that bind her arms. I've wasted enough time; fear motivates me to move faster despite my waning energy, and fortunately my work, though sloppy, is still effective. When she's free, she tries to climb her way out of the pit, whipping her fin around to gain momentum, I'm guessing, and clinging to the side to push herself up. Her fin gets too close to the fire and she lets out a small cry. I stiffen, my gaze falling back to Rolan then Chut, waiting for one of them to awaken and find me at my task.

Rolan sits up, and my breath catches in my throat. He's looking right at me, our eyes lock, but his are glossed over with sleep. His head wobbles just a bit to the left when he says, "Good eating, that one. Delicious." Then he lies back down, sniffing and stretching as he adjusts himself on the thin mat he'd been lying on.

I can't risk that happening again. Next time, he might come to completely.

I'm going to have to carry her. Or, at least, drag her. And I'm going to have to do it quickly. But first, I must unleash more spectorium.

No, first, I must move her away from the fire pit. After I've dragged her several feet, my energy is gone, and I feel faint. Frantically, I stumble to behind my boulder and drop to my knees, digging a deep, deep hole. The spectorium gushes from my palms, filling the hole with molten liquid. I cover it over before it cools, fumbling with the task. This is taking too much time. Two more holes I dig, and by the time the third is filled, I've regained my full strength. I'm hoping the sacrifice of time is worth the payoff in energy to finish this escape.

Returning to the Parani, I tuck my arms under hers and hoist her up. She's much too heavy for me to throw over my shoulder as Rolan had. Cursing my weakness, which has nothing to do with actual spectorium, I try other ways to lift her but fail. This is costing us too much time. I must tug her across the desert sand and hope for the best. She seems to understand that I'm helping her; she holds to me tightly, her head resting against my chest. Her webbed hands feel confident on my back, and she makes no sounds even though I know the rocks and pebbles on the ground must be scraping her fin. I hope that all the rumors about the tough skin of a Parani are true and that her discomfort is not as much as it appears to be.

Her dragging fin makes a slithering trail in the sand heading toward the river, one that Rolan and Chut will easily be able to follow.

We must move faster.

We both grunt as I stumble in general and fall twice. The river is not far ahead, just several more paces, when I hear yelling behind us. We have not been fast enough.

My muscles ache and my wrists shake with their new task, but I hoist the Parani higher on my torso and dig my feet to gain more traction in the sand. My breathing comes in gasps, and my companion begins to whimper again. She knows we won't make it, just as I know.

We reach the water's edge and I all but dump her in, stomping and splashing into the water as I pull her in deeper. "Go!" I scream, chucking the blade into the river behind her.

In her dark eyes, I see the glow of our captors' torches gleaming behind us. If she doesn't go now, they'll catch her again.

A hand clamps down on my shoulder. A big hand that could only belong to Chut. "What do you think you're doing?" he roars. "That's our food you're letting go!"

But I'm not letting her go. That is to say, she's not leaving.

Oh no.

A webbed hand pulls hard on my wrist, jerking me away from Chut. She brings it to her mouth and I'm sure she means to bite me so I struggle against her. Now that we're in her element, she's able to overpower me, and using the strength of her fin she surges forward. With a quick motion, her tongue lashes out over my palm. Once, twice, shaping an X of venom there. Then she disappears under the surface, hardly making a ripple in her wake.

I can't decide which hurts worse, the sting of the Parani venom disintegrating the skin in my hand or my ribs from Chut's jostling gait as he walks me back to camp thrown over his shoulder. We meet Rolan halfway. His eyes are dark again, full of venom themselves, and now they have puffed rings beneath them from being awoken so suddenly.

"You're going to pay for that," Rolan growls.

Chut hauls me all the way back to camp, muttering and cursing under his breath. I have the sense that Chut and I are no longer friends. A Parani feast meant a lot to him, and now I've let her go.

I made the wrong choice. I saved a thankless Parani. And she's given me a painful reminder of my generosity.

Chut sets me against the boulder and turns to Rolan. "What will we do with her now? We've no more rope."

Hands on hips, Rolan snarls down at me, teeming with agitation. "How did you get free?"

"I had a knife hidden in my skirts."

He narrows his eyes. "Another secret compartment, is it?"

I shake my head. "A pocket. Nothing particularly secret about it. In my undergarments." It's a good lie except I hope they hadn't inspected my person while I was unconscious. If they had, Rolan will call me on it now, the way he had when they'd ransacked my satchel.

"I should have told you about it. I'm sorry," I say, keeping my voice calm and respectful, and lowering my head. Wrath practically emanates from Rolan and a bit of fear steals through me. I no longer have Chut's favor. He'll agree with whatever punishment Rolan decides is appropriate, I'm sure. At the moment, I can't imagine a punishment more painful than the venom burning in my palm even as my fingers grow numb.

"Temple of Theoria, do you spew lies as a trade, then? Chut, check her undergarments to ascertain she's not hiding any villages or horses in there." He turns to me with a wicked grin. "It's the least we could do."

Chut hesitates. "I can't do that, Rolan. She's a proper mistress."

"Proper mistresses do not carry knives, Chut."

"It's not fitting, Rolan. It's just not fitting."

Well then. Perhaps my lie was not as clever as I'd thought. Chut may not be willing to violate decency, but Rolan appears more than eager. He moves toward me and I stiffen, my instincts screaming at me to fight. But I must win their trust again. I need them to take me to Anyar. They're capable of feeding themselves, obviously, and so they could feed me. Keep me in fresh water. For the money they expect to fetch for me, they would probably even carry me if I became too exhausted to keep up. And without Forging, I will be too exhausted.

I must let Rolan put his hands on me.

Grabbing my wrists, he pulls me to my feet. He's thorough, patting down every inch of my skirts, turning me around and around. When his hands slide down my breasts, down my bottom, I cringe, knowing heat fills my cheeks when I face him again. His mouth is downturned when I finally muster the courage to meet his eyes.

"We've no rope, as Chut said, Mistress Sepora," he says, balling his fist.

I swallow. "I won't escape. I promise. I know it's safer for me to travel with you. I'll not venture off."

He tilts his head at me. "A truth, for once in your life. Why the change of heart, mistress?"

"I'm safe with you," I admit, baffled at his constant perceptiveness.

"But you mean to escape once we reach Anyar?"

I lift my chin. "No."

He throws his head back and howls into the crisp night. "We would be rich, mistress, if we could only sell your lies."

12

TARIK

TARIK REMOVES THE JEWELED NECKLACES DRAPED along Patra's head and back. She fully shakes her body, her fur undulating in waves, as if she's shuddering off the last bit of weight of her stately burden. He feels as relieved as she does. Today is one of the precious few he has to himself, and he intends on taking up the Healer Cy's invitation to visit him at the Lyceum. Only, he has no intention of going as pharaoh. Against Rashidi's wishes and ranting and stewing, he dons a blue beaded bib collar—a symbol that he is merely a royal servant. A high-ranking one, but a servant, nonetheless. It's liberating to wear only the collar and the basic linen shendyt wrapped around his waist reaching just to his knees, rather than the robes and the golden headdresses and the fanciful gold-flecked paint his face and body must endure while holding council or court or being king in general.

Patra follows him throughout the palace, her ears perked at attention and her steps more calculated than usual; she knows this is the way they go only when they're escaping their normal routine and the palace and the monotony of being a royal cat. He wishes he could let her loose to nurture her instincts to hunt instead of being hand-fed the choicest of meats day by day, brushed and combed and petted and groomed to no end. Sometimes he thinks it a disservice to keep cats in such splendor and comfort when their thriving depends so much on their instincts to survive, and to do it well. But to change such a traditional law, to ban the keeping of cats as protectors would throw the Superior class into a frenzy, one that he cannot afford right now. The Superiors must remain happy, else the threat of them moving to a more accommodating kingdom becomes very real.

The kingdom of Hemut has already lured many of the Superiors into purchasing ice caves and into taking frequent respites there, despite the bitter cold and the icy terrain. Though, as Tarik recalls from a visit he made to Hemut with his father in his childhood, the chill of the air is easily forgotten compared with the magnificence and beauty of the ice structures and buildings there. He and Sethos still talk fondly of the Frost Shoots, a mountain carved with many slides for the youth of the kingdom to play on. And besides, one can put on many layers of clothing, while in Theoria, only so much can be taken off, as a matter of etiquette.

Tarik glances to Patra then, noticing the sleek movement of her shoulder blades drawing together and melting apart as she takes each step. He always recognizes when she grows restless; the outings are as good for her as they are for him. They've been doing it since he was just a boy of perhaps thirteen, the two of them together, a boy and his cat, and while his father didn't exactly approve, he never stopped them. That may be why Rashidi huffs and puffs but never insists that he stay inside the palace where a pharaoh can be safe and sound and bored to weeping.

Of course, Rashidi is in no position to insist that he do anything anymore—a fact that Tarik is just desperate enough to remind him of. Advisers may not forbid kings anything.

Yet, with privilege comes steep responsibility, and as Tarik slips past the last set of guards at the servants' entrance of the palace—who know not to bow to him as he leaves—he feels some of the pressure lift from his shoulders as if evaporating into the dry desert air.

The shortest route to the Lyceum is to cut directly through Anyar's Bazaar, and Tarik couldn't be happier. Late at night, one of his favorite views from the palace is from the balcony on the west tower, which overlooks the vast Bazaar. Even from his vantage point and late into the darkest hours, he can smell the spices on the breeze swirling up to him, can hear the soft music mingle with children's laughter as the booth keepers tuck their families into bed for the evening. The Bazaar used to glow brightly with spectorium at each booth, small dots of mostly white but sprinkled with specks of purple and blue. Now, only the wealthiest merchants have it and in small abundance. What they do have glows purple in the night, a dying supply of luminous security and power and prominence.

Soon the Bazaar will be lit by fire, and citizens will carry torches around instead of lanterns illuminated with spectorium, which isn't in itself a terrible thing. The people used fire for centuries before spectorium was discovered and culled for its power, and they can certainly make do with it again. It's not ideal, to trek in the direction of their ancestors, but it's the only option they have at the moment. If it keeps his subjects fed and warm, who is he to complain?

But the Superiors, they will complain. Once the last splendor of spectorium has died out and the mechanical contraptions they use to amuse themselves fail for lack of power, they will grow edgy. Father always said that if the Superior class is not entertained, they will entertain themselves with ideas of overthrowing the throne. He said it is a natural inclination of people, to want to rule. And because the people of Theoria do not yet know what sort of king Tarik will become, the Superiors could easily play on the citizens' fears and worries for the future, and steal the throne from beneath him.

What they don't know is that Tarik would be glad for the relief. Becoming pharaoh, being responsible for so many lives . . . it's not as glorious as the Superiors think it. Perhaps he should turn the throne over to them for a time, see if they can solve this spectorium conundrum and while they're at it, tackle the plague harvesting victims from among them. Then perhaps they would be more humble when making assumptions about what the royals are and are not doing for the people.

Outside the palace walls, the well-worn dirt path, fresh with chariot tracks, meanders its own way into the Bazaar of Anyar and eventually branches out and finds its way to the Lyceum. It's the same path used by visitors and invaders alike, the only road etched into the sand on this side, the only manageable way to come and go without being bogged down by the soft waves of the desert.

The Bazaar, when he and Patra arrive, thrums with trade and bartering and life itself. A pulse runs through the booths and tents in the form of commerce, buying and selling and negotiating. Patra weaves in and out of the crowd beside him, never more than inches away from him and on high alert at all times, but still fascinated and taken in by the smells and the sounds and the bustle. Fabrics, spices, vegetables, grains, jewelry, gems, fish, baskets, and pottery make up the medley that is the Bazaar, and Tarik wonders what it's like to stay here all day and watch the people carry on as if their lives didn't depend on it. People tend to give him a wide berth, for even though he's not browsing as pharaoh, his rank is obvious by his dress and harassing such a one is punishable by flogging.

He passes through, avoiding the women who would sell themselves to him and steering clear of the merchants who overzealously push their goods, trying to lure him to their tents and booths with offers too good to be true. They do not seem to care that any Lingot within earshot can hear the deception in their alluring pitches.

At the end of the market, the Lyceum of Favored Ones is visible to the north and the closer Tarik draws to it the more he finds he admires what the engineers have done to improve upon its appearance. It used to be a large, uninteresting square structure that loomed over the Bazaar in a dark and uninviting way. It reminded him of a prison instead of a place of higher learning, a concept he'd always associated with brightness and clarity. Once the attendance of the Favored Ones started to wane, it was decided to enhance the presentation of the school, make it more attractive for its potential pupils. The endeavor worked very well. His latest report from the Lyceum was that they were in full attendance and might soon require an extension of their already massive structure.

Now, instead of the dark, mud-colored blocks of desert sand, the face of the building is almost white with sun-bleached limestone harvested from the southern mines of Wachuk. Large rounded columns guard the front of it, offering inviting peeks of what's to come. Tarik ascends the grand stairs leading to the entrance and finds Cy the Healer waiting for him there. Cy doesn't recognize him at first, though, bidding him a good day and most likely expecting him to pass by, but when Tarik settles next to him on the limestone bench, Cy is forced to reconsider the person he thought was a stranger. The boy gives a sideways glance at Patra and recognition takes over his expression.

"Don't call me *Highness*," Tarik says quickly. "And do *not* bow."

Cy licks his lips. "That doesn't feel right, High—"

"Tarik."

The young Healer shakes his head. "I don't think I can do that."

"Of course you can. You're Cy. I'm Tarik. Now, let's get along with this, shall we? I'm curious to see what you have to show me."

Without further hesitation but not without a hint of awkwardness, Cy leads him and Patra into the Lyceum. The rooms are spacious and open and separated by grand archways. The marble floors resound in muted clicks beneath their sandaled feet as they weave their way past classrooms with open doors and ones with shut doors and one with no door at all. Cy bids him to ascend another set of stairs when they reach the north wall, and they climb several levels silently. Tarik feels uncomfortable since Cy is so obviously uneasy with the informal nature of his visit. Still, Cy must get used to such things. It would be a pain to make ceremony out of each visit he makes to the Lyceum, especially since he intends to do so more often to check on his young friend's progress. Whether that is an excuse to get away from the palace, Tarik isn't sure. Others cannot lie to him, but on occasion he finds that he can fool himself.

When they run out of stairs, Cy bids him down a long hallway that would be dark if it weren't for the lanterns of blue, dying spectorium lining the walls. "That spectorium could be put to better use," Tarik mutters.

Cy gives him an amused glance. "Yes, High—Tarik. It could have, were it used before this stage. But I've found that in this form, with the power dwindling so rapidly, the spectorium is of little rejuvenating use."

"Rejuvenating?"

Cy grins. "Yes. You'll see. Come."

At the end of the hall, Cy comes to a vast wooden door, locked by a wooden barrier on the outside of it. Tarik scowls. "I was under the impression that we had called for volunteers, not prisoners."

"Forgive me, uh, Tarik, but if we allowed him out of the room he would terrorize the entire school. Trust me, things are as they should be."

A faint scream echoes from the other side of the door, and there is an urgency in the way Cy lifts the board from its position obstructing entry and sets it hastily to the side against the wall with a loud "plunk."

Once inside, they happen upon a young boy, possibly six or seven years in age, screaming at a capacity unhealthy for his lungs at an exasperated servant who holds a tray of fruit and meats. "I don't want fruit. I told you, I want custard," the boy says, on the verge of sobbing.

"Healer Cy says you must eat for your health while you're here, young master. Please, you adore grapes. Won't you have some?"

"No!" The young master slaps the tray the servant offers; she recovers quickly as though she's used to such outbursts.

"Enough!" Cy roars, impressing even Tarik with the manfulness of his tone. "Juya, you're in my care until you're completely well. What would your father say?"

Juya the young master juts out his bottom lip, which quivers under the weight of Cy's stare. "But Cy, I'm better. You see?" He pulls down his cheeks to expose as much of his eyeballs as possible. "The redness and swelling are gone. And I've stopped bleeding." Juya scowls at his servant accusingly. "At least, that's what she said."

The servant, an older woman with more wrinkles than patience, sets the tray down on Juya's bed and brushes her hands together as if washing them of the situation. "I'm going to speak to your mother about your tantrum, Master Juya." She wags a finger at him. "Your mother will surely be ashamed."

"Don't tell Mother!" Juya says. "Look, I'm eating the grapes, Taia. I'm eating them. See?" He shoves three big ones in his mouth and proceeds to speak around them. "They're good, too. So good."

She eyes him. "Well. Maybe I'll not have to speak to Mistress Suyan after all."

"No," he agrees. "You don't. See?" More grapes, and this time, he picks up a generous sliver of meat and wiggles it at her. "I'll even eat the veal."

Taia nods. "Good. That's a good little master."

Tarik wonders if he himself acted that way when he was younger and cringes when he realizes he just might have. Only, his aversion hadn't been to eating, it was against taking baths. He hated going to the baths with his mother and bathing with all the women instead of being able to go with his father and bathe with all the men. But his mother insisted the men didn't talk of anything suitable for a boy's ears—which, of course, made him want to accompany them even more.

Cy walks to Juya's bedside and lifts the boy's chin as he chews. "It is quite remarkable," he says. "The swelling is almost completely gone, in a matter of a sunrise and sunset." He turns to Tarik. "You see, Juya's father, a Superior nobleman, volunteered him for our experimental treatments with spectorium. This boy was on the verge of death just two days ago, I swear to you. I thought we would lose him the night they brought him." Juya's eyes grow big at this revelation.

Tarik steps closer, bidding Patra to stay at the door. There is dried blood encrusted around the boy's nostrils, and a bit of the same at his ears; his shoulder bones jut out sharply and his arms could be fully grasped by the hand of the child. He did suffer the worst part of it, Tarik can see. Still, with a little weight put on, the boy would otherwise appear in perfect health, not sickly by any means. It's difficult to imagine that he was slipping away into death just two days prior, when right now all he wants for is a thorough bath and food. Plenty of food.

"Who is this?" Juya says.

"Pharaoh heard of your illness and sent me to make sure you were comfortable while being treated," Tarik says. "I'm his servant."

Juya allows himself the luxury of taking in the sight of him. Satisfied, and a bit smugly, he says, "So, the pharaoh has heard of me? I'm not surprised. My father is the wealthiest noble in Theoria." At this he sniffs. Tarik discerns that the boy is telling the truth—or at the very least, the boy believes what he is saying.

Tarik raises a brow but says nothing. He hasn't a clue who the boy's father is, and furthermore, is not aware that there *was* a wealthiest noble in all of Theoria—or that the title deserved special attention. It must be the sort of thing the Superior class finds useful and perhaps even entertaining. "The Healer Cy has been so kind as to explain to me your treatment, so that I may relay that to the Falcon King. Would it be acceptable to you, young master, if I were to stay for his examination so that I may report to pharaoh of your good condition?"

"Of course," Juya says generously. "You may stay."

Cy sets about inspecting the boy, feeling at his jawbone, pressing into his stomach, testing each limb by bending and stretching it. All the while, Juya does as he's instructed as if humoring an irritating relative or acquaintance. "I don't have to take the needle again, do I, Cy?" His voice cracks just a bit.

"Needle?" Tarik says.

Cy nods. "Our method, the method that seemed to have worked

on young master Juya here, is that we heat the spectorium back into liquid form, and then inject it in his most apparent vein."

"I glowed," Juya says proudly.

"He did glow somewhat," Cy says, frowning. "We could see everywhere his veins carried the spectorium. It was . . . quite fascinating. In fact, I think we could use that for future cases in which we have a need to find a blockage—"

"You injected spectorium into the boy?" Tarik says, mesmerized. He couldn't help but hold a new respect for Juya. "Did it hurt?"

"It burned. I cried. Only a little, though."

Tarik looks at Cy. "But wouldn't the spectorium cool inside his body and harden again?"

Cy smiles. "It would, yes. But you see, the blood is thinning as it is, and the spectorium helps it to thicken. Though I did have to mix it with red sage leaf to prevent the hardening, and a root balm to coat his veins to prevent burns inside the body."

"Why does the spectorium work?" Not that Tarik wants his young friend to think he doubts him, but in order to continue to allow such treatments, he feels he should understand it himself. "I'm no Healer, keep in mind. But I'm sure the king would like to know, don't you?"

Cy purses his lips. "Well, to put it plainly, it's as if Juya's body needed a boost of power. By all accounts, other than a weakening and dissipating of the flesh and, of course, blood loss, I can't find any other symptoms except lack of energy. It's quite mystifying, really."

"And so you turned to a source that created energy."

Cy nods quickly. "But I did test it on sheep before."

"I wasn't aware any sheep had been sick."

"No High—Tarik. I tested to make sure the liquid wouldn't solidify once in the body."

Tarik feels the blood drain from his face and pool in his hands and feet. "You mean to say you didn't know what would happen to the boy after you injected him." He didn't intend to raise his voice, but the alarm got the better of him.

Cy raises an eyebrow. "I mean to say that I knew what would *certainly* happen to him if I *didn't*. This plague is not to be trifled with. His father was willing to try anything to save him."

Cy's words fall on Tarik's ears and ring true. Everyone involved believed the boy would die. A last-minute effort on Cy's part had saved him. He should be thanking the young Healer and complimenting him on his ingenuity rather than questioning it. "Of course. Well done, Healer Cy."

Cy beams. "Thank you. May I—that is, I'd like for you to send a message to the Falcon King. Would you ask him if I could repeat the experiments on other willing patients?"

"I'm sure the king will agree to this, but I'll deliver your request."

Tarik is able to find his way out of the Lyceum on his own. He doesn't want to keep Cy from his needy patient any longer, and he has much to think about—and company would tend to distract him.

"What am I to do, Patra?" he says, turning his path back to the market. "Spectorium is the solution, and it's the one thing Theoria doesn't have."

But Patra offers no answer on their way back to the palace.

13

SEPORA

I CAN'T STOP THINKING OF THE LAST TIME I SAW my father. Of his expression when I Forged a sword and pointed it at his face. I had refused to Forge for him any longer and he'd been about to strike me, I could tell. And so I'd Forged the sword faster than I'd ever Forged anything in my life. That is when I made the decision I would not be a waif like Mother, that some things are more important than obedience. He'd had me imprisoned immediately in the highest mountain of Serubel, in a cell with an iron gate and open wall in the back, in case I chose to jump from it and plummet to my death. He never believed I would. I know he thought that after all my royal comforts were taken away, I would submit to his demands. He never expected Mother to come to my aid. I can only imagine his outrage at discovering that indeed, I had taken my own life. Or at least, so I hoped it appeared.

It has been three suns and three moons since Rolan and Chut captured me, and if the great River Nefari weren't still to our right, I'd say we were lost. My face stings from the certain sunburn I've acquired, and my feet are swollen so as to protrude from my worn servants' slippers. I stumble to catch up, trailing my captors by several feet while they talk and banter between themselves. They have not bothered to tie me up. Each night Rolan asks if I will escape, and each night I tell him I am much too tired to do anything but sleep. This seems to placate him.

I wonder aloud how close we must be to Anyar, but neither of them answers. Surely we're close enough for Rolan to allow my face to heal and my feet to rest. Too, I must look a mess in this tattered clothing.

Rolan is a trader. Indifferent and logical. Surely he'll see the reason in those things. Perhaps he didn't hear my question before, though, so I try Chut. "Chut," I croak. "Please stop. I must relieve myself."

Chut does indeed stop and calls ahead to Rolan, who must have heard but kept going. "Says she needs to relieve herself. Again." I try not to smile at the irritation in his voice. It's true; I make them stop often. But I must Forge at every opportunity if I'm to keep my energy up.

"You just did, moments ago," Rolan says, stopping. The corner of his mouth tugs up in an ugly grin. "You're slowing us down. Perhaps that is your plan?"

"It's been longer than moments," I tell him. I should know. I've been tracking the movement of the sun, and expelling the spectorium once every hour or so, as far as I can tell. If anyone wants to get to Anyar, it's me. But I can't risk leaking the element at night while I sleep, either. I think of the royal toddler who leaked in his bed and almost blush. I've been able to control my Forging since I was four years old. Not a single accident since then.

"Funny that," Chut says, clutching my chin with his big hand, but not ungently. "One would think she'd be as exhausted as we are, but look at her. All . . . spry and chipper."

"Well." I snap my chin from his grasp. "If you had to walk around in flimsy slippers, you would not think so at all."

Rolan contemplates this. After several moments of assessing me, he says, "We'll make camp here. We're just outside of Anyar." Relief billows through me like a welcome breeze. He looks at Chut. "I'll take the spectorium to the Bazaar and trade for some food and proper clothing for her. We'll break our journey here and rest up."

Chut nods down at me. "Can't imagine she'll fetch much, dressed like that. Those eyes, though. Aren't they something to behold?"

To my surprise, Rolan agrees. "The only breathtaking thing about her." With that, he turns to the horizon ahead and leaves us.

I look up at Chut, shielding my eyes from the sun directly overhead. "I need to relieve myself," I remind him. Abruptly, he turns his back to me.

The rule is that I'm allowed privacy as long as I keep talking. As soon as I stop, they'll turn around to make sure I've not run off. So as I dig my hole for the spectorium, I begin to babble on about being raised in Serubel. I tell Chut about the Serpens, one of his favorite things to hear about—especially the legend of the Scaldlings—and I tell him about the rope bridges and the Great Falls, which pour into the River Nefari.

To my relief, Chut never questions why it's taking so long. The hole is deep and I fill it to the brim with spectorium, not bothering to shape it, just letting it pour from my hands and cool in the hot desert sand. I cover it over with sand and relieve myself quickly on top of it, so that the sloppy mound is not subject to investigation. Not that I believe Chut to be instinctively curious, but just in case he's hungry and brilliant at the moment—and therefore in the mood to ask questions.

When I've finished, he offers me a sampling of food, which consists of cactus stripped of its thorns, a few slices of dried fish, and some sort of berry that I'd been tempted to eat earlier but wasn't sure if it was poisonous. *It would have been nice to know*, I think as the juices make a pleasant explosion in my mouth. All these resources I'd been passing by with a lamenting stomach. I would not have survived if I hadn't been captured.

"Pace yourself," Chut says as I struggle to chew my mouthful. "Or you'll lose everything you've taken in."

As I eat, Chut hurls questions at me. "Why did you let her go?" he says, his brows drawn together.

"Her eyes," I say, which surprises us both. "She understood what was happening to her."

"Well, of course she did. Same as she understands what happens to the people she's probably eaten in her lifetime."

I hadn't thought of that. Of course, he's right. I offer him back the berries I shouldn't finish, lest I vomit. He accepts them, popping one into his mouth thoughtfully.

"I hope you learned a lesson," he says a bit smugly, nodding at my hand, which still throbs with pain from the venom. "Parani are not stupid. And they are not friendly."

We sit in silence then and wait for Rolan to return. He takes a long time, and it makes me wonder how big the Bazaar is, how busy it could be. If the crowd is large enough to slip off into.

Rolan returns as the sun is setting, a great pack strapped to his back. He eyes me inquisitively as he sets down his load. "You've thinned out some these past few days," he says warily. An understatement, we both know. Our rations have been light, to say the least. "Did you eat?"

I nod.

Out of the pack, he retrieves a handful of leafy stalks, a tiny glass jar of white powder, and a small clay cooking pot. "These will ease the blisters on your face," he says, shaking the leaves at me. "And I'll brew something that will help your swelling ankles. Chut, start a fire. We'll need to boil the leaves first. Draw out the medicine."

"We've no more flint," Chut informs him.

"I've procured more for us, friend." He tosses Chut two sizable rocks. Chut does not have the coordination to catch them, but picks them up from the sand and wanders off, I suppose to collect something parched enough to support a fire.

While the pot is cooling, Rolan pulls what looks like linen from his pack. "I've brought you some proper attire. Your gown is filthy, and besides that, there's far too much of it."

He walks it to me. I begin to unfold the garment and am horrified when there is very little to unravel. I hold it up, unsure if I'm looking at the top or the bottom. "Where is the rest of it?"

"That's it."

"I cannot wear this," I tell him. Surely Mother did not have this in mind. Surely the Serubelans in the Baseborn Quarters do not demean themselves with such scanty attire.

"You'll wear it," he says, and spits in the sand next to me.

"This will barely cover me," I protest, handing it back to him. He pushes it toward me again.

"Well now, that's the point, isn't it? How can I lure a buyer for you all covered up like a temple widow? Though I'm sure that creamy skin of yours will fetch a high price. That sort of coloring is rare in Theoria, even among the freed slaves."

I'm not sure what a temple widow is, but apparently it is someone who dresses with some semblance of modesty around others and has little need for leaves to heal a sunburn. Yes, Theoria is hot and I've not experienced a moment where I'm not sweating. This garment would offer a measure of relief from the sweltering air, but is it really considered proper here to reveal so much of one's body? How vile Theoria must be!

And why am I asking such silly questions of myself? According to Rolan, I'm to become the mistress of a merchant. Should I not be more worried about that?

But I'm going to escape, I tell myself. And soon, before we get to the city of Anyar.

Chut returns and coaxes a fire to life in a rudimentary pit he's dug. Rolan sets about crushing up the leaves and boiling them, then hands them to me to press upon my face. I'll admit, it does instantly draw out the heat from my cheeks. As if for good measure, he dumps the rest of the leaves in the pot and boils it some more. After a while, he blows on the top of the green frothy concoction, wrapping a piece of linen around the pot for a barrier between it and his hand. He drops a clump of what looks like sugar in it, then adds the jar of powder, swirling it around for a few seconds. He hands it to me gently, letting me take it from his hand. "Careful. It's hot. Just sip it."

I'm horrified to have to be drinking something hot in this heat. It seems like a punishment instead of any sort of cure. "What is this? It smells awful." Thanks to the sugar, it actually smells sweet, ugly as it is, but I want to be difficult for Rolan. I owe him that much. And besides, I've become accustomed to lying as a first instinct.

"It's goat vine. It will hydrate and speed along the healing process of your burns. You'll need to drink it all."

But I'm already downing it. The brew is delicious and soothes my parched throat even as it scalds it. The bits of leaves get stuck in my teeth and Rolan instructs me to chew them, to make use of the entire blend. I'm half inclined to thank him, but I just cannot bring myself to do it. The only reason he is helping me at all is to recover a high price for all the trouble he's taken in keeping me. We must be close to the city; they want their precious cargo to heal before presenting me at the Bazaar.

"Are you not going to drink some yourself?" I ask, even as I tilt the pot higher to corral the last drop in it. But the thought is fleeting; the brew overtakes me.

In my vision, the world disappears into a shrinking hole, the last of which surrounds Rolan's grinning face as I pass out.

14

TARIK

RASHIDI ALLOWS HIMSELF INTO TARIK'S CHAM-
bers unbidden. Tarik lies in his massive bed, in the very space
his father used to lay. It's an eerie feeling, sleeping in the room
where his father had died, in the bed where his father had wasted
away to bones. Rashidi ascends the stairs and seats himself in front
of Tarik on the edge of the bed. Tarik doesn't look at him, only continues to pet Patra, who lies beside him, and stares at the mural
painted on the high ceiling above.

"The caravans have been dispatched to Pelusia and Serubel,
Highness."

"We need the Serubelan spectorium, Rashidi. You should have
seen the boy Juya. He had been on the threshold of death and healed
completely within two turns of the sun."

Rashidi sighs. "Of course, I could not have seen the boy, sire, as I
tend to stay in the palace where I belong."

"I must know my people," Tarik says. "And the only way to truly
do that is to be among them." That's the most noble reason he has

for leaving the palace, but there are more selfish ones, too, and they both know it. Besides that, Rashidi does not stay in the palace so much as he claims. He is, after all, an advocate of the people of Theoria. His duties require him to be among its citizens.

Rashidi doesn't argue—something that suggests he has ulterior motives for personally delivering the message about the caravans. Tarik tenses and waits. Rashidi clears his throat. "As your trusted adviser, Highness, I must recommend sending a caravan to Hemut as well."

Tarik slides a cautious glance to his friend. "Why is that?"

"To open the discussion of marriage talks, of course."

He shoots up, startling both Patra and Rashidi. "And who does Sethos want to marry?" And at fifteen years? Oh blast, what has his brother gotten himself into? Had Tarik not been clear when he said he didn't need anything else to worry about? Surely Sethos did not make a fool of himself over the attractive emissary who'd presented in court? "It was not *my* idea to invite her to the palace dinner," Tarik grumbles to himself. Only a blind man would not notice the attention Sethos had given her.

"You misunderstand me, sire. The bride I have in mind would be for *you*."

Ah, so. Rashidi is of the same mind as Sethos; they both wish a woman upon him. Marriage even. Another mouth to feed, feelings to consider, a costly wedding no doubt. All at a time like this? It's nearly unthinkable.

When Tarik doesn't answer, Rashidi continues, "You'll need an heir as soon as possible. What if—and it's a terrible thing to say, sire, so please forgive me—you were to contract this awful plague? Then the bloodlines would stop with you."

"There would still be Sethos," he says dryly.

Rashidi sniffs. "I've no doubt your brother has already started some errant bloodlines of his own, Highness. But you well know the law. The firstborn son—"

"I know the law, Rashidi. But why are we in such a rush? I've barely taken the throne. Father is still warm in the tomb. Besides, Father married for love. Why can't I?"

"Your father did not marry for love. As I recall, he did happen to fall in love with your mother after they were wed, which is a rare and fortunate circumstance. I'm afraid marriage is not about love."

Tarik lies back down and turns away from Rashidi. Patra is still purring and sees fit to readjust her position, too, so that Tarik has better access to scratch behind her ears.

"Princess Tulle is very beautiful, you know."

In all the five kingdoms, Princess Tulle's hand is the most sought after and has been since Tarik was a boy. Her beauty has inspired songs even in Theoria, and most of them are about how every man who encounters her will be heartbroken eventually, either by her inability to reciprocate his feelings or because she is to marry a mysterious, faraway prince. Her father has waited until a suitable match could be made; he must have had Tarik in mind all along, which makes his head throb with pressure. Tarik scoffs. "What do I care of beauty?"

"The Superiors care very much for beauty. And they adore the cold climates of the ice kingdom. What they care for, you should care for."

"How do you mean?"

"More and more of them are taking their wealth and resources— including what's left of the spectorium—to the kingdom of Hemut. If we are in control—er, that is to say, if we have an alliance with that kingdom—then perhaps we can see some of that spectorium return to Theoria."

Tarik wants to fight against his adviser's logic, but when he lays it about like that, what choice does he have? He sighs into the dry night air. Once the spectorium runs out, and the Superiors have none to trade in Hemut, will the ice kingdom turn them away? If that happened, some might actually try to relocate there, taking their other resources and commerce with them. The last thing a plague-stricken Theoria needs right now is a failing economy to kick them in the stomach. "A pity the princess of Serubel fell to her death. I would offer for her directly. We need all the spectorium we can get our hands on. Did she have a sister, by chance?"

"I'm afraid not, Highness."

"Unfortunate. I'd get dressed and accompany a caravan this very night."

"It is regretful that you don't feel the same of Princess Tulle of Hemut. Your enthusiasm would go a long way in securing the marriage."

"They'd be foolish not to want to align with us. We're the most advanced kingdom of all the Five. I'm just afraid our citizens will think it foolish on *our* part to share our majesty with an inferior kingdom." Pompous words, he knows. But he can't allow Rashidi's logic to dominate the conversation.

"Our citizens well know we're surrounded by inferior kingdoms. Would you rather I send a Lingot to Wachuk and inquire of one of their many princesses? To say the least, we'll always be assured there will be food on our table." At his joke, Rashidi chuckles.

Wachuk is by far the crudest kingdom of all the Five. The women are known to be unkempt and dirty, often not bathing for weeks.

They take multiple husbands and divorce often, and only bother to bear children in between their many hunting expeditions. Tarik has seen a Wachuk woman. She was more muscular than Sethos. He shudders.

"Send a caravan to Hemut," he blurts. "Let us see what they say."

15

SEPORA

SOMEONE CALLS MY NAME, BUT I CANNOT ANSWER. My eyelids flutter but will not open. My mouth rejects words; my throat is too withered dry to form them anyway. I become aware of someone patting my cheek, the action graduating to a stinging slap as I regain my wits. I try to fight back but hear myself moan in indignation instead. Saints of Serubel, why can I not open my eyes?

Then I remember the goat-vine potion. Rolan telling me to drink it all. Chew the leaves, he'd said. It'll heal you, he'd said. Ha! I remember the swift feel of ease and contentment fall over me, my eyelids heavy against the brightness of the sun.

Oh yes, the potion. I've been knocked unconscious, only not by the hand of a brute this time. I took the mixture with my own steady hands and nearly thanked Rolan for it in the process: foolish, foolish.

Sounds. Sounds echo all around me, far away at first, then right upon me as though men, women, and children have all gathered around me, all gibbering in their Theorian tongue. Feet shuffling, metal clanking, the far-off bray of horses, water sloshing around. A medley of noises that could only mean one thing.

I'm at the Bazaar.

I'm at the Bazaar.

I must get out of the Bazaar!

Forcing one of my eyes open, then the other, I pull my hands to my face to try to stop my head from spinning. Finally my vision adjusts, and a few arm's lengths away, I see Rolan and Chut talking to a man. The man wears a black metal beard jutting from his chin, a painted cylinder that reaches from his jaw almost as far as his belly extends, nearly caressing his chest as he speaks. Chin pieces are a sign of Theorian wealth. And so are the sort of headdresses this man wears. I've seen them in paintings back home, and on some of the wealthy Theorian merchants who dared to request a sitting with my father to negotiate the price of spectorium. Not to mention, what Aldon taught me about this society. We did not have an extensive lesson on Theoria per se, but we did cover their wealth and haughtiness in multitudes.

I have to get out of here.

Wriggling my toes to assure myself they work, I perform the same exercise on the rest of my body. Ankles, knees, hips, arms, shoulders—moving them all just slightly enough to test their ability to function without drawing attention to myself. Occasionally Chut glances my way, and I become still as a corpse, fighting against the adrenaline surging through me. I'm almost shaking with the need to flee.

That man, that wealthy Theorian man wants to buy me, an unconscious girl whom he's never met. Theoria is a despicable kingdom for allowing such things to happen in their boundaries and in public. The Bazaar is not only for trading goods, but people as well. Aldon did not tell me about this. All he taught me was the language, though I never thought I'd have to use it, and the history and the political interests he thought a princess should know.

Well, a princess should certainly know of *these* things as well.

My mind thrums with the sum of it all. The Warrior King has died and the Falcon King has taken his place, an eighteen-year-old boy who probably couldn't find his way out of his own palace to inspect the goings-on of his kingdom. If I ever get to meet this Falcon King, I'll knock him on his rear for allowing such things to occur. For women to be exploited in such a way. Given and taken as gifts. Utterly unacceptable.

Satisfied that not only should I run, but also that I'm capable of doing so, I jump up. Chut reacts immediately, coming toward me with open arms, meaning to secure me. I nearly fail to dodge him as I take in the crowd around me. I'll stick out sorely with these clothes—wait. My clothes. I'm not wearing servants' attire anymore. I'm wearing one piece of linen folded around me to cover only the most pertinent of areas. When did this happen? And why am I allowing it to distress me when I should be interested in escaping?

Rolan takes advantage of my hesitation, grasping my arm and jerking me backward. I use the momentum to force the crown of my head into his nose as he leans down and gain an instant release. Chut hurries forward arms wide, and again I dodge him, thankful that he's as slow on his feet as I'd hoped.

I take off running, past the wailing children, past the braying horses, past a woman pouring water from a bucket and a man showing a piece of glittering jewelry. But the Bazaar only becomes bigger and bigger, no matter where I turn or how fast I run, there is no end to it. I dare not look back, dare not become discouraged by the sounds of feet falling in pursuit of me. Booth after booth, tent after tent. It's a maze of entrapment. I begin to feel dizzy, and wonder how long I was unconscious. How long has it been since I Forged?

My feet do not sprint as they should. I've the feeling the booths do not whir by me because of my great speed, but because of my body's need to release spectorium. I must find a safe place to expel it. I must find a safe place for *me*.

And fortune does not favor me this day.

Ahead I see soldiers. Surely they will help me. Surely this practice of selling people is not truly legal in Theoria. It is a secret business of sorts, an operation in which only thugs and thieves partake. After all, Chut and Rolan do not strike me as upstanding citizens. "Help me," I yell at them, not slowing until I've pitched myself into the arms of the first soldier I come to. He's just as surprised as I am.

"Help you, mistress? What is your need?"

"I've been kidnapped," I tell him breathlessly. "And they're chasing me."

There is shouting behind us and someone yells, "Hold her! She's the property of the Falcon King! Do not let her escape."

The voice does not belong to Chut or Rolan but to an older man. Perhaps the wealthy man I saw before? I do not know. All I know is that the soldier wraps his arms around me and to my horror, keeps me in place while my captor approaches. His black metal beard arrives long before he does.

"The Prince Sethos means to give her as a gift to His Majesty the Falcon King. For his harem," he informs the guard. Prince Sethos? The Falcon King? His *harem*? I try to recall what exactly a harem is, and my mind refuses to fully comprehend the idea. To fully comprehend my truly horrific luck.

The man with the beard comes to us, and as I squirm and writhe in the soldier's arms, screaming as loud as my breathless lungs will allow, he reaches his hand out and clamps it on my shoulder.

My vision is an instant tunnel, growing black around the edges. What did he do to me?

I reach for the explanation, but it eludes me. In fact, everything does. All I remember is falling against the soldier behind me, limp as a string. I'm reminded of the goat-vine potion Rolan gave me as the brilliant colors of the Bazaar fade to gray and black.

I AWAKEN TO A BEAUTIFUL WOMAN STANDING over me. She holds a cloth in one hand and with it, reaches for my face. Sitting up, I shove her hand away, more forcefully than I'd intended, and she laughs. "I wondered when you would wake," she says. "I've wanted to see your eyes since you arrived. You have the whole of us curious."

Even her voice is beautiful, her words lilting around us in the open room. She has long dark hair bound in sections down her back, exquisitely long lashes, and eyes bluer than the sky in Serubel. She sits next to me on a couch, effectively blocking me from getting up to flee. I wonder if she did it on purpose. I fold my knees into my arms, just to put that much more distance between the two of us.

"They were right," she says. "No one has eyes like you."

"Where am I?"

She laughs again, and the world seems to get brighter. How can one person be so enchanting? "You are privileged with being the newest concubine of the Falcon King's harem. Perhaps now that you're here, he'll pay us a visit. You are a gift from his brother, after all. He would not be so rude as to neglect the gesture."

"A *concubine*?" And what's more, I'm a mere gesture of goodwill between brothers. Saints of Serubel, how could I let this happen?

Mother would expire directly were she here to see this. I was to go to the Baseborn Quarters where I would not stand out. Now I'm a concubine of my father's own enemy, and rumors have already spread about my silver eyes—at least, throughout the harem. How long before the rumors reach outside the walls of Anyar? How long before my father finds out I live?

I bite my lip, disappointment at my utter failure stinging my eyes.

She allows me to curl up and my shoulders pinch together. "Ow," I say pathetically. I remember then that the man with the metal beard squeezed me there before I blacked out.

"Should I call for a Healer?" the woman says. I suppose her to be at least twenty years of age, if not slightly older. She giggles at my apparent perplexity. "Who would have thought that the king would prefer plump women?"

Well. My mother always said I had the curves of the River Nefari, but compared to this girl, anyone could be considered plump. Surely they feed the concubines of the harem?

But at the moment, I need not concern myself with the malnutrition of concubines. My concern is for Forging. I have no idea how long I've been unconscious, how many hours or even days the goat potion kept me idle. I do feel quite faint but cannot discern whether it's the goat potion still in my bloodstream or my need to Forge.

"I must relieve myself," I tell her. "Privately."

She purses her lips. "Cort said you were a flight risk. You should know that if you try to escape, there are guards at every entrance. Don't bring harm to yourself."

Why she should care if I bring harm to myself I'm not sure. "I need to relieve myself," I tell her again.

She nods behind us, to a vast room without a door. "We have

running water in there. The seats by the fountain are most comfortable."

Running water. Our castle in Serubel had running water that eventually spilled into the River Nefari, but there were some structures where the waste simply splattered down to the Underneath. "Where does the water empty?"

She looks at me as though I've grown a second nose. "What?"

"The . . . the refuse. Where does it go?"

"Surely you're not thinking of escaping through the—"

"Of course not!" I tell her quickly, though that could have been a thought. What is a little refuse compared with being defiled as a concubine of the Falcon King? "I'm just curious to get to know my surroundings, if this is to be my home." Lying has become a part of me, I realize. I wonder if there will ever be a time when I don't have to lie to survive.

She smiles. "It empties into the River Nefari." She grasps my hand, which looks horridly puffy in hers. Though I daresay a twig would appear puffy in her grasp. Still, I wonder just how "curvy" I really am.

"My name is Gonya. What is yours?"

"Sepora. Gonya, I—"

"Yes, yes. Go relieve yourself."

I ALLOW THE SPECTORIUM TO POUR FROM MY palms, not bothering to shape or mold it. It steams as it hits the water and disappears, headed toward the River Nefari. I'm careful to release it in small pellets so as not to clog the pipe when it hardens in the water. This is much better than having to bury it, as I would have to in other, less luxurious waste holes or in the desert as I've done for the past weeks. Indeed, the marble columns and gold-plated orna-ments remind me that I am in the Theorian palace, that I am property of the Theorian king, and that the Theorian king has much more wealth than I ever imagined. All of this to accommodate a place to relieve one's self? What must the throne room look like?

The many curtained seats here in the lavatory lead me to wonder exactly how many concubines the king cares to keep. And why he would possibly need another one, when he has someone like Gonya to occupy his time.

As if I thought her into existence, she appears in the open door-way of the lavish room, her expression filled with worry. I'll not allow myself to like Gonya, I decide. Because I will not be staying here long enough to make a friend.

I halt the expulsion of spectorium from my hands and absorb the leftover liquid back into my palms. Standing, I greet her. "Gonya, hello. I was just finishing up here." If she wonders why I was kneel-ing in front of the water hole, she doesn't say as much.

"Well then, come with me," she says. "I'll show you around and introduce you to the rest of us."

The rest of us.

Allowing Gonya to whisk me past plush, colorful couches and rooms separated by sheer drapes and floors inlaid with what appears to be gold, we approach an outside area abundant in sunshine and barely dressed women. Guards stand on either side of the entrance, spears and shields at the ready. The sound of falling water and the heavy scent of orchids assault our senses before we ever reach the gar-den itself.

All of the glorious concubines lounge, each of them in their own state of relaxation and skillful undress, around a clear shallow pool that seems to glitter as though gems were spread precariously along the bottom of it. Some of the women dangle their feet in the water and talk among themselves. They wear a variety of paint on their faces, mostly red on their lips but with vibrant, rich colors and kohl designs around their eyes, artistically drawn to rival any creation adorning the castle walls back home in Serubel. Each woman drips with jewelry, gold, and gems pressing at their necks, wrists, even their ankles. More baubles hang from one woman than my mother has in her entire collection.

Mother would chafe at the sight of such wasted luxury here. I can't help but agree.

Conversation tends to halt as we make our way to the back of the sanctuary where a catlike woman reclines on what I'd consider a small throne overlooking the rest of the gathering. This woman wears much more jewelry than the others, in addition to a headdress made up entirely of Defender Serpen scales shimmering brilliantly when she turns her attention to us.

I'd heard Theorians have the barbaric tradition of killing Serpens just to adorn themselves with their scales, but I'd never seen such a spectacle in person. Nurturing an immediate dislike for this woman and thanking the saints of Serubel that I did not bring Nuna on this journey, I take in the rest of her with enough scrutiny to match the ability of any Seer Serpen. Wrinkles tug at the woman's eyes, which are made more noticeable by the thick black paint encircling them, drawing out the deep emerald color around her pupils. She wears no red on her lips, and she should, for if there were any mouth in need of beautifying, it would be this woman's. As it is, she molds her face into a scowl as Gonya and I draw closer.

"So, the prize of the harem has awakened," she announces loudly. She may like me even less than I like her.

"Tuka, this is Sepora, our newest member," Gonya says diplomatically.

"So, the boy Falcon King wishes for a newer, younger variety even though he hasn't even bothered to inspect his existing coffer of women." Tuka leans back, taking in a slow breath. She used to be a beautiful woman, and in some ways, she still could be, if she did not allow bitterness to strain all her more attractive features.

"Sepora," Gonya says, her voice slightly shaky, "this is Tuka. She's the eldest of His Majesty's harem, and Favorite One of the Warrior King."

So, Tuka is jealous of my age. To her, I am a threat. She was the favorite of the Falcon King's father, and now I am the first addition since he passed away. If I could muster up some affection for this woman, and if I intended to stay here a moment longer, I would assure her I had no ambition whatsoever to take her place as anyone's favorite. Already, the king would do well to stay away from me. In fact, perhaps if I told her this, she would help me.

"I don't want to be here," I tell her bluntly. "I will leave, if you'll show me the way out."

Amid the whispers all around, Gonya says, "Sepora! You mustn't say such things, lest His Majesty finds out."

I turn to her. "I should like to speak to His Majesty," I tell her. "I was purchased in the Bazaar."

Gonya waits, as if I'm going to say more.

I flush. "Did you hear me? I said I was *purchased*. Me. A person, not a horse or a cow or a—"

"Yes, yes," Gonya says quickly, grabbing my forearm and gently squeezing it. "I did hear you, Sepora." But by her expression, she underestimates the seriousness of the matter. "But leaving the harem is only a decision the king himself would allow, and it isn't likely he would bother himself with such a notion, as it's such a privilege to even be here."

I raise my chin, trying my best to appear regal and above her words. A privilege to be a slave? Has everyone gone mad? "How can I summon this Falcon King?"

Tuka bursts out laughing in genuine glee. Two of her chins jiggle with liveliness. "You wish to summon the king?"

"I do."

"And what will you do when you have his full attention?"

"I'll demand my release, of course." Even I wince at the severity of my answer. Perhaps, if I were smart, I wouldn't be declaring what I will and will not demand before the king in the company of such obviously loyal followers. My father did not keep a harem. But if he did, he would not put up with such insolence from one of his women.

I can see in her eyes that Tuka is happy with her successful provocation of me. "Guard!" she calls, and my stomach sinks, seeming to settle somewhere in my toes. One of the guards at the entrance of the lush sanctuary approaches. "How may I be of service, Mistress Tuka?"

She smiles at him. "The Mistress Sepora here wishes to summon the king."

The guard looks from Tuka to me and back again. Confusion emanates from his very being. "How do you mean, Mistress Tuka?"

She laughs. "Sepora, do tell us how you mean to summon the king."

"I . . . well, I . . . do you have parchment paper and ink?"

The guard scratches the back of his neck with the ledge of his shield. "I could obtain that for you, Mistress Sepora, if you wish."

Perhaps being a concubine is a privilege after all. Parchment and ink are expensive commodities in Serubel. I wonder how it fares in Theoria where there is no immediate supply of trees for the paper. As it were, Serubel had to trade a high price for it with Wachuk, which is even farther south than Theoria. "I do. Wish, I mean. For you to obtain that." So much for regal.

I can feel the weight of Tuka's stare on me. What I want most is the courage to deliver a glare back in her direction, but I'm so out of sorts at the moment that I can't scrounge up the bravery. I resolve to be better at that—courage. As I'm already a master of the lie.

"You heard her," Tuka tells the guard, slapping her knee. "Fetch the materials right away. We are all anxious to see the king's response to Sepora's urgent summons." Tuka is far too amused at my expense.

And after a week's worth of days, I figure out why.

The king simply does not answer summonses from his concubines. Each and every day, I bide my time, learning to paint faces as the other girls do, mostly practicing—and failing—on Gonya; I swim in the sanctuary pool; I eat my meals in silence, except for the times when Tuka sits next to me, prodding me with "And has His Majesty answered your most recent requests yet, Mistress Sepora?"

And each and every day, the answer is no.

By now I've been fitted and supplied with a new wardrobe so that I'm just as scantily and beautifully dressed as the other women. Colorful linens and silks and fabrics I've never seen before, and I have my choice among any and all of them. Fine jewelry from the kingdom of Hemut, rich in diamonds and rubies and any other kind of jewel one can fathom. Gold from the banks of the River Nefari in the southern kingdom of Wachuk. A maid to sculpt my hair into submission, braid it into art, and adorn it with flowers and sweet-smelling perfumes, should His Majesty the Falcon King care to visit and actually choose me from among the other gems of his harem to keep his esteemed company.

All this preparation for a chance visit from him, and he won't even respond to an actual request for his presence. No matter how urgently I address the letters. No matter how prettily I write them, or how angrily they are composed. No matter how I provoke him with my words. He'll not answer.

I'm confident that even my father would answer the last letter, if it were only to demand my head from my shoulders.

And so life exists this way until one day, while lying in the sun, I muster up an idea. A long shot, not my best of designs, but it's something. When I had first arrived, the harem had been abuzz with the recent events; the king had sent soldiers to collect all the spectorium in the harem, which had, by all accounts, been a massive haul. The spectorium had been embedded into ornaments and decorations to embellish the walls, had been thrown into the pool for added sparkle, in addition to being used for lighting in every room of the wing. The sudden and unexplained removal of all that glows had caused a stirring of curiosity—and a little outrage—among my fellow concubines, but it didn't take me long to figure out why he'd taken it. Without me, the kingdom of Serubel is not making any new spectorium, and the surrounding kingdoms will have been running out.

Including His Esteemed Majesty the Falcon King.

And so while I bask in the sun, using my finger to trace the now healed X carved by venom into my palm, a thought occurs to me. Letters will not get the attention of the king.

But spectorium will.

16

TARIK

TARIK DROPS THE CORRESPONDENCE HE'S BEEN reading and stands, sending his seat behind him flying backward. "What do you mean there is fresh spectorium in the harem?" Tarik nearly shouts at his guard. "There is no such thing as fresh spectorium anymore." He should know. He's been trying to get his hands on some for weeks for Cy's healing experiments. The weaker the spectorium, the weaker the healing results have been. And the spectorium they have left is doing nothing but weakening now.

The guard steps back. "I saw it with my own eyes, Highness. White spectorium, a huge mound, on the Concubine of the King's throne."

"Why on her throne? Where did she get it?"

"She claims not to know, sire. The women say it just appeared there overnight. The guards have no recollection of anyone coming in or out throughout the night. The women believe it to be a gift from you."

Impossible. This, of course, must be some sort of mistake. The only news he'd heard from the harem of late was that a few of the women had contracted the Quiet Plague, and a eunuch Healer had to be fetched to care for them. The harem had grown quite the burden indeed. "Have this so-called spectorium brought to me at once. And question all of the women in the harem. Someone had to have seen something. Who was the first to see it?"

"It was Mistress Sepora, Highness."

"Sepora." He pulls his great chair back to his marble desk and sits thoughtfully. "Why does that name sound familiar?" Then he glances down at the correspondence he'd been reading just moments before. It was, in fact, from the Mistress Sepora. Her handwriting is very loopy and her Theorian is broken, but he didn't detect any deception in her words. The problem is, there are too many of her words. Each day he receives a new parchment from her. And each day he begins to read it, but much more important matters of the kingdom usually take precedence and he ends up discarding it halfway through reading. "What do you know of this Sepora?" he asks quietly.

"She's the most beautiful in your harem, Highness. A gift from your brother."

Oh yes, he remembers now. Sethos had gifted him a new concubine, and Tarik had suspected that he was really gifting himself, in the event that Tarik let him make a secret visit to the royal harem. Tarik waves his hand. "I care nothing of her beauty. What do you know of *her*? Is she the mischievous sort?"

"No, sire. She is . . . well behaved."

The truth. So the guard is not enamored with her and trying to protect her. Likewise, he's telling the truth, or what he assumes to be the truth, about the mound of spectorium. "What do you make of this?" Tarik asks him.

The guard shrugs. "Sire, perhaps someone has gifted you with it, and somehow it ended up in the harem?"

"But you say no one was seen coming or going? Anyone sending me such a rich gift would have announced it to the rooftops, and yet I have no such declaration. Someone has gifted me with the most valuable resource in the kingdom, and no one is taking credit for it? Find my adviser, Rashidi. And bring that spectorium at once."

17

SEPORA

THE FALCON KING NEVER SHOWS UP TO RETRIEVE his spectorium. Ten of the king's soldiers arrived in his stead and hauled away every last pyramid of spectorium from our quarters without explanation or commentary. The women of the harem were left in a state of dizzied disbelief as their pride took nearly unsustainable blows. It was then that I realized their luxuries meant nothing so much as attention from their king.

And so my plan did not work.

Now, as I sit again in the sun, watching Tuka bat dismally at fruit flies buzzing around the perfumed sculpture of her hair, I realize what must be done. The king will never come to me in the harem. Therefore, I must go to him.

It will have to be done in the light of day, because without spectorium glowing in the halls and entryways, I'll never find my way out of this wing and to His Highness. After all, if the harem is this big, I cannot imagine how enormous the rest of the palace must be.

But the light of day has its own dangers; the guards will see me coming. No, they'll hear me coming, for all the linens and fine fabrics used for my clothing rustle stiffly even in the smallest of breezes. No, if I'm to make it as far as the exit of the wing where two guards watch over the king's women, I'm to make the trip noisily. It cannot be helped.

And so where I cannot have stealth, I will need speed and cunning. And today is as good as any.

Having Forged more than usual in the lavatory this morning, I've gained plenty of energy for my endeavors today. I wait for the highest part of the sun to pass and then make my way toward the exit. As I suspected they would, the guards hear me immediately and turn around. I make no fuss about having been caught already. "Mistress Sepora, you know you're not permitted in this part of the wing. Return to your sunbathing," one of them tells me kindly.

Still, I keep walking toward them, which obviously makes them uncomfortable. "Mistress, you must return to the sanctuary. It is simply not fitting for you to be so close to the palace hallway. What if someone were to see you? Think of how displeased the king would be."

"Of course, you're right," I say pleasantly but continue forward. One of them swallows, and the other squares his shoulders. They look like brothers, these guards, similar in build and color, with matching helmets and weapons—spears and shields, and neither of those ready enough for what is about to happen. "I'm just curious," I say to them. "Why has the king himself not come to the harem?"

But by now I've come close enough to execute my plan and so while they're racking their minds for a proper answer to my question, I begin to sprint toward them, gaining on them faster than even I thought possible. Running across rope bridges my entire life has made me nimble on my feet, but when the guards make their ready, I'm suddenly not as sure of myself as I was before.

Two men against one girl, and yet I keep the pace, maybe even hastening it, if that were possible. *I will never get around them*, I think as my approach grows imminent. They are rigid in stance and ready for my body to crash into them, to seize me, to return me to the harem and report my behavior to the king.

But this time I intend to be the one to report to the king.

So then, I decide I must simply go *under* them.

Within arm's length, one of the guards braces himself, spreading his legs far enough apart so that I can slide neatly between them—and out of the wing. I don't take the time to look behind me to gauge my pursuers; I pick myself up from the floor and run.

Of course, I have no idea where I'm going and I suspect that any second now a spear will pierce my back and my outing will have been for nothing. Before, when I was planning all this, I didn't account for the fact that escaping the harem's wing might be punishable by death, and so I make a jagged path as I run, hoping that my sharp, unpredictable movements will save me from being impaled.

But I don't have time to contemplate my stupidity; as I run, more and more guards come to the aid of the two I left behind. I hear one of them breathlessly explaining to another that I'm an escaped concubine, and immediately, the pounding of several feet come to a halt in their pursuit, which I would normally find curious, but at the moment all I can think is how grateful I am that I have a mere dozen guards giving chase instead of fifteen.

The palace proves too great for me; the halls all look the same and go on and on for days as I run, sprinting between guards, twisting and turning out of their grasp as I make my way deeper into the maze. Columns of marble rise from the floor, and I approach a hall where the natural light of day gleams brightly and the sheer curtains give way to gentle gusts of wind coming from the south side, floating up and down like an apparition.

And from those curtains springs my captor.

I slam into him, the biggest guard I've seen yet, and instantly his arms embrace me, and no matter how much I wriggle and squirm, he's got good hold of me, a strong, tight hold that I almost feel is meant to snuff the life out of me.

"Hold her steady!" one of the guards behind us yells, and my detainer clinches down even tighter.

"What is the meaning of this?" he says, flustered when I bite down upon his hand. Instantly he turns me in his arms, slapping me across the face. Hard.

The room spins, the columns seem to become one with the curtains, and the colors dance around me, mingling with spots of blackness. I struggle to hold on to my consciousness and listen to what is being said of me, to what will become of me, and it's then that I hear, "Take her to the king."

I've done it. I'm to see the king.

18

TARIK

TARIK LEANS BACK IN HIS SEAT, ASSESSING HIS oldest friend and adviser from across the table. Patra reclines at his feet under the marble table, purring contentedly. "Your age is showing, Rashidi," he says gently. "It is time we acquire an attendant for you."

Rashidi scoffs. "I do not need an attendant, Highness. It would be an inconvenience for me to have someone always underfoot."

"I've given you immense responsibilities. More than you had before, with Father. Perhaps we could obtain a Healer to assist you in your duties. A Healer could also—"

"I'm in no need of a Healer or an attendant," Rashidi says. His brows draw together. "I have a very particular way of accomplishing my tasks, and an attendant would just get in the way. Your father never made me take on an attendant."

Tarik shakes his head. "But he did apparently speak to you of it."

Rashidi's mouth becomes a straight line. He obviously knows his answer will tell on him either way. To Tarik's amazement, he chooses the truth. "He wanted me to, Highness, but I did not have the time for it then and do not have the time for it now."

"You don't have the time *not* to have an attendant." This is the third time they've had this conversation since his father passed, and every time Rashidi offers an exhaustive list of reasons why he doesn't need an attendant. Today, he's narrowed his point to lack of time.

Pride of the pyramids, but he's a stubborn old man.

The ornate door to Tarik's private meeting chambers bursts open then, startling them both. Guards file in, enough guards to alarm him, and he stands in unison with Rashidi.

"What is the meaning of this?" Rashidi demands as the last guard enters the room, hauling something over his shoulder. Rashidi peers closer at the silk-sack-looking thing with legs slung over the guard's broad chest. At once, Tarik notices that the sack draws a breath and releases a feminine sigh. Rashidi's nostrils flare. "Is that a *concubine* you've brought here for all the world to see? Have you a death wish for us all?"

Tarik resists the urge to roll his eyes. The law states that any man who sets his eyes upon the king's concubines will be thrown from the Half Bridge, eaten alive by the hungry Parani waiting in the water there. He'd much rather have the entire harem stolen away than allow any of his loyal soldiers to die for looking upon any of his royal assortment of women. And to think Rashidi assumes he would punish *him* for seeing one of them is utterly ridiculous.

"Who is in charge here?" Tarik says, mustering up his patience. *Aside, of course, for me.*

One of the first of the men to enter the room steps forward. "Majesty, I'm Dogol. I guard the harem wing. This—that is, Mistress Sepora escaped this morning."

"*Escaped*?" Rashidi says, incredulous. "Why in the name of Theoria would she want to do that?"

Sepora. The irritatingly persistent one who does nothing but send him letters scrawled with terrible penmanship and broken Theorian. The one who begs urgently for an audience with him. The one he's been considering sending back to his brother, since Sethos is the reason for the nuisance in the first place.

The one who first discovered the mound of spectorium that morning on the Concubine of the King's throne.

The guard had said she was not prone to mischief. The guard had been wrong.

Tarik shakes his head, sighing heavily. "She finally got her audience, then. Set her down in the seat there." He points to the empty seat across from him, beside Rashidi. "How is it that she escaped?"

The large guard complies with his king, plopping the girl in the chair and giving her cheek a gentle slap. "Mistress Sepora," he coaxes, his jaw locked in frustration. Tarik can tell he does not want to be gentle, yet she is, after all, property of the king. "Mistress Sepora, you must awaken." He looks back to his king, cringing with his answer. "She somehow made it past the guards of the harem wing. We've had a fine time chasing her around the palace."

Tarik pinches the bridge of his nose. "An agile concubine. Who would have thought?"

"Highness—" Dogol begins, but Tarik waves him off.

"It was a jest, Dogol. Please, try again to wake her."

Dogol gives her a good shake, but still it takes a few moments for her to come to, and when she does, Tarik must find the discipline not to stare at his own concubine. Her eyes shine astonishingly silver, and her hair, though woven into an intricate braid around her head and splaying freely down her back, is a striking white blond. Her eyes are lined with a metallic pewter paint, enhancing their color tenfold. He knew she was beautiful as she slept; he wouldn't expect anything less of one of his concubines and, indeed, of such a gift from his brother. Yet, as lovely as she is while sleeping, she's nothing less than stunning when she opens her eyes.

It's a wonder Sethos did not keep her for himself, Tarik thinks dryly. Instead of risking the chance that Tarik would not let him into the harem to see her.

Once the girl is fully responsive, she rubs her jaw, on which Tarik can see she has a slight bruise. He wonders just what kind of resistance she offered, to be struck so hard.

"Mistress Sepora, is it?" he says. "Tell me why you're here and not enjoying the sun in my sanctuary."

Sepora sits up straight, squaring her shoulders, aligning them almost perfectly with the back on her chair, which makes her appear regal somehow. "Who are you?"

Tarik blinks. His own concubine does not know who he is. Well. She is new, after all. And obviously Serubelan, at that, if her coloring is any indication. "I'm the recipient of many parchments delivered at all hours of the day, mistress. Urgent messages from you, as they were."

She mulls over this, absently rubbing her shoulder and working her jaw back and forth. Tarik will get the name of the man who thought it was imperative to knock her into semiconsciousness. How could she have been that much trouble?

"You're the Falcon King?" she says finally. She raises a brow. "You do not look like a boy." With this, her eyes drip down the length of him, making him itch to stand taller. Something about her scrutiny finds fault with him, he can tell. Perhaps she was expecting a toddler still suckling at his mother's breast. He's glad to disappoint.

At least she speaks Theorian fluently, even if her written communication is somewhat flawed.

"You escape the harem, and now you've a mind to insult the king?" Rashidi hisses, rage shaking at his hands. "What kind of disrespectful—"

"Enough, Rashidi, please," Tarik says mildly. "Recall that she has just been revived from a coma."

Rashidi all but pouts. "Forgive me. Your patience is remarkable, Highness."

"As is your indifference," Sepora says and stands, making the guards behind her uneasy. Tarik cuts his eyes to them to stay back, as she places her palms flat on the marble table separating them. She leans in.

She is something to behold, this Mistress Sepora. She cannot be as old as he, Tarik calculates, perhaps younger by two years. Maybe three. Her eyes have a wild look in them, aside from their being absolutely silver.

"You're speaking of the scads of dispatches you've sent me," he says, amused.

"Of course I am. If you are responsible for the harem's every comfort, how could you—"

"One could argue, mistress, that the harem is responsible for *my* every comfort."

She crosses her arms but cannot hide her blush. "Yes. Well. They are eager to see to your comforts, I'm sure. If you should show up now and again."

"They? Are you saying *you* are not interested in seeing to my comforts, Mistress Sepora?" He can't help but goad her. He wonders if her eyes change colors when she's angry. A ridiculous notion, of course, but a nonetheless intriguing one. Storms, he decides. Her eyes remind him of the rare handful of storms he's seen in Theoria.

Her nose lifts slightly and she sniffs. "Absolutely not, Highness. I've been trying to secure my release for weeks."

The truth. Interesting. Rashidi is nearly rocking on his heels in fury. To Tarik's knowledge, a concubine has never tried to escape the harem. It's a story his father would have told him, a story that surely would have been passed down from generation to generation of inheriting kings.

Tarik is not sure what he finds more amusing—Rashidi's ire or Sepora's outspokenness. "Did you know, Mistress Sepora, that in Theoria, it is a great privilege to be considered beautiful enough for the king's harem?" he says gently.

"And I thank you for that great privilege, Highness." Insincere at best, he concludes. "But I did not come to Theoria to be beautiful, nor do I consider it a privilege to be sold at the Bazaar like livestock."

Tarik almost chuckles at the hissing sound Rashidi makes with his teeth. His poor adviser can barely contain himself. "Such practices have been tradition since before my father's father was king." He's not sure why he's explaining himself to a concubine to begin with, and especially in front of his men. He rests his gaze on the guard who claimed to be in charge. "You're dismissed, Dogol. I'll see to it that the mistress is returned to the safety of the harem."

Dogol nods but doesn't move from his place against the wall. "Are we to report to the Half Bridge, Highness?"

Ah. The men are not as fascinated with Sepora's accusations as Tarik is, but are more concerned for their lives. As they should be.

Tarik focuses his attention back on Sepora. "I don't suppose the king of Serubel keeps a harem?"

"Of course not," she says. "We, that is to say, the king considers it a vile practice."

"And how do you know what the king does and does not consider vile?"

"It is an assumption, Highness, since he does not keep a harem of his own."

A lie. Tarik is not sure what to make of it. The weight of the untruth reflects in her voice and in her eyes, yet the words hardly carry the seriousness of how her lie seems to affect her. She is truly hiding something with those words.

Curious.

"Are you aware of the punishment for a man if he were to lay his eyes upon any of the king's concubines?" He'd feel silly referring to them as *his* concubines, because he never intends for them to be his; they will always, in his mind, belong to his father. He'll make them comfortable and keep them entertained out of respect for the Warrior King, but he has no time for anything more. Especially if he is to entertain a wife soon.

She swallows. "I don't know what you mean."

Tarik gestures around the room. "All of the men you see here? They are all to die because of your carelessness. Each and every one of them has seen you, Mistress Sepora; indeed they've apparently chased you far and wide, and were, by all accounts, forced to handle you. They are all deserving of death, according to the law. What think you of that?"

Her breaths come in shallow gasps. "I think, Highness, that it is unfair," she says quickly. "It's not their fault I escaped."

"Actually, it is," Rashidi counters grumpily. "It is one of the two duties they have. Keep you in; keep intruders out. It's quite simple really."

Sepora's eyes grow as wide as the gems sprinkled in her hair. Her lovely pale complexion falls even more pallid. "What of the guards who bring us our meals? And the ones securing the wing? They've seen us all."

"Eunuchs," Tarik says. "A eunuch is—"

"I'm quite aware of what a eunuch is, Majesty," she says quickly. Her eyes glint in the sunshine pouring in from the windows and Tarik is again captured by her glare. "I was not aware of any such law, or I would have gone about things differently."

"Do tell."

"Oh, is this really necessary, Highness?" Rashidi waves his hand impatiently. "Take her to your bed if you wish, Highness, and she'll tell you all the stories you wish to hear. As it is, these men are waiting to know—"

"Yes, of course," Tarik says. He turns to Dogol. "As Mistress Sepora was only trying to secure my attention and not the affection of any of my guards, they are all pardoned for their transgression today, and I would like to formally thank them for their efforts. An extra pittance will be added to their monthly pay. You are all dismissed."

Sepora breathes an obvious sigh of relief as the men file out of the chamber, alive and well. "Thank you, Highness," she says when they're gone. "My apologies for the trouble." Sincere this time. It appears the mistress cannot decide if she's pleased with him or miffed.

And he cannot decide which he prefers just yet. "Please, sit. We have some details to untangle, I think."

"Details," Rashidi mutters.

"The only details I wish to discuss are when and how I may

secure my release, Highness. Surely you can see I do not belong in your harem."

"Indeed. And why is that, Mistress Sepora? What have you against a concubine?"

She lifts her chin. "Nothing, of course." A lie. Not that he cares in the least how she feels about concubines, or even why she doesn't want to be in the harem. It is solely for entertainment purposes that he keeps her talking just now. And to his delight, she seems easy to bait, even as she tries to be diplomatic. "But," she continues, "I've traveled a long way from Serubel and I'd very much like to finish my journey. I'm for the Baseborn Quarters." The truth.

The only Serubelans in Theoria Tarik knows of are the descendants of the freed slaves who chose to stay after their release rather than return to their own primitive kingdom. They've chosen to make careers out of building the pyramids, working for a wage instead of the whip or whatever small reward their old kingdom used to offer. If one must labor, he thinks to himself, it is better to labor in a kingdom enlightened with knowledge than one darkened with ignorance. They have become a vital part of the Theorian economy, and not only because of their skill in handling spectorium; the task of building the pyramids has long been looked down upon as being an inferior duty, which requires almost all labor and no thought.

But Tarik views things a bit differently. After all, his best pyramid architect is Serubelan, and she is by no means inferior. Thus far she's been able to outdesign all of the past royal architects and her knowledge of the uses for spectorium is beyond extensive. She is a valuable asset to his kingdom, indeed.

He openly studies Mistress Sepora for a time, until she appears uncomfortable under his scrutiny. What to do with a concubine who does not want to be a concubine, but would instead suffer an uncomfortable life in the Baseborn Quarters? Ah, if only he could give up the "privilege" of being king. But obligation and duty have much more power than "want."

Still, Sepora offers something of a reprieve from the burden, from the weight of his responsibilities. For the first time since his father passed, he's genuinely amused. What will she say next? What will she do? And those eyes of hers. A silver medley of truth and lie all swirling behind long black lashes. He's momentarily saddened that she does not want to stay here in the palace. But neither can he blame her, under the circumstances. "I have a problem with releasing you," he says finally. A solution looms before him, and he tries not to smile. "You see, you were a gift from my brother. My brother has never given me a gift before."

Sepora's jaw visibly clenches. "I was not his to give, Highness."

"I'm under the impression he paid a very high price for you, mistress."

"That's not the point—"

"How long will you let this she-demon speak to you in such a way?" Rashidi says, pounding a fist on the table. "She needs to be taught some manners, at the very least, but more than that, the respect that any king of Theoria is due. She is simply ignorant, and I'm horrified your brother would send you such a rotten gift. Then again, Sethos always was one for practical jokes."

Sepora rears back, taking in the enormous breath she'll need to retaliate. Tarik is delighted. Yet, her tone does not match her expression when she says, "I'm very familiar with how a kingdom should be run, sir, and how a king should be addressed." The truth. Intriguing. And a little insulting. Still, he can tell she's holding back her true ire. "But His Majesty's brother took what was not his, and that is not how I was taught even a prince behaves."

Rashidi's face grows red enough for Tarik to fear heart palpitations in his adviser. "Rashidi," Tarik says gently, "please do not be offended on my behalf. I find Mistress Sepora's honesty quite refreshing. Though, of course, you're right, old friend. She does need to be taught manners and she'll need to be informed of the way of things in Theoria, if she's to remain here in the palace for any length of time."

Rashidi nods. "Yes. And taught by someone who isn't afraid of this little snippet. Someone who will have the discipline to handle her tantrums. Obviously, the guards are not capable enough."

"But it has to be someone wise and knowledgeable as well," Tarik persists agreeably. "Her Theorian scribble is atrocious."

Sepora scowls. "It's quite adequate," she says defensively.

Rashidi calms down slightly, accepting Tarik's silent invitation to be dignified. "Of course, Highness, though I can't think why a concubine should have a need of pen and parchment. And someone with an army of patience. I'm afraid I can't think of anyone offhand—"

"She'll be your attendant," Tarik says, clapping his hands together to hide his soft chuckle.

"What? No, Highness—" Rashidi is shaking his head profusely but Tarik has already decided. Rashidi needs an attendant. Sepora doesn't want to be a concubine. But sending her away from the palace would be a slap to his brother's pride. He must be able to produce her at any moment, were Sethos to ask of her. Of course, Sethos having access to her unsupervised is out of the question.

"Yes, she will. It's the perfect solution, don't you see? You need an attendant, and Sepora here is already well informed of how to run a kingdom. How do you come by that knowledge, mistress? Were you a servant in a highborn household in Serubel?"

She blinks at him. Once. Twice. Gearing up for a lie, he can see. "I . . . I . . . yes. A servant. I was a servant."

"Excellent. You'll be paid for your labor, of course." He allows his gaze to linger on what she's wearing—and appreciate what she's not. "Pride of the pyramids, you can't go traipsing about the palace in that scanty concubine attire, I'm afraid. But as a royal servant you should be properly dressed and groomed. Yes, and you'll have your own quarters away from the harem and an attendant to teach you how to dress and present yourself. I'll have a guard collect your things from that wing. Whatever is presentable, anyway."

"Highness—" both Rashidi and Sepora are saying. Rashidi has actually scooted his chair away from the young mistress.

"And you may have every tenth day off, starting in the morning. Do you require a royal escort, Mistress Sepora?"

She blinks. "I . . . an escort, Highness?"

"Yes. You'll want to explore the kingdom, I presume?"

She lowers her eyes, barely containing the disbelief on her face. "You are correct, Highness."

"Well then, the Baseborn Quarters are quite a distance from the palace and are known to be a rough place to visit at times. I'll arrange an escort for you."

"Oh, that isn't necessary. I'm perfectly capable of taking care of myself." Something she truly believes. But he'll not accept an argument on that point. Someone of her magnificence will surely be bothered on the long crude road leading to the Baseborn Quarters.

"I . . . I'm afraid I'm not qualified to be Rashidi's attendant, Highness, though it's a great honor to be considered."

"Really? And why is that, mistress?"

"You see, I was an attendant to mostly females in the royal castle.

I'm not accustomed to caring for the needs of a male, and certainly not one of Rashidi's great rank and esteem."

Rashidi beams at this.

But Tarik is troubled by this new set of lies. He must clear things up immediately, if Sepora is to stay. "Mistress Sepora," Tarik says. "Do you know what a Lingot is?"

19

SEPORA

EARLY MORNING DRIZZLES INTO MY BEDCHAMBER a little at a time, the rays of gentle sunlight poking and prodding at my eyelids, bidding them to open fully. I'd been secretly pleased about being given a chamber facing the east; sunrises have always been something of a phenomenon to me. Back in Serubel, when I could steal away, I used to take Nuna out in the dark hours of the morning, to the highest mountain to watch the sun peek from the horizon and fully realize itself mere minutes later. It was, by far, the most relaxing part of my day and somehow made the long hours of Forging more bearable.

I throw the silk covers back and pad with bare feet toward the balcony of the chamber. My chamber is simple, save for the view, with only a bed, a settee, an ornate trunk, and a small room snuggled into the corner, sectioned off by a single sheer piece of hanging fabric that houses a bath and washbasin and a lavatory—which I've already ascertained empties into the Nefari.

The most exquisite feature of the room, save the promise of daily sunrises, is the gold-framed, full-length mirror beside the bed. A luxury for a servant and a bit out of place, I decide, as I lean my elbow against the stone railing and sigh contentedly at my good friend, the sun.

"Mistress Sepora," someone calls from inside my bedchamber. "Mistress Sepora, are you here? We've come to dress you. Oh, what if she's escaped again?"

"Someone would have noticed," says another feminine voice. "His Highness set an extra pair of guards at the end of the wing, remember?"

The king had said he would assign me a servant, but two or more? A servant with servants—who has heard of such a thing? "I'm here," I say.

Then their words register and a small smile spreads across my face. The Falcon King does not yet trust me, if he's posting guards at the end of the wing. And what reason have I given him to trust me? I escaped his harem, putting the lives of many of his guards in danger. Then I lied to him about almost everything yesterday. Him, a Lingot. I've never met a Lingot before—though perhaps Rolan had been one—and the very idea of it fascinates me. Someone who can speak all languages and can discern a truth from a lie? Could that really be possible? I'm tempted to lie to him from here on out, just to test his abilities—and if possible his patience.

The Falcon King is entirely too collected for my liking. And far too handsome for my comfort. The black paint circling his eyes does make him look fierce and intimidating, but under his scrutiny—when I dare to meet his eyes—he has a kindness that reflects back at me. A kindness that one does not expect of a Falcon King. Especially after all the horrid things my father said about his father. I would be wise, I decide, not to underestimate this new king of Theoria. After all, my father could not have conjured up ideas from nothing, and if the

Falcon King was groomed for kingship by the Warrior King, surely he will rule with the unjust, outlandish methods my father—and my tutor, Aldon—always spoke of.

It's difficult, though, to feel gratitude toward a man—or is he truly a boy, like they say?—who keeps a harem as he keeps a stable full of horses or a field full of grazing cows. Though truth told, while they are there for his convenience, his harem seems to garner no attention from him.

As I ponder over that, one of my apparent servants peeks onto the balcony. She has dark hair and skin, and big impressive brown eyes with long lashes. I would not call her beautiful per se, but her features command attention and interest.

"Mistress Sepora?" she says. "My name is Anku and this is Cara." She gestures to the girl beside her, who is, shockingly, Serubelan. Cara is a bit shorter than me, but with the same hair color and same distinctive pinched-looking nose native among Serubelans. Even her name is common among the farming class. Is she a freed slave, then, forced to stay here and work? I resolve to find out later, if we have a private moment without Anku. As it is, Cara stares at me now in a way that makes me uncomfortable. There is a hint of recognition in her eyes. Does she know who I am? Surely not. Not if she's been raised in Theoria since the slaves were freed all those years ago. She might not have even been a slave herself; perhaps she comes from a slave family who stayed. She looks a bit young to be of the slave generation.

"We are pleased to be at your service this morning," Anku is saying, motioning for me to follow her.

I comply as they lead me back into the bedchamber. Cara pulls some delicate blue cloth from a satchel she brought and lays it out before me on the bed, careful not to make eye contact with me.

"We just need to fit you with an ensemble or two before you depart today," she says. "His Majesty gave strict orders to make sure you would be identified as a royal servant before you left."

After what feels like an eternity of fitting and taking in and hemming, I'm fully dressed. Without asking, they each grab a shoulder and turn me to the mirror so I can inspect myself. Not terrible for servant attire, if I'm being honest. It's a blue knee-length dress, with sheer blue fabric hanging down to my calves. Around my waist is a golden belt—surely it's not genuine gold, or I'll be robbed straightaway upon leaving the palace—and a large beaded necklace that resembles in shape the bib a young child would wear before taking in a meal. A simple striped blue-and-gold headdress is stationed atop my hair—which itself has been arranged into a labyrinth of curls and braids. I can't help but notice that my attire is more intricate and detailed than the simple blue dresses of my servants back home. And it is a relief to find that it is much more conservative than the attire fitted for me in the harem—and by Rolan.

"The headdress is important," Anku informs me. "It denotes a higher standing among the royal servants, since you are the attendant of the royal adviser."

Ah, Rashidi. Rashidi, who argued to near death all the reasons why I'd be inadequate as his servant. Because of that, I'm going to prove him wrong. Why shouldn't I? I'm being fed and housed in the palace, and given leave to explore the kingdom of my own accord. I doubt even Mother could imagine how well this venture has turned out. I've traded the fate of the Baseborn class for the fate of a pampered servant.

And not just that. The thought is not lost on me that although I reside close to my father's enemy, I am in a much better position to help Serubel than I would have been eking out an existence in the

Baseborn Quarters. Surely that means all is not lost. Surely once Rashidi learns to trust me, he'll divulge information that I could somehow pass on to Mother. And surely Mother will know what to do with the reconnaissance.

I must have taken too long to respond, because both Anku and Cara both stare at me, curiosity etched in their expressions. "Thank you for your help," I tell them quickly.

"Of course, Mistress Sepora." Anku strides over to the corner of the room, where she retrieves a large embroidered tassel that had hung close to the wall. She shakes it at me. "This is your bell, mistress. If you require anything at all, you may ring it and we will be at your service."

"Oh, I'm sure I can manage without too much assistance." Even at home, I did not use my servants as much as I could have.

She smiles. "We're told you're fond of writing to pharaoh. Do let us know if you require parchment."

I flush. So, rumors spread in the Theorian palace the way they did in Serubel's royal castle. By Anku's tone, she's merely jesting with me, but Cara turns up her nose in disapproval. Perhaps she feels I'm betraying Serubel by keeping up correspondence with the king. Perhaps she is jealous of my privilege. Whatever the case, I don't want to make an enemy out of her. I'd quite like to have a friend here in Theoria, and it's refreshing to see another Serubelan here.

"Thank you, Anku, but I doubt I'll have need of speaking to His Majesty further."

A pity, to say the least. I've all sorts of lies I'd love to deluge him with. But for now, he has given me leave and an escort to explore Anyar—but the smarter course, I decide, is to become acquainted with the palace itself. Besides, I still have a wretched taste in my mouth from my first experience in the Bazaar of Anyar. And I certainly do not want to risk another run-in with Rolan or Chut.

"Cara," I say, using my sweetest tone. "Have you many duties today? I'd much prefer to tour the palace and wondered if you'd care to accompany me."

But Cara frowns. "I'm afraid I've too many chores to attend to, mistress. Perhaps one of the guards—"

Anku nudges her in disapproval. "Of course Cara may accompany you today, mistress. It would be my pleasure to assign her duties elsewhere. As I said, we are at your service."

CARA, AS IT TURNS OUT, IS A TERRIBLE GUIDE. She rushes us through corridor after corridor of the palace, spouting off the least information possible before moving along to the next hall. She emanates a sort of staunch discontent with me, and by midday, I pull her aside.

"Cara, do tell me what the matter is," I say. "You've hardly spoken to me, and I'd hoped we could be friends."

She casts her glare toward the floor, but I do not get the sense that the action springs from shame, but rather from dislike of me. "What are you doing here, mistress?" she says finally. "Are you here to bring an end to Serubel?"

I gasp. "Why would you say such a thing?"

She meets my eyes then, her mouth set in a straight line. "You're a Forger. I know it by your eyes. If you Forge for the king, he'll have no need to trade with Serubel. Our homeland will go to ruin."

"How . . . how do you know what I am?" No one knows what I am, save for Father, Mother, and Grandfather while he lived. Not even the people of Serubel know exactly where the spectorium comes from; they are all told there is a mine deep within the mountain of the palace that yields the kingdom's most precious element.

She looks over her shoulder and pulls me farther to the side, behind a tall marble column. "My uncle was a Forger, mistress. And he kept it a secret, for he knew the Warrior King would demand him to Forge day and night for Theoria. They all keep it a secret."

All? Saints of Serubel. "How is that possible?" I breathe. "Forgers come only from the line of royals."

Cara nods gravely. "The Good King of Serubel visited long ago. He fell in love with my uncle's grandmother, a servant in the palace. Together they birthed a child." She sighs. "My uncle kept it a secret all his life. He could have been rich, you know. Traded all that spectorium for a better life. But the Good King warned him to keep it a secret. He said spectorium, if fallen into the wrong hands, could lead to harm to Serubel."

The Good King. My great-great-grandfather. My throat has suddenly gone as dry as The Dismals. Could it be? "Your uncle. He's passed on now?" I ask, noting that she had said "kept" instead of "keeps."

She nods, lowering her eyes. "Indeed he has, mistress. Just recently, I'm afraid."

"I'm sorry to hear that." Truth told, I'm not sure if I'm sorry. I still don't know what to make of all this. My grandfather fathered an illegitimate child—a Forger, nonetheless. Does Mother know? Is that really why she told me to seek out the Baseborn Quarters? Surely not. Surely she would have told me to look for my relatives.

Relatives. If the Good King was her uncle's grandfather, then does that not make Cara my cousin somehow? I swallow hard.

"Are you also the bastard of a royal?" she asks knowingly, oblivious to my internal turmoil.

And what shall I say? Mother instructed me to keep my identity a secret. While Cara discloses much to me now, I cannot risk opening up to her. Perhaps the Falcon King already knows what I am. Perhaps he has appointed Cara as my servant to glean information from me, knowing I would trust another Serubelan. Knowing I would trust my own supposed cousin. After all, he is a Lingot. He discerns much. Too much.

I cannot take such a risk, I decide. "I think . . . I think I must sit down," I say, breathless.

She leads me to one of the many resting benches we've passed in our journey through the palace. We sit, and she pats my hand sympathetically. "Forgers are scarce," she informs me. "To see another one is very unusual."

"Are there more of them here in Theoria?"

She pinches her brows together. "My cousin Bardo, my uncle's grandson, is but a boy. Eight years old, he is. But he was born with those silver eyes. I've heard of others, too. It's rumored that the king's architect is a Forger. That's why she's so gifted in constructing the pyramids of spectorium. I've never met her to confirm it, though. And I rarely see my family, being as I work in the palace. Traveling to the Baseborn Quarters would take an entire day, and I've only one day off every so often."

"Does . . . does Bardo know to keep his Forging abilities a secret, then?"

Cara nods solemnly. "Of course, mistress. They all do. My question is: Do you?"

"Yes," I say firmly. But I'm not willing to discuss it further. After all, there is a chance that none of this could be true. There is a chance that the Falcon King has recognized me for what I am and has chosen to draw me out in this way, knowing I would never admit to such a thing to him directly.

"The young king appears to be wise, but even if he weren't, he's still a Lingot. You must take care, Mistress Sepora. Serubel depends upon it."

If she only knew. "I . . . I am not feeling well after all," I say. "Perhaps you could take me back to my chambers to lie down?"

"Of course, mistress." I do not miss how relieved she sounds to rid herself of my company.

20

TARIK

TARIK AND PATRA FIND SOLACE TOGETHER ON the terrace of the grand garden of the palace, his oasis in the desert that is Theoria. The palace boasts other smaller gardens in each corner, and an indoor courtyard that flourishes with plant life and is used for entertaining, but the grand garden is by far Tarik's favorite. It is the most private of them all, but perhaps is most endearing to him because he had helped his father oversee the construction of it not long before King Knosi's last trip to Wachuk. Together they watched the gardeners install the greenery, mixing the dry sand with rich fertile soil, and witnessed the sun and water—diverted to the garden in the form of a small stream—coax unlikely life from the land. It had been a peaceful, slow process, and it makes Tarik feel as though he'd accomplished at least this small feat, despite the mountains of responsibilities he'd inherited in the days since.

The setting sun seems to extract the heady fragrance of the lotus flowers, the sweetness of the plant wrapping itself around him, reminding him that the lotus had been the main flower at his father's funeral, and that in a way, it symbolizes a great change in his life. The calming, earthy scent of chamomile keeps his panic at bay, and the scents are some of the many reasons he chose to visit the garden this evening.

That, and his servants keep falling ill with the Quiet Plague. The illness runs rampantly throughout the palace, and in a way, Tarik feels it is safer to be among the silence of the flowers and shrubs than the silence of the plague. Just this afternoon, his messenger Dolis fell faint, only to encounter a nose bleed soon after and need the aid of one of the three Healers that Tarik now keeps in the palace at all times. Though resting and being treated with the utmost care, Dolis is having a difficult sickness. It is a trying circumstance for Tarik to hear the reports of his palace Healers, especially when etiquette stops him from personally visiting Dolis, whom he secretly considers a friend.

With these heavy thoughts, Tarik is sitting on a bench sharpening his handmade arrows, Patra contentedly grooming herself at his feet, when Rashidi seeks him out. He'd intended on watching the sunset alone with his feline companion but knows he must make an exception for his best adviser. Pushing the intoxicating aroma of the garden—and the new meaning it carries for him—out of his foremost senses, he focuses his attention on his old friend's tired movements.

"Has your attendant returned from her outing?" Tarik asks without looking up. He hadn't meant to ask about Sepora first thing, and is surprised with himself that of all the problems and pressing matters he could have opened with, he chose to ask after a recently discharged concubine.

"Indeed she has not."

Tarik smiles at hearing relief in the older man's voice. "You know, it was a compromise, Rashidi. I'll take a wife. You'll take an attendant. Do you see how that works?" Again, he pushes the subject of Sepora. Why?

"Unfortunately, I do, Highness."

Tarik chuckles, setting his newly sharpened arrow into his quiver and retrieving a dull one from the pile next to him on the bench. It had been a while since he'd practiced his archery. It was his one fighting skill he'd mastered over Sethos, and if he intends to keep hold on that claim, he needs to practice on occasion. Not that he'd intended to practice this evening. The mood of the garden didn't lend itself to violence but rather the keen concentration of producing arrows worthy of flight. "What brings you to see me, Rashidi?"

"Forgive me, sire, I do know you like your evenings in silence."

That is true. Silence has become his most treasured jewel, even above meals. It seems that every other part of the day he has someone speaking to him or, in some cases, at him. Anyway, he's desperate for a few stolen moments to himself, even if they must be stolen away from Rashidi at times. But for the most part, he knows those are the small luxuries he has left in life. "You are always the exception, friend."

From the corner of his eye, he can see Rashidi fidgeting his hands. Rashidi never fidgets. He remembers a time when Rashidi had to inform his father that his favorite cat had died—and Rashidi had been the one to kill the beast, as he had turned on a guard. Rashidi did not even blink when delivering the news. For him to be fraught with anxiety now makes Tarik very uneasy. "The caravan is all set to depart for Hemut in the morning," Rashidi announces, his voice more galvanized than his manner.

"Excellent." When Rashidi says nothing more, Tarik looks up at him. "Is that what you've come to tell me?" *Have I become such an ornery tyrant, then, that my most trusted adviser cannot inform me of the goings-on anymore?*

"No, Highness. I've come to make a request."

Tarik braces for an argument. *Nothing like bickering with your highest adviser to ruin a good sunset.* By the Great Pyramid, if this is about taking on Sepora as an attendant . . .

He glances up and past the garden wall, attempting to gear up for the worst from his adviser. The large heavenly orb has already made it halfway down in its journey; Tarik's eyes feel heavy. He allows his shoulders to hunch a little, since only Rashidi is here to see it. Still, he has much correspondence to attend to before he retires to his chambers. A king does not resign with the sun. And apparently he does not find solace in the garden anymore. "You need an attendant, Rashidi, and Mistress Sepora's as good as any."

"That's not my request, sire. Well, not exactly."

"What do you require of me, then?" His voice is sharper than he'd intended. But Rashidi has a gift of presenting matters in a way in which Tarik cannot refuse. And exhausted as he is, he's in no mood to be mentally bested at the moment.

"If I may, Highness, I'd like to accompany the caravan to Hemut tomorrow."

This is unexpected. "Why?"

"This is one of the most important decisions of your lifetime, Highness. It doesn't feel appropriate to entrust this sort of measure to anyone beneath me. I'd like to act as ambassador on your behalf. King Ankor is known for being disagreeable."

"Our ambassadors are quite capable of handling such situations."

"He's also known to hide his true intentions."

"You wouldn't rather send a Lingot, to discern any kind of deception?"

Rashidi nods, folding his hands behind his back. Absently, he begins to pace back and forth in front of Tarik, the rustling of his long robes the only sound in the garden. "I'll be happy to take one with me, sire. But I feel it's something I should do myself. Your father would send me, were he here. He sent me to negotiate for your mother."

That was different. His mother was a Middling here in Anyar, and negotiating with her family to become the next queen of Theoria had been an easy task. Still, there is something distant and nostalgic in Rashidi's eyes. "Are you being sentimental, Rashidi? Or are you trying to get out of training your new attendant?"

"A little of both, I'm afraid."

Tarik laughs at the truth in the words. "And what shall I do with her while you're away?"

"Since you're so set on my acquiring an attendant in the first place, you could see to her training yourself. Er, that is, of course, if you wish, sire."

"You want *me* to train *your* attendant?" The idea brings mixed feelings. Sepora is vastly amusing to him, and he'd welcome the distraction from the more mundane aspects of his duties. Yet, the mundane aspects of his duties require his full attention—something Rashidi well knows.

"It's just that I cannot fathom what you would have her do for me, Highness. Only you could know that. And if only you could know, who better to train her than yourself?" If Rashidi were trying to make excuses, that would be one thing. But everything he says is true. Everything he says he sincerely believes. Including the fact that he's being sentimental.

"I hardly have the time."

"I'm aware of that. But I'm afraid having an attendant underfoot while I'm negotiating with Ankor would be cumbersome, to say the least. I know she claims to have served a high-class household in Serubel, but she's unschooled in *our* ways. What if she does something to offend the king or his daughter? I could not withstand the embarrassment on behalf of Theoria. I'm afraid my patience for such things has worn thin in my old age."

The idea of Rashidi embarrassed would be exceedingly entertaining is Tarik's first thought. But if Sepora accompanies him, Tarik will not get to witness her unpredictable antics. What could a girl who escaped his harem—and sent half the palace on a merry chase—be capable of doing in a foreign royal court? The endless possibilities almost make him smile.

Almost. But Rashidi is far too serious at the moment to insult him with a grin.

"Very well, then," Tarik says. "She'll attend to me while you're gone. Of course, when I have time to devote to the task."

"Many thanks, Your High—"

But before he can extend the rest of his gratitude, the great double doors of the west wooden gate to the garden open, exposing a view of the outside palace wall for a fraction of a moment before guards begin filing in two by two, weapons at the ready. Patra is on her feet, the hair bristling on the back of her neck. "Easy," Tarik tells her, even though he feels the same way.

The guards form a line with Tarik at the end and center, none coming forward to explain the reason for the interruption. He sighs. His evening was apparently destined to be ruined anyway, even if Rashidi had not come to him. He sets down his arrow and stands. Patra leans in closer to him, allowing her side to brush against his hip. If he were to give off even an inkling of unease, she would put herself between him and his own guard.

One of the soldiers approaches, an officer as indicated by the decorative sword he carries. The man takes a knee before him, nearly tucking his chin into his chest in reverence. "Your Highness, permission to speak, sire."

"Of course," Tarik says.

"Sire, we've shot down a Serpen north of the Nefari tributary. It was leaving for The Dismals."

"A Serubelan Serpen?" Tarik says. "Why would one be so close to Anyar's border? Was there a party with it?" Did King Eron want to speak with him after all? Had he sent a party out to meet with him just as he had sent a caravan to him for the same reason? Tarik sucks in a breath through his teeth. *Now we've shot down one of his Serpens as a welcoming act. This won't go over very well.*

The gates open to their maximum capacity, and a dozen or so guards grunt and groan as they pull the dead Serpen into the garden for his inspection. The long blue body is limp and makes a track across the green grass his gardeners have worked so hard to cultivate. But Tarik is in no position to mourn over grass. His military, acting under his general command, has just shot down a Serpen.

They settle the beast between two great fountains, off to the side. "Why would you shoot it down?" Tarik says, trying to mask his irritation. "Could you not have followed it to its conclusion?"

"Sire, it's a Seer Serpen. It can be used for spying, among other things." The officer appears apprehensive now under the weight of his king's questions.

"What have you done?" someone cries from behind them. Tarik does not have to turn around to know that the Mistress Sepora has returned—and that she is very upset at the sight before her.

He opens his mouth to greet her but shuts it just as quickly. After all, she did not greet him, she addressed *his* officer in *his* garden during *his* inquisition. He doubts this sort of behavior is acceptable even in a highborn house in Serubel. Not that she cares one bit. The girl actually pushes past him and stands before the officer. She crosses her arms, and Tarik gets the distinct feeling it's because she's trying to keep from putting her hands on his high-ranking guard.

"Why would you kill him?" she says. "Seers are gentle creatures."

The officer alternates his surprise from Sepora to Tarik, clearly unsure whether he should answer the question. "Mistress Sepora," Tarik says more gently than he should. "This is not your concern."

She turns around, tears in those silver eyes of her, and something within Tarik becomes restless. "But Highness, he's harmless. Seers do not even possess the convenience of teeth."

And what, he's supposed to chastise a crying girl? Not his mother's son. *But I am supposed to be acting as my father's son! Will my reputation survive the patience I allow her?* "My guard here suggests Seers are used for spying. Is that true?"

She hesitates, wiping away a tear with the back of her hand. "Yes, they could be. I'm not sure what . . ." But she trails off. And it's clear to him she knows exactly "what" she was going to say, yet she doesn't expound. He wonders if he prods her privately if she'll tell him. He doubts it. "But there was no need to kill him," she continues. "His information can be obtained from his eyes. If he were still alive."

"How do you mean, Mistress Sepora?" the officer asks. By the way he says her name—he caught on rather quickly to her name, Tarik thinks—he's already quite taken with her. Tarik frowns against his will.

Sepora takes a step closer to the officer, gently touching his hand to get his attention. *As if she doesn't have it fully already.* "You see," she tells him, "Seers have more than just exceptional vision. Their eyes are able to capture what they see. While they're alive, that is. You can remove their eyes and place them to smoke over a fire. An image of what they saw last will appear in the smoke."

Tarik had heard of this but never thought such a remarkable

thing could be true. He'd never seen a blue Serpen before—except in the rudimentary paintings of the former slaves descended from Serubel. They'd taken to painting the inside of the pyramids they'd built with their own hands and their art was so beautifully executed that no king had had the mind to stop them. Too, he'd seen what was supposed to be blue Serpen scales adorning the headdresses of some in the Superior class—Serpen scales were considered as rare as the rubies of Wachuk's Death Caves. But after many strolls in the market and hearing the merchants' cries of the scales ring false in his ears, he'd concluded that there was no such thing as a blue Serpen.

"After a few turns of the sun, their eyes will grow back again as if you'd never harvested them," Sepora is saying. "Just as the brown lizard will regrow its tail after the cutting off of it."

"With respect, Mistress Sepora," the guard says, "the beast is still alive."

Her eyes light up, and she pushes past both Tarik and the guard and sprints to the downed Serpen, the sheer parts of her dress flowing behind her. *No one cares to stop her*, Tarik thinks dryly. It's as if she's cast a spell upon them all. Even Rashidi has kept quiet throughout the entire affair. No doubt from impatience and horror, if Tarik had to guess.

Tarik follows her, bidding his guards to fall behind him. He listens as Sepora softly coos words of encouragement to the great beast, though it remains unresponsive. Her head barely reaches the top of it, even as it lies limp and unalert on the ground. "Sepora," he says gently. "You realize we do have to harvest the eyes. I must know who sent it and why. Tell me the best way to do it. Is it very painful for them?"

She frowns up at him. "Not as much as one would imagine. They are bred for this very thing. Still, do you have anything to sedate him with?"

"I'll call my Healers at once." He shifts from one foot to the other. Her body language suggests that this beast she's never even seen before is very important to her. He wonders if it reminds her of her home kingdom. It surprises him to realize that he doesn't want her to miss her home. *What has gotten into me?*

"Sepora, do you know how to train such a creature?"

She pulls her focus from the Serpen and fixes it on him. "I had a Defender Serpen in Serubel. I taught her tricks. But this Seer has already been through training. You see, Serpens tend to bond with their person. I'm not sure I could sway him to obey me."

"I require that you try. Our military could benefit from a Seer."

She bites her lip. He prepares for the argument he can tell is just at the end of her tongue. He can allow her only so much headway in front of his men—and Rashidi. But her rebuttal does not come. For that, he is endlessly thankful.

"Of course, Highness," she says, bowing her head in submission. "As you wish." Her tone carries a hint of excitement, something he's sure the others surrounding them cannot detect. Another thing about which to be grateful—the fact that Sepora's submission stems not from her genuine obedience, but from her enthusiasm over the beast. Pride of the pyramids, but what is to be done about her?

"Good. Meet me in the east courtyard in an hour's time." He turns to his officer. "Have a fire built there. We shall discover what this Seer beheld."

21

SEPORA

IN SERUBEL, COURTYARDS ARE QUIET, ETCHED-OUT places of beauty carved into the mountainside. There are wooden benches and birdbaths and vines full of fragrant blooms crawling up the surrounding bluffs. Here in Theoria, the east courtyard of the young Falcon King's palace is nothing but a stone wall surrounding highly tread-upon dirt that resembles a battleground rather than a courtyard. I suspect this is where the king's soldiers train for combat; I can't think of another reason why the sand would have such an unkempt look compared with the smooth, windswept neatness of the rest of Theoria's desert.

In the center of the bleak courtyard, a great fire laps at the early evening sky, the burning wood resembling the beams and poles of structures rather than firewood cut for the purpose. I suppose in Theoria they would have to trade for wood with Wachuk, whose forests provide a complex variety of tinder, since forests are nonexistent within this desert kingdom's borders. In Serubel, we, too, traded for wood from Wachuk but not to heat our hearths; Serubel has enough wooded mountains for keeping fires. We needed the kind of wood used to make quality parchment, and so we traded for that.

Next to the sizable inferno in the courtyard, Rashidi and the boy king stand, talking between themselves, their faces drawn into expressions of solemnity.

I will myself to approach them, though I'm not ready for the questions the smoke will incite. Is my father looking for me? Does he know I live? Or does he search for Bardo, the boy Forger? Or the architect? Or any of the secret Forgers hiding in Theoria?

I cannot shake the feeling that the smoke will reveal that the Seer spied me from above, following me as I wandered behind Cara, who toured me through the outer courtyards and gardens of the palace. Surely the guards would not allow a Serpen to fly so close to the king's residence. And certainly I would have noticed a Serpen overhead—wouldn't I? But indeed the guards had said it was flying *away* when shot down. And they would have shot it down well before it penetrated the sky above the palace. Still, unreasonable fear makes its way through me. What if it slipped past them undetected? What will I say to the king, whose Favor gives him the ability to dissect the lies I so desperately want to tell? Will he return me to my father? Will he hold me and demand a ransom from my kingdom? What will Mother say?

I envision Mother's lips pressed tight with disappointment, sighing heavily as I'm returned to the castle in this scandalous state of undress. "You've failed," she'll say. "You've failed, and now we have war on our hands."

Or possibly the Falcon King will keep me, when he sees what value I have to the king. Possibly he'll ask me all the right questions, and I'll have to admit that I am—or thought I was—the last Forger. Or worse, he'll ask if there are others, and my answer will betray them all. Because of me, the youngest Forger will grow up as I did, a slave to producing spectorium, a mere vessel used for his abilities.

My heart twinges at the thought.

I'm so consumed by my fears that I don't notice the king and his grumpy adviser have approached me. Indeed, I don't notice until the king places his hand on my shoulder, sending a shiver through me. It's silly for me to respond this way; he's never been anything but civil to me. It's just that in his hands lies the power to send me back to my father. That in itself is enough to cause me to fear him, but it is not lost on me that if he does send me away, he'll risk his own kingdom, too. A kingdom that, as far as I can tell, doesn't deserve the atrocities of the war my father has planned for it. Still, I've been here for a very short time, I remind myself. Hardly enough time to make such judgments. Hardly enough time to throw my lot in with this peculiar boy king.

"Sepora, are you well?" the king says, his brow furrowed. If he weren't the king, and I merely a servant to his servant, I would think him genuinely concerned.

"I worry for the Seer, Highness." Which is essentially true, just not in the way I mean. Yes, a small part of me worries for its health and fate, but that is just a sliver compared with the worry I have over what it has seen. Of what it will reveal here today.

I've no experience in dealing with Lingots—at least not successfully. How much of the truth can he discern? How much does he know is missing from my confession?

The Falcon King scrutinizes my face, and I know he finds conflict in my answer. Yet, he keeps it to himself. "I'm told the surgery went well, and the beast rests peacefully. The Healers found scars where the eyes have been removed before, so I'm hopeful the procedure will be but an inconvenient routine for your beloved beast. Please come to the fire, so we can examine the smoke."

I try to swallow the dread, but it becomes lodged halfway down, bringing my voice to an uneven pitch. "Of course, Highness." I follow behind them both, striving not to step on Rashidi's stiff train as it drags after him in the sand. It's curious, how Rashidi wears a tunic and robes with his shendyt, all in varying colors of blue, while none of the other Theorians wear this much attire. I wonder if it has to do with his position as adviser, and I grow all the more inquisitive. A gold rope drapes about his neck, and he wears rings on both hands. His sandals are simple leather without any embellishment, though, and his head is shaved all over except for a patch over his right ear, where he binds it with a small gold clasp. I'm not sure why I notice so much about him now, but his attempts at trying to put distance between me and the king could not be more obvious.

What's more, I'm not sure what the king is expecting of me, especially considering we're surrounded by dozens of His Majesty's royal guards. All truth told, the king would not need his guards to come to his aid. He seems perfectly capable in size and strength to render me nothing more than a passing nuisance, even with the training I received in Serubel to protect myself.

Other men and women attired differently from Rashidi have assembled around the fire. They seem to adore wearing as little as possible. The women have small strips of fabric crisscrossed over their chests. The men wear only shendyts, the guards with the added sheathed swords and shields tucked at their backs. Truly, Serubelan dress would be much too stuffy for this weather. Rashidi must have some sort of ailment brought on by the cold, since he wears more than is really bearable in this heat.

It occurs to me then how much the blaze warms my cheeks; the size of this fire is meant to create smoke for all in attendance to see. In Serubel, we did such things without ceremony in any hearth convenient at the time, and of course, large enough to hold the eyes. In the palace, the only hearths I've seen are pristine and clean and bereft of any signs of use. I wonder if the winter months here will change that. I wonder if winter exists in Theoria, as it does in Serubel.

After a few moments, the eyes of the Seer are brought, still bloody, on an intricately carved clay platter that takes two men to carry. Carefully, they hoist their load onto the fire, small embers of orange erupting beneath the weight of the tray and disappearing with a sizzle into the night. With apprehension, I watch as the eyes turn cloudy and then glow a brilliant red, signifying their imminent release of smoke. Murmurs begin to circulate in the gathered crowd, and I close my eyes against the anticipation. None of the outcomes I imagine will end well for me. The overwhelming urge to run overtakes me, and I begin to back away from the fire.

But the Falcon King notices immediately and slowly shakes his head at me. Of course he expects me to flee. I've told nothing but half-truths in his presence, and after all, I did already take flight from his harem. Becoming attendant to Rashidi had not been my choice, and I'd made that clear. If only the king weren't so attentive to me at times such as these. But he is wise to keep watch over me. I would do the same, under the circumstances.

The smoke begins to swirl and thicken into a ball of vapor over the platter, and images finally materialize. At first, they are blurry and separate as each of its six eyes comes into clarity, but I know all too well how quickly that will change. The images will converge together, giving us a panorama of what it is like to fly. Watching the smoke will seem as real as being there with the Serpen itself. It is, in a way, stepping back into time.

First, a vision of a man dressed in traditional Serubelan war attire. I recognize him immediately as my father's highest general. He reaches a hand toward the Seer, affection apparent on his face.

Saints of Serubel, they've captured General Halyon's Seer.

I fight the urge to flee again as we all watch the Serpen take flight, leaving the soldiers beneath it appearing as tiny freckles on the desert sand. Trained to peer down, it absorbs the landscape, crossing over the River Nefari quickly—the war party must have been just north of the tributary that separates the sprawling desert in half. It passes a lone, immense building, then what I assume is the Bazaar. Any second, it will turn east, toward the palace. Any second, it will have me in its sights.

Instead, though, it passes the rough road leading to what I assume, from the scant tents and blond residents below, is the Baseborn Quarters. I hold my breath, just knowing that Father has discovered a blond-haired citizen with silver eyes, a hidden Forger, perhaps even little Bardo. But the Baseborn Quarters come and go. After that, more of the desert. The Seer passes the occasional band of travelers but doesn't swoop to investigate. It certainly has a destination in mind; I recognize when it begins lifting its nose to smell the air around it. In the distance, structures appear, dark structures that look as though they've been burned. As the Seer approaches, it slows its speed, plunging into a downward spiral until it hovers just above the ruins.

"Kyra," Rashidi hisses to the king.

"Kyra?" I ask, sifting through all of my history lessons with my tutor, Aldon. Kyra had been Theoria's capital long ago. It had been razed by Scaldlings in the Great War between the kingdoms. Serubelan history teaches it as one of our greatest military achievements, though Theoria's retribution for the act ultimately won them the war—and all their Serubelan slaves.

The Falcon King tilts his head as he scrutinizes the smoke, as if trying to discern the Seer's thoughts. For a brief moment of panic, I wonder if a Lingot has the ability to do just that. But then I remember, the king explained that he cannot discern the thoughts of beasts.

"What interest do the Serubelans have in a burned city?" he says, turning to me. "Mistress Sepora, do you recognize the man who dispatched the Serpen?"

I nod, feeling the desperate need to lie cling to my insides. But I am defenseless against the king and his Favor. "It's General Halyon, Highness. High commander of Serubel's army."

This appears to surprise him. "Do you have any idea why he would be so intrigued by a city left in ashes?"

At first I shake my head. Then I realize I do know what Halyon wants. What Father wants. Why a city of ashes and destruction would interest him so.

Scaldling venom.

The king must see the realization strike me; he steps closer to me, the shadows from the fire dancing around his face, his normally brown eyes reflecting the orange of the flames. With the gold paint covering his body, he seems to glow. Again, I want to step away from him, from his knowing eyes. "What of it, Mistress Sepora?"

How can I answer? How can I manage myself around his Favor? I decide omission is my best strategy. He cannot discern a lie in what I do not say. "It's not that they wish to occupy the city, Highness. It's the ashes they're after."

His mouth falls slightly ajar. "The ashes? Why?"

I sigh. "Because, Your Majesty, the ashes contain Scaldling venom. And it's highly explosive." So much for omission.

22

TARIK

THE COUNCIL ASSEMBLY LASTS WELL INTO THE night, and Tarik would like nothing more than to leave the throne room and retire to his bed. He'd been quiet but attentive, allowing his company to toss about ideas of what the Serpen's vision could mean for Theoria. Most were in agreement; it meant the kingdom must prepare for war.

So then, we are to battle a plague and *the kingdom of Serubel all at once. So much for having a Silent Reign, as did my father.* The only thing silent about his reign so far is the plague itself, sweeping through his citizens as though carried on the wind, and now his entire assembly must contemplate how to prepare for conflict while the plague ravages through the ranks of the Majai. Lucky for them, the Majai army resides at the Lyceum with the other Favored Ones and have Healers to tend to them at the snap of any commander's fingers. But with Majai weakened with disease, they are unable to keep up with their training. And their training has never been so important as now.

But there are still questions burning within him, questions his assembly cannot answer, questions that he dare not pose to them at all, lest he incite a panic. As his best advisers and scholars exit the throne room at last, all appearing just as exhausted as him, Tarik bids Rashidi to come closer. Once the great doors close behind the last of them, Rashidi allows himself a sizable yawn before approaching.

"Yes, Highness?"

"Summon the Mistress Sepora."

"At this hour? Highness, she is most assuredly sleeping."

Tarik shakes his head. "No, she's not. I could tell by her expression she was disturbed by the Seer visions. She'll still be awake. And I want to know why."

It takes the better part of an hour for the Mistress Sepora to appear before him. She appears bedraggled, her eyelids heavy, as if her eyelashes are weighted down. Her glorious hair falls around her loosely like a cape, crinkled from the braids she wore earlier.

"Forgive me for disturbing your sleep, Mistress Sepora."

She sighs. "I wasn't sleeping, Highness."

Just as he thought. "I've more questions for you."

She nods. So, she'd been anticipating more inquiries. Could that mean she'd held back something in the courtyard? And would it be such a surprise if she did, with so many onlookers in attendance?

"May I sit, Highness?" she says. "I'm afraid the day's events are taking their toll."

"Of course." He'd forgotten she'd spent the day exploring the palace, in addition to all that had taken place with the capture of the Serpen. She's so weary that before he can have a seat fetched for her, she ascends the stairs two at a time and sits on the top one, closest to his throne. Careful to keep her legs tucked beneath her, she folds her arms about her, as if chilled, looking up at him expectantly. "How can I be of service?" she asks.

A certain radiance has left the girl who escaped the harem, and he can't help but mourn the loss of it. Perhaps she really is tired and not defeated, which is the impression she unknowingly gives now. Still, he must tread carefully around her sudden willingness to cooperate. He well knows being overly helpful is not a dominant characteristic of hers. At the same time, she could be eager to have be done with this inquisition. And he can't blame her in the least. "As you know, my assembly has just convened. The majority of my advisers are under the impression that Serubel is seeking to start a war. What are your thoughts on that?"

She hunches over, resting her elbows on her knees. For a moment, she seems to consider what she'll say, then appears to abandon it in favor of saying the closest thing to nothing. "What does it matter what I think?"

"I didn't say that it does."

"Then certainly you'll not mind if I do not answer."

"I didn't say that it *doesn't* matter, either."

She huffs. "I'm but a servant. I do not have such lofty thoughts as a king and his adviser."

Oh, but she lies. Sepora does have an opinion on the matter, a very strong one, which makes Tarik want to know it all the more. Before he can persuade her, Rashidi ends their game.

"Have out with it at once," he barks. "The king is not to be trifled with, and at this late hour. Pride of the pyramids, but you could test the nerves of a priestess."

Her shoulders fall, her lips forming what is a considerable pout. "I'm afraid I agree with your advisers," she tells Tarik, careful not to grace Rashidi with an acknowledgment.

"Why would they want a war with us?" Rashidi asks. "Surely they've kept the records of such follies in their histories."

Sepora casts him a glare, her previous sparkle shining through once more. Tarik suppresses a grin. "Perhaps they're seeking to make *new* histories," she snaps.

"Tell me," Tarik says. "Tell me why they would start a war."

The Mistress Sepora sighs, fixing her stare on the marble steps below her. "It is no secret that King Eron thinks Theoria is condescending and deserving of a reckoning." She agrees with "condescending" but has a disdain for the word "reckoning." Curious.

"He would risk the lives of his citizens because of this narrow-minded view?" Rashidi says, contempt unhidden in his features.

Tarik holds up his hand. Calling Sepora's king narrow-minded is not the way to lure the truth from her. "Please, friend. Let her speak."

"Apologies" is what he's hoping Rashidi grumbles under his breath.

"You're asking me to betray my kingdom." The angst in her eyes tells him she's fighting her own war deep within. She still has loyalties to her old home. He can understand that. But her loyalties cannot take priority over the safety of his kingdom.

"Perhaps if I know his reasons, I can prevent deaths in both our kingdoms."

"If Theoria is so superior, why do you wish to prevent another victory for your histories?" There is a bitterness in her voice, telling of hurt pride and long-entrenched prejudices. The Serubelans did not take kindly to their defeat many years ago. Perhaps with time, Sepora will come to see that her enmity is unfounded.

Perhaps, that is, if they are not forced into another war with her homeland.

"There are no victories in war, Mistress Sepora. There are only kingdoms that suffer fewer casualties."

She runs a hand through her thick blond hair and pulls it around, absently braiding a small piece of it. A few long moments pass before she speaks again. "He wishes to control Theoria. To rule it, as he does Serubel."

Rashidi barks laughter. "Is he mad? He actually thinks he would win against us?"

Tarik holds Sepora's gaze. Her eyes tell him that she believes it possible. "How could you know his intentions?" he asks softly. "The king would not share that with just anyone, especially a servant."

She nods, as if she'd been waiting for that question. "I lived in the castle, Highness. I worked very closely with the king." Tarik is taken aback by the truth in her words. She lived in the castle and worked closely with the king? He glances at the guards standing at the door of the throne room. They've heard the entire conversation, yet he trusts their discretion. It is possible that a servant such as Sepora overheard things not meant for her ears, just as these guards have.

But it is also possible that she did not.

"Are you a spy, Mistress Sepora? Sent here by King Eron himself?"

At this she smiles. He tries to recall seeing anything so beautiful and he cannot. Feeling a bit rattled, he shifts in his seat. Rashidi steals a curious glance at him, at which he scowls.

"No, Highness. I am most certainly not a spy. Do you ask if I would try to warn Serubel of an impending attack? Of course I would." Another truth.

"Why did you come here?"

"I was being mistreated by the king. He demanded too much of me, gave me more duty than I could handle. I was not happy there." Again, an honest answer. He doesn't know what to make of it. How could one so young be such a trusted asset to a king?

"And are you happy here?" He nearly groans at his bluntness, not daring to look at Rashidi. His friend is most likely very amused by the direction in which this interrogation has taken. And why wouldn't he be? He's never shown interest in any female before, save for Patra.

"Happier than I was in the harem," she says.

Rashidi rolls his eyes. "Splendid," he says superficially. "Highness, if the Serubelans want a war, I suggest we prepare for one. In fact, I suggest we attack first. By now they'll have realized their Serpen is not returning to them. They'll have surmised what happened to it."

Tarik shakes his head. "We cannot attack based on assumptions, Rashidi. The Mistress Sepora has been helpful in deciphering King Eron's intentions, but we cannot know for certain what they truly are until he makes another move." He drums his fingers on the armrest of the throne. "Before your departure for Hemut in the morning, send a messenger to the Lyceum. Tell the Master of the Majai to prepare for war. Double the guards at all the walls and set up vigil at Kyra. Keep the archers ready and watching the air for more Serpens."

"If this venom is so explosive as the Mistress Sepora says, should we not keep our structures wet? I could send a messenger to the chief engineer, have him construct something to increase the water flow to the cities. Cease the public fountains and baths."

Tarik wrinkles his nose. "Keep the baths, but do everything else. And dispatch messages and soldiers to the outer cities. They'll be the first victims of this idiocy but also our first line of defense." He leans back, searching his mind for more ways to prepare for an attack. One lingers at the edge of his thoughts, yet he's hesitant to give it consideration. It is a long shot, after all, and so unviable that Rashidi would possibly laugh him out of the room. But all possibilities must be put forth. And if the responsibility of protecting the citizens falls on his shoulders, he should do everything in his power to do so. Only, this is not something that necessarily falls within his power. "You know, it's a shame we cannot harvest the nefarite," he says hesitantly. "With enough of it, we could fortify our weapons. They would be impenetrable, even to firepower."

At this, Sepora sits a little straighter. "Nefarite?"

He nods at her. "Yes, mistress. Nefarite is an element found in the River Nefari. It is protected by the Parani. It can withstand a blow from all other elements, even spectorium." There was a time when the River Nefari was bereft of Parani, when they preferred the waters of the southern kingdom of Wachuk, and when nefarite was abundant and widely used in Theoria. He'd even inherited a sword forged from nefarite, an heirloom passed down through generations of pharaohs. The day his father presented it to him, he'd taken him into the courtyard to demonstrate its strength. King Knosi had a block of spectorium placed before them and with one heaving slice through the air, he'd cleaved the block in two. It had made an impression on Tarik, one that he carried until this day. His father had told him that once the Parani arrived upon the scene, they made the river too dangerous. Sending laborers into the river among them had caused dire results. Nefarite was all but lost to them.

"Protected how?"

"By the fact that they'll eat any sort of flesh unfortunate enough to cross paths with them."

Rashidi shakes his head. "We've no one to spare in order to excavate it. It would be risking more lives than it could potentially save. Our histories prove that."

"We could divert the river, dry them out," Tarik says, though the consequences of taking that sort of action would reach far and wide. By diverting the river, he would also be lowering the levels needed to sustain the crops of the Middling class. The crops needed for their survival and for Theoria's food supply.

"How much nefarite is in the river?" Sepora is asking. "Enough to protect everyone? Enough to spare Theoria?"

Tarik sighs. "We're not sure. Rashidi is right; it's too risky. There are enough Parani within Anyar's limits alone to consume the flesh of the entire city."

She tilts her head. "They cannot be made to see the necessity of harvesting the nefarite? Perhaps peace could be reached—"

"Ha!" Rashidi slaps his knee. "Peace! The Parani understand peace the same way a cow understands the scrolls of the dead. Impossible! Do they not even provide a basic education in Serubel, then?"

She arches a brow. "Even the crudest of educations include good manners, which you—"

"Oh, enough," Rashidi says, waving his hand. "This is getting tiresome." He looks at Tarik. "If you ever want to gift me with something, her tongue would be what I want most."

Sepora sniffs but says nothing more.

"I'm afraid Rashidi is right," Tarik says, ignoring her sudden ire at the words. "The Parani cannot be bargained with. It was just something I felt obligated to mention out of duty, really. To explore every avenue of possibility."

But the words seem to fall on deaf ears. Sepora stands abruptly, energized anew, tucking her hands behind her back. Something has struck her, he can tell, an idea or an inspiration, and he's far too curious about it for his liking. "May I be excused, Highness?"

She's tired. He's tired. Rashidi is tired. All good reasons to want to excuse her. Still, he searches for a justification to keep her here. And he finds none.

Perhaps agreeing to train her was not such a good idea after all. Not if his mind is occupied by little else—especially since she cannot be trusted, having worked so closely with the king. After all, she'd admitted she would warn Serubel of an attack, and that had been the truth. No, he must keep his guard up where this one is concerned. He must keep his wits about him. "Good night, Mistress Sepora."

23

SEPORA

I AM FAR BEYOND EXHAUSTION WHEN I REACH MY bedchamber, but my mind still whirs with the conversation I had with the king and Rashidi. Theorians believe war is imminent. I'm not sure what my father hopes to accomplish with the Scaldling venom now that his supply of spectorium is finite and the power from that supply is swiftly ebbing. What I do know is that if my father still wants the venom, enough to take the risk of reaping it from the burned city of Kyra well within Theorian borders, then he still feels he has enough spectorium to start a war with Theoria. It's possible he thinks his victory will be swift, that his cache of spectorium will be enough for his purposes.

What he doesn't know is that I've just advised his nemesis to prepare for war. And that I'll do anything in my power to stop the violence.

My mother thought my leaving Serubel would prevent a cold war from becoming inflamed. She was wrong. But now that I'm in Theoria, out of Father's reach, I'm still not helpless to prevent unnecessary violence and inevitable death. Part of me wants to believe I've done my part by warning the Falcon King of the possibility of an attack, to believe that I've done all I can. The other part, the bigger part, knows that I haven't.

And I am afraid.

The pressing question, though, the one spiraling my thoughts and coiling my stomach, is how much *am* I willing to sacrifice? Shouldn't I be willing to sacrifice everything to save many lives, even if those lives belong to Theorians? The words of the king resound in my head, making me clench my teeth with certainty. *There are no victories in war, Mistress Sepora. Only kingdoms that suffer fewer casualties.*

Which means there will inevitably be Serubelan casualties as well. Rashidi had been right; the Theorians had shown their mightiness in the past. At this point, the Falcon King is not considering making an offensive attack. At least, he's not willing to discuss such an attack in front of me, as Rashidi is. In fact, all the king does speak of is defense and, given the generosity I've observed of his nature so far, I'm inclined to believe his claims of wanting peace. Of deflecting outside invasion. And if he's to be trusted, if he's more of a ruler than my father has proved to be, then I must help him.

No, not him, not exactly. I simply must prevent war. There is a difference between aligning myself with my father's enemy and with preventing a devastating conflict between two powerful kingdoms.

Still, I can't supply the boy king with spectorium, not with the quantities of Scaldling venom he has at the tips of his fingers in Kyra. And not with Rashidi so eager to attack. I could never risk Serubel in that way. And I could never risk becoming enslaved as a Forger again.

So, I must not give him a means to attack. But that doesn't mean I cannot try to give him a means to defend his people—and for at least long enough for Father to run short of Scaldling venom, spectorium, or both.

THE SPECTORIUM I FORGED AND RELEASED IN THE lavatory in my bedchamber gives me scads of nervous energy that my body almost cannot bear. Still, this mission will require all the energy I can muster, and though I'm nearly shaking with the power surging through me, I make do as I meander through the darkened corridors of the palace.

This late in the evening, the servants' entrance on the west wing is guarded by only one soldier to monitor the comings and goings of the king's fleet of laborers. The man wears a helmet and a sheathed sword around his light blue shendyt—the color of the royal guard, I've surmised—and does not hide his surprise as I approach. "Mistress Sepora," he says. "You'll not be slipping between *my* fingers."

That I recall, I've never met this particular guard. He could have been one of the many who gave chase in the palace after my escape from the harem, or perhaps he'd heard the tales of that afternoon from his cohorts. I fight the urge to cringe. This may be more difficult than I'd anticipated. I hadn't expected to walk out of the palace without an explanation, but I also didn't expect to be greeted by a guard assuming that I'm attempting to escape.

I lift my chin. "I'm sent on order of His Majesty."

He raises a brow. "Sent where?"

"To the Lyceum. I must fetch a Lingot there."

"The Falcon King is a Lingot. For what would he need the services of another, and at this hour of the early morning?"

Wrath is what I would display were my story true. Wrath is what I must display now. "You dare to question the king's request? Is the king's private business subject to your approval, then?"

He licks his lips, letting a breath out through his nose. "You're the one I question, Mistress Sepora. Not His Majesty."

"And what is the penalty for hindering a servant of the king from accomplishing his bidding?"

His shoulders hunch slightly, and I know I'm close. "I'm attending to His Highness in the absence of the adviser Rashidi, who left hours ago for Hemut," I continue. "I'm to report directly to the king if I happen upon problems and other such nuisances as this, and now, of course, I'll have to wake him. A pity to be sure, since he's most likely just fallen asleep after yesterday's alarming and taxing occurrence." By the look of horror in this guard's eyes, I've just secured my freedom. The true pity here is that I cannot lie convincingly to the king himself; I'm apparently highly skilled at it with unFavored ones.

"No, Mistress Sepora, there's no need to wake our good king. Please, though, allow me to procure a chariot and an escort for you. The Bazaar is rife with troublesome sorts this time of morning, and a chariot would spare you much time."

I dare not smile, though the triumph stirs up feelings of giddiness. A chariot and an escort is more than I could have hoped for. Instead, I act as though I've been inconveniently delayed. "Very well, then," I say, inspecting my nails out of boredom. "But do hurry. I'm to report back to the king at sunrise."

"Right away, Mistress Sepora."

The chariot ride to the Lyceum is shorter than I had expected. I'd hoped for more time to construct what I will say to the unfortunate Lingot I select for my journey. I need an experienced one, which means I must be careful what I say. Persuading a guard is one thing. Lying to a Lingot is quite another.

The Lyceum is a monstrosity even in the shadows cast by the moonlight, with stone walls and magnificent archways and torches of fire lighting each domed entrance. As we approach, it becomes bigger and bigger until I feel a bit overwhelmed by it. It's as impressive as the palace, even if not as sizable.

We have nothing like the Lyceum in Serubel. It is the responsibility of parents to teach their children to read, write, and develop a skilled trade as they have time for it in the home. All the children, too, are trained in basic combat with a sword and bow and arrows, a tradition passed down from our very earliest ancestors. We have no lavish structure devoted solely for the purpose of learning, as Rashidi so kindly pointed out earlier. Leave it to the Theorians and their quest for knowledge to make such a building more luxurious than even the royal castle in Serubel. And yet the bitterness I'd felt before about their lofty ambitions does not arise; indeed, I feel a stitch of admiration for the structure and its purpose. Perhaps Serubel should encourage education. Perhaps if it did, Father could not so easily persuade his council, his army, to incite war with such a powerful kingdom.

I swallow, hoping my companion doesn't notice my apprehension as he pulls to a stop in front of the great structure. The guard sets the reins of the chariot on the front panel and bids me to wait there while he fetches a Lingot for the king's business. He disappears into the shadows at the top of the steps.

It's the best possible outcome I could have hoped for, not having to persuade the Lingot myself to come along with us. The charioteer believes me to be on the king's business, which I hope means the Lingot will hear the truth in his words, instead of the lie in mine. The Falcon King had explained to me that sometimes he can detect deceit even in the words of a third party, though delivered through ones who believe their message to be true. My hope is in the fact that it means that sometimes he *cannot* catch the lie in these cases.

After what seems like a handful of eternities, the guard returns to me, a young woman following close behind. She wears blue robes, the color of the servant of the king, and seems to yawn incessantly. She's very pretty, around my age, but her hair is short and dark, spearing this way and that in a barrage of spikes. At first, I imagined that in her haste she hadn't the time to tidy her hair, but in the lightening sky of early morning I see that she in fact arranges it in this way.

I will never get used to the Theorian sense of fashion. The women either wear their hair very long or cropped close to the scalp. The men either shave themselves bald or leave long patches of it, to be braided, dangling from the side or the back of their heads. In contrast, Serubelans strive for a more modest and less eye-catching approach to personal grooming. I glance down at my clothing now: a thin linen shendyt wrapped around me fully and tucked into a belt. The fabric doesn't reach but mid-thigh, and it exposes my shoulders and collarbone. I'd be publicly flogged for wearing this in Serubel.

"Good morning, Mistress Sepora," the Lingot says. "I'm Master Saen. I'll be accompanying you at the king's request. Where shall we be going?" *Master* Saen? A kingdom where women can be sold into harems, yet also honored as a master of their trade? Saints of Serubel, but I will never understand the workings of Theoria.

Still, it appears the deception worked. Now I must play a game with Master Saen, and it is not lost on me that this game may very well get us both killed. I think of Mother and wonder if she would think the sacrifice of one Forger and one Lingot worthy of averting a war. Undoubtedly, she would. But when does the calculating become cold instead of useful? *Have I misplaced my trust in Mother's judgment?*

"To the Half Bridge," I tell her.

She exchanges looks with the charioteer. He holds up his palms. "I was not aware of the destination, Master Saen."

Saen casts a doubtful look at me. "What would the king require of us both at the Half Bridge?"

It is a tricky question. I decide to leave the king and his requests out of it altogether. And so I start our dance of words. "Thank you for coming, Saen. It is imperative that we open communication with the Parani. For the sake of the kingdom. I shouldn't be telling you this, but the king believes we are in danger of attack from the Serubelans." I feel the charioteer eyeing us curiously as he helps Saen aboard the chariot.

She grasps the handle in front of us as the chariot takes off and casts me a nervous look. "Why would he think that?"

I explain to her about the Seer, about the images his eyes produced, about the conversation I had with the king and Rashidi. "So you see, Theoria needs to extract as much nefarite from the river as possible," I tell her. The chariot hits a bump and we both startle. "That's why I need to open up communication with the Parani."

The morning sun peeks from the east behind us, and in her profile I catch a glimpse of a scowl. "The Parani are nothing but feral beasts, Mistress Sepora. They do not speak a language. I'm afraid you've come all this way for nothing." *And unnecessarily disturbed my sleep* is what she doesn't say aloud. One does not need to be a Lingot to discern the irritation in her voice and stature.

I shake my head. "No, I don't think I have. You see, I've heard one of them speak, more or less. I think it's enough for you to decipher." If a Lingot can translate what the tribes of Wachuk say with their clicks and primitive growls, surely a Lingot can interpret the high-pitched wails of a Parani. The people of Wachuk believe that words are meaningless without action, and so choose to sign their words with their hands, and the occasional grunt, where just hand signals alone will not do. If a Lingot can decipher that, a Lingot can understand a

Parani. At least, that's what I'm counting on, among other things that make my stomach churn with trepidation.

She blinks. "Speak? What do you mean?"

And so I tell her only some of the story of how I came to be in Theoria. I tell her about Rolan and Chut, about how they captured a Parani and how I came to free her. I show her the X etched forever-more into my palm. It seems to burn again with the new attention.

Saen observes me as one does a person who has lost her mind. I cannot fault her on it. Not when I question myself whether this is a reasonable venture.

The soldier pulls us to a halt. We have arrived at the Half Bridge. Excitement and dread vie for my focus. I try to force the bile back down my throat as I step from the chariot and wait for Saen. Together, we walk a long, slow, and tortuous path down the bridge. It creaks beneath us in places; there are soft spots in the wood where I sink a bit, then others where the wood has risen slightly and I tend to trip on those. Saen is more careful than me, allowing me a slight lead down the bridge.

"I still don't understand why we're here," Saen tells me as we stroll as though we're taking in the scenery. Neither of us is eager for our task. Saen, because she doesn't know what lies ahead. Me, because I do know.

We reach the end, and neither of us can help but look down into the water below. It's a long drop. I imagine criminals walking to their death on this unfinished bridge, of them forcing themselves to jump or taking the chance of being run through with a sword by the guards as they push them ever forward. Perhaps it would be better to be on the verge of death as you hit the water. Perhaps being on the fringe of dying ebbs the pain of being eaten alive.

Even now, the Parani smell our presence, hear our steps upon the bridge. The rising sun's fingers touch the surface of the water below us. Fins and spined heads make frantic waves in the water, a frenzy of carnivores waiting with obvious impatience for the flesh standing above them, for the potential meal watching them from above.

I close my eyes.

"We've no nets, no hooks, no bait. How will we secure a Parani?" Saen says, wringing her hands. "I think we need to obtain help for this task."

"We are not here to secure a Parani," I say softly, taking in a deep breath.

And I hurl myself from the pier.

24

TARIK

WHEN SEPORA DOES NOT APPEAR FOR DUTY in the morning, Tarik sends a servant to fetch her from her bedchamber. After all, he reasons, she's used to the indulgent, relaxed schedule enjoyed in the harem. Rising each morning with the sun, and especially after yesterday's events, including their late evening discussion, will take some adjusting to.

Still, if she's going to attend to Rashidi and Rashidi is going to attend to him at court, then she must be present during these sessions. He well knows listening to noblemen and women complain of their petty woes is not the most interesting subject to learn on her first day, but he holds court thrice a week and she'll need to keep up with the goings-on. Ideally, she would just retrieve parchment, history scrolls, or decrees of law when Rashidi needed to consult them to fulfill his task of advising the king. And, of course, she would be responsible for the occasional refreshment when Rashidi inevitably wore down in the afternoons. But what Tarik looks forward to while his adviser is away is to discern the difference between how he holds court and how King Eron rules. Perhaps he could gain a glimpse inside the ruler's head and determine what kind of man he is. His father always taught him to rule openly with a stern hand and secretly with a soft heart. Does King Eron follow this philosophy? And who better to answer that question than Sepora?

When the servant returns without Sepora, he feels his stomach tightening with dread. Did he push her too far last night, prying her from the comfort of her bed for a relatively intrusive interrogation? Or had Rashidi's callous yet empty threat of attacking her kingdom been too great a burden to bear? Or worse yet, had she escaped to seek out the Serubelan army who sent the Serpen?

No, of course not. She wouldn't return to a king who mistreated her. And he believes King Eron did mistreat her. She hadn't been lying about that.

"Perhaps she's gone to attend to the Serpen," he tells his servant. "She'll be in the north courtyard, in the stables." Of course, they'd had to relocate many of the horses to accommodate the length of the one Serpen. A Serpen who, by all accounts of his Healers, should be fully awake and rested by now. Still, it was his Healers who were supposed to check in on the beast first thing, not Sepora.

He'll have to chastise her, he knows, or his guards and servants will think him weak. He's already permitted her too much leniency in her speech and actions, earning him questioning glances from the court and glares from Rashidi, and now she's late in attending to him. No doubt the entire palace is murmuring about how gently he handled her in the garden yesterday; he cannot allow such gossip to continue. Despite his curiosity about the Mistress Sepora, he simply must gain control over his reactions to her, however intriguing she may be.

But when the servant returns once again without her, his patience begins to wane. His father's words echo in his mind yet again this morning. *Stern hand, soft heart.* But how can he have a soft heart for such blatant disregard for his orders?

He simply cannot overlook this offense.

"Find her," he instructs. "Interrupt whatever task she's at. And bring her directly to me."

25

SEPORA

I HIT THE WATER FEETFIRST AND SINK FOR SEVERAL long moments until my feet touch the slimy bottom. My first instinct is to push off the mud and return to the surface, to slink back to shore without making a commotion, without disturbing the underwater residents. Yet, that would be impossible. After all, they've been waiting for me. They've watched me watching them.

And cowering now will not accomplish the task I've come so far to execute. Rising to the surface. Swimming to shore. The only life those actions will save is mine.

And that is not acceptable. I had been too cowardly to take my own life back in Serubel to prevent a war in the first place. I'll not have any more blood on my hands. The risk I'm taking is worth the lives I could save.

Without warning, I feel a sting at my calf and let out a panicked scream, sending bubbles floating in a heavy stream up to the surface. All at once, the stings cover my body, and I feel sharp teeth and venom embed into my arm, my stomach, my back. Shallow bites here and there, leaving behind their rage but not taking anything away. My flesh remains intact. And painful.

They are not eating me, I realize. Not yet. They merely taste me, and most likely enjoy the muffled screams I emit with each bite, each cry of agony I can't hold in. I'd hoped for either a swift resolution or a swift death, and I'll not attain either if my only accomplishment is yelping like a weakling. Floating about, sustaining nibbles to my person is not why I came.

I'm no longer a coward, I tell myself against the barrage of pain deluging my body. I stood up to my father, my mother. I admonished the Falcon King. I jumped from the Half Bridge. Wouldn't all those things qualify me as brave? I have to believe that they would. And I have to believe that now that I've gone this far, I can finish the task at hand.

I hold up my palm, the one with the X on it, wondering if bravery equates with foolishness.

Saen had called the Parani primitive and feral and beasts. It's easy to believe her now. I cover my face with my other arm, surprising myself with my vanity. All of these shallow bite marks will leave scars, venomous trenches just like the one on my palm. But to have a scar on my face . . . could I endure such a thing? My father had a visitor once who had a long bulging scar running down his cheek. The servants had all been afraid of him, and when my mother introduced me to him, I'd cried to be dismissed. Could I endure that kind of reaction from strangers forevermore?

All I know is that if I must die, then I will. But if I survive, I'd like to do so with my eyes and nose and mouth fully intact, my cheeks unmarred. So while my arm sustains bites and stings, it stays up to cover my face, and the shame of such an act soaks through me all the while.

The intake of breath I took before I hit the water begins to fail me. It occurs to me that if I don't die from being consumed by the Parani, I'll surely drown. My lungs burn and my heartbeat slams heavily against my chest, resounding in my ears with a quickening rhythm. Around me, the water swooshes and churns, and I've no inkling how to count how many Parani there could be swarming about me; all I know is that they've stopped biting me.

I allow my arm to fall away from my face and try not to take in a breath of river. At least a dozen of them surround me, of different sizes and builds from what I can see through the murk. Some dance as shadows behind others, farther than my vision will afford me. They are all easily twice the length of the average man, though, and that makes my pulse race all the more. What strikes me as most intriguing is that they all have expressions on their faces, not animalistic at all, but human expressions, the same as the Parani I saved from Chut and Rolan. Some of them seem disappointed, some of them curious, some of them hungry. But, they keep their distance, as if I've pointed a weapon at them.

In an instant, webbed hands grab at my waist and I'm jettisoned upward, to the surface. As my head breaks through the waves and I gulp for air, the Parani who led me to the surface also pops its head up. Though I can't tell for certain, it appears male to me, with features more squared than the Parani I stole away from Chut and Rolan. He dips his chin back toward the water beneath us and I nod. As quickly as we surface, we plunge below with a speed as though I'm being pulled by the weight of three Serpens.

As I'm dragged farther and farther, I see that more Parani have assembled. They communicate among themselves in what sounds like different pitches of the same whine. I wonder if it weren't for the water if these undeveloped noises would actually resemble words or phrases.

A language. A communication more complex than the braying of a mule or the purrs of one of Theoria's giant cats. A communication as complex as ours.

The Parani who seems comfortable with hauling me around pulls me to the middle of the crowd. He makes a series of sounds and gestures with his hands, clearly indicating me while he "speaks." Another Parani treads water to move forward, also a male I think, and he takes my hand and opens it to reveal my palm. He whines at me, and I'm sure it's a question, but I've no idea how to answer. I have come here utterly useless.

My lip quivers as my body fully realizes the pain I'm in from the bites. I try to hide my discomfort from their searching eyes, but surely they must know what they've done. And they must have a horrible relationship with Theoria indeed, to intentionally do that to a person.

I want to convey that Saen and I mean only peace, that we have a reason to intrude into their territory. I want to convey gratitude for not being eaten—well, mostly not eaten, anyway. The stings all feel like hot barbs lodged in my skin. I can't imagine what they would do if I vomited in front of them, but that's exactly what I feel is going to happen. I try to remember how long the pain lasted on my palm and it must have been a few days before it eased entirely. Days. I do not have days down here.

I must summon more courage, more fortitude, if I am to follow through.

I place my hands together and nod toward them, hoping they'll grasp that I want them to watch. The spectorium leaks from my palms, simmering the water about it even as I struggle to superheat it in order to mold it. I have a captive audience as I pull and push at the glowing element that lies somewhere between a solid and a liquid, malleable and yet runny in places that have not cooled. I've never

Forged underwater before, never had to, and so it's a remarkable challenge not to let the current interfere with my designing. I rub my thumbs against the glowing element, swiping it with my fingers and pressing it into itself until I have the crude shape of a Parani—the young female I helped to escape. I hope they recognize her when she is finished; I am vain when it comes to my sculptures as well. I wait until it solidifies completely before offering it to the male treading water before me, not unaware that I am again running out of air and quickly.

He accepts it, handling it gingerly at first, the glow of it illuminating the crowd around it, which moves in, all in various states of what appears to be awe. Fighting against the blackness speckling my vision, I point toward the surface. The male Parani passes the sculpture to the closest one beside him, who swims away with it, a small throng breaking off and following him in a flurry of fins. The large male grabs my wrist, pulling me upward again.

When we break surface, I point to the top of the Half Bridge at the same time I hear Saen screaming. "Mistress Sepora, get away from it! Can you swim?" Her voice is full of panic, and I can't help but feel guilty that I've dragged her from her warm bed to witness what she must have thought was a suicide.

"He's not going to hurt me," I shout back, startling the Parani next to me. He backs away. "I'm sorry," I tell him softly, kicking my feet harder so I can raise my open hands at him in a show of amity. I point up again, at Saen, who lies on her belly on the Half Bridge, dangling her arms down as though trying to reach me and fish me out of the Nefari.

"You'll have to come down here," I call up.

She stops waving her arms and appears to brace herself on the wood beneath her. "You've gone mad, mistress. Positively mad."

"How else are you going to communicate with him?"

"They are *beasts*," she insists. "I won't understand him." Frustration and fear laces itself around her words. By this time, a small assembly of people have gathered around her, peering down into the water and exchanging whispers.

"They understood that they shouldn't kill me," I reason. Lingot that she is, Saen should know that I'm telling the truth.

"Perhaps they don't prefer the taste of you."

"Have you ever known Parani to be selective with their meals?"

Saen huffs. Clear indecision wrenches her brows together. She keeps me waiting several more moments and the Parani grows impatient beside me, giving me a small whine of what I sense is complaint. "Mistress Sepora," she says. "I—I cannot bring myself to jump."

"Then climb down."

The Parani gives me an uneasy look as Saen begins to descend down the wooden beams of the Half Bridge. I nod to reassure him, uncertain of what else I could be doing differently.

"It's suicide!" someone shouts from above.

"Come back, Mistress Saen. You can't save her now," someone else insists.

"You'll be devoured alive," a young girl shrieks.

"Oh, do shut up!" I yell back. "Have none of you something else to do?" Of course they do. Their busy day should be starting. Surely they have mouths to feed, work to be done. But what else could be more interesting than not one, but two royal servants offering themselves willingly to the likes of a vicious Parani?

Saen's motions are tight and hesitant as she grips the poles and beams on her way down, taking care to clutch them for several more moments than necessary to gain her balance. When she finally reaches us, I can see how loathe she is to slip into the water. She licks her lips

and clings to the last beam, looking at the Parani swimming appre-
hensively beside me. "He . . . he doesn't seem to want to hurt me,"
she says, unsure. "But what if I'm reading him incorrectly? He is after
all an animal—"

"Look at his face," I tell her. "At his eyes."

She fixes her stare on him long enough for my companion to
think her rude. The Parani whines to me again, and Saen freezes, eyes
wide. "He . . . it can't be."

"What?"

She shakes her head, then leans her temple against the beam, never
taking her eyes off the Parani. Several more moments pass, just as
several ranges of emotions overtake her face, the last one resting on
curiosity. "He called me a coward."

26

TARIK

"WHAT DO YOU MEAN, *I* SENT HER ON AN errand?" Tarik beholds the guard in front of him as though he's grown an extra pair of eyes. The giant guard squirms under the weight of his stare.

"She insisted you'd sent her to the Lyceum. I called a chariot for her, Highness." He worries his hands together. "I'm sorry, Highness. She said she'd wake you and tell you I was not complying with your orders. I would never—" Tarik allows him to babble on about his dutiful loyalty, which turns out to be very real. This guard would not dream of disobeying his king.

He closes his eyes against the irritation he's trying to keep out of his voice. This guard—what is his name, Guner?—is the victim here, after all. The victim of a clever little sphinx who is apparently very good at lying. "Did she say what I sent her to the Lyceum for?" What an absurd and telling question. If he'd wanted to hide the fact that Sepora had committed an offense against him, he isn't doing a very clean job of it.

"She was in need of a Lingot, I believe."

"I am a Lingot, Guner."

"Yes, Highness. And a very good one, I'm sure, Highness. It's just that I assumed the task she was assigned was too mundane for you, Highness, and so—"

Tarik waved him off. "Very well, Guner. Very well." And what else is there to say? The man had acted on what he truly believed were orders from his king. If Rashidi were here, he would pass out forthwith. *What was I thinking, recruiting a mischief maker like Sepora to assist my closest friend? What kind of judgment does that show on my part?* Father would certainly extract the title of Falcon King from him if he were still alive to see this.

He wonders how the Mistress Sepora fared with the Lingot she engaged for her foolish adventure. Surely the Lingot would hear the lie in her tone, no matter how smoothly Sepora delivered it. There are ways around speaking with a Lingot, he knows. But his training at the Lyceum taught him to recognize such trickery; perhaps Sepora drafted one of the newer pupils who cannot yet identify the deception.

And, pride of the pyramids, what is she up to?

Tarik wishes he could bury his face in his hands but doing so in front of the entire court would be inappropriate at best. If anything, he should be burying his face because of the increased percentage of cases of the plague brought to his attention at court. Of the way the noblemen and women look at him askance, as though he knows the cure but is hiding it from them. The Superior class has been exceptionally difficult to appease. Their children, their servants, their spouses, all contracting the plague and needing to know what their king is doing about it. And what can he say but "All I can," and assure them the Healers are working tirelessly on a cure.

And now this. This spectacle of Sepora in court, or rather, *not* in court.

The entirety of the situation is his fault, he knows, and his to repair. If only he had listened to Rashidi and sent Sepora straight back to the harem where he could have doubled the guard and kept her safe yet secure. If only he had thought with his mind instead of his eyes that day. If only she didn't have such discerning silver eyes and such an enchanting temper.

Enchanting? Fool! Oh, how he would punish her for this. He would have to think long and hard for a discipline worthy of such an act of—

"Highness, that's the charioteer I sent her off with," Guner says, pointing to the back of the throne room at the man stalking toward them.

"Forgive me for interrupting your court, Highness," the man says breathlessly. "But the Mistress Sepora has jumped from the Half Bridge."

27

SEPORA

I CLIMB THE BANK OF THE RIVER, JUST ENOUGH to sit at the water's edge. Saen follows, hoisting herself next to me in the mud. "He says this is far enough away," she tells me of our Parani companion. He'd wanted to leave the crowd of spectators—both Parani and people—to gain some privacy for our talk. I'm grateful he's willing to speak with me at all. I've caused quite a commotion among his kind, and some of them clearly do not approve. Saen said she'd overheard one of them say that this Parani—whose name she'd gathered is Sed—was foolish for communicating with us.

Sed stays in the water, a few arm's lengths away. He keeps his eyes trained on Saen, clearly curious as to her ability to translate. He opens his mouth, letting out a crude series of whines that from far away could be mistaken for the frantic neighs of a goat. She nods at him, then turns to me. "He would like to know our purpose."

"Tell him that we need nefarite. We'd like the permission of the Parani to harvest it from the river."

The wails she returns to him sound nasally and lack fluidity, and her voice cracks a bit as she finishes. She winces. "I'm afraid I'm not very good at this," she says.

"You're doing well," I tell her. "And I'm grateful for your efforts."

Sed speaks again, this time gesturing with his hands. "He says that we ask much of them, when we've mistreated them for as long as their memories stand."

As long as memories stand. These are not beasts. A cow does not remember even what it ate the day before, let alone annotate the history of its own kind. I want to point this out to Saen, but by her expression, she has already come to this conclusion herself. I endeavor not to smile.

"Mistreatment? How so?" I ask. Instead of mistreating the Parani, Serubel avoids them. Going to the Nefari involves going to the Underneath, and Serubelans would much rather stick to their mountains.

It is then that I realize Saen is giving me a quizzical look. I think of the question at hand, the charge against Theoria for mistreating the Parani. And I remember the way Chut and Rolan had handled their catch. They were going to let her die a slow, tortuous death. And, from what I'd gathered in my own experience with the Parani, the Theorian criminals pushed from the Half Bridge fare no better. The small bites still prickle in my arms, my legs, my back. The Parani take their time in killing their meals—at least, their human ones.

Saen's mouth becomes a straight line. She doesn't want to ask my question—of course, she'll already know the answer, having grown up in Anyar, and from our conversation on the chariot ride here.

"We need to know everything we're up against, all of their grievances. We need a starting point for negotiations." Ha. Negotiations.

As the servant of a servant, what am I in the position to negotiate for? But surely I didn't misread the longing in the king's voice. If he could get his hands on nefarite, he would save his people from certain destruction.

I want to believe that if he could, he would. It occurs to me that I want to believe much of this boy king.

Saen sighs against my reasoning, but proceeds to render my intentions to Sed. He looks at me for a long time. Then he speaks for even longer. It must be a burdensome list of complaints he has to lodge against Theoria. This is not good.

Finally, Saen turns to me. "He says we've diverted the river in too many places, causing the water levels to become too low. Many fish have died off, and they hardly have enough to feed their young ones from day to day." She cringes. "He said the food we offer them from the Half Bridge comes far too infrequently to be of any help."

The food from the Half Bridge. At first, I actually think the Theorians take the time to feed them. I quickly realize, though, that he speaks of humans who have been deemed unworthy of keeping their lives. The criminals sentenced to death. I shudder.

"He thinks of us as food," Saen says, her tone full of warning. "They are beasts. We should leave here."

"Have you ever spoken to a cow before, Saen?" Ah. Her beliefs are more deeply entrenched than I'd given her credit for. "Have you ever addressed a sheep or even one of the giant cats you Theorians are so fond of?"

She scoffs. "Of course not."

"Yet, here we have a Parani who is telling us of the devastation we've wreaked among his kind, and you can turn a deaf ear to that? Has a cat ever told you how much he adores his morning meals? Has a cow ever complained of being milked?"

She purses her lips.

"Think of what this means, Saen. We can communicate with them. Perhaps we can form an alliance with them. They are the guardians of the Nefari—what opportunities could we glean from this? Don't you think the king would want to explore the advantages of such an alliance? And think of your reputation," I say, making a play for her vanity. "You are now the first Lingot to ever communicate with a Parani. Doesn't that mean something to you?"

Her expression softens. "I hadn't thought of that."

"Tell him that I will speak to the king of this, and that I will return with an answer for him. But tell him I need a gift of good faith to bring to our leader, just as I've given him one."

She blinks. "What gift did you give him?"

I want to tell her that it was a gift of meat—something I should have thought of doing much sooner—but I know I cannot lie to this woman. It was too bold of me to have Forged something for Sed, knowing that communications could be opened up between us and having no way to silence him on what he saw. I've risked much this day and only now realize that the consequences might not be worth the exposure. What if he refuses to negotiate with us? What if the king refuses? I've put myself in the middle of a centuries-old strife, and my fate lies with a Parani who doesn't speak any of the languages I know.

Fortunately, though, Saen herself must not be that curious about my supposed gift because she rolls her eyes at my silence and begins to relay my message to Sed. He answers, shaking his head.

Saen's brows knit together. "He says the nefarite is to be respected. That it is the Great Judge."

"The Great Judge? Of what?"

She asks, but he only shakes his head again.

I don't know what to make of it. Perhaps the Parani worship the nefarite, just as the Hemutians worship the great whales in the sea bordering their kingdom. Perhaps they think of the nefarite as a living element, the way the people of Wachuk believe fire must be alive, because it eventually dies. After all, they reason, everything that dies must have once lived.

"Tell him that we will respect the nefarite. That he will come to see that we are not evil, that we mean them no harm." Or at least, I sincerely hope we don't. The Falcon King must make the decision for his kingdom. I cringe at the thought that this all could have been for naught.

Saen gives me a sidelong look. "Very well," I say. "Tell him that we *no longer* mean them any harm." It's then that I wonder if Lingots *can* lie—and if Saen will think she is lying when she says this. What an unfair advantage if Lingots have that ability, to lie yet discern the lies of others.

Sed takes his time mulling over this. Finally, he answers with a short staccato of grunts, after which he disappears into the water. The circles left by his departure spread and dissipate before reaching shore. Have we failed, then?

"Where has he gone?"

Saen brings her knees to her chest and rests her chin on them. "He's gone to fetch you some nefarite. Then he wants us to be on our way."

And so we shall.

THE CHARIOTEER HAD ABANDONED US; THE WALK back to the palace was a long one. Saen and I had parted ways before ever reaching the market, and she'd been ruffled that she had probably missed some of her classes as the Lyceum. The sun shone midday above me as I left the Bazaar, with the palace in view ahead of me.

I resolve that on my days of rest, I'll explore Anyar until I know it as I know the rope bridges of Serubel. If this is to truly be my new home, I must start acting like it. As it is, I hope the king will accept the rock of nefarite I clutch in my hand as a peace offering for not attending to my duties this morning. Still, I know I must be punished for what I've done. I've lied under assumed orders of the king, and I've delegated palace resources for my own personal use.

My father would find me deserving of imprisonment. I wonder what the Falcon King will decide. He seems to rule differently than my father does, with a lighter hand and a patient countenance. I would accept most any physical punishment, even a healthy flogging, if only he wouldn't send me back to the harem. Pain is something I can grow to accept; even now the Parani bites all over me feel as though I've been branded in half-inch increments. The treachery of boredom, though, I cannot survive.

When I reach the palace walls, a cry sounds from one of the towers and I recognize my name being shouted in every direction. I have definitely been missed and probably searched for.

And I am most certainly in trouble.

28

TARIK

THE TWO GUARDS PULL THE MISTRESS SEPORA across the throne room to Tarik, and it appears as though she's grateful for the assistance, her sandals dragging at the toe with each step. Her hair is a tangle of what appears to have been a braid at some point, wisps of it flying this way and that. The silver paint lining her eyes now streaks her face in rivulets as though she's slept in it or not washed her face properly after wear. Small yet eye-catching wounds pucker her skin in places on her arms, her legs, her shoulders, some of them inflamed and giving evidence of the almost certain pain she must be in.

Tarik is irritated that his initial ire seeps from him as he beholds the very public mess that is Mistress Sepora. Perhaps he should have had her brought to him in his private day chambers to spare her this open humiliation in front of such a crowd. But a private meeting, a private confrontation about her offenses will not satisfy the curiosity of those present, of those who have witnessed the frenzy of a morning in search for her, of those who yearn to hear her punishment for having brought the king so much trouble and interrupting his morning of court. And a private audience with her would most definitely start petulant rumors that the mistress has a measure of control over him—which is not something he wants nor can afford in this climate of power changing hands, of him taking over the kingship. The king has been wronged, and some sort of discipline is in order, even if it appears as though the offender has already punished herself in some way.

He squares his shoulders, careful to arrange his expression into one of indifference. The morning of searching for her has already given the impression that he deems her more important than she really is—or should be. Whether this is true he'll reflect on at another time. "I could not help but notice you did not report for your morning duties, Mistress Sepora," he says, trying very hard to sound bored. "I do hope your outing today is worth the punishment you must suffer for your transgressions."

She nods. "I do, too, Highness."

"Indeed. Well, let's have it, then. Do explain your actions today. As far as I can tell, you've lied to one of the royal guards and endeavored on a false mission in my name, which included stealing a chariot and recruiting a Lingot from the Lyceum." He swallows. "And rumor has it that you've thrown yourself from the Half Bridge." Which is technically not a crime, but something he's outrageously curious about. "What is your plea to these charges?"

"They're all true, Highness." Frustration swirls in his stomach. He didn't want those things to be true. He didn't want her to be guilty of punishable crimes.

Whispers erupt among the guards, the noblemen and women surrounding them. Tarik feels eyes on him, watching keenly for his reaction to Sepora's astonishing admission. He gives them none, though the pit of his stomach now lies somewhere in the vicinity of his ankles.

On the one hand, he's glad she didn't try to lie and add to her trespasses, and on the other, though he knows it to be true, he cannot believe, not really, that someone would willingly jump from the Half Bridge unless they intended suicide—which has been known to happen on occasion. "Those marks all over your body. What are they?"

"They are Parani bites, Highness." Gasps burst forth from the very captive audience. At least Sepora has the good sense not to speak out of turn, to try to defend herself against what she'd just admitted were justified charges against her. He remembers the last time she was brought to him before an audience and the boldness she'd shown in defending herself. Now she just appears humble and dutiful and sapped of bluster.

It's a bit disappointing, not to see her usual fire.

"If I may, Highness, I'd like to speak to you privately." Ah, the brazen Sepora he thought he knew after all, speaking out of turn at last. How refreshing—and utterly inconvenient.

He shakes his head. "I'm afraid a private meeting is not possible. There are many here at court who wish to know what will come of these crimes, and I'm of a mind to yield to their inquiries." She should be more afraid or at the very least intimidated by his words, yet a certain energy keeps her standing upright when clearly the girl is exhausted.

She holds her hand out in front of her and opens it to reveal a silvery rock speckled with white and black flecks. Tarik has seen a similar rock before; his father kept it in the form of a sword on a mantle in his bedchamber, a gift given to him from his bravest warrior who withstood the dangers of the Nefari to obtain the element to make it for him. Tarik inherited this lump of earth, and he values it greatly. Because this unimpressive rock is nefarite.

"I've been on a mission in your name," Sepora says evenly. "And although it was in many ways a lie, there was still truth in my deeds. I did these things on behalf of Theoria, and though I'll gladly accept your punishment, Highness, I do think what I have to say warrants a private audience."

His eyes lock with hers. She believes what she says. Giving her a private audience will show weakness on his part, he's sure of it. But not giving her a private audience may be more detrimental than a handful of rumors. Surely he can thwart gossip of his weakness some other way, in some other show of power. Sepora believes that what she has to say is for his ears only and she's holding the largest piece of nefarite he's ever seen, aside from his own. She's covered in Parani bites. And she's done it all on behalf of Theoria. He settles his gaze on the guard next to her. "Accompany the Mistress Sepora to my day chambers and stay with her until I join you."

HE PACES BACK AND FORTH BEHIND HIS MARBLE table, striving to find the patience to even speak to this girl who has caused disruption in his previously peaceful palace. King Knosi would not stand for such behavior and yet, he cannot conjure up the appropriate anger for the situation as he beholds her posture, so pitiful and defeated since the last time she sat in that very chair. She has been through much today, and though it appears she did indeed perform these tasks on behalf of Theoria, she has still broken more than a handful of laws while doing it. If only Rashidi were here to listen to her story, to advise him on how to proceed. Rashidi would know how to handle Sepora objectively. Or would he?

Yet, what is there to handle? There is no deception in her story. This girl has single-handedly opened communications between their kingdom and the keepers of the Nefari. She stole a chariot, a Lingot, and jumped from the Half Bridge to bring him his own lump of nefarite—and with it the promise of much more. The last person to do so was honored as the king's bravest warrior. Tarik doesn't know if he should behold her with awe or if he should shake some sense into her.

Though the latter seems more appealing at the moment.

"Highness, you've said nothing of the terms of the Parani. Did you not want the nefarite from the river after all?" It's her way of breaking the silence, he knows. Her voice is tired and she staves off a yawn with the back of her hand. She is woefully unafraid of him.

Stern hand, soft heart.

He stops pacing and takes his seat across the table from her. Of course he wants the nefarite. But there are so many things to consider. So many things to weigh against one another. "Did he say how much nefarite we could obtain?"

She shakes her head. "When he gave me that"—she nods toward the rock on the table between them—"he said there was much more."

"How can we trust that?"

"I told you. Saen the Master Lingot believes he tells the truth."

Of course. Saen would have been sure to pick up on the authenticity of the Parani's promise. The idea of communicating with a Parani at all still has his head spinning. "How did you persuade the Master Saen to accompany you?"

"I didn't. The charioteer did. I assume his belief in my mission convinced her?"

Tarik nods. "It's possible." The charioteer believed her, and so his story was probably persuasive to Lingot Saen. What amuses him is that Sepora herself is not sure how she managed to pull off that stunt. She is genuinely asking him whether that could be the case. So for his most trusted adviser, he has procured a reckless, thieving, headstrong liar. Rashidi will be thrilled.

"You still didn't answer my question. Will you negotiate with the Parani?"

Tarik adds "pushy" to Sepora's list of qualities as he leans back in his chair. "It's not something I can answer right away."

She sits up straighter. "But you need the nefarite. That is what you said. You need it to protect yourself from the Serubelans." A brief expression passes over her face when she says "the Serubelans" and Tarik thinks it might have to do with the fact that she did not seem to include herself in with the kingdom, though it would be unwise for him to think that she doesn't still. They have simply come across a mutual desire: to prevent war between the kingdoms.

"It would be helpful, but at what cost?" That is the true question. "The Middlings will be the ones to suffer if we close one of the tributaries. Without the water the channel brings, their crops will die." How can he take away the livelihood of so many? By far, they make up most of Theoria's population. A loyal working class of people who rely on the River Nefari for their food, their water, their trade. "We were actually thinking of diverting *more* water to their crops."

As much as it baffles him to be having this conversation with a mere attendant, he still feels as though it would be a natural thing for them to discuss. She is the attendant of his adviser after all, and in his absence, could he not analyze things with her in his stead? And, it is not to be overlooked that she is the very reason they must discuss it at all.

Sepora shakes her head, pulling her hair around her shoulder and attempting to rebraid it. She seems at ease with him, and he's not sure how he feels about that. He's not sure how he *should* feel about that. Even before he became king, people treaded carefully around the

Falcon Prince, simply because of rumors of his discernment and most likely because of the fact that he would one day be king. Sepora clearly hides something deep within her, yet she is honest in her dealings with him now. "What of the Parani?" she says. "If you divert more water, their food supply will dwindle and they'll completely die off."

"You say that as if it were a bad thing." He can only view the Parani's nonexistence as a positive in the grander scheme of things. Their presence has been a nuisance for centuries.

"They're not beasts, Highness," she says. "I think we have proved that today."

"They're not people, either. More specifically, they're not Theorian, and therefore not my concern." His father would be proud by the way he handled that. "Theoria must never perish," King Knosi had always said. "No matter what the other kingdoms do."

Sepora narrows her eyes. "You could do that, Majesty. You could divert even more water away from them, watch them die slowly." She spits the last word as if it tastes sour in her mouth. "But doing so would nullify this offering of peace." She picks up the rock from the table and tosses it back and forth between her hands. "It will take years for the Parani to die off completely, and if I understand correctly, you do not have the luxury of years to prepare for a war."

Ah, but negotiate with the Parani? What would his father do if beset with such circumstances? This leader of the Parani, Sed—and pride of the pyramids, Parani have *names*?—has proposed that the Theorian kingdom should divert more water to their territory, giving them more room to swim and grow, as it were. This will detract water from the Middling crops, Tarik knows. Sed proposed that Theoria stop fishing so heavily, to include refraining from fishing from the main banks of the Nefari completely. This will greatly affect his fishermen working to sell their catches daily at the Bazaar. They will have to fish along the tributaries, and their catches will need to be preserved with salt—something the Pelusians do in order to trade their ocean hauls—which will also affect the Middling class. The Superiors will surely complain of not having fresh fish at their disposal at all times. And the Baseborn Quarters will be forced to pay more for the fish, since it costs more for the Middlings to salt them.

Tarik could not help but notice that Sed made no mention of whether they would continue to receive gifts of condemned prisoners being thrown from the Half Bridge. He has half a mind to ask Sepora about that very thing. Indeed.

And so, in exchange, the Parani will not harm a single Theorian who steps foot in the Nefari for any reason.

It is a sound bargain, Tarik knows. But that doesn't mean he should allow Sepora to dominate his conversation, not when she's permitted to dominate his thoughts so often.

Tarik crosses his arms at her. "This war you speak of. Is Theoria to be the only target?"

"The first target, Highness. King Eron will take down every kingdom until he rules them all."

"You seem to know him very well."

"I know him better than most."

The truth. Curious. "And what would you have me do, Mistress Sepora?"

"I did not jump from the Half Bridge for nothing, Highness."

He grins. "And what if you did? What if I refuse to negotiate with the Parani?"

"Then you are much less intelligent than I'd estimated."

"You'll not speak to me like that." He says it gently, more gently than he should, but for now he's just grateful there are no onlookers to witness her disrespect. Rashidi would have her head if he'd heard those words from her mouth. *Why am I taking such abuse from my attendant's attendant?*

She sighs. "I'm sorry, Highness. I'd assumed you, as a Lingot, prefer directness instead of dancing around a matter."

Another truth, and one he cannot refute. He does grow bored of false flattery and reverence. And if he's being honest, her audacity is one of her more entertaining flaws. Still, she speaks of the matter as though experienced in it herself. He's sure many Serubelan noblemen tickled her ears hoping to get in a word with the king. Or perhaps they tickled her ears for different reasons. Flattery does come to mind, but not of the false variety. A compliment to the mistress on her beauty could never be unfounded.

Annoyed with himself for allowing his mind to wander, he reaches across the table, a silent request for the rock in her hands. When she passes it to him, their hands lightly brush and he swears he sees her shiver, but her expression never changes. He turns the rock over and over in his hand, as if it holds the answers to all of his questions.

And indeed it might.

"The Middlings," Sepora says after a while. "They're farmers?"

He nods. "And fishermen. They trade most of their goods at the Bazaar and eat the rest of them. Why?"

"Perhaps they could tend to a different harvest?" She eyes the nefarite in his hand.

He thinks on her words, pursing his lips. "You're suggesting I use the Middling class to reap the nefarite from the Nefari. And how shall I pay them? As you know, we've a shortage of spectorium and the last time I checked, nefarite is not edible. Not only that, we need the crops they reap from their fields to feed *us*."

At this she rolls her eyes, and Tarik could not be more delighted.

Finally, someone who truly does not toy with him or give him undue credit. Even Rashidi at times can be overwhelmingly praiseful and, if not, then painstakingly diplomatic. Sepora is neither of those things.

Get hold of yourself, fool. After all, you are delighted with a servant who insults you to your person!

"Nefarite is not only valuable to Theoria, Highness," she says, somewhat condescendingly. "Especially if Eron's plans are to move on to the other kingdoms. You simply must inform them of his intentions. They'll be knocking down the palace doors for nefarite once they realize the danger they face. The Middling class might find it more profitable than their wheat and corn, if you let them keep a percentage of it. And, of course, we can trade nefarite for food." Curious that she uses the king's first name without his title. She must have been very close to him indeed.

"You're sure you're not a spy?"

Slowly she stands. With her hands she brushes the length of her arms, pressing her finger on each of the Parani bites. She lifts the skirt of her dress above her knee, tracing a finger in a zigzag pattern along those bites as well. Afterward, she gives him a look that clearly says his question is nonsense. "What must I do to prove I'm not a spy?"

"I just cannot imagine what makes you so eager to remove your loyalty from your people and give it to me." It's something he's given more attention than is due. Why would she be so forthcoming with information? Why would she be so willing to help save Theoria? "Do you not care about the lives that would be lost in Serubel were we to make an offensive attack to catch your former kingdom off guard?"

She places her hands on the table and leans in toward him. Her eyes shine like silver fire, her cheeks pink with barely disguised fury. It's a sight to behold, Mistress Sepora on the edge of a tantrum. "I'm not giving you my loyalty, Highness. I'm simply trusting you to save lives. You yourself said that no one truly wins a war. I did not believe an offensive attack was on the agenda."

"It isn't. But you should not be so reckless with your trust."

She opens her mouth but shuts it again, and Tarik wonders if she was actually going to argue that she wasn't reckless and thought better of it. He grins again, ready to tease her for it, when Sethos opens the door unannounced and strolls in. When he sees Sepora, he stops dead.

"It seems I've interrupted. . . . What exactly have I interrupted?" he says, his glance shifting from Sepora to Tarik. His attraction to the mistress is plain on his face.

Annoyed beyond explanation, Tarik longs to run a hand through his hair, but his headdress will not allow it. With one swift motion he removes it and tosses it on the table. Sepora's mouth drops open, and it occurs to him that she's never seen him without it. He can't care about that now. Standing upon ceremony in the privacy of his chambers and in the presence of his younger brother is more than he can bear at the moment. "Sethos, do come in," he says dryly. "The Mistress Sepora and I were only discussing the fate of the kingdom. Would you care to join us?"

Sethos strides to Sepora and takes her hand in his. Tarik tries not to grimace. "Mistress Sepora, it is, of course, a pleasure to meet you. Are you one of His Majesty's new advisers, then?"

She gives Tarik a questioning look.

He waves his hand in response, as if batting a fly. "Sepora is your gift to me, brother. She didn't want to reside in the harem, however, so I gave her to Rashidi as an attendant."

"You *gave* her to *Rashidi*?" Sethos says, incredulous. "Did it occur to you that *I* would have taken her? Pride of the pyramids, Tarik, look at her."

"I was not aware you required an attendant at the Lyceum." Oh, this is going to be great fun. He can see the fury unfurling in Sepora's expression as they speak of her as though she's not present.

"An attendant? Well, that's one way of putting it, I suppose—"

"Or perhaps a sheep or a goat?" Sepora spits. "Or perhaps a bushel of apples, or something just as meaningless that can be bought and sold at the Bazaar?"

Sethos tilts his head toward her. "Your tone would have me believe you're angry with me. Which is nonsense, of course, because we've never met. Not to mention, females are never angry with me."

"*Females?*" By this time Sepora is nose to nose with Sethos, and Tarik can tell his brother is on high alert. It is the Majai training in him. Before Tarik can protest, Sethos catches Sepora's wrist and wrenches her around, pinning her arm against her back. She lifts her leg almost naturally, her heel catching him in the tender part of his goods, and he lets out a growl as he repositions the mistress to a safer hold.

Tarik purses his lips as Sethos contemplates aloud what to do with his new captive. "Have you gone mad?" he tells her. "Is that any way to treat the brother of the king?"

"You," she says, nearly growling the word. "You grabbed me first!"

"You were about to do something you shouldn't. I was protecting you." Sethos casts a glance at Tarik. "Is she always so ornery?"

"I'm afraid so."

"Let me go, you sniveling, vile—" Sethos does as she asks, pushing her away from him so hard she nearly trips. She turns then, and Tarik thinks she just might fling herself at his brother. As amusing as that would be, Sethos's defensive instincts are uncanny; he may end up hurting her without meaning to, were he actually attacked.

"Mistress Sepora," Tarik says quickly. "I've an idea about the Parani."

She turns to him, breathless and distracted. "What?"

"The Parani. We were discussing what we could do to form a truce with them, if you'll recall." That's not exactly what they were discussing when Sethos interrupted them, but it's as good a subject as any to address.

"You what?" Sethos says, holding up a hand in warning to Sepora. Obviously he can read her body language as well. Sethos slightly shakes his head at the mistress. "It will not be worth what you're thinking, Mistress Sepora."

She huffs. "Are you a Lingot, too? Is *everyone* in this place a Lingot?"

"I've decided to slaughter some cows," Tarik is saying good-naturedly. Both Sethos and Sepora give him their full attention.

"Cows? For the Parani?" Sethos says. "I don't follow."

But Tarik keeps his gaze trained on Sepora. "We'll close the tributary to the Middling fields, but it will take some time to do. In the interim, we'll slaughter some cows and throw the meat from the Half Bridge in a show of peace. What think you of that, Mistress Sepora?"

Forgetting Sethos, she takes her seat again and folds her hands in her lap, nodding. "Yes. Yes, I think that would be very good, Highness. And the Middlings' crops?"

"It will be as you suggested. They'll keep a percentage of the nefarite, and we'll start trading it to other kingdoms. It's a well-known resource, and its value is irrefutable. It should be easy enough."

She lifts her chin. "And my punishment?"

"Well, I don't suppose throwing you from the Half Bridge will work," he says, amused at her appalled expression. He mulls over the question, though, trying to find the right balance. She committed these offenses for the sake of the kingdom. Still, she'd plowed ahead thoughtlessly, without care for the consequences in the event she didn't get exactly what she wanted. But his court expects a punishment. An idea comes to mind, and swiftly he grasps it with both hands.

"I will require you to train the Seer Serpen to listen to your commands. If we are to go to war, it shall be *our* spy." It's the perfect solution, really. His court will see it as an insult to her to train the beast to work against her own kingdom, and she will see it as a reward for what she's done. Her affection for the beast had been evident since the moment she laid eyes on it. And he will do much to emphasize the Parani bites she's already suffered, which mar her skin in puckered welts even now. Very few Theorians can say they have suffered a Parani bite and lived to speak of it, after all. They'll be horrified with the idea, Tarik is sure.

Even now, Sepora's eyes light up. He can tell she's trying to look thoroughly chastised but is failing quite miserably. She stands. "Yes, Highness. May I be dismissed, Highness?"

Dismissing her would be the right thing to do, but he's not finished with her just yet. "One more thing, Mistress Sepora."

"Yes, Majesty?"

"I am not so reckless with my trust as you are. There will be two guards posted at your door and escorting you to your duties in the morning until further notice." She bows her head in acceptance, but Tarik can see the defiance in her eyes. She does not care for the latter requirement. But Tarik has met his threshold for caring what displeases the mistress for the moment. The last thing he needs is for her to get another brilliant idea and steal away from the palace on some martyrly quest.

When she's gone, shutting the door quietly behind her, Sethos turns to him, grinning. "Do you hate Rashidi, then?"

Tarik laughs. "When Rashidi returns from Hemut, she'll be fully trained and ready to serve him. He'll thank me for recruiting her."

"I'm no Lingot, brother, but even I can recognize a lie when I hear it. Now, tell me about the Parani."

29

SEPORA

CARA AND ANKU CALL MY NAME JUST AS I EXPEL the last of my morning's spectorium down the lavatory. I resolve to wake up early each morning for this; I simply cannot get caught Forging, even if Cara knows what I am. Expelling in the evenings and in the mornings has served me well so far, but I must take care to be more cautious—especially since the door to my bedchamber does not lock from the inside.

For the next hour, they both fuss over me to no end. They've somehow prepared several ensembles for me to wear to court, all of which are made of blue linen but with differing designs. Some have gold embroidered into the waistline; some have extravagant beaded bib collars; and others have the sheer, flowing material that will trail behind me. It's the latter of the dresses they choose for me for court today. After I'm dressed, Anku takes great care in arranging my hair and Cara paints my face with silvers and blacks and blues. When I look into the mirror, I do not recognize myself. My eyes are lined with black, my face is brushed with silver, and blue dots form an almost imperceptible mask around my face. What an odd sense of style these

Theorians have. Then, I've seen what the king wears. Gold and black mostly, and I hadn't even realized he had hair until last night when he removed his golden headdress. Not that I imagined him bald, but, well . . . I didn't imagine his hair to make him appear so . . . attractive, disarrayed as it was.

"Are you sure this is what a servant is supposed to wear?" I ask, holding my arms out and inspecting the sheer material that looks like draping wings behind me. It's a ridiculous thing for an attendant of an attendant to have attendants. But then I remember that I'm acting in Rashidi's stead, and he most certainly has attendants.

Anku shakes her head. "You're not just any servant; you're a royal adviser. Since Master Rashidi is away, you're taking his place."

"I'm Rashidi's attendant," I say, purposely leaving off the master part. I don't care if Rashidi is a Healer, Majai, and Lingot all wrapped in one grumpy old being—he's not *my* master. "I'm not an adviser of any kind."

Cara places hands on hips. "The Falcon King himself requested you to be dressed properly for court, Mistress Sepora. If you please, you can take issue with him."

"The guards are ready to take you," Anku says. "Court will open shortly."

COURT IS FANTASTICALLY BORING. EVEN THE Falcon King appears disinterested in the petty plights of his citizens. And who am I to point accusing fingers? These noblemen and women can hardly eat their morning meal without finding something over which to squabble. Still, Anku had called me a royal adviser. If I'm to act in Rashidi's stead, perhaps I should actually advise the king of my opinion. The problem is, I'm not familiar with Theoria's laws, and the ones I am familiar with, I find utterly ridiculous. What is also ridiculous is the fact that it is almost always one person's word against another. If the king himself were not a Lingot, who could decide such a matter?

I lean in toward the king, and he discreetly lends me his ear. "Are there not other Lingots who can handle these affairs, Highness?" I whisper. "You've an impending war to think of, and these are such trivial matters that do not affect your kingdom as a whole."

He looks up at me, apparent amusement dancing in his dark eyes. "That is precisely what I've been telling Rashidi. Unfortunately, he holds more traditional views."

"Who is pharaoh, you or Rashidi? You've inherited a kingdom during a season of change," I tell him quietly. "Perhaps the way you rule requires change as well." But then I am presented with a new scroll and a new case I must announce before the court.

After a few more cases, the king gestures for me to come closer. I lean in, preparing for him to ask me a question about the case, and frantically try to recall the last time I paid attention. It is difficult to care about such frivolous quarreling. "I think we shall make this change," he whispers. "We'll test it out while Rashidi is away. If it succeeds, he has no leg to stand upon. Send a message to the Lyceum that we're in need of three Lingots to hear the cases of the court. Tell them to assemble in the morning and be ready for a long day."

"Yes, Highness."

After court, I follow the king to his day chambers. When we're alone, he immediately discards his headdress and ruffles his hair. I look away, unsettled by the ease in his posture and the casualness in his voice as he offers me water. A king, offering a servant a drink. My father would never do such a thing. He would see it as a sign of weakness. I can only help but see it as kindness.

It is not good that my father's nemesis is kind. I stop myself. *Do I not believe him to be my nemesis as well?* Surely I do. Surely any enemy of Serubel is an enemy of mine. What has become of my resolve?

Yet, I cannot bring myself to attach such a negative feeling toward this royal boy.

The Falcon King comes to sit at his marble table across from where I take my usual seat. He scrutinizes me for a long time, tilting his head in curiosity. I take care not to shift in my chair. I feel as though I'm telling secrets just by sitting there and allowing him to dissect even the smallest of my expressions.

"What do you know of the shortage of spectorium?" he says finally.

A difficult question, one I'd hoped he would never ask, but then I've always been one for wishful thinking. And I've always been one for preparing for the worst. "I know that King Eron will be stock-piling all that he has."

"For the war, you mean. There are rumors that the king has run out of spectorium and that is why he hasn't traded it. Could that be true?"

"Yes."

"Have the mines run dry with it, then?"

Ah, how to answer. I could lie and say yes, but he would detect deception in that, I'm sure. But the truth is so jarring and exposing. Can I tell him of Forgers? Can he be trusted with the biggest secret of Serubel? Yet, what choice do I have? He will discern either way. "There were no spectorium mines, Highness." It unsettles me, the admission. What I've unveiled to his knowing ears.

"What do you mean?"

I bite my lip. This line of questioning is getting dangerous, but

I've a feeling he'll not back down from it. I must tell him the truth in increments without giving myself away. Without giving the others away. Short, precise, evasive yet true answers. That is my strategy. "The Princess Magar made spectorium, Highness. She was a Forger, the last known Forger in Serubel, I'm afraid." I try not to think of the others as I say this. After all, they are not in Serubel. I hope this cloaking with words succeeds.

If the king has an internal reaction, it doesn't show on his face. This makes me nervous. How could he not react to a revelation like that? How am I to play this game if my foe is unreadable? "And what exactly is a Forger?" he says, pressing his fingertips together.

And so I tell him. I tell him of the history of Forgers. I tell him of my grandfather and of the way the king forced this poor Magar to Forge all the time. I tell him of how unhappy she was. I tell him all these things, and instead of feeling guilty, I feel as though I've been freed from heavy chains.

"You knew the princess well."

Accidentally, I do shift in my seat. The action does not go unnoticed by the king. Nothing goes unnoticed by the king. "Very well, yes."

"Why do I detect deception in your words? That is unlike you, Mistress Sepora."

What else can I say? This is a game I cannot afford to play. He has enough Scaldling venom to make Serubel a mere memory, if only he knew I could Forge the spectorium needed to do it. He has made it clear he will call me on outright lies, and now he detects deception in words that are technically true. A dangerous game, indeed. And an interesting one. "I don't like discussing the matter of her death." Which is true, and mostly because it makes me homesick. Surely he must hear the truth in that. Surely his Favor cannot be so masterful as to perceive my treachery.

"Her death must have devastated you." Again, hardly an outward show to match his voice.

"It was very sudden."

He tilts his head again, and I wonder what he must be thinking. What is it like to know nothing but the truth all the time? I wonder if there are truths he would rather not know. "Are there any Forgers left?" he says.

"I told you, Magar was the last of them in Serubel."

"So there is no other way to get spectorium?"

Blast him. He is not called the Falcon King for nothing, I realize. There is no way to evade, no way to dance around this question. "I would not tell you if I knew."

"Ah, but you do know, don't you?"

"Yes."

"There is another Forger."

"I did not say that. Magar was the last known Forger in Serubel."

He leans back, scrutinizing me. "You purposely speak in riddles, mistress. That can only mean you think I'll use the spectorium against King Eron in the impending war. I was under the impression that you trusted me more than that."

"By your own words, I am reckless in doing so, giving my trust so freely, Highness. I'm simply trying to improve upon my flaws, you see."

He laughs and the sound is actually quite enchanting. Immediately I don't like how it makes a certain warmth steal through me. "You are right not to trust so willingly. But I'll let you in on one of my own secrets, Sepora. There is a Quiet Plague stealing through Theoria. My father died of it." He waves his hand in the air, likely in response to my shocked expression. "Oh, I know. The rumors are that he contracted a disease from Wachuk on his visit there. It isn't true. Most of the people have not encountered it yet, but if my Healers do not find a cure for this Quiet Plague of ours, hysteria will settle in and chaos will ensue. Many Theorians will die. Fortunately, I have a brilliant young Master Healer working tirelessly so that this does not happen. So far, he has helped some to survive. And do you know what he needs in order to cure them?"

I close my eyes against what I already know he's going to say.

"Spectorium, Sepora. We need spectorium."

"I am not a Lingot," I tell him. "I cannot mull words in my head and separate the truth from the lies. You may tell me what you wish, Highness. But I've seen what mixing spectorium with Scaldling venom will do—and you have an abundance of that. I cannot—will not—help you raze my home to the ground. Your Healers are the best in the five kingdoms. Everyone knows that, and it is no great secret that Theoria is not humble in announcing it. I'm sure your talented Healers will find another way to handle this Quiet Plague." With this I stand. Any more direct questions and I'll be placed in some dungeon, Forging the weapon that will bring my home to nothingness. "Please allow me to take my leave, Highness. The day has been long, and I still must visit the Seer for his daily training."

"I find it curious that you will jump from the Half Bridge and risk your life to save Theorians, yet you'll not do the same when it comes to a mere plague. Lives are lives, no matter how they are lost."

When he puts it like that, I have nothing to say. And so I don't. "My leave, Highness?"

He nods, his mouth a tight line. "Our day is clear tomorrow, Mistress Sepora, since we've assembled Lingots to manage our court affairs. I'd like to give you a personal tour of Anyar. Please meet me at the servants' entrance of the palace shortly after dawn and borrow your attendant's attire for the day. You are dismissed."

30

TARIK

TARIK WAITS WITH PATRA AT THE SERVANTS' entrance, engaging the guard there in a bit of informal banter. The guard is uncomfortable, he can tell, and nearly unwilling to address his king so casually, but under strict orders to do so, Tarik has left him no choice.

"Will you be needing a chariot?" the soldier says, not quite meeting Tarik's eyes. He can tell by the abrupt way he ended the question that he put much effort into not addressing him as "Highness."

"I thank you, Ptolem, but I've already arranged for one. You've not seen the Mistress Sepora this morning, have you?"

Ptolem grimaces. "I've not. I don't know whether to let that one come or go, truth be told. None of us trust her beyond our own arm's length." Immediately his face falls. "My apologies. Of course my opinion is not worthy of your ears."

Tarik laughs. "The Mistress Sepora can be an intricate creature to decipher sometimes, even for me. I think, though, that perhaps she is becoming more tame."

"I'll keep that in mind," a feminine voice calls from behind them. Tarik can't help but be miffed when Patra leaves his side and nuzzles Sepora's hand, blatantly asking to be petted, and even more put off by the fact that Sepora doesn't shrink back from the beast but wraps her arms around the great cat. He's also a touch miffed that though the mistress does not wear the makeup and the elaborate adornments required of court—or the harem, for that matter—she is still breathtaking in the plain blue attire worn by palace servants of the king. Perhaps it's the way her hair is loose and falling about her shoulders, or the way her silver eyes glint in the morning sun.

Perhaps I should get my thoughts about me instead of ogling her the way Patra ogles cutlets of meat.

"Are you ready for your tour of Anyar, mistress?" he says lightly.

She smiles at him, nearly stealing his breath. Not for the first time, he is thankful that the Mistress Sepora herself is not a Lingot.

"I am, Highness."

"Ah, but we must leave *Highness* and *Majesty* and *All-Knowing Ruler* behind us here. We are but servants to the Falcon King, on his errand throughout the city today."

"*All-Knowing Ruler?*" she says, her brow rising just a bit.

He laughs. It is good to tease and for his teasing to be appreciated. As it is, Ptolem licks his lips nervously at her doubtful expression. "Let us go, before Ptolem expires and we have to carry his body inside."

He grabs her hand then to pull her forward and, as soon as he does, regrets it. She is soft and inviting, and though she breaks away in the slightest of pulls and keeps her eyes trained on the path ahead of them, he knows she felt something in their touch as well.

Today might prove to be a long day after all—and revealing, if nothing else.

THE BAZAAR IS BUSTLING AS USUAL, THE AIR HOT and dry and the wind just strong enough to be a nuisance, pelting them with tiny grains of sand that infiltrate their mouths as they speak, their eyes before they can blink away the irritant, and their noses so that they sneeze midsentence. Still, Tarik finds all those things to be insignificant inconveniences if compared with the growing enthusiasm he feels for Sepora's exclusive company. Even Patra seems content to walk between them as if it were the most natural thing in the world for her to do.

He would be a fool to lie to himself about such a thing as his fascination with the mistress, when clearly he hangs on her every word and dissects her every smirk and smile in a way he's quite sure has nothing to do with being a Lingot.

"So if not as Highness," she whispers as they approach a booth, "how should I refer to you?"

"My name is Tarik," he says, suddenly wanting to hear her say it. What an odd thought, to want to be addressed so informally by someone who just days ago would have called him something very crude if she'd had the chance. He remembers her ire at being held in the harem and nearly bursts out laughing. A harem would be boring to someone as interesting as the Mistress Sepora.

"And no one recognizes you here?"

"Of course not. What business would I—the pharaoh—have at the Bazaar, dressed like this, without even a speck of body paint?" Still, he keeps his voice down, decreasing the grandeur of the statement.

"And Patra?"

"I am the king's servant, taking His Highness's cat out for much needed exercise."

"Are servants of the king supposed to act so presumptuous, then, Tarik?" He doesn't miss the demure way she shades her eyes with her hand as she teases him. And he doesn't miss the casual way she says his name, though he can't decide if she's testing it out to see if she's pronounced it correctly or if she's trying to discern whether it fits him. Either way, Sepora is at ease with him, despite his rank and station and responsibility.

Either way, Sepora is not here with the Falcon King; she is here with Tarik. And he enjoys that more than he should.

31

SEPORA

I'M NOT SURE WHAT I'M DOING, BANTERING WITH the king as though I've known him since infancy. Perhaps it is the way he wears no paint this day, that his skin is a deep olive color, or that his eyelashes stand out more without the charcoal lining his eyes. And where I thought the body paint embellished his muscles, I'm surprised to find that the king is, in fact, built as a warrior. Built as I imagined his father would have been. Indeed, the paint hides his superior physique. But still, there is more. There is an ease about him, a poise that belies peace with his lot in life—a poise I never saw in my father—and also a desire to get away from it every now and again. The latter is evident in the way he handles the children who swarm about him, asking if the Falcon King has sent him along with prizes for them from the palace.

From his rope belt he pulls a purse, a mere cloth tied at the top with string woven through it, and he opens it to reveal a small fortune in gold coins. As the children squeal, he retrieves one, holding it in the air so that even the highest of jumpers can't quite reach it.

"Shh, shh, quiet down now," he tells them. "And has the wind carried off your manners with it? Did you not notice I come with company today?"

An overwhelming sense of shame emanates from the throng of children, and the king laughs. "Well, don't be shy, you bunch of wildlings. This is Sepora, and she is also a servant of the king. She'll be accompanying me often, so you may as well get used to her."

One of the smallest of the bunch steps forward, a little short-haired girl with a front top tooth missing, a rather shabby white linen dress, and a cloth tight about her right arm, signaling that she is of the Middling Quarters. "You're pretty," she informs me bashfully. "I like your eyes."

"Thank you," I tell her, feeling a blush warm my cheeks, even in the hot desert sun.

The king hands the small child a gold coin. "See? Was that so difficult?" He looks around the gathering, apparently for more volunteers. "Does anyone else have anything to say or ask Sepora?" the king asks. "I've got a gold coin for the next person to ask her a question."

A boy this time, with all of his teeth and an extra chin, pushes to the front of the group. His shendyt is a pale lavender and his arm bulges out of the silver armband he wears, signifying his status as a Superior, as Anku related to me. "You look like the freed slaves. Are you of the freed slaves?"

"No," I say, not appreciating his bluntness. Then I reprove myself; if the boy cared about Theoria's apparent caste system, he would not be bothered to play with children of the Middling Quarters. Cara informed me that they do not intermix with the underclasses, as they call them. But this child is not concerned with classes at all. He doesn't care if I'm a freed slave. No, he is simply a child being a child. "I'm of Serubel," I say, less gruffly.

"Why did the king send you with Tarik? Will you always come with him?"

The king laughs and hands the boy a gold coin. "The king thought I needed help. What do you think? Should I keep her along with me?"

"I think you should marry her," says the first little girl. "You and she would make beautiful babies."

The king ruffles her hair and winks at her. "I think Sepora is far too clever to want to marry the likes of me," he says lightly. "Anyone else?"

I try to imagine my father doting on a group of children like this in our marketplace and can't. He never even doted on me, his own flesh and blood and royalty, nonetheless. I'm not sure why I keep comparing the Falcon King to my father, but every time I do, I find my father lacking. Not that I thought my father was ever the affectionate sort, but for him to act so warmly toward anyone beneath him would be, well, beneath him.

Perhaps this is a game the pharaoh is playing with me. A game for him to win my trust and tell him how he can acquire his precious spectorium. If only I were a Lingot, able to discern if there is deception here.

Still, it does not take a Lingot to see these children are very familiar with their king, though they only know him as Tarik. He has done this many times and long before I ever arrived in his grand Theorian harem. No, this is not a ploy to gain my trust. This is the king's way of enjoying himself.

I try not to find that enchanting.

After each of the children has earned their gold coin by asking me questions, they are on their way, leaving the pharaoh and me to wander the Bazaar by ourselves. "They can be overwhelming," he says after a while. "But I do find their innocence and inexperience to be refreshing."

"Yes, I noticed."

He raises his brows. "I didn't mean to ignore you, mistress."

I smile. "That's not what I meant. I just—I'm glad you were having a good time."

"I still am." His eyes lock with mine, and I can't help but feel infused by heat that has nothing to do with the Theorian sun. I find this version of the king to be most unsettling. In fact, I find it unbelievable. He truly is not the Falcon King today. And I do not feel like a runaway princess of Serubel. Today we truly are Tarik and Sepora, enjoying a day at the Bazaar.

It is a dangerous thing, to let one's thoughts linger.

"Tarik, so good to see you!" a voice calls from the booth before us. Giving a lighthearted laugh, Tarik breaks our gaze and greets the man behind the table of necklaces.

"Cantor, how are things with you, my friend?"

Cantor is happy to relay that his wife and children are doing well, business is thriving, and his cat, Jesa, just had a litter of three and is making excellent work of motherhood. I find it endearing that Theorians are so smitten with their giant cats. I'm a bit jealous, too, that the kingdom of Theoria approves of pets in general. In Serubel, a pet is just a nuisance, another mouth to feed.

It is not long, though, before Cantor lets his gaze fall on me, in an obvious request for an introduction.

Tarik obliges easily. "This is a fellow servant of the king, Sepora. Sepora, this is Cantor, my good friend who fashions the most exquisite pieces of jewelry for the Superior Class, made from Wachuk turquoise."

I bow my head, uncertain of what else is required of me. Cantor bellows his laughter. "No need to be shy, Sepora," he says. "I'll not bite, and especially not with Tarik standing there looking at you with such longing. A man knows when to step down."

It is Tarik's turn to feel the heat of his own kingdom's blasted sun. "I . . . er, that is to say . . . I thought I saw a fly in her hair," he stammers.

"It was," I tell him. "I've heard it buzzing in my ear all day." Letting the king of Theoria off the hook is not something one takes lightly and we both know it. He nods to me slightly, thanking me silently for his discretion. Still, his eyes hold a certain sentiment that extends beyond gratitude. Upon seeing it, I look away, my stomach swirling with an unfamiliar feeling.

Cantor seems to want to talk further, but Tarik seems eager to pass to the next booth, and then the next, making quick introductions and trivial exchanges until we've reached the end of one stretch of the Bazaar. There are four more rows of booths and tents, and I wonder if Tarik intends to take us to each and every one when he says, "On a normal visit to Anyar I would make my entire rounds, but today I wish to visit with Cy the Healer at the Lyceum. I'll introduce you to the rest of the merchants another day."

Another day. He wishes me to accompany him again. I'm not sure how I feel about that. I'm not sure how I *should* feel about that. These are his private moments that he steals for himself, I can tell. Special excursions meant solely for his pleasure and rejuvenation. Why he would want me with him I'm not sure. I've made myself a pest, a prickle in his foot at the very least.

We head north then, taking what I recognize as the path to the great Lyceum where I'd recruited the Lingot Saen for my impossible task of wooing the Parani. That morning I'd remembered every bend in the roadway, every sizable mound of sand we passed, as one would when one believes one may be about to die. Even now, as we walk down the beaten path, I feel squeamish as I contemplate what could have happened to me. And then I berate myself for all of a sudden turning coward again.

Tarik eyes me curiously but says nothing. I'm a bit unsettled at how easily I refer to him as Tarik in my mind instead of the king, and once again I'm confronted with how I *should* feel about things instead of how I actually *do* feel about things. I hope I don't slip at court and call him by his given name; I know that seeing him as Tarik, instead of the king, has left an immense impression within me, a much deeper impression than watching him deal with the mundane matters of court as pharaoh. I wonder what the punishment for such a thing is here in Theoria, calling a king by his given name.

I wonder what my father would do under such circumstances. And I shudder.

32

TARIK

CY GREETS THEM EAGERLY IN THE OPEN COURT-yard in the middle of the Lyceum. Groups of Majai train one-on-one close by, and by the center fountain a group of Healers—recognizable by their lavender attire—recline for what appears to be an out-of-doors lecture. All of these things Tarik notices, and so does the Mistress Sepora in wide-eyed awe, yet it is the grimace on Cy's face that commands most of Tarik's own attention.

Tarik feels himself tense. How many lives has the Quiet Plague claimed now? How long before it becomes a noticeable threat among the citizens of Theoria, before it is talked about in the Bazaar instead of litters of kittens or children acting foolishly? These are questions he wants to blurt at Cy, but instead he makes hasty introductions for Sepora.

"My pleasure, of course, Mistress Sepora," Cy says. "You've quite the reputation here at the Lyceum. Master Saen chatters on about how clever you are and Majai Sethos about your beauty."

Tarik grits his teeth at the latter; Sethos and his infatuation with Sepora has become a bothersome thing. Just this morning he sent word that he'd like to have a meal at the palace soon and hopes that Sepora may attend. *If he thinks I'm giving her back to him, he's lost his mind.*

Cy beckons them to an assembly of stone benches in the middle of the lavish courtyard. "I've news, Highness—er, Tarik. I've been seeing more of the Middlings at my door."

"I was afraid you might say that," Tarik says, feeling a scowl on his face.

Cy nods. "It is spreading, but not in the way that you think."

"How do you mean?"

"Are you familiar with the Owinat root?"

Tarik raises a brow. The Owinat root, when ground and used as a tea, has hallucinogenic effects. He's well aware that it's a highly sought-after plant, used for leisure among all the classes. It's sold widely in the Bazaar, and though not outlawed, it is traditionally considered in poor taste to hold company while under the tea's influence. Though Tarik was not there to witness it, it's rumored that a Superior merchant attended King Knosi's court after having just drank the stuff, and was so addled that he stumbled to the throne and dared to stand eye to eye with the pharoah—a crime punishable by ousting at the Half Bridge. His father had spared the man's life, but stripped him of his fortune and title. Gossip holds that the merchant dispatched with himself shortly after. Gossip that rings strikingly true to Tarik's ears.

There is not a Theorian who does not know of the Owinat root and its effects.

But there *is* a Serubelan who does not. "What is Owinat?" Sepora says, mispronouncing it slightly.

Cy clears his throat. "Well, you could say that it's a sort of a scandalous plant used for ill intent at times. It can ease the pain of some chronic illnesses, but when abused, it can cause quite the addiction to it."

"And what does that have to do with the Quiet Plague?" Tarik asks. "Are you saying the Owinat is an alternative solution to spectorium?"

Cy shakes his head. "Quite to the contrary. I think the symptoms the classes are presenting are very similar to the symptoms of withdrawal from the Owinat root. It appears our citizens are withdrawing from something, but what, I couldn't say. Likewise, I still can't explain why a dose of injected spectorium helps them. It is a powerful elixir, that."

Tarik runs a hand through his hair. "You're saying they're withdrawing to the point of death?"

"I'm afraid so. And there's more."

"Tell me."

"Since the spectorium eventually dies, I fear that once it's injected, it, too, will wear off in the patient's body. I'm afraid it's only a temporary solution. What I'm trying to say is, we need a constant supply of it, if not to power our city, then to power our citizens."

A constant supply of spectorium. Something they may never have again, unless . . . His eyes lock with Sepora's. "Not to worry, Cy. Sepora and I are working on a solution to this very problem, aren't we?"

But she doesn't answer, only raises her chin a bit. Oh, how can he trust her if she acts in such a way?

"Cy, I hate to take you away from your work, but I'd love to show Sepora how thorough you're being in finding a cure for the Quiet Plague. You see, she is capable of finding . . . *unconventional* solutions to problems as well, and I think she'd appreciate seeing the progress you've achieved. Do you mind showing us what you're working on now?" Out of the corner of his eye, he sees Sepora tense.

"Of course not, High—Tarik. Please follow me."

He leads them south and through the usual labyrinth of halls and archways and stairs until they come to a set of double wooden doors. Apparently Cy's work has been given additional space; Tarik is pleased to find the room they enter now is large and echoes with busyness, with at least twenty beds lining the walls in increments about two arm's lengths apart. Each bed holds a body, and each body reveals clear symptoms of the Quiet Plague. Other Healers weave in and out between the cots, some with water jugs, some with clean linens, and more still with steaming bowls of what appears to be liquefied spectorium glowing purple in the dim lighting.

Sepora stops cold. "I don't want to see this."

Tarik grasps her hand gently and is struck again at the revelation that her touch sends chills and heat throughout him all at once. He tries to discern a reaction from her, anything to suggest she feels something of the same, but his Lingot perception returns to him with nothing. "I think it is only fair that you see this," he says. "The king would want it." Very much so. She should see the effects of the Quiet Plague up close and personally, should see the speed at which it takes its victims and the speed at which spectorium returns their life to them. She should put faces to this plague, put faces to those who might not otherwise live without this resource whose whereabouts she keeps hidden.

She inhales a long yet impatient breath, but when she releases it slowly and steadily Tarik can tell she's ready to cooperate. Cy bids them to follow him to the corner of the room, to where a middle-aged man lies on the cot, his thin linen sheet draping halfway on his legs and halfway onto the floor. His blank stare, which is fixed on the ceiling, and his shallow, whistling breaths give the impression he's concentrating on not dying. There is dried blood crusted around his nostrils, in his ears, at the corners of his mouth. His lips are stained red with it. To Tarik's knowledge, however, this is not something that happens when one withdraws from use of the Owinat root. Cy believes his theory; Tarik cannot be so sure.

Sepora is not unaffected by the sight, Tarik can tell. Her rigid posture, her squared shoulders, her slightly upturned chin. All of it practically announces to him that she is very affected—and that instead of softening to the man's plight, she's attempting to steel herself against it. He's not sure if bringing her here was the right thing after all. He knows the Mistress Sepora to be very stubborn indeed, and if she sets her mind against helping him she will follow through.

Something more is needed.

"Children," Tarik tells Cy. "Show us some children."

Sepora gasps. "No, please. I don't want to see any children."

But Tarik is already leading her across the room behind Cy, where a small girl lies on a blanketless cot. Her long black hair is damp with sweat and dark circles shadow her eyes. "We are about to administer the spectorium," Cy says softly. "Soon you will be feeling much better, child."

He gestures for one of the lesser Healers to come forth. "Heat the spectorium and inject her." He turns back to Tarik and Sepora. "I invite you to come back within two days' time. We'll not be able to contain her, so abundant with energy she'll be."

"And if there were no spectorium, Cy?" Tarik asks, hating himself for it. It is cruel of him, especially after all the mistress has done to help Theoria. But if Sepora knows where they can find more spectorium and still refuses to share that knowledge, she must come to a full realization of the consequences of withholding it. She must know that withholding spectorium means tolerating death—and death does not discriminate. "Or if the spectorium had been given time to dwindle into blue, its last and final stage?"

Cy's expression falls grim. "We can only use purple spectorium, or white would be best if it were available. Blue does little but prolong the suffering. If there were none at all, though . . ." He shakes his head.

Sepora wraps her arms around herself, staring down at the child half-alive in the cot. At this, Cy offers her a kind smile, one full of more wisdom than should be possible at thirteen years old. "Bravery comes in all forms, mistress. You are very brave in your own right, jumping from the Half Bridge as you did. But sometimes facing the death of a child makes us all cowards. And perhaps it should."

With that, Cy excuses himself.

33

SEPORA

B Y THE TIME WE REACH THE GREATEST OF ALL
the pyramids, night descends upon us as the sun drizzles below
the horizon, as though sinking into the River Nefari ahead of us. As
we make our way to the entrance of the great structure, I can't help
but reach out and touch the wall made of spectorium, which glows
purple into the lavender evening. I've never seen anything so immense
constructed by spectorium before; no wonder Father had me working
so diligently day and night. It had to have been constructed within a
short time indeed; that it still glows purple means that it was Forged
just months earlier.

"You have enough spectorium here to cure all of Theoria," I tell
Tarik, not a little irritable. "Why keep monuments to the dead when
the living needs them more?"

He brings the small fire torch in his hand closer to my face. I step
back, not because I'm afraid he'll burn me with it, but because I'm
afraid he'll burn me with *him*. Every time he touches me I feel melted
in place. The way he places his hand on the small of my back to guide
me in a certain direction. The way he grasps my hand when he wishes

to emphasize a statement. The way our arms brush together when we're in close quarters at the Bazaar. I swear by Serubel I've not blushed so much in my entire existence.

He seems to take a small satisfaction in the fact that I lean away from him slightly. "These are not just monuments to the dead," he says, amused. "This is where we *store* our dead. And there is an even greater purpose than that here." He turns and points in the direction of the Bazaar. "You see, the people of Anyar wish to see their loved ones again. Our Healers work to find the cure for death. The spectorium pyramids protect the bodies from the desert elements in a way that no other resource does. Our engineers have found that building spectorium upon itself, in this shape, creates a preserving power. It's fascinating really, but very boring if you've no mind for the workings of things."

I'm not sure if I should take offense at such a statement. Theorians, after all, believe they are the only among the five kingdoms to ponder over "the workings of things." Still, I'm curious. "Which of the two are you? Fascinated or bored?"

He shrugs. "It depends on the 'things.'"

He sets his torch down next to the wall, digging a hole for the handle to keep it standing up and ready for later use. I follow him inside a long hallway illuminated purple. Both of us seem to blend in with the walls, and I must focus on his muscular silhouette ahead of me in order not to lose him in the brightness. He reaches a hand and traces it along the wall as though we are in the dark instead of stark light.

"What are you looking for?" I ask.

"There is a small lever here somewhere. Ah." His hand disappears into the wall and when it reemerges, the wall beside me begins sliding to the right. The sickening sound of stone scraping stone saturates the air and even in the iridescence I see Tarik grinning at me. "Does Serubel not have anything like this?"

I raise a brow. "Of course not. We're sensible. We bury our dead and are done with it."

He snorts. "There are many things about our society you do not know, and I'm afraid once you learn them, you'll have to find something else to do with that pretty little nose of yours besides keeping it upturned."

"Do enlighten me, Great Majesty Tarik."

He laughs. "I try all day to get you to call me Tarik, and you somehow manage to mock me while doing it. Well played." He extends his hand to me, and I don't want to take it. He must see this for he nods upward. "We've many stairs to climb, and the last thing I need is for you to tumble down them. Take my hand for support. Please."

"Where are we going?" I can't imagine more steps than required to navigate the Lyceum. Though, before the spectorium shortage, they were working on creating spectorium-powered "lifts" to get them to each floor.

"I am going to show you," he says, taking the first step up the narrow stairwell, "the most breathtaking view of Anyar. Now, if you could withhold your questions until we reach the top—"

I snatch his hand into mine and pull him upward myself, ignoring the heat lacing up my arm. His laughter trails us as we climb and climb and climb. Even climbing the stairs and rope bridges back home could not have prepared me for this steep ascent. My thighs and calves burn, and for once it has nothing to do with the Falcon King. "You're right," I tell him grouchily. "It is breathtaking indeed."

"Nothing worthy is ever easy, Mistress Sepora." Though he sounds a bit winded himself.

"So noted, Highness."

At the top of the stairwell, in between the blur of the walls and stairs, a black hole begins to appear and the closer we get the more stars I see freckling the night sky, their whiteness just barely contrasting against the purple gleaming in my face. The hole materializes into an open, arched doorway, and as we reach it, a small balcony spreads before us, one I couldn't see from the bottom of the structure. It is just enough room for perhaps five people to stand.

One cannot help but notice the intimacy of the space, and one cannot help but blush all the more for it. I'm only glad the glow from the pyramid shields my stained cheeks, hopefully the only visible indication of my distress.

Ahead of us—and far below us—is the truly magnificent city of Anyar, recognizable by chunks of lights spread across patches of desert darkness. In the middle is the Bazaar, all dotted with the lights of fire lamps and spectorium torches lined with the shadows of tents and booths. If I squint hard enough, I can see the palace just beyond that, a glowing blue silhouette against the night sky, though not because it's constructed of dying spectorium—somehow the engineers have found a way to make the fire from the torches burn blue and green. It really is a magnificent sight.

The Superiors' Quarters glow brightly beside the palace, and although most of the structures glow blue, some do not glow at all, but are rather lined with plain firelight. And though I know it is there, I cannot see the Middling Square north of there. Hard workers that they are, the Middlings do not waste fire or spectorium or for that matter sleep in these hours of the night.

I've been to all these places today, as Tarik had promised to show me, but none of them by far match the beauty of all of them bunched together yet separate under the night sky and in the stillness of the evening from atop this pyramid.

Tarik nudges my leg, and I see that he has already taken a seat along the edge. He gestures for me to sit beside him, something I was afraid would happen. It is one thing to do the bidding of the king. To follow his orders and treat him as others do day in and day out. But without his gold body paint and face paint and ornate attire and the immense headdress he's required to wear at court? Without his kingly posture and formal, commanding voice and his unwieldy indifference? Then he becomes Tarik. A boy with a humble smile and readiness to bow his head toward a stranger. Tarik, with his easy laugh and mannerisms, and playful scolding. His beautiful brown eyes and disobedient hair and melting touch.

He looks at me now as though he can read what I'm thinking. Hoping that Lingots do not have this unfair hidden ability, I do as he says and sit, taking care to keep my eyes on the city instead of on his face.

"Sepora," he says softly.

"Yes?"

"What do you think of our ambitions to cure the dead?"

The question is unexpected. I turn to him. His eyes meet mine and hold my gaze, and I feel pressured to keep steady, to not look away. I feel it's a sort of challenge he's presenting me, and if I pass . . . I'm not sure what happens if I pass, but I'll not fail, that's all I know. "I think that it's absurd. Dying is a part of living."

"It doesn't have to be," he says gently. "You say it so boldly now, but tell that to a mother who has just lost the newborn she's carried in her stomach for months on end. Could you do it? Could you say it to her just as you said it to me?"

I shouldn't have said it to begin with. Not when Tarik has only just lost his own father. "No."

Tarik sighs. "Neither could I." He is quiet for a long time then.

"But what you said below is right. Though it's not a monument to the dead in itself, it is a sanctuary of sorts for them. And we need to focus our attention on the living for now. I think I shall give the order to disassemble the pyramids tomorrow."

"No!" I grab his hand without thinking. It surprises us both. "Tarik, please. If you believe your Healers can bring the dead to life, then . . . then . . . I mean, what of your *father*, Tarik?"

He stiffens, lifting his chin just a bit as the king in him spills out. "That is exactly why they must be disassembled. My father would want that, if he knew his people were facing such a future and they needed spectorium. He would be angry that I held out this long."

And that's when I see the whole picture, every last painted swoop of the brush. I drop his hand. "Are you . . . are you *toying* with me?" I scoot away from him.

"How do you mean?"

"Did you bring me here just to woo me into telling you where you can find your precious spectorium? Did you bring me here to push me over my edge, to soften me up?" I feel so betrayed. So foolish. This entire day has been dedicated to soliciting my knowledge, of plundering my secrets. He wanted me to meet his people, to feel sorry for them, to see them dying in the Lyceum and want to help them. He brought me here to see the beauty of a city that could die if I don't help them. He brought me here to place the responsibility of it all on my shoulders.

Just as my father would have done.

I see the exact moment realization strikes him. His face changes from confusion to rage and then, to my surprise, softens into laughter. "Spectorium," he says, more to himself than to me. "I could see, of course, why you would think that."

"Well?" I demand, unamused. I'm not even sure what I'm asking, just an explanation perhaps, or better yet, a confession.

He slides to me then, closing the distance I'd put between us. I have nowhere left to move. Does he mean to push me from the top of the pyramid if I refuse to help him save his people?

"Yes," he says, leaning toward me. I feel panic and something else I cannot name ricochet throughout me. "And no." His eyes fall on my lips, and I know my cheeks will certainly explode with the warmth filling them. Fears of our lips brushing together replace fears of falling to my death.

"Yes, I did bring you here to woo you," he says softly. "But no, not for the spectorium." And he lowers his mouth to mine.

Tarik waits for me then, our lips barely touching, as if asking a question without words. He waits for me, letting me know that my answer will determine if this will be our first kiss or his last effort at one. He waits for me, tiny me who is about to tremble from the ledge under the scorching heat of his touch.

And I make him wait too long. He pulls away, sliding back a few inches, a small rush of cooling desert air filling the space between us. And that is when I decide that kissing the king would have been a foolish idea. That kissing a pharaoh, the enemy of my father, a man in the position to destroy my home and everything in it would have been a very brainless thing to do. That kissing a man who keeps a harem would have been nonsensical.

I ease away gently, so as not to insult him, but I take care to make my movements precise, delivering with them my decision. I shall not kiss the Falcon King.

He gives me a self-deprecating grin, his eyes full of a sentiment I can't quite place. He scratches the back of his neck, the muscles in his arm bulging with the action. "Wise, brave Sepora," he says softly. "You were brave enough to flee from tyranny in Serubel and brave enough to jump from the Half Bridge and brave enough to withstand the pitiable advances of a foolish boy king. I have faith that you will find the wisdom to this conundrum you have unfurling inside you."

"Conundrum?"

He nods. "The conundrum that keeps you from saving us from the Quiet Plague."

He stands then, and extends his hand down to me and pulls me to my feet. I allow him to lead me into the pyramid, but that is where his ability to compel me stops. I cannot—will not—allow him to coerce me into Forging for him.

Not when this very pyramid could be disassembled. He is wrong; I have no conundrum. Not one that has anything to do with saving lives, anyway.

FOR A SPYING SEER SERPEN THAT ONCE BELONGED to the highest general in Serubel, the beast is much more tame than I'd expected it to be. I can't remember what General Halyon called him, if I ever knew at all, and so I've decided to name him Dody, because after days and days of feeding him and caring for his newly developed eyes, he seems to have developed at least some sort of affection for me. Even now, when he sees me approaching his stall in the makeshift stable built for him, he becomes restless, his tail whipping about just as Nuna's had when I came to get her for an outing.

He gives off a litany of snorts of what sounds like excitement. Perhaps it's the rudimentary saddle I carry with me, the harness I'd been fashioning for him as he healed. Nuna and I had bonded so thoroughly that we had no need of saddles or harnesses; she would respond to pressure from my legs against her neck and verbal commands we'd developed over our time together. But Dody must go back to the basics of preliminary training—or rather, he must become accustomed to a new handler. The basics, I'm sure, he knows well, since a harness and a saddle are standard military accessories for Serpens in the king's army. But he definitely recognizes the possibility that today he may fly again. Dody is not quite as big as Nuna—none of the Seers have ever compared in size to the Defenders—but he is just as beautiful and just as capable of flight.

And I truly hope that is the case, as his eyes have healed quite nicely, along with the arrow wound he took to the underbelly. That had been minor, just enough to fell him; the rough, calloused skin of his belly had protected him from deep penetration.

Today we shall see what Dody is capable of, if he will respond to my basic commands. Tarik had shown me around the city of Anyar by foot; if I can get Dody in the air, I can experience it all by flight, and I'm curious to know if the view will be as breathtaking as the one from the great pyramid a few nights ago.

Ah, that night. A night ending a wonderful day. A night ending my only chance to see what the Falcon King might have tasted like. Relief and regret vie for my consideration over the matter, each of them presenting reasons why I should or should not have kissed Tarik.

But it is no matter. The moment has passed, and it will not present itself again. The king all but said so himself. In the days since our visit to the city, he has been nothing but polite, and, of course, kingly when required to be at court and during visits with his closest council members. In those few moments of privacy we share together between our duties, he mentions nothing of that night, nor do I, though it seems to hover in the air around us as if something remains unresolved from our outing that day.

But it is not unresolved. We did not kiss. We will not kiss. And that is how it should be.

34

TARIK

TARIK WOULD LIKE TO THINK HE DOES NOT know why his steps take him toward the new Serpen stable on the far side of the west courtyard. But lying to himself is not a habit he wants to cultivate. And so, he admits the reason he approaches the stable now has long blond hair, silver eyes, and a maddening pair of sensual lips.

The reason he'll tell her, however, is that he merely wishes to check on the progress she's making with the Serpen beast. After all, the creature could be a valuable asset to Theoria if war were indeed to erupt, and for the past few days, she's been able to take it to flight. It is a reasonable excuse to come to the stables, he thinks as he pulls open the door of the wooden structure. A reasonable excuse to ensure that his new attendant is taking her punishment seriously—and enjoying it.

The wide door creaks open and swirls of dust rise up around his sandals. Tarik does not need to call out her name to know that she isn't here—and neither is the beast. The stable is as silent as the tombs in the pyramids. He walks the length of it anyway, staving off his disappointment; he must have just missed her. There are fresh track marks in the sand, one set of human footprints, the other set a long slithering trail leading to the stable door. They have already gone.

It is just as well, he decides as he shuts the door to the stable. Being with the Mistress Sepora gives him a reprieve from the often overwhelming demands of his obligations, of course, but perhaps he doesn't need a reprieve. Perhaps he should command more focus instead. Perhaps he should employ the mistress in other activities throughout the day, activities that keep her from constantly being at his side.

Then again, perhaps he should think on it more.

As he makes his way to the closest palace entrance, a dark shadow flits across his path and feminine laughter trickles down from the sky. "Highness," a familiar voice calls from above. He looks up to see Sepora mounted upon the Serpen beast, guiding it into a consistent circle just above his head. "I was not expecting you," she says, her voice teeming with excitement and pleasure. "Stay right there. I'll bring him down for your inspection."

He crosses his arms and grins—though his stomach tightens at the thought of her falling from such a height—as she maneuvers the great creature to a skidding stop before him in the courtyard sand. It's a vision to behold, a beast such as that with the ability to land as gracefully as Patra parades by his side through the palace. Tarik finds Sepora's smiling face as the dust cloud clears. Her cheeks are stained red from the wind and her hair likewise is a mess. And of course, she's stunning, in every sense of the word.

Gingerly, she hops off the beast's neck, murmuring words of praise to it as she would a child. After the Serpen is sufficiently rewarded with Sepora's attention, she turns it at last to Tarik, striding to where he stands.

"It seems you're taking your punishment very seriously," he says. "What a pleasant surprise."

She smiles up at him, breathless, as she attempts to pull down her hair and arrange it into something more manageable. It splays across her shoulders in a magnificent deluge of white curls from her previous style, before she gathers it all back up in one hand again and twists it into a bun atop her head. "Come with me," she says excitedly. "Let me show you what Dody can do."

"I can see well enough from here, mistress."

"Surely the *Falcon* King is not afraid of heights?" But her smirk is playful. "I'll not take you higher than the great pyramid, I promise. You seem comfortable enough at that height, are you not?"

It is the first time she's mentioned their shared evening on the pyramid. He'd been wondering if she'd forgotten. *What does it mean that she hasn't?* He shifts his weight from one foot to the other. "It's not the heights that make me nervous; it's entrusting my life to a Serubelan beast sent here to spy on me."

She looks over her shoulder at the Serpen rolling over and over contentedly in the courtyard sand, as though it is attempting to scratch an allover itch. The creature is quite oblivious to present company. Sepora raises a doubtful brow at Tarik.

He sighs. "Say I accompany you on a flight. Where will we go?"

He is surprised and more than a little pleased at her boldness when she takes his hand in hers and begins to lead him toward the beast. "We'll fly over your kingdom, Highness. For your inspection, of course."

"Say I get injured. Can you imagine the months and months of scolding from Rashidi?"

"It will be worth it. And you won't get injured. I'll harness you to me so that we are both secured by the saddle. The only way we'll go down is if your brainless guard shoots us to our deaths."

"Say I—"

She tugs harder on his hand. "Say you come with me and have a marvelous time."

"That, I think, is a given."

She doesn't turn to look at him as she leads him toward the Serpen. She mounts the beast first, in one agile jump, using the low-hanging stirrup of the saddle to hoist herself up. Once settled, she extends her hand down to him, as if he could actually reach it.

"Where will you have me?"

"I must use the saddle to guide it. He knows my basic commands. You'll need to sit behind me, and I'll use this belt to strap us together and to the saddle." She pulls on the leather strap to show how sturdy it is, but Tarik is already pulling himself up by the stirrup and positioning himself behind the saddle. It's actually not uncomfortable, though his legs are set a bit wider than they are when he rides horses or camels.

Settling behind her, he inches as close to the back of the saddle as possible. She wraps the belt around them both, cinching it tightly so that his chest presses in against her back. "Highness," she says, "you may want to hold on to me, at least while we take flight."

Needing no further encouragement, he slides his hands around her waist, even as he feels the shock of doing so rock through his body. Where his body has hard lines, hers is soft, curving underneath her dress. Reveling in the feel of her, he perhaps lets his hands linger a bit too long at her hips before he remembers his manners. He tenses, waiting for her to stiffen at his boldness, but she merely leans down to Dody, whispering something in his ear. In an instant they become one slithering mass circling the courtyard, gaining speed, and Tarik's hold on Sepora tightens as the beast lifts them from the ground. For a time, they spiral into the air until Dody straightens his course and takes them over the palace walls.

Because of his proximity to her, Tarik can feel when Sepora's legs apply pressure to Dody's neck, obviously signaling him to fly north. As the breeze of their speed hits him, he's overcome with the aroma of orchids and lavender oils and something else he can't quite name and he must fight the urge to lean in and fully take in the scent of her.

"Where shall we go first, Highness?" she says.

"I'm entirely at your mercy, mistress."

"Very well." She seems pleased, almost as if she expected him to say that.

Dody responds to an imperceptible signal from Sepora and turns west. They reach the Bazaar in no time, and Sepora brings the beast lower when she spies a gathering of children on the edge of the marketplace.

"No," Tarik says quickly. "I'm dressed as king. They cannot see me like this."

"You think they'd recognize you in all that glittering paint?"

"I don't want to risk the chance. You know, speaking from a Lingot's point of view, children are sometimes the most perceptive among us all."

"Very well, Highness." She drives them upward again and in the direction of due west, leaving the bustle—and wondering youthful curiosity—of the Bazaar behind. She cuts slightly south and over the Baseborn Quarters. Unlike the tents of the Bazaar, the tents here are light and drab in color, bleached by the sun and tattered at the corners, some with holes peeking down into the dismal households. The blond-headed residents move quickly in and out of the way of each other, trading and bartering for things too mundane, things too ordinary to find at the Bazaar. Frivolity here could mean the difference between eating a meal or going without; children do not play, but rather linger at their parents' side, waiting to be put to good use.

A few of the young ones do take pause to point and stare into the sky at the spectacle the king of Theoria is making with his servant girl Sepora and her Serpen. Pride of the pyramids, but Rashidi would eat his own headdress were he here to witness such an exhibition. Of course, his adviser does not make a nuisance out of himself where his occasional visits to the Bazaar are concerned, but that is mainly because Tarik is not visiting as king but is dressed in servants' attire. Now, though, Sepora has picked him up from the palace courtyard, and he is fully painted and adorned as the Falcon King. And the Falcon King goes nowhere without ceremony, armed guards, and a thoroughly self-assured expression. To see the king smile is a rare gift.

One that he wishes he could bestow much more often.

Tarik wonders what Sepora sees when she looks at these people. Does she see herself as one of them or consider that she's risen above them in so many ways? But no, that would not be fair to say. Some of them have proved themselves worthy of earned scholarships to attend the Lyceum. Yet, they always come back to the tent village where their people are. They never make homes for themselves among the Superiors or Middlings. Always here, in the Baseborn Quarters.

Tarik has always wondered why the freed slaves stay, why they choose not to return to their homeland of Serubel when they seem to have such loyalty to one another. Does that loyalty no longer extend to their home? They have nothing in the way of belongings to miss and could easily trek north up the Nefari and follow it all the way to the floating mountains where they are from. Are they happy here, eking out an existence so far from their kingdom? Why else would they stay?

By her expression, Sepora is not enjoying the view below. Her mouth is downturned and her shoulders square as she takes in the sight of her people. Coming from the everyday splendor of life in the palace, this must come as quite the shock to her senses.

"Perhaps the next time we leave the palace we will visit the Baseborn Quarters instead of the Bazaar," he tells her softly. "We'll bring two satchels of coins, to make up for lost time."

If he didn't know better, he would say she leans back into him slightly when she says, "Yes. Yes, let's."

Veering north, she leans forward and whispers something in Dody's ear. Swiftly, the beast spirals, turning them upside down more times than Tarik cares to count. He gasps, clutching onto Sepora, unsure whether he does so out of need to save her from falling or to lock himself in place, and admits that it's a little of both. The spiral becomes tighter and his stomach feels tickled to near implosion and he lets out a laugh. Sepora straightens them then and grins back at him. "I call those Daring Dozens," she says. "The first time I did it was an accident. I confused my directions for my Serpen, Nuna, and we coiled through the air like a spring. You took your first one very well. I vomited."

"How old were you?"

She laughs. "It was just months ago."

"You were trying to make me ill, were you?"

"Just curious to see if I could."

"Disappointed?"

Absently, she pets Dody's neck in front of her. "No, I don't think

I am." Without elaborating, she increases their speed until her hair threatens to spill out of the unkempt bun atop her head.

In the distance, Tarik can see the pyramids come into view. In the daylight, their dying purple spectorium shines gray underneath the sun's scrutiny. As they approach the valley of burial grounds, his gaze cannot help but fall first to his father's pyramid and next to the pyramid where he and Sepora nearly shared a kiss.

Nearly. But the mistress would not meet him halfway, would not meet him at all, in fact. How can he convince her of his intentions? And are his intentions entirely good? After all, Rashidi could be in Hemut at this very moment, negotiating a marriage contract between himself and the Princess Tulle. Should he just let things be as they are? Is it wise to pursue a woman for himself while the crown pursues another?

"Shall we call on the nefarite quarry, perhaps?" she says. "You've not made an official visit, and the Middlings would be proud to see their king himself curious as to their progress."

"Rashidi would swallow his own headdress if I were to visit without ceremony."

Sepora laughs. "All the more reason to do so?"

He grins to the back of her head. "Of course."

It really is a magnificent view, taking in the city of Anyar from the back of a Seer Serpen. The Lyceum, always so large and imposing, now appears to be the size of a single room in the palace—albeit a big room. They leave it behind in no time, and soon are back at the Bazaar. Still abuzz with life, small specks of people migrate through their daily lives as though ants in an aboveground colony.

The large, ornate structures of the Superior class loom in stark contrast to the tiny, dreary tents of the Baseborn Quarters. These quarters are quiet, bereft of life, probably because of hours spent drinking and dancing and whatever else his Superior citizens find to entertain themselves during the cooler hours of the night.

Instantly, an imbalance in his kingdom makes itself known to him. The spectrum from rich to poor is simply too vast. He must take steps to correct this. It will be yet another argument to have with Rashidi. But to Tarik, the healthier *all* the classes of the kingdom are, the healthier the kingdom itself will be. To his knowledge, his father never bothered to enrich the lives of the Baseborn class. Perhaps this aspect of kingship has been neglected for far too long.

What if Sepora lived there among them? What if she chose to leave the palace and flock to her people? Could he stand for her to live in such striking poverty?

He tries to convince himself that his decision to help the Baseborn class has nothing to do with Sepora—he tries and fails. Perhaps it's not entirely owing to her, but to say she has nothing to do with his decision to redirect some of the kingdom's wealth there would be a lie.

When they fly over a particularly lavish building with gold-plated rings circling the four surrounding towers and a colorful center garden worthy of a spot in the palace, Sepora smiles back at him, apparently oblivious to his darkening mood. "Isn't it lovely?"

He scowls. "It would be lovelier if the Superiors could awaken at a decent hour in order to participate in the goings-on of the kingdom. It seems they only do so when they've a mind to come to court and complain."

She sighs. "Are you Theorians not capable of looking at something and appreciating the beauty of it without having to analyze it to bits?"

This surprises him. His people have keen intellects, but that does not mean they are not capable of appreciating beauty when they see it. "That's a ridiculous question."

She nearly turns around in her saddle. "Name one thing!" she says accusingly. "Name one thing of which you can appreciate the beauty without dissecting it into fragments."

Swiftly, his mind conjures up thoughts of nature, the stars in the sky, and the flowers in his gardens at the palace. He thinks of great man-made structures and natural ones that formed over centuries of exposure to the conditions of weather. He thinks and thinks, but there is nothing that his people have not made a science of in some way or another.

Except one thing. One very beautiful thing.

He leans toward her ear, making sure to touch his cheek against her lobe. "You."

"What?" she says.

"You, mistress. I do not question your beauty or how you came to be in such great supply of it. I simply allow myself to admire it."

And so he answers both their questions. He can admire beauty without overanalyzing it.

And he does intend to pursue one woman while the throne pursues another.

35

SEPORA

TODAY TARIK WISHES ME TO FLY HIM TO VISIT the Baseborn Quarters—which is why I wait rather impatiently in my bedchamber for Anku and Cara to arrive with my breakfast. I'm not interested in the honey cakes and oil they'll most assuredly bring; I need to speak with Cara in private before we depart this morning. I need to know what to expect once the freed slaves see my silver eyes—and I need to know how to act around them without giving away Bardo's secret, all while dancing around the king's inconvenient abilities.

As soon as my door opens, I snatch the tray of breakfast from Anku, catching her off guard so that she stumbles back. "Well," she huffs, "someone is hungry this morning. Are we late with your meal, mistress?"

"Of course not. You're never late."

"I see you've already dressed yourself," she says, leaning against one of the bedposts. "Perhaps today we could braid your hair and then make intricate swirls—"

My hair is a haphazard mess, in what I hope resembles an attempt at an elegantly folded bun, but more important, what I hope will keep it out of my face as we fly Dody. To arrange it into anything "intricate" would be a horrible waste of time once we leave solid ground. "Actually, Cara was just telling me about a new style she learned. Cara, would you stay behind and show me? Anku, thank you for breakfast. You may go." Cara told me nothing of the sort, but I must get her alone.

Of course, I did not mean to dismiss Anku so callously, because out of the two she is my favorite, even if only because Cara barely has the enthusiasm or mind-set to say three words to me each morning. The truth is, Cara makes me nervous whereas Anku makes me feel at home—a sad irony, to be sure.

Anku wishes me well for the day and leaves, but shuts the door a bit harder than usual, and I cringe at Cara for it. We wait for the sound of her footsteps to disintegrate down the corridor before speaking.

"You've upset Anku," Cara says, crossing her arms.

"I needed to speak with you in private."

"So it seems."

Cara still does not like nor trust me, which makes it difficult to trust her, even if she is Serubelan. But today, I have no choice but to confide in her. After all, we both have the same objective: to keep Forging a secret. "I take the Falcon King to inspect the Baseborn Quarters today. He is particularly drawn to children; I worry we will come across Bardo and the people will try to lie to the king about his silver eyes. If they do that, he'll come to be even more curious about Bardo than if they had not lied."

"The king never visits the Baseborn Quarters. Why is it that he's doing so now that you've arrived?"

The question is an accusation, one that I don't appreciate but one that I feel a tinge of guilt for. After all, I should have known better than to lead Dody to the quarters. I'd been hoping Tarik would see the living conditions there and perhaps do something to improve them. It never occurred to me that he would want to visit them for a closer look. But knowing Tarik, and the way he cares for people, I should have known that would be his inclination.

Absently, Cara moves her hand to her throat and sits upon my bed. She nods. "Perhaps you could talk to the king. Tell him you are not feeling well?"

"You know he would discern the lie."

Cara folds her hands in her lap and stares at the floor for a long time. I want to shake her and tell her we do not have time for panic. But as it turns out, she is not panicking at all. She looks up at me again, a determination in her eyes. "I have some herbs I use for medicinal purposes. I can make a tea that will make your sickness very real, mistress. The king will postpone the visit until we think of something else."

"He may go without me."

She shakes her head. "It is well known in the palace that the king does not go very far without you. He will postpone the trip. In the meantime, I will try to get word to my family there that you may be coming."

"How quickly can you get the tea ready?"

Cara rises and strides to the door. "Take off your clothes and pull your hair down. It must be the truth when I report to the king that you are not dressed. The delay will allow some time for the tea to steep. After that, you'll fall ill quite quickly."

And with that, she shuts the door.

THE WORD "ILL" IS A GRAVE UNDERSTATEMENT for how I feel. I've done nothing but wretch for the past two days, barely able to swallow water in the tiniest of sips. Though custom does not allow Tarik to visit me personally—for which I am thankful—he has sent Cy the Healer twice to my bedchamber to ascertain that I have not contracted the Quiet Plague.

As Cy leans over me now, he shakes his head. "You've lost quite a bit of weight in these past two days. But you say you've not noticed any bleeding? None from the nose or the ears?"

"Take a look for yourself," I tell him weakly. "My stomach is simply sour."

Sour. That is what Cara was when she made this concoction for me. She probably enjoyed stirring the herbs together she knew would make me sick. We will have to talk, she and I. We will have to discuss this lack of trust between us. If we are to work together for a common cause, surely there is a better way to go about doing it.

After Cy's inspection, he nods, satisfied. "It seems as though the king has been fretting over a common stomach ailment, though you've one of the worst cases I've seen."

"The king has been fretting?"

Cy grins. "Well now, I suppose kings do not *fret*, do they? That just would not do. So then the Falcon King has been *brooding* over your sudden illness."

Brooding. Indeed.

"And how long will I feel this way?" Though the question would be better posed to Cara.

"I would say you have another day, maybe two, and after that you'll start feeling warm-blooded, at the very least. Do not worry so much about eating; you should drink as much water as you can, and I will send a tonic from the Lyceum that will help your dizziness. It will also make you sleepy, but promise me, mistress, that you'll take in water every time you awaken."

"I promise." Saints of Serubel, but I promise. Cy had said I'll be feeling this way for a day, possibly two. Surely enough time will have passed for Cara to get word to her family and, somehow, to the rest of the Forgers.

One day, I tell myself, I will meet these people, I'm sure of it. I hope they appreciate all I've done here to protect our abilities.

Just then, the door to my bedchamber creaks open. Patra slinks in, followed by one of Tarik's personal guards. "Please excuse the interruption, mistress, Healer Cy," he says, nodding to each of us. "But the Falcon King has sent his cat along to Mistress Sepora in order to keep her company during her distress," the guard says.

As if following orders, Patra leaps onto my bed and makes herself comfortable beside me, her head at my feet and her tail tickling at my nose. She is already asleep by the time Cy gathers his things and leaves my room.

36

TARIK

T ARIK WATCHES FROM HIS DAY CHAMBER BAL-
cony as Sepora glides Dody by him through the air, making
loops as though the creature itself has no backbone. She has trained
Dody well and thoroughly, and today a soldier accompanies her on
the flight to learn how to manage the beast. From the looks of things,
Sepora is having a ravishing time in giving the unfortunate Majai an
awful fright with her scandalous Daring Dozens. He clings to her for
life itself, though using her as an anchor is foolish as the soldier weighs
thrice as much as she.

Sethos leans on the balcony beside Tarik, watching the debacle
unfold in the air. He makes his admiration for Sepora known a little
more every day, and it has started to wear on Tarik's nerves. "I'd
hoped by now you would have come to your senses and given her
back to me," Sethos says lightly, swirling the drink in his golden chalice as if more interested in its contents than the conversation at hand.
But Tarik knows him better than that. If Tarik gave the word, Sethos
would have Sepora out of the sky and in his arms faster than she
could gasp.

"You should get that notion out of your head, brother."

And ah, my senses, Tarik thinks. *Or perhaps it would be more accurate to say the lack thereof.* It has been two weeks since he tried to kiss Sepora, and still he cannot get the scent of her out of his head. Chamomile mingled with orchid and something else that addles his brain every time he thinks of it, every time she brushes past him or stands in the breeze by the window of his day chambers or leans across him to advise him in the throne room.

Which is more often than she really should. She is not, in actuality, Rashidi, after all. But every errand he finds for her to do in Rashidi's stead, he then finds another person who could do it in *her* stead, so that she might remain close to him, though not just because he enjoys her company but because he values her insight into the matters of the kingdom. Where he felt he could spare Rashidi, he retains Sepora to gain her insight on the matter. She has a way of looking at things from unique perspectives, no doubt from her time spent serving the king of Serubel.

Rashidi will not like it, Tarik knows. When he returns, he will be put out immensely. Sepora brings traditions and suggestions from a foreign land and adhering to them—in Rashidi's eyes—will seem as though Theoria's own tradition of ruling is outdated, or worse— ineffective. It may even appear to Rashidi that Tarik is questioning his own father's way of governing. But King Knosi did not have to contend with the Quiet Plague. In fact, his entire reign was called the Silent Reign, because so few troubles overtook the kingdom while his father ruled.

But with new problems come new solutions, and Tarik is not interested in clinging to custom if it means losing his people. Some traditions are to be respected—but so is common sense. And common sense tells him that to defeat his adversary in the plague, he'll have to do much more than consult his scholars and hold continual councils.

And so far, Sepora's input has been invaluable. The council of Lingots is just one example of her wisdom. Each day, they assemble and sort out the lies from the truth, the justice from the injustice. Each day, they deliver a verdict for all cases, and each day, Tarik has more time to spend on more important matters, such as harvesting the nefarite and keeping the Parani happy and monitoring the progress Cy makes with the Quiet Plague.

As Sepora still refuses to divulge where he can find more spectorium—or that is, the one who has the ability to Forge it—he made the decision to disassemble one of the newer pyramids and give the remains to Cy at the Lyceum. Rashidi will be livid, he knows, and he'd hoped Sepora would come around before his adviser's return, but he is due back any day and the kingdom has finally run out of scraps of spectorium. He'd had no choice but to disassemble the pyramid and consolidate the preserved bodies of the dead ones into another pyramid close by.

Though he has nothing to *fear* from Rashidi except a temper tantrum, there is one thing he is not looking forward to upon his old friend's return: the *disappointment* on his face when he tells him of the pyramid. When he learns that Sepora could have prevented it, he will refuse her as an attendant and probably call for her arrest.

And what will Tarik say to that?

He cannot openly admit that his interest in Sepora runs far below the surface of his outward exchanges with her. Rashidi will think him a walkover, even if he never says it aloud. A king who is ruled by a servant.

As he gazes down at Sepora as she lands the Serpen beast in the courtyard, he knows he must keep his emotions in stricter check. After all, if Sepora truly had the best interest of Theoria in mind, she wouldn't hesitate to reveal her secret source for spectorium. If she truly did not want to see his people suffer, she could end it easily, of that he's sure.

But she does not. And so, he must hold it against her in his mind, even if his heart will not agree.

Sepora waves up to them from the courtyard, and Sethos takes a swig from his cup. "She's really a fearless little thing, isn't she," he says.

"Of what does she have to fear?" *Sepora is treated well, lives within the palace walls, and is given time to herself regularly. She has access to the kingdom's best cooks, servants, and of late, its best Healer. If anything, she lives as though royalty,* he thinks dryly. *And who is to blame for that?*

Sethos grins at him. "From me? She has nothing to fear. From you? It appears she'll soon be burdened with boring, lengthy words of sentiment. You realize you could try and hide it. She doesn't have to ever know you're a sniveling lovesick whelp."

Tarik scowls. "Why don't you try and hide your arrogance? Or do you consider arrogance to be a worthy trait?"

"It's better than being a whelp, I think." Sethos takes another sip from his chalice as Sepora disappears under the awning beneath them. She'll arrive in his day chambers soon, and Tarik doesn't want this to be the conversation she walks into.

Tarik turns and strides to his desk. "Haven't you heard? I'm to marry the princess of Hemut. I've only just received the correspondence this morning. Rashidi sends word that negotiations are going well." In truth, he's surprised to have found the correspondence waiting for him in his day chambers as it takes at least ten days to reach

Hemut by caravan. Rashidi wasted no time in his negotiations, apparently. And neither did the king of Hemut.

Sethos takes the seat across from him, throwing his legs over one side of the chair. It is things like these that betray how young Sethos still is. "Ah, the rarest beauty among all the Five. And the most vain. An Ice Princess in the truest sense, I think. How sad that you must take such a cold and unwelcoming wife."

Tarik raises a brow. "You haven't seen her since we were children. Surely you're not still holding a grudge?" The Princess Tulle had been the first female who'd ever enchanted Sethos. He'd spent all afternoon once picking flowers from a garden, but when he presented the gift to the young princess, she'd been horrified, accusing him of stealing beauty from its natural state. Sethos had been inconsolable for days.

Sethos sniffs. "A grudge would suggest I think of her at all, which is certainly not the case."

"I see."

"At any rate, you should have kept Sepora in the harem," Sethos drawls. "A wife is for heirs. A concubine is for enjoyment."

"As amusing as they are, I must ask that you defer your revolting comments until another time. As it is, I've much work to do."

"Is that why you don't come visit me at the Lyceum? Thrice you've been to see Cy and not one of those times have you sought me out to break the midday meal. Why is that?"

"I come as a servant of the king, Sethos. Taking in an unannounced meal with a prince of Theoria is hardly appropriate."

Sethos appears unimpressed. "You could pretend to bring me messages from His Royal Highness. Really, Tarik, be creative."

Tarik leans back, inspecting his brother. "It's not me you want to see, though, is it?"

The corner of Sethos's mouth raises slightly. "Perhaps if you had white hair and silver eyes—"

"Ahem," Sepora says from the door. Her cheeks are windburned and her lips are stained with the red of adrenaline. "Perhaps I should come back?"

"Oh no," Sethos says, standing. "My brother would not like that."

Tarik gives him a withering look, but it falls on Sethos's indifferent expression. He pulls the chair out and gestures for Sepora to take his seat. "Please, mistress, do me the honor."

Sepora rolls her eyes at him, and he laughs. "There is nothing I can do to impress you, is there, mistress?"

"I'm afraid you've already made an irreversible impression on me, Prince Sethos."

His face pinches together. "Please, call me Majai Sethos. Or just Sethos. 'Prince' sounds so . . . domestic. As though I laze around all day and have grapes fed to me."

This time she laughs. Tarik quells the envy he feels at their easy banter. But to Sepora, Sethos's advances have a clear purpose. To the mistress, his brother's intentions are transparent and though despicable, she's able to deflect him well enough. But if Tarik teases her, he gets the sense that she's suspicious of his intentions, that he's only softening toward her in order to persuade her into revealing her secret to him.

He knows that Sepora is not so reprehensible that she'll withhold the information forever. If they in fact run out of spectorium—which will take dismantling all the pyramids in Theoria—and people do begin to die again, she will tell him what he needs to know. He's sure of it.

At least, he wants to be sure of it.

"Sethos was just leaving," Tarik announces happily.

Sethos cuts him a threatening look, and Tarik ever so slightly shakes his head. If Sethos outs him in front of Sepora, he will pay a high price. Technically, a prince of Theoria should not reside any place other than the palace. Tarik could change his circumstances faster than Sethos could finish his sentence to the mistress. And Sethos would be the victim of endless teasing from the other Majai who "rough it" at the Lyceum.

"It was a pleasure watching you with the Serpen," Sethos says, taking Sepora's hand to his lips. "As always."

"Enjoy the rest of your day, Majai Sethos," she says, nearly wrenching herself free from his grasp, which makes him grin all the more.

"The same to you and to you, *Highness*." He pauses at the door. "I think I shall dine at the palace tonight. Mistress Sepora, would you like to join my brother and me for the evening meal?"

She gasps. "I'm the attendant of the king, not a guest, Majai Sethos." This she says through gritted teeth.

"Well, you certainly couldn't come as *his* guest, but there are no rules worth mentioning that you could not be *my* guest. Besides, I've grown quiet of late. The kingdom has been expecting at least a small scandal from me for a fortnight. You would be doing me a favor in helping me keep my reputation tarnished."

To Tarik's dismay, Sepora laughs. Yet, she looks to him for the appropriate answer. This presents the perfect opportunity to do the right thing. To decline his brother's invitation on Sepora's behalf. He could cite extra work he's assigned her, or even the fact that she's been so ill lately and needs her rest. But it's *because* she's been so ill, and he hasn't actually *seen* her eat anything yet that he's inclined to agree to his brother's suggestion.

Tarik sighs. "I was going to let you rest this evening, but if you've the inclination to dine with us, you certainly may. I'll have a Serubelan menu prepared for our meal."

Both his brother and Sepora gape at him for long enough that he waves them off in dismissal. "Sepora, do you not have messages to fetch from the Lingot council? Sethos, do you not need to travel back to the Lyceum and scrounge up something formal enough for dinner at the palace?"

Sethos shuts his mouth, opens the door, and leaves.

Sepora takes steps to follow him, but Tarik stops her. He bids her to sit once more.

She settles in her chair and quietly sets to unfastening her braid, only to rebraid it again. Is she nervous? Is she taken aback by the fact that she is now forced to dine with his brother? Whatever her issue, she chooses a traditional Theorian hairstyle this time, and it appears she has been practicing. The braid falls around her head as a halo, and the small wisps of hair that loosen themselves from the structure make her look young and completely breathtaking.

Tarik clears his throat. A breathtaking adviser. How fortunate he is.

"How was your time with Dody?" he asks, hoping to catch a trace of the banter she enjoyed with his brother.

"It was wonderful," she says, her eyes lighting up. "He's very attentive and a fast learner. Although I cannot say the same for the Majai you sent along with us." She frowns. "I don't think he's the right fit for Dody."

Tarik laughs. "You'll not think anyone besides you is a right fit."

"It's just that you Theorians don't respect a Seer for what it is. You have your precious cats." She gestures toward Patra, who lies uninterested beside the desk. "But you see no value in a Serpen." She purses her lips then, and Tarik is astounded by how much he can be affected by her pouting.

"I've given you the task of picking the perfect rider for Dody," he says. "If you're not up to it, perhaps I'll—"

"Oh, I'm up to it. I just . . . well, why couldn't I be the one to ride him?"

"On a mission? Absolutely not." He doesn't mean for it to come out as harshly as it does. But there is no way he's risking Sepora's life to spy for his kingdom. What if they were to get shot down from the sky? Pride of the pyramids, the thought makes his heart race.

"Why not? I'm the best rider by far."

"It's too dangerous."

"More dangerous than jumping from the Half Bridge?"

He hates when she brings that up. She has been the one to keep up communication with the Parani, she and Master Saen, and while he doesn't like the idea of her entering the River Nefari and its potential dangers—she still carries the venomous scars all over her body from her first encounter with them—he can't risk losing his new-found partnership with the Parani, either. And Sepora happens to be the only person to whom they will speak. "That's different and you know it."

She sighs. "I suppose I'll have that Majai—what was his name, Sodi?—back in for another session next week. If I have to choose from among rocks, I suppose a polished one will have to do."

Tarik laughs. "You are spoiled beyond belief."

She appears put out. "May I be excused? I must call Anku and Cara back to prepare me for the suddenly lavish evening I'll apparently be enjoying."

"Of course, mistress." He cannot help himself from watching her saunter to the door.

And he wonders just what a Serubelan menu will entail.

37

SEPORA

I STEP CLOSER TO THE MIRROR, UNABLE TO RECOG-nize myself in the reflection staring back at me. Anku and Cara have really outdone themselves, having been caught up in the idea of a Serubelan dinner—only they've done it in the ornate style of Theoria. Were I actually in Serubel attending a royal dinner, my gown would completely cover me, mostly likely be made of red and gold velvet to symbolize the colors of our kingdom, and my hair would be braided modestly. I wonder if Cara even knows the tradi-tional dress of Serubel, and I highly doubt it. As it stands, my hair swirls atop my head, constructed and laboriously shaped to appear as one of the mountains of my homeland. Small, beautiful flowers and vines are scattered over it, a touch Cara added, to represent the flora of our homeland. But by far the most amazing component of this creation is the miniature silver Serpen with sapphire-encrusted eyes encircling my mountain of hair, its wings made of fine silver tulle that spring to motion at the turn of my head, giving the effect of the Serpen fluttering its wings.

Silver paint lines my eyes and spreads out over my cheeks in an elaborate design of tiny vines entwined elegantly down the length of my neck. To finish the effect, my lips are also painted silver, and Anku assures me the paint will last throughout dinner by adding a horrible-smelling glossy balm to it with the tip of her finger.

My reflection shakes her head at me. I look like a silver figurine, a doll, ready to brighten some wealthy child's mantel or lie upon the child's silken bedding as she plays with other toys not so delicate as me.

"Don't you feel that it is a bit . . . elaborate for a simple dinner with the Prince Sethos and the Falcon King?"

Anku seems taken aback. "I was given to believe you were a guest at the royal table." Her hand covers her mouth in horror. "You're not just attending to them, are you?"

I feel the heat in my cheeks almost instantly. "I am Prince Sethos's guest." There is shame and pride in the words. Shame because I know Sethos's intentions are less than honorable toward me, but pride because I am a petty thing who has never been a guest at a royal dinner before and would love to know what it is like in a foreign land. At home, it is quite boring.

Anku nods once, tightly. "Well then, you must dress as any other guest at the royal table shall dress. It is an honor most attendants never enjoy, mind you. You've certainly seemed to impress the right pair of brothers in Theoria."

Another blush. I will never survive dinner in this state of mind.

SEVERAL TIMES I CATCH THE FALCON KING gazing at me, but apparently speaking to me is not on his agenda this night. It is true, then, that I am only the guest of Sethos, for his brother has barely spoken at all to anyone, while Sethos engages me endlessly. Tarik merely pushes the simple beef and cabbage—a staple Serubelan dish—around his plate in what appears to be disgust, while Sethos asks me how my communications with the Parani fare. "Well," I say, not a little surprised the younger brother is capable of serious conversation.

"It was a brave thing you did," he says, scooping up a bit more of the overcooked vegetable into his mouth. "You've no idea of the significance of this treaty with the Parani. Even if we were not on the verge of war, I'm sure there are many more uses for nefarite that remain undiscovered as of yet. Our engineers will be delighted to have their day with it, when it comes."

"I hope that is the case." I know my answer is sweeping, but I'm not sure what else to say. I had not expected Sethos to offer any sort of substance in the way of conversation this evening; I'd merely expected to deflect his advances. It's obvious he's genuinely interested in what I have to say.

"How are your scars healing? Oh, don't worry, they're not as noticeable as you think. It's just that the subject of the Parani reminded me what a great risk you took in securing that treaty for us and the personal injury you endured. I don't believe I've ever formally thanked you for that," Sethos says, and I'm sure my eyebrows are somewhere near the top of my forehead by now.

Even Tarik is surprised, if not a little grumpy. "You are very talkative this evening, brother. To what do we owe this honor?"

"Why, Highness, we've a special guest among us. The last time anyone harvested nefarite from the river, our father threw him a great banquet and declared him our bravest warrior. And what have we done to honor the Mistress Sepora?" He shrugs. "And before I left the Lyceum for dinner tonight, I happened to have brushed up on my etiquette." Sethos turns to me. "Dinner at the Lyceum consists of lining up at the table while they slop something resembling food onto your tray and you have less than five breaths to eat it or you go hungry."

"I'm sure you can hold your own," Tarik drawls.

Sethos grins. "Of course I can. You see, Sepora, a soldier may not have a proper meal for days, especially while traveling, so it's important not to get used to fine dining and the like. That's why I never eat at the palace."

"You seem quite at your ease to dine finely tonight, brother," Tarik says.

"Well, I did say that I brushed up on the delicate matters of a royal dinner, did I not? You may be surprised to know, Highness, that conversation is an important part of the meal." Sethos winks at me then, and I hide my giggle into my linen napkin.

Tarik rolls his eyes and takes a sip from his chalice. "It's just that when I try to engage you into speaking with me of our economy and the impending war, you seem horribly bored with it all."

"Perhaps it is you I'm bored with. How can I be bored with such a lovely dinner companion as the Mistress Sepora?"

Ah, there is the Sethos I know. But somehow, it is difficult to despise him at this moment. "Why did you choose the life of a Majai, Sethos?" I ask, surprising not only myself but everyone at the table.

Sethos is glad for the question. "You could say the life of a Majai chose me. Growing up, it was very obvious that life in the palace did not suit me. I was always endeavoring to escape to the Bazaar and always picking fights with the other children there when I did. One day, a Master Majai became privy to a fight where I had taken on several boys much bigger than I. He escorted me to the palace to speak with my father, to persuade him to send me to the Lyceum for training. It did not take Father long to realize that I needed an outlet for my . . . energy. So, he agreed I would become Majai."

"Your father was a great warrior. Did you inherit his skill?"

Sethos nods. "I would like to hope so. My father could have been Majai, you know. If being the king did not take up so much of his time."

"He trained his own personal guard," Tarik says, a tinge of pride coming through his voice. "He was the only king to ever do such a thing." He turns to me, a gleam in his eye. "Up until that point, only Master Majai were in charge of training the king's personal guard."

Sethos laughs. "I heard the only time the guard would not protect him was from Mother herself."

Tarik grins. "That is true."

"It's as it should be," I say. It's the first time either of them have mentioned their mother, who passed away years ago when the brothers were very young. According to Anku, she contracted a fever, went to sleep, and never woke up. I wonder how it affected the two. As of now, they seem to have grown to accept it. I would wonder if they remember much of her, but there is a certain fondness in their voice when they speak now.

"Indeed." Sethos chuckles, raising his chalice in salute. "Indeed."

The last course is brought to us then and while Sethos devours a rather large piece of maple cake, Tarik turns away dessert altogether. I find myself disappointed in the realization that he must not have a taste for Serubelan food. I'm not sure why I wanted him to enjoy it, perhaps because it's a part of who I am—and he seems to enjoy me well enough.

But I must stop thinking along those lines. It has been weeks since the king tried to kiss me that night on the pyramid, and every day since then I have wanted him to try again. Yet, I've squandered all the chances I've had to give him some sort of sign that he should make another attempt. That he should take it further than telling me how lovely I look or how clever I am at court or the simple act of brushing my hair to one side when it fell into my face. But each time, he stops. Just short of where I want him to stop.

Perhaps by now his interest in me has waned altogether. Perhaps that is why he's so quiet this evening. He didn't seem particularly pleased when Sethos invited me as a guest. And could I blame him? I've been as cool as a winter morning in Serubel toward him.

Oh what a fool I am to be thinking of this instead of paying attention at the royal dinner table. That I should be pining away for a king who has lost interest in me, and ignoring a prince who is very interested in me.

"You've hardly eaten a thing, brother. Are you falling ill?" Sethos says around a mouthful of maple cake—one of my favorite dishes from Serubel. "You know, I rather enjoy this Serubelan fare. We should have it more often."

"Do you intend to dine at the palace more than once every two fortnights, then?" Tarik says dryly.

"If Sepora will join us, and we can experiment with more of these Serubelan delicacies, then why not?"

Tarik sits straighter in his chair and folds his hands in his lap, ignoring his brother's enthusiasm. He gives me a somber look. "I hope it wasn't a mindless thing to order a Serubelan dinner this evening. It was meant to honor you, not to make you homesick. You've barely touched your food. And you're not drinking enough water."

So. The Falcon King is still paying close attention to me. "My stomach is not quite fully recovered yet, Highness, but it's very kind of you to think of me for the menu this evening. I'm honored."

But the last of my sentence goes unheard, as a tray of food is tossed upon the table, and the face of a servant lands in my lap. Blood seeps from his nose, and it trickles from his ears. His mouth is open, and his eyes stare at me but do not see me. Quickly I cradle his head in my hands before it can slip away to the floor, where the rest of his body wants to slink at an odd angle.

Instantly Tarik and Sethos are on their feet and at either side of me. Tarik takes the adolescent boy from me and eases him gently to the chair next to me, setting his head to rest on the back of it. The boy's eyes roll back inside his head.

He has the Quiet Plague.

"Guards!" Tarik says. "Take him to his quarters and fetch the Healer Cy immediately." To me, he says, "Sepora, you must move away from him."

But I cannot. I cannot move at all. For this boy has the Quiet Plague and is dying in front of my eyes. My thoughts punish me as I ponder what would happen if Cy did not have the spectorium he needed to help him. If he were completely out, as I know one day Theoria will be, this boy would not live. He looks only to be a bit younger than Tarik.

And what if Tarik himself were to contract the illness? And why should I care so much about this king? I should stop this nonsense and quickly, before it upsets my reasoning abilities altogether.

I contemplate this as the guards usher the servant boy away, and still more when I feel the king's eyes on me. I cannot think that one day it will be him. Because perhaps it will be, and I will still have to keep my secret a secret.

My Forging has never been so much of a burden as it is now.

Tarik's lips press together in a line. "I apologize, Mistress Sepora. I did not know he was even ill. You're looking pale. Perhaps we should cut the evening short so you can get some proper rest." And he adds, though not unkindly, "And so you can think of the matter at hand more thoroughly."

He wants me to reflect upon the boy and what could happen if Theoria were out of spectorium. Did he plant the boy here to further his own purposes?

Could Tarik be so cruel? Up until now, I thought not. But the boy was serving me, was he not? Could that be so coincidental?

My temper begins to get the better of me then, filling my cheeks with a different kind of heat than Tarik usually incites.

"Nonsense," Sethos says, slapping the table. "What she needs is physical exertion to get her mind off of what happened. Why would you want her to dwell on such unlucky events, brother?" Sethos pats my hand in an almost childlike way. "You'll see, Mistress Sepora. Physical exertion works for me every time."

I try to discern if I should be insulted by just what type of physical exertion he has in mind, but Tarik shakes his head at me. He does not believe his brother to have stepped out of line. Relieved, I turn to Sethos. The threat of the Quiet Plague amid our dinner does not seem to bother Sethos. Of course, he does reside in the Lyceum. He's probably well acquainted with it, sharing the same space as the Healers do. I clear my throat and try to focus on the conversation at hand. "Physical exertion? How do you mean?"

"I shall teach you to fight with a sword," he says with finality.

With his fingertips, Tarik massages his temples. "That, of course, is out of the question."

"Why?"

Only, the question did not come from Sethos—it came from me.

He turns to me, incredulous. "You *want* to spend time with . . . er, that is, learn to fight?"

I cross my arms at him. This boy king would control my every step if he had the chance. And so, he will not. "And why shouldn't I learn to at least protect myself the Theorian way, if I'm to reside in their midst?" I wonder if the king even realizes that I can fend for myself with a sword as it is—as long as I'm fighting in Serubelan form.

"You live within the palace walls, Sepora. You are well protected."

Sethos shakes his head. "That's unreasonable, to assume a mistress as beautiful as Sepora would not need to learn defensive tactics, at least enough to help her make an escape to safety."

"Any man who tried to attack Sepora would be thrown from the Half Bridge," Tarik says through gritted teeth.

"But that would be after the fact, now wouldn't it, brother? The damage could still have been done."

"Of course you may train me to fight," I tell Sethos hurriedly, before Tarik can reject the matter again. "The sooner the better."

His expression lights up in delight. "How about now? Are you finished with your dinner? You'll excuse us, won't you, Tarik?"

Before the king can put a halt to it, Sethos is already dragging me from the dining room and imparting the best possible way to angle a kick to a man's groin.

38

TARIK

SEPORA ARRIVES FOR DUTY ALMOST AN HOUR late. She wears the same attire she wore the evening before for her Serubelan feast. Only now she looks quite a bit more disheveled. And irritatingly happy. Her hair has been let loose from its exquisite styling and now cascades around her shoulders in waves of white. Her dress is spotted with dirt in places and torn a bit at the hem. The silver Serpen she wore in her hair was carefully bent to wrap around her arm. Tarik cannot stand the thought of who helped her accomplish that feat.

Withholding his scowl, he instead pours Cy a goblet of water and offers him some fruit, astonishing the two attendants standing beside the refreshment table, who probably had been waiting for Tarik to issue those very instructions. "You may go," he clips at them. After all, it is better for a king to employ his hands for the good of his guest than to throw the entire tray of food at the wall—which is exactly what he feels like doing. But such a display simply won't do, since Cy is here to instruct him on how his ill servant fared through the evening, and besides that, Tarik had personally invited him to join him this morning.

Blast it all, but he wants to shake Sepora and demand to know whether she spent the entire evening in the company of Sethos.

But he already knows that she, of course, did. Because even if he hadn't been kept informed of her whereabouts, he still couldn't ignore the correspondence waiting for him on his table when he arrived at his day chambers this morning. Sethos had sent him quite the persuasive and humble request asking to visit Sepora more often and spend time training with her—for her own sake, of course. "We've taken quite a liking to each other, brother, and you cannot deny her beauty warrants undue attention. She must be able to defend herself when the situation calls for it," he'd written.

We've taken quite a liking to each other. Since when did Sepora develop a liking for Sethos? Surely not in the span of mere hours.

"I'll prepare that," Sepora says quickly, rushing toward the table of refreshments against the back wall of the day chamber. She snatches the goblet from Tarik, brushing her fingers along his accidently, and glances back at Cy, smiling. "I've found that the figs are quite delicious. Would you like one, Master Cy?" she says.

Figs. Delicious. Surely she jests. But in the merry mood she is in, she'd find a pile of Patra's—

"It must be the time of year," she says more to herself than to anyone in the room. "It's cooling off now, especially during the evening. Why, last night it was . . ."

She stiffens at his side, pausing before she looks up at him. He feels his jaw clench when their eyes meet. "Last night must have been quite exhilarating indeed," he says, sweeping his gaze over her unchanged clothing. "Perhaps you would like some time to freshen up?"

She smiles sweetly, a lie he recognizes right away as counterfeit. "Highness, I'm surprised to see you up so early as well. You looked so tired and put out when we left." She is mocking him. And to what does he owe this new delightful tendency?

Cy clears his throat from across the room, and Sepora uses it as her prompt to bring him his food and drink. If Cy weren't here, perhaps he and Sepora could have a direct conversation. He'd been hoping to speak with her anyway, and so he'd cleared his schedule this morning. Tarik feels the need to warn Sepora that when Rashidi arrives, she must not inform him she knows how to procure more spectorium. Tarik does not need another crisis within the palace walls at the moment.

Tarik follows her back to his desk, where he takes his seat. Folding his hands in front of him, he tries to focus solely on the young Healer instead of the girl with the silver eyes, his eternal conundrum, who stands just beside them, looking on with expectation.

"Cy, do continue," Tarik says. "You were saying something about repeat cases?"

Cy nods, biting into the fig. "Yes. Your boy last night was a repeat case; I'd treated him at the Lyceum a while ago. It seems that the spectorium improves the patient's health for only a little while. Once the life of the spectorium dies out, the life of the patient follows suit. More spectorium must be administered, which, of course, we are glad to do. But I'm afraid I must have a continual supply of it."

Tarik does not need to look at Sepora to know she has stiffened where she stands. He feels everything about her, including the tension emanating from her now. Cy licks his lips and takes another bite of fig. "I'm sorry, Highness. I thought spectorium would be the answer. But it is temporary at best because of our supply of it."

Temporary. Unless they have a continual supply of it. He looks at Sepora. She's already staring at him, her chin jutting out. She is not convinced. "There are many more pyramids that can be broken down and distributed," she says.

"Yes," Tarik agrees. "There are. And where do you propose we put the bodies of our dead loved ones, mistress? Bury them in the hot desert sand so they can rot for eternity?"

"It's not ideal, but there is enough spectorium in the kingdom for Cy to continue administering while we look for another solution—"

"Not ideal? What is not ideal is that we will lose our dead ones *and* our living ones all in the same breath if this is not stopped," Tarik says. "That, love, is the opposite of ideal."

Sepora's mouth snaps shut. He's never called her "love" before, and he never intended to use it sarcastically. But pride of the pyramids, where has she been all night? Only part of the evening with Sethos was spent in training. Where did he whisk her away to when they'd finished? Sethos must have assumed Tarik would keep watch over them, and if anyone knows how to dodge unwanted spies, it would be his younger brother, always up to no good.

Tarik wants to ask, wants to know if she was with him all night, and yet he doesn't want to ask. Because he will discern the truth no matter what her answer. And he may not like the truth.

No, he'll hate it.

Sepora blinks several times, and Tarik gets the sense that she's on the verge of tears. Regret churns his stomach. He is taking out his jealousy on her, and he knows it. He is acting a fool. "Please allow me to apologize, mistress," he says softly. "I meant only—"

"No."

Through his teeth, Cy sucks in a breath as he looks up at Sepora.

"No?" Tarik repeats back to her. The word feels so foreign in his mouth. How easy a transition it has been to become accustomed to always having one's way. The word "no" has not been something he's told often.

"No," Sepora says again. "I will not allow you to apologize."

Cy stands quickly, dropping the fig on the tray in front of him. "I've forgotten I've something terribly pressing I must attend to at the Lyceum, Highness. Do you mind if I could be excused?" *Ah, Cy, but the damage has already been done, whether or not you are excused.*

Tarik's gaze never leaves Sepora. "Yes, of course, Cy. I'll not keep you from your work."

Still, Cy is wise beyond his years to want to escape what happens next. Sepora has defied him in front of one of his subjects. It's a grave matter, and one that he cannot ignore. One that he doesn't want to ignore. Sepora has pushed him far enough.

As soon as Cy closes the door behind him, Tarik is at his feet and striding toward her. To her good credit, she takes a step back. But only one. He closes the distance between them until their noses almost touch. She doesn't look away.

"Where were you last night?" he blurts. It's not what he intended to say. He meant to demand an explanation for her defiance or something important such as that. Blast it all, he can't remember why exactly he crossed the room, only that he needed to cross it.

"Where were *you* last night?" she counters, her breath pushing against his lips. The faint smell of orchids nearly consumes him.

"What right have you to ask me that?" he says, finding his senses.

"The same right you have to ask me."

"You're an attendant. I am the king. Perhaps you don't understand proper etiquette. Perhaps I've allowed you too much leniency—"

"Do not dare speak to me of etiquette and leniency!" She pokes a finger on his bare chest, smudging the gold paint there. "You refused Sethos's request to train me. Why?"

His mouth falls open. She knows about his brother's request—and the fact that he refused it within minutes? And worse, she *consents* to spend more time with Sethos? The girl who would not be a possession in the king's own harem, the one who decried the very same prince of Theoria for the indecency of being put in such a position? What has his brother done to change her mind so swiftly about him? *What has he done in the space of hours that I could not do in the space of weeks?* Fury laps against his insides. He takes a step away from her to contain his temper. "What is so special about Sethos that you would spend every free moment with him?"

"Since when do you care how my free moments are spent?"

Tarik's stomach clenches with her words. But she continues, "Surely you can see the wisdom of training. Besides, your brother is not so bad as I'd once thought."

The more time she spends with Sethos, the more likely she is to be swayed by his charm, by his skill in seducing women. *Over my embalmed body.*

"The answer is no."

"Why?"

"Let it be, Sepora."

"I deserve an answer. Why will you not allow me to pursue happiness?"

"*Happiness?* What have I withheld from you?" he says, incredulous. "I've risked my reputation to give you what you wanted. Everything you have asked for I have granted. You should have been flogged more times than I can count on one hand!"

"You've withheld one punishment and given me another, then!"

"You are being irrational. Surely you recognize Sethos's true intentions. Apparently you've no idea of his nature."

She crosses her arms. "You're the Lingot. Did you discern anything amiss with him? In the message that he sent you? Was there anything misrepresented?"

He could lie. He wants to, badly. Sepora is not a Lingot, and he could easily tell her that he sensed something was off with the request. But he won't. Sethos believes Sepora needs training—and that they are "quite taken" with each other. He sighs. "No. It was written with candor."

"So then it is settled."

"When Rashidi returns, he will need you. You've not even begun to realize the full scope of your duties." Yes, that's true enough. Though Rashidi would rather let her spend all her time with Sethos than rely upon her for anything.

"Rashidi hates me."

"He's overly excitable sometimes."

"Very well. I shall ask Rashidi for *his* permission."

Blast. Rashidi will give consent quicker than he would send her back to the harem. "It is not Rashidi's decision." At least, it's not anymore. He pulls his headdress off and runs a hand through his hair. "You . . . you care for Sethos, then? In the space of a few hours, he has changed your mind about him?"

She takes a step back. Realization strikes him as an arrow. He's chosen the right line of questioning to get himself out of the corner and her into it. "You *do* care for him?" he persists.

"Yes," she says, lifting her chin.

"A lie." He steps toward her. She tries to back away again but he grabs her arm, holding her in place. "Tell me you care for him as he cares for you. Convince me of it, Sepora."

"He is a good man."

"He's but fifteen years old. Hardly a man. Why? Why him?" He pulls her closer. Her breath is rushed and shallow. This debate is taking much out of them both. This debate pushes them both toward an edge they cannot afford to traverse.

"Tell me you love the princess of Hemut," she says, desperation in her voice. "Tell me you *want* to marry her." The princess of Hemut? What does *that* have to do with *this*?

"I will not say that. I cannot say that." It will never come from his lips. It will never be the truth.

"Yet you will marry her." She does not like this. So much so that her lips quiver on the words. Is that what this is about? Has it come down to this? She wishes to expose his raw jealousy in order to hide her own? Hope wrestles through him, untwining the tightness in his chest.

Sepora, jealous of another woman. Utterly ridiculous. He must end this madness. He must bring them both relief. "It is not Princess Tulle that I want, Sepora."

Through the leftover silver paint, her lips are red, run through with the heat of their conversation, the passion of their argument. He grabs her other arm and pulls him to her. She pushes against him, but he'll not allow her to budge from his grasp. "Let me go," she says, even as she stills.

"Never." His mouth covers hers. She writhes against him at first, but it lasts for all of a breath of a moment before she melts upon his chest. Kissing Sepora is nothing like he thought it would be.

It is so much more. Her lips are soft, so soft, and before he realizes it, his hand is tucked behind the nape of her neck, pulling her closer until her hair spills around them both. She smells of chamomile and fragrant orchids and something else that nearly renders him senseless.

They'd argued before, but the time for that is over. Now they converse in a language without words, in a language that is unmistakable, an interchange of hunger and need and pent-up passion, and for all that is sacred, she kisses him with truth.

This is how Sepora feels about him. Him, not Sethos.

39

SEPORA

I DO NOT HAVE TO BE A LINGOT TO KNOW THAT Tarik is asking me a question with this kiss. That behind all the possession and the jealousy and the desire there is something gentle in the way his mouth moves on mine, probing and inquisitive and strong and powerful. I will make him ask it, though, out loud. I want to know that he'll never let me go, not because I know where to find spectorium, but because he's in love with me, the way I am with him.

But for now I do not press the issue. Not when I've only just disintegrated in his arms, not when I've only just got a true taste of him, not when his scent intoxicates me beyond my wits. His hands work through my hair, using it as something to grasp me tighter, to pull me closer, and I moan against his lips. I'm on the tips of my toes, needing all of him pressed against me, needing him in every sense of the word. Beneath my hands his biceps flex; beneath his, my skin burns hot.

To my dismay, he is the first to break away, and he does so

breathlessly. His eyes are open and so then mine must be. He untangles himself from my grasp and takes three steps back, looking as bewildered as I feel. He shakes his head. "You are not very good at persuading me to let you go."

"Tell me why I should stay," I say, my arms aching with the emptiness he leaves behind. "Tell me why I should not spend more time with Sethos."

He comes back to me then, grasping one of my hands, and with the other he runs his thumb along my bottom lip. "You will never kiss Sethos the way you kissed me."

I cannot tell if it is an order or a statement, or perhaps a smidgen of both. I press my forehead into his, sighing. "You'll not tell me, then."

"On the contrary. I'll tell you anything you want, if you'll keep looking at me like that."

"I'll not ask again."

He leans his head back and laughs. "This is your way of asking? Hmmm," he says. "I'll have to tread carefully here; I can tell." He pulls me toward the balcony and leans an arm on the railing, observing me with not a little amusement. I can't help but notice his lips are still swollen from our kiss, and I wonder in what state of dishevelment I'm in myself. "You think I want you because you know how to acquire more spectorium."

I blink. "Yes. That is, I want to know if that's the reason."

"This is possibly the only time I have ever wished you to be a Lingot. Then you would know that is not true in the least."

"I am not a Lingot. I'm afraid I require a full explanation."

He smirks, pressing a kiss to my hand. "You must consider that if I wanted, I could have pressed you to tell me. There are ways of making a person talk, as much as I hate to admit knowing of them."

"You are not a cruel king. I have never been afraid of that." I try to ignore the fire his lips left on the back of my hand, the way his thumb traces circles on it as his touch lingers. I find that I do not want him to stop, that I don't want to lose this proximity to him, both physical and emotional. I feel he's an open scroll right now, rife for the reading. He'll tell me anything, if I ask it of him.

And I would likely do the same. It is dangerous and exhilarating at the same time.

"How shall I explain this?" He gestures toward the sky. "Having you on this balcony with me makes the sun shine brighter. Your laugh is a cool breeze on a scorching day. The throne room, full of its problems and complaints and inquiries and stifling etiquette—your presence seems to hush all of that. You have taken a bleak existence, a life of duty, and made me eager to wake up to it each and every morning. Your kiss, mistress, is like taking possession of something that has always been mine. Tell me, Sepora, what of that has to do with spectorium?"

I watch his lips as he says this, wishing I were a Lingot, both longing for a deception and at the same time, relieved that there is none. This will complicate things for me. It already has.

He is not my father. He is not cruel, and he does not seek war. He cares for me. He's just said as much, even if not with the exact words I long to hear; there was no mistaking in the way he kissed me. I've not had much experience in the ways of men and women, but I should hope I could recognize a false kiss when one crossed my lips, and that there was nothing deceptive about it. "So then, where does this leave us—"

But the question falls short as the door opens and the voice of

Tarik's trusted commander, Morg, calls for his king from inside the chamber. He finds us on the balcony, and by that time we've put an acceptable distance between us. "Great Pharaoh, please forgive the intrusion, but there is something you must see. Please, if you will, come with me to the far courtyard."

40

TARIK

THE CIRCLE OF SOLDIERS STANDS IN FULL MILItary attire in the courtyard, wearing the standard light blue shendyts, leather weapons strapped tight across their chests, shields hoisted upon their backs. The mid-morning sun casts a half-moon shadow that Tarik and Sepora must cross to penetrate the rows of waiting guards. Sepora trails slightly behind him as they follow Morg to the center where two warriors, breathless no doubt from practicing, bow deeply to their king.

"Highness," Morg begins, "today we begin training with the weapons shaped from the nefarite."

Tarik nods. He'd known that. From the look Sepora gives him now, he'd failed to mention that to her. Had he done it unconsciously? Or had he wished to spare himself the unease of telling her that they are in the act of producing weapons for the purpose of war with Serubel? "Yes. How goes the progress?"

Morg hesitates. "Highness, not very well. If I may, I've arranged a demonstration. If you and the Mistress Sepora will stand back for safety's sake and allow our soldiers some room?"

They do as they're asked, Tarik feeling the need to tuck Sepora behind him and feeling doubly frustrated when she defies him by peeking around his shoulder for a good view. Still, he understands her curiosity; she has been involved with the development of the nefarite from the beginning, from the time she brought the first rock of it to him after she hurled herself from the Half Bridge. She is invested in this venture, and what's more, she genuinely cares about the safety of the Theorians against Serubel's newest weapon.

There will certainly be a high price to pay for failing to mention that they'd already begun developing their own.

Morg nods to Tarik. "Majesty, we find that the nefarite is not strong but fragile." He then nods to the two soldiers, Majai by their dark blue shendyts and matching face paint, in the middle of the circle of the rest of the men and women warriors. One of the soldiers holds his shield up, and the other charges toward him, grunting with the power and speed he's gaining in the sand. This one brings his sword down upon the other's thick round shield with a horrendous clash. Tarik gasps, as does Sepora, when the sword forged with nefarite shatters, spraying fragments into the surrounding dirt. It is then that he notices that there are many, many bits of nefarite scattered throughout the courtyard. This demonstration is the last of numerous failed attempts at practice with the new weapons.

Tarik narrows his eyes, turning on Sepora. "This nefarite is more feeble than a sword made of wood."

She winces, obviously having already drawn the same conclusion herself. "You think the Parani negotiated a sour deal."

"It appears so." It is something he doesn't want to think about at the moment, and especially in front of such a large crowd. But if the Parani have truly bartered with false intentions, then there must be retribution. Their leaders knew what he had intended to use the nefarite for; what good is an element that shatters upon contact in a war? What's more, he changed traditions of Theoria for this, uprooted nearly the entire Middling class for this, risked Sepora every time she went to mediate on his behalf. He had hoped this would work. His hope had obviously not been fulfilled.

Sepora steps out from behind him. "But Master Saen spoke with him. She would have detected any deception."

"There are ways around such detection, as you may well know, Mistress Sepora. And you must think, this language is vastly understudied. Mistakes could have been made."

She flushes, tilting her head up at him. Ah, but those silver eyes catching in the sun have him nearly speechless. As does the way she bites her lower lip, especially since he is now acquainted with how that lip tastes. "She was very direct with him at all times, Highness. Something here is amiss." She turns to Morg. "The shield there. Is it not constructed from nefarite as well?"

Morg nods. "It is, mistress. Which is truly the mystery of the situation."

"And were they built in the same way, with the same process?"

"Exactly the same."

She strides to the soldier with the shield, and though it's too heavy for her to handle, the warrior allows her to inspect it closely. Running her fingers along it, she mumbles something to herself that Tarik cannot quite make out. She picks up fragments of nefarite from the dirt, allowing the sand to sift through her fingers in order to better look at the remnants of the swords—of the scores of swords. Finally, she looks up at Morg again. "Have any of the shields failed?"

He shakes his head. "No, mistress. Not one."

Her eyes lock with Tarik's. "I've an idea of what is happening here." She stands and walks back to him. "The Parani told Saen and me that nefarite is the Great Judge. We didn't understand his meaning at the time. We thought perhaps the Parani worshipped the nefarite as a living element, as the citizens of Wachuk worship fire. Now I'm quite sure that is not the case."

"Tell me your thoughts, Mistress Sepora. I don't think I'm following." The idea of nefarite, a basic element, holding the ability to judge a man is not something he'll readily accept—though, of course, he's not sure that's what Sepora is trying to relay. And he's quite sure Sepora didn't mention this detail before, nor did Saen; sometimes he can discern the truth from third parties and he's quite certain he would have picked apart this detail for what it appears to be: superstition.

"I cannot be sure, Highness, but it appears nefarite *is* a judge after all, in some way," she says. "The shield is used for protection, the sword for attacking. The shield withstands a blow, while the sword shatters. It distinguishes between good and evil. The shield is used for good, the sword for evil."

"Spectorium is the only living element, Sepora. It has been an accepted fact for ages upon ages."

Her bottom lip juts out, and Tarik is sure he's going to have to haul her back to his day chambers if he doesn't want to stir a scene here. "It has been ages since anyone has actually possessed nefarite, is that not true?"

Well. He supposes the sword he inherited from his father doesn't count for much in this discussion, since it was never made into anything of purpose. Still, his father did cleave a block in two with it. It was not fragile at that time. "That is true, mistress."

"And so, we cannot really be sure of its properties just yet, wouldn't you agree, Highness?"

He smiles. She really would make an excellent adviser. *What would Rashidi do if I appointed her as such?* "We cannot assume anything at this point, however. You will go back to the Parani, Sed. The Master Saen will accompany you. Tell Sed what has happened here and see what he says." He would accompany her himself were it not considered a task beneath him. It reminds him that he must take a day off soon and whisk Sepora back into the city with him.

She bows her head slightly. The act is insincere at best, and he nearly smirks at her, catching himself at the last moment. As it is, he raises a brow. "Of course, Highness," she says demurely. "Right away."

41

SEPORA

I MAKE MY WAY TO TARIK'S DAY CHAMBERS, HOP-
ing to catch him in a private moment. That is always the hope of
late, to hold the exclusive company of the king, even if for only a
few stolen moments at a time. It is the only chance I have to make
his lips my own, to see whether he will conquer me or I him in our
brief exchanges.

Disappointed, I find Tarik is not alone; Cy the Healer and Morg
the military commander sit at the great marble table teeming with
parchments and scrolls. Upon seeing me, Patra meanders over from
the sliver of sunlight streaming in from the balcony and pushes her
head into my palm. Tarik tosses me an amused look before he greets
me formally. Cy and Morg stand at my presence. When they do so,
Patra abandons me again in favor of her cozy spot by the terrace.
Tarik has offered several times to acquire a cat for me, but I find that
I'm quite taken with Dody and his care. A cat would just be a burden,
I think.

"Ah, Mistress Sepora has returned from the River Nefari," Tarik says. "What news do you bring? I was just informing Cy of our Great Judge."

I wince internally, noting to myself that I'll need to give the king a proper scolding later, especially after speaking with Sed again today. Well, after *Saen* had spoken with him, at any rate. Tarik simply must show his new allies more respect, though it was in question for a while whether the Parani had truly sided with us. Still, mocking what they consider a Great Judge simply will not do. "As it turns out, Highness, it is as I assumed. The nefarite will fail if used for purposes other than good."

"Fascinating," Cy says, eyes wide.

"So all the nefarite we used to forge the swords with is now worthless?" Morg says.

Tarik attempts to answer, but I accidentally interrupt him, earning a look of disapproval from Morg. Cy seems unaffected by my disgraceful behavior; I'm afraid he's most likely used to it by now. I sit in on almost daily meetings with him and Tarik regarding the plague—at Tarik's insistence, of course, in case I care to cave on the matter—and Cy has grown quite accustomed to our exchange in banter. I don't think much is lost on Cy, indeed. "I asked Sed if all was lost, and he said the element should be salvageable from the swords. You can melt them down and use them for other purposes, and the nefarite will regain its strength."

"Interesting," Tarik says, leaning across his desk. "We've no need of more shields. I suppose we can trade the old swords to Wachuk for more silver for new swords." Trading useless swords would be a sour deal negotiated by Theoria. Or perhaps I underestimate Tarik. Perhaps he reasons that if used for hunting game to feed their people, the swords would not be so fragile for the citizens of Wachuk. Surely the Great Judge would deem the swords worthy for this use.

"Our soldiers are already fully dressed with nefarite shields, Highness, that is true," Morg says thoughtfully. "But perhaps we need one shield for *all*." Morg pauses then, as if still forming the thought in his mind.

"I'm listening," Tarik says.

I take my place at the king's side, trying and barely succeeding in not staring at him. He is fully dressed in his royal attire, which is not how I prefer him, but I cannot help but notice the way the gold body paint accentuates each of his muscular cuts along his arms and stomach. Things I should not be thinking of at this important moment.

"We could use the nefarite to fortify the city," Morg says, drawing my attention back to the matter at hand. "If it indeed acts as a protector against attack, we could mold a layer to each of the structures in the city, beginning, of course, with the palace."

Tarik nods. "Yes. That's an excellent idea. Do we have someone experienced enough to do this?"

"I'll send word to your Serubelan architect, Highness. If she cannot complete the task herself, she will select a pupil who would fit our needs. My only hesitation is that she is of the freed slaves. Where do her loyalties lie?"

Tarik looks at me. "I've no doubt of her loyalties. She will do as we ask."

Is he speaking of me, or this grand architect of the freed slaves? There seems to be no malice in his voice; it is not a command, for his eyes still resonate with playfulness. Perhaps it is a question for later. I tuck it into the recesses of my mind and allow myself to feel some relief at the conversation. It really is a splendid idea, fortifying the structures, and for once I'm forced to acknowledge that perhaps Morg is not as bloodthirsty as I first supposed. Perhaps he truly is interested in defense, rather than attacking my home kingdom.

Then I realize that Cara said the king's own architect is a Forger. What *will* she think of the king's command? Will she truly be as loyal as he supposes? After all, Cara herself had been concerned with the fate of Serubel. Do all the freed slaves and their descendants share this concern?

"Of course," Morg says, moving along with his strategy against Serubel. "We'll need to test it out against the explosive properties of the Scaldling venom before we go to all the trouble. If it is useless against the Serubelans, we need not waste time in pursuing this avenue of defense."

I tense at Tarik's side. He does not miss it, but he'll not meet my eyes. "Agreed," he says, and I resist the urge to hurl myself at him. He's well aware of how I feel about harvesting the Scaldling venom from Kyra. If he has no ill intent toward Serubel, if he means to only defend against attack, then he should leave his scorched city the way it is. "But we needn't harvest much of the stuff for our purposes," Tarik amends when I cross my arms. "A bit of the venom dust and melted spectorium should tell us if we're wasting our time."

"Of course, the spectorium we have is not fresh, so the effects of the mixture will likely be diluted," Morg is saying.

"The Serubelans should be running out of fresh spectorium themselves," Tarik says. Immediately he realizes his folly. Will he now explain to Morg about the late Forger princess? That there is another Forger somewhere in the Five Kingdoms. Perhaps he'll not have to. Perhaps Morg will overlook this slip up. But it's too much to hope for. The brazen commander always pays close attention to his king. To my dismay, Morg's head wrenches upward. I brace myself for the inquisition I'll receive at his hands.

"Is that so? How do you know this?"

Tarik smiles. "Surely you do not think I wouldn't have my own informants, Morg. There are those loyal to my father, and those loyal exclusively to me." So, Lingots do have the ability to lie.

And Morg must not be a Lingot. The warrior sniffs, clearly taken aback. "You've put me in charge of protecting Theoria. Please consider that withholding information that affects my ability to do that is setting me up to fail, Highness."

"Of course I do," Tarik says, his voice nurturing. "But I find that due to my inexperience, I need the council of many rather than just one. How am I to find my own way, otherwise? And I was not keeping the fact from you. Why do you think we are having this meeting?"

A diplomatic response to be sure. But Morg does not appear pacified. Yet, for all his dismay, he says, "Of course, Highness."

"May I have a supply of nefarite for the Lyceum?" Cy says, startling us all with his enthusiasm. I had nearly forgotten he was in the room.

"The Lyceum will be one of the first structures to be coated with it," Tarik reassures him. "We must protect the work you're doing with the Quiet Plague."

"Yes," Morg says, nodding in approval. "My ranks have not gone untouched by this nuisance, and young Master Cy was quick to take up against it. I am eternally grateful."

"Yes, well." Cy does not seem to know how to smoothly accept a compliment. He shakes his head, turning back to Tarik. "No, Highness, I meant for my personal use. For experimenting."

"Experimenting for what?" Tarik says, not unkindly. "Your time is better invested in seeing to the needs of our people at the moment. Experiments outside of that seem frivolous—"

The young Healer hesitates before interrupting, but does so nonetheless, looking to Tarik for forgiveness and approval. "If it's all the same to you, Highness, I'd rather not say for the time being. My ideas and speculations are very broad, and I must think on it more before explaining it fully, but rest assured it *does* have much to do with helping our citizens."

Tarik drums his fingers on the table, no doubt processing Cy's words, turning them over in his mind to find the truth or at least something worthy enough to indulge his young Master Healer. He has much respect for Cy, and I can tell he wants to give him ample room for his ingenuity. "How much do you need?" Tarik says finally, amid another sniff from Morg.

"Perhaps three or four swords. I can melt them myself. I think that will be sufficient for what I have in mind."

"It is decided, then," Tarik says, standing. "Cy may have a few of our worthless swords. We'll test the Scaldling venom against the shields. Soon we will have some answers."

42

TARIK

A SMALL GASP RESOUNDS FROM A FEW SEATS down on the balcony and Tarik becomes acutely aware of Sepora standing behind what would be Rashidi's high-backed chair. She grasps the wings of the chair, her knuckles growing white with the force of her grip. Tarik follows her line of sight to the soldiers in the yard as they make ready for the demonstration of spectorium and Scaldling venom. Her glorious hair is woven into an intricate braided masterpiece atop her head, the sheer bits of material and gold chains flowing from the creation dangling loosely in the wind. She's distracted, preoccupied, and biting her lip in a way that makes him want to go to her. He knows what she's thinking, what is passing through her mind at this moment as she stares down at the soldier in the yard melting purple spectorium in a large metal pot.

Despite his assurances to the contrary, she believes Theoria will move against the Serubelans using this new concoction of venom and spectorium—what the more experienced soldiers are calling cratorium, for the deep cavities the mixture leaves in the ground. She believes he would make cavities of the Serubelan army this way.

It bothers him that Sepora still doesn't trust him. Not enough to tell him the identity of the last Forger. Not enough to know that he has no intention of using this horrible weapon against her precious Serubel. He'd hoped by now they'd have progressed, that he could confide in her the way he wants to and that she could confide in him. But still they hold back, each one cradling their own secret feelings as though they do not know each other at all. As if they do not find ways to see each other every day, to touch their lips together, even if for the briefest of moments.

If only she could trust him. Then he would trust her. Then he could tell her that she saved him. That before she came along, he had been existing, moving like one of the many mechanical creations the engineers contrive, only instead of being powered by spectorium, he was powered by sheer obligation, going through the same motions over and over again as though a windmill or the wheels of a chariot. Only when she escaped the harem did this mundane survival finally turn into a life. One he'd be happy to share with her—for as long as she'll have him.

How can he tell her? *Should* he tell her? He isn't sure, and it is not something about which he can confer with Rashidi, even if he were here. His old friend would not approve of this secret romance with a royal servant—especially if that servant is Sepora. Nor would Sethos understand, as his view of women extends just below his waist, never reaching his heart or his mental faculties. And pride of the pyramids, his brother couldn't utter anything about Sepora without his feelings for her tainting his words.

As it is, they've kept their relationship hidden from Sethos's eyes. His brother just lost his father. Tarik will not hurt him with losing Sepora as well. When the time comes, then he will tell him. And he will make his brother understand.

Tarik is drawn from his thoughts at the sound of a trumpet bouncing in a rhythm of high-pitched bursts throughout the track, which brings the entire royal balcony to attention. This used to be his favorite place as a child, coming here to the complex to watch the chariot races with his father. The king and his guests had a balcony entirely their own overlooking the center of the track, where warriors would chisel away at each other's defenses or chariots would whirl around dangerously to get just inches ahead of the others.

Now, some of the council members choose to stand, while some take seats lined close to the balcony's waist-high edge. Sepora takes her place to stand beside Tarik's chair, absently gripping the balcony ledge before him and almost blocking his view of the procession below. She simply must calm down, but exchanging words with her at this moment, at her height of anxiety, would not be good for either of them. She would say something out of turn, and he would be expected to correct her for it. As they both watch with keen interest, soldiers prop up large shields reinforced with nefarite across the yard as targets for the volatile mixture. Sepora had already instructed the soldiers on how it is to be done, emphasizing that they must release the blended spectorium and venom quickly, lest they risk burning themselves. Tarik had noticed a small burn on her hand before; he wonders if she sustained it while helping King Eron fashion a spectorium explosive. He wonders if that contributed to the reasons she left. He wants to ask her but dares not. Though she stands so close to him, she seems so far away at the moment. He would like her attention during this experiment, to confer with her on the results, to hear her thoughts on the matter. To hear her concerns. Because from what he gathers by the way she chews at her bottom lip, Sepora is very concerned.

Other soldiers ready the catapults, while the one standing guard at the melting pot waits for his orders. Morg, who stands tall and unshakable behind the catapults, signals for the observation to begin. Tarik cannot help but clutch his chair as the melted spectorium is poured into the first catapult. Another soldier reaches into a leather satchel and pulls out what appears to be just a pinch of venom dust; he sprinkles the spectorium with it as though he were adding flavor to it. Slowly he backs away, appearing entranced by the reaction taking place within the bowl of the catapult.

"Quickly!" Sepora calls down, now standing in front of Tarik on the balcony, all but blocking his view. "You must release it quickly."

Tarik stands then, unsure if it is out of support for her or out of sheer curiosity of his own. One of the soldiers raises his sword and cuts the rope, sending the mixture soaring into a glowing arch toward the first shield on the opposite side of the yard. It falls just short of its mark, landing in the sand in front of it. The rest of the attendees stationed on the balcony stand and wait for the impending blast. Just when Tarik thinks the test is impotent, the liquid pool explodes in a rush of smoke and sand hurled many feet into the air. When the dust clears, there is a substantial hole in the courtyard. An impossible hole, reaching at least an arm's length deep into the dirt. A hole that could one day symbolize where some of his soldiers used to stand, were the Serubelans to use it against them. He tries to stifle the thought.

Morg appears unimpressed; Tarik gets the sense his senior commander has already extensively investigated the cratorium mixture beforehand and found this first test lacking. He seems determined for results, as he calls for the catapult to be loaded again and adjusted for distance. This time, the deadly compound reaches its mark, the explosive flattening the nefarite shield to the ground. Still, when a nearby soldier holds the shield up for inspection, it is fully intact. Unmarred even, as far as Tarik can tell from where he sits. The only evidence that remains is merely the fallout of the explosion in the sand around it.

With a grimace, Sepora leans in, to speak for Tarik's ears only. "Highness," she says, "they must add more venom dust to the spectorium. We must know what the shields can truly withstand."

He raises a brow. "You think they can make something stronger than that?"

"I think they will try." There is fear in her voice and in her eyes. A fear that makes him sure she has seen something more dangerous than what has been presented here. Again, his eyes flit to the scar on her hand.

He nods and places his palms on the ledge. Morg already awaits his next command. "This time add more Scaldling venom dust to the mixture," he calls down. Morg nods, obviously pleased with his new order, and relays it to the soldier at the next catapult. Melted spectorium is poured into the bowl of the contraption, shimmering metallic in the sun. And instead of a sprinkle, an entire handful of venom is thrown in behind it. Morg and his assistant back away, swiftly this time, and the rope is cut, sending the liquid cannon slamming into the second shield. It explodes upon contact, a burst that takes Tarik's breath away and pounds in his ears, lobbing the heavy slab of nefarite even farther back than the previous one. A silent awe blankets the courtyard.

When the soldier retrieves the shield, he looks to Morg, eyes wide. "It is unscathed, Commander."

Morg looks to Tarik again, waiting for further direction.

"I believe we have seen enough," Tarik announces, folding his shaking hands behind his back. "The shields will stand against the venom dust."

His soldiers, however, will not.

MORG LEANS BACK IN HIS SEAT AS HE SPEAKS from across Tarik's desk. The commander of the Theorian army wears a contented look upon his face.

"We need a weapon such as that," Morg says. All the while, Sepora bites her lip, refusing to make eye contact with him—or for that matter, anyone else in the room.

"We have an excellent defense, but war is not only composed of defense," Morg continues. "We've no reason to believe we'll not need to counterattack our enemy. This cratorium could save lives. It could win us the war."

"As of yet, there is no war," Tarik says. "We've not seen a single sign of aggression from the Serubelans."

Morg sighs. "By the Mistress Sepora's own admission, there is an imminent strike. I'm afraid we cannot ignore that, Highness; we need an offensive strategy as much as we need a defensive one. It would show weakness on our part not to annihilate the Serubelans if they dare to attack us. Weakness is something we cannot afford. It is something *you* cannot afford, as a new king." The words would have been out of turn, if they were not said so sincerely.

"It would also show that we are peaceable," Sepora says, crossing her arms. "That Theoria does not want a war."

"Peaceable?" Morg says, incredulous. "We've already shown ourselves to be peaceable when we sent an ambassador to Serubel to speak to the king. He flogged the entire caravan and sent them away! Do not speak of peace to me." He looks to Tarik. "Forgive me, Highness, but the Mistress Sepora is not Theorian. It would be difficult for her to remain objective in this matter."

"I may not be Theorian, but I do care about lives," she clips. "And

if I understand correctly, war results in casualties from both sides."
She looks pointedly at Tarik.

"This is true, Mistress Sepora," Morg says. "But we already have
a plague sweeping through our people. We cannot afford to lose more
of them to a war in which we are only spectators. If we do not retaliate, other kingdoms may view us as vulnerable. Vulnerability attracts
the attention of power-hungry rulers, I'm afraid."

Tarik cannot ignore this logic. Of course Sepora is worried for
her kingdom, but if she is to adjust to life here, she must start thinking of Theoria as her home. This is not something to discuss in front
of present company, however. When he steals a private moment, he'll
reason with her further.

"Everyone has made valid points," Tarik says. "I must think on it
more before coming to a decision. Please leave me; I'll be alone with
my thoughts now."

Sepora is not happy to be among those dismissed, but to her good
credit she doesn't resist; she follows dutifully behind Morg as he exits
Tarik's day chambers, her expression pinched into a scowl.

Yet, Tarik knows what he must do. And Sepora will not like it.

43

S E P O R A

AFTER TOSSING AND TURNING IN MY BED FOR what seems like several forevers, I finally surrender to the anxiety. The moon spills in from the balcony as I slip into my clothes and open the door to my bedchamber. Thankful that Tarik had already dismissed my guards a few days ago, I roam the palace of my own free will, trying to get my bearings on where exactly his bedchamber is. I pass guards who give me curious looks but say nothing. Either they've been instructed to remain at their posts or they do not deem me their responsibility.

I wrap my arms around myself; I had never thought the palace cold before. Indeed, it can be quite stuffy in the halls where there is no access to the outside breeze, pockets hidden away where the heat has a chance to build and simmer. But there is something about the palace that has grown frigid, and I cannot help but think it has to do with the discussion of the Scaldling venom earlier today in Tarik's day chambers. With the excitable way Morg spoke of an attack on Serubel. With the way Tarik seemed torn in his decision.

Indeed, I am chilled from the inside out.

Once I make it to the west wing, I stumble upon two rows of guards leading up to large, wooden, and intricately carved double doors. A pair of Theorian soldiers blocks the entrance to the room; this must be the king's private chambers. Who else would require need of such protection? Taking a deep breath, I pass each guard without looking at them, holding my head up high as though I've come here for a purpose, as though I've been summoned by the king himself.

Of course, I have come here for a purpose, but not a purpose the king will want to hear. The guards allow me to close in on the door, but the men there move together in unison, crossing their long spears so as not to allow my passage. "Mistress Sepora," one of them says, "the king is in private discussions with his council and is not to be disturbed."

"What council? I am his council until Rashidi returns."

The guard nods. "Rashidi joins him now."

Rashidi is back? Perhaps now is not the right time to speak with Tarik. Rashidi will have much to relay to the king from his visit to Hemut. And Tarik will have much to relay to his adviser. How will he explain our relationship? How will Rashidi react? My first thought is to postpone my meeting with Tarik until we can swindle a private moment from his busy days. But with Rashidi back, there will be very few private moments. I will become his attendant, instead of Tarik's. I will see to Rashidi's needs, his errands, and his commissions. Or he may dismiss me altogether.

"The king is expecting me," I lie, hoping none of the guards within earshot are Lingots. I bristle at the fact that none appear to be. Tarik would do well to post Lingots at his door, in case any who he trusts means to harm him. I understand the need for Majai; but a royal guard should be well rounded with different skill sets for different lines of attack. Perhaps I'll speak to Rashidi about it in the morning. If there is one thing the adviser and I agree upon, it is the importance of the king's safety.

"He did not tell us of your visit this evening," he responds, gripping his spear tighter. No doubt this man has heard of my escape from the harem, of my escape from the palace to speak to the Parani. No doubt this man trusts me as much as he trusts a one-wheeled chariot to get him to the Bazaar.

Just then, the door behind them creaks open, and Tarik steps out, bereft of paint or gold adornments. His gaze locks with mine, and I can tell he has not slept. I can tell much weighs on his mind. Small, faint blue rings circle his eyes and his hair is a bit disheveled as though he, too, has been tossing and turning. Rashidi must have arrived not long before me; Tarik has not had time to gain any sort of composure.

"She may come in," Tarik says tiredly. "Let her through."

Immediately the guards separate and make room for my passage. Tarik shuts the door behind us. His bedchamber is enormous, with several sitting areas, a table and chairs, what appears to be a lavatory in the far corner, and an immense bed surrounded by four columns and steps leading up to it. Gold statues of warriors guard the walls between each entrance to the long balcony where sheer white curtains sway gently in the night breeze, letting rivulets of moonlight in. On the ceiling is a mural embellished with gold, depicting what appears to be a battle. Theorians, of course, conquering whomever it is they are in conflict with.

The room is intimate yet stately, and luxurious in every way.

I feel Tarik looking at me, and I turn to him. "It was my father's," he says, nodding around us. "Rashidi insisted I use it, but I much prefer my old room on the other side of the palace. Too much space for thought in here."

"A king must have space for his lofty thoughts," Rashidi calls from the corner behind us. He sits in a chair, cradling his long golden staff in the crook of his arm. He appears perhaps more tired than the king himself. He must have arrived late this evening.

I bow my head in greeting to the old councillor. "I am glad to see your safe return, Rashidi."

He tilts his head at me. "Are you, though?"

A blush heats my cheeks. What does he know of the king and I? Or perhaps he's merely referring to our very mutual distaste for one another. "Of course," I tell him. "This is a time where the king needs his most trusted adviser."

"And what lofty thoughts weigh on your mind tonight, your Highness?" I ask, turning to Tarik.

"Several, I'm afraid. And I'd wager the same thoughts that brought you to my bedchamber, mistress."

He places his hand at the small of my back and ushers me to the sitting area closest to the balcony where Rashidi is already seated. The old adviser steals a disapproving look at me as Tarik takes a seat across from me. I well know it is not proper for a mistress to visit the king's bedchamber in the middle of the night, attendant or not. It is not proper in any kingdom, I should think, for a woman who is not his wife—or concubine, as it were—to visit. Certainly in Serubel it is not. But we are well past the point of what is proper and what is not. Tarik is right to keep his distance. This conversation cannot be tainted with my feelings for him. By his feelings for me.

"Have you made a decision regarding cratorium?" I ask.

"I have." He leans forward, folding his hands carefully in front of him, his elbows on his knees. "Sepora, you must understand that I cannot overlook the counsel of my military commander and my closest adviser."

So. Rashidi agrees with Morg. And Tarik agrees with them both.

My heartbeat falters, once, then twice. Tarik is very good at not taint-ing this conversation with his feelings for me. I must now do the same.

"You're going to use it as a weapon, then." My lungs feel heavy in my chest, as though full of water, and at any moment they could slip into my stomach and down to my knees, drowning me completely. "Against Serubel."

"If they use it against us, yes. We must fight back. The ways of Theoria dictate that. It was never really my decision to begin with. If I have a way to protect my people, I must use it, Sepora."

"You have the nefarite to protect them."

Rashidi sighs. "If we do not attack those attacking us, we show vulnerability to all the surrounding kingdoms. We open ourselves to further assault. The Falcon King cannot allow that."

"It is for nothing, then. Everything I've done for you," I say to Tarik. I will not grace Rashidi with my glare. He is not the one deserving of all my ire just now. I stand and walk toward the balcony, grasping a curtain as though it could hold me up were I to collapse into my emo-tions. I hear Tarik behind me, feel his breath on the back of my neck.

"I have responsibilities, Sepora," he says, his voice pleading. "I have responsibilities that tie my hands in this matter."

"You are the most powerful man in this kingdom," I tell him softly, trying to concentrate on the moon overhead instead of the warmth of his body behind me. "Maybe in all the Five. And yet your voice does not outweigh that of a war-hungry commander and a grouchy old man?"

"I have served as royal adviser for two generations," Rashidi says indignantly. "As it were, you've interrupted an even more important conversation than the well-being of a kingdom that means to attack us."

"That conversation can be heard at a different time," Tarik says sternly. Then his voice softens as he speaks to my hair again. "Morg is not war-hungry. He has his duties, as do I. And this time, those duties align with each other. Rashidi may be grouchy, but his loyalties lie with Theoria. I must trust him."

I've given this man, this boy king too much. I've given him nefarite. I've told him about the Scaldling venom and spectorium. I've told him about the Forging. I've warned him of my father's impending attack. I trusted him with all of it and in so doing I've handed him the means to defeat Serubel. To kill my people.

I cannot bear the thought of it. Not at this moment. Fighting angry tears, I step away from him. It is better to put physical distance between us since he is bent on putting a different sort of distance between us. How can I trust him now? How can I serve him if he will use me in this way? "And what conversation have I rudely interrupted?" I whisper, knowing Rashidi would rather be sentenced to a life in The Dismals than tell me.

But Rashidi is all too happy to relay his news. "My journey to Hemut was a success. His Majesty the Falcon King will take Princess Tulle of Hemut as wife within four cycles of the moon."

I shut my eyes against the words. Of course that is what they were speaking of. Rashidi's purpose was to unite the kingdoms of Hemut and Theoria. That is where he has been these four weeks. What better way to do that than marriage? And of course that is why Tarik wanted to speak to Rashidi about it at a different time; for Rashidi's ears only. No doubt he planned to seek me out and tell me privately, to be gentle and kind about it the way he does when we have a disagreement. But this is not a disagreement.

This is yet another betrayal.

"We must make this an elaborate wedding, Highness," Rashidi is saying. "And I had the thought that, if you were willing, we could send King Ankor a supply of spectorium and venom dust, and show him how to create the cratorium. After all, when we are united, the kingdom of Hemut will be in danger of attack as well."

Arm the Hemutians against Serubel as well? I have met my threshold for patience this evening. I have met my threshold for patience for an entire lifetime. Turning to Tarik, I press my back into the wall, all but rejecting his closeness. His eyes hold a sadness that I feel deep within my own chest. But it is no matter. Not anymore. "Am I a slave, Highness?"

"Of course not," he whispers.

"Then I may leave if I wish?"

"Sepora—"

"Surely you don't expect me to stand by and watch you bring my people to their knees. I certainly was not going to stand by and watch my kingdom attack yours without warning you." Of course, that's not exactly how it unfolded, but it's how it turned out in the end. And surely he does not expect me to watch idly as he weds the Princess Tulle. But that is not for Rashidi's ears. Even now, even when all has been exposed between us, it is still only between us.

He runs a hand through his hair. "You speak as though I am the one who started this war. Remember, it is your king who means to—"

"It makes no difference. I'll not stay here and watch either of you die. Not the Serubelans, not the Theorians. I came here to prevent a war. I've failed. I have no purpose here anymore."

"Purpose?" He raises his hand to brush his knuckles along my cheek. It takes all of my willpower not to shudder under his touch. Rashidi stiffens in the corner. A king does not touch his attendant so. Tarik would break with etiquette now? "Your purpose here is to keep me sane. To keep me balanced." He smiles. "To keep me in my proper place."

I wrench away from him and move across the entrance to the other wall. "Words! I do not have the luxury of being a Lingot, Highness. Words mean nothing to me. Actions mean everything."

"Sepora, don't do this."

"And what of the king of Hemut? You're sending him a supply of cratorium? Rashidi has secured you a bride and a powerful ally for war. How delighted you must be."

"We are necessary allies, Sepora. My enemies are now Hemut's enemies." The louder I get, the softer his tone. I'll not let him soothe me. Not when so much is at stake.

"Why? Why must you collaborate with him when you have all this at your disposal? You have nefarite to protect yourselves. You have cratorium to fight back. What is the point of aligning with Hemut? This is not their fight."

"It is not their fight, but it will be," Rashidi cuts in. "He is to wed Tulle. The Falcon King must make heirs. He must keep his lineage intact."

And that is when the breath is truly knocked out of me. I would love nothing more than to fling myself at Rashidi for his callousness. *Heirs.* Tarik must take the Princess Tulle to his bed. And where does that leave me? Where has it ever left me? It leaves me as a lovesick fool. A servant who has been stupid enough to fall in love with a king. "You'll marry the Princess Tulle after all, then?"

He nods slowly, his eyes never leaving mine. The boy king appears mortified. I wonder if I reflect his expression. "I need Hemut's army as much as I need spectorium."

"How could you give your affection and attention to me, knowing you would marry another?" All of the kisses, the caresses, the secret smiles shared between us. All the time I spent thinking of him, wishing to be in his presence, longing for his touch.

He takes a step forward and I hold up my hand, halting him. "I thought you knew, Sepora. Marriage is merely a means to unite kingdoms. It doesn't mean anything. *She* doesn't mean anything."

"And what of this heir you're expected to produce?" He doesn't have to respond; we both know the answer. I shake my head. "And you would expect me to stand by and wait for you to return to me after spending the evening with her?"

Rashidi has the good sense to keep his meddling mouth shut. If he suspected something was amiss between the king and me, there is no room for doubt now. But I no longer care what this looks like to him. I no longer care because I have been betrayed in the worst way and I will have my answers.

"I had not thought of it that way. It is a matter of duty—"

"Duty? And if I had the same duty? Could you wait for me while I passed the time in another man's bed?"

Tarik's face grows hard, and I know I've hit my mark. "You've no reason to share another man's bed."

"I'm not your concubine, Tarik. I'll not share you with anyone, king or not."

His face softens. "These are the way of things. It is the only way we can be together. I thought we had an understanding."

My laugh is sharp and full of bitterness, bereft of humor. "I thought so, too. But alas, we are not to be together, Highness. I leave as soon as dawn breaks."

Tarik runs a hand through his hair. His face tells me he is not surprised. "Where will you go?"

"That is not your concern." And, I'm not sure where I'll go. Not Hemut, not in a century of centuries. I cannot return to Serubel. I would never survive in Wachuk with their crude and coarse ways of living. Perhaps I'll travel to Pelusia. They can survive without spectorium; I'll not be of any political use in Pelusia—and I'll be well away from the prying fingers of this impending war.

Tarik wipes a hand down his face. "Sepora, please. You must understand—"

"What I understand is that you intend to make war on my people and that you will soon marry Princess Tulle and bring her here, into your bedchamber. If that is not the case, please do correct me." When he says nothing, I glide past him and make my way toward the great double doors of the chamber.

"I cannot let you go, Sepora," he calls after me. I can tell he is close on my heels. His hand grasps my wrist and he whirls me around. His eyes brim with sleeplessness and agony. I cannot help but look away. I'll not be ensnared by him again. Not ever. "Please, Sepora. Don't do this."

I glance past him, at Rashidi. The old man stands now, watching us intently. He fidgets his hands. No doubt he knew the king and I had grown close while he was away. But his expression suggests that this is too close for the adviser's comfort. I look back at Tarik. "You have your obligations. I have mine." I open the door then and leave him behind.

DAWN BREAKS INTO MY ROOM, UNWELCOME AND unneeded, as I've already packed a satchel and dressed for my journey by the light of my own fresh spectorium. *Let the prince think on that for a bit. Let him think his precious, mysterious last Forger has visited me during the night.*

I half expect my door to be barred shut from the outside, to in fact become a prisoner in this palace yet again, but it opens easily and without noise. There are no guards keeping watch, no one to stop me from leaving. Perhaps this will be easy. Perhaps Tarik finally sees reason in my words, that there is nothing left for me here. He is not mine; I cannot be his. And he will eventually attack my people, instead of merely defending Theoria against them.

My sandals fall softly on the stairs as I make my way down to the kitchens of the palace. I'll eat breakfast here and take some provisions with me. After my stomach is full and my satchel fuller, I leave that wing of the palace and step out into full morning sunshine. The corral where Dody the Serpen is kept is just beyond the training courtyard; it should only take me a few moments to reach it but I find that my feet drag in the sand.

I must leave, I tell myself. I must stand my ground. If not in this, then what else is there? Why did I leave home in the first place? I'd wanted to save lives. To prevent war. Now I've helped to ensure it will be worse by tenfold. It will be more than war. And it will not come without a cost. What if Tarik is injured? What if the palace falls?

These are things I cannot dwell on. I've done all I can.

I swing open the door to the corral—and nearly touch noses with Tarik.

"You could have asked," he says, nodding toward Dody behind him. "I would have given him to you."

"I thought you would try to stop me." Never could I have guessed he would provide me with the means to leave; I'd decided to steal Dody the moment I decided to abandon my life here. I couldn't very well negotiate The Dismals by myself again. Or the people I might come across, who could be far worse than the likes of Chut or Rolan. Better to fly over The Dismals this time, than to trek through them.

Still, I should have known Tarik would not keep me here as a prisoner. He is not unjust in that way. He is not my father.

His shoulders slump. "It is impossible to make you stay, yet impossible to let you go. Why is that, Sepora?"

But I don't have an answer for him. I hoist the satchel higher on my shoulder, waiting for him to step aside. When he does, I'm careful not to brush against him. A few days ago, I would have taken every opportunity to touch him, to revel in the feel of his skin against mine. Even now, I want him to tell me something that will set everything aright, something that will overturn my overwhelming urge to flee, something that will draw me into his arms and keep me there forever.

He says nothing.

"Hello, young sir," I coo to Dody. He nuzzles his nose into my hand, reminding me of Patra. Dody has grown on me, yes. But he will never be Nuna. "Ready for our journey?"

I hoist myself onto him and settle into the groove behind his head. Pulling on his ear to instruct him, he moves forward, slithering past Tarik and out of the corral.

"Where will you go?" Tarik says, walking beside us as we circle the courtyard for a brief warm-up.

"I don't know."

"A lie."

"Why should I tell you? Do you mean to keep watch on me, then?"

His guilty expression suggests he had every intention of it. "Let me send someone with you. For protection."

"I can take care of myself."

"You were captured in the desert and sold into my harem last time you were looking after yourself."

I bite my lip. "Well then, I've valuable experience in such matters now."

He moves fast, impossibly fast, to grab my ankle, halting Dody from making another circle around the yard. The only men I've seen who can move like that are Majai. "Tell me what I can say to make you stay," he pleads, his jaw clenched. "Tell me what I can say to convince you of my love for you."

My love. He's not spoken the word aloud before. Hoping he returned the love I have for him was not something I'd dared to do.

I want to scream at him for making this so difficult. Why did he have to come here today? Why did I have to see his face again, his eyes, his lips? Why must we both endure this torture? "For all your privilege, Highness, it seems you are not at liberty to tell me what I need to hear." That he'll not counterattack Serubel. That he'll not marry Tulle. And not just Tulle. That he'll not marry another, ever. That I am worth more than a dozen heirs to him.

But as he said, his hands are tied. They are tied, and so mine must be.

"Do you have family in Serubel?" he says, running beside us now as we move to take off. Again, his speed surpasses my expectation. "I can guarantee their safety," he's saying. "I'll have them brought here at once, before the war even starts. I'll protect them as my own."

"My family cannot be protected," I say, looking away from him and into the sky. I know this truth will puzzle him. What family cannot be protected by the Falcon King? *My father is your nemesis* is what I want to tell him. But instead I fix my gaze on a cloud in the distance. Dody's wings flap intensely and in a matter of moments we are gliding through the air. We must pick up more speed to breech the wall ahead of us.

"Wait! Sepora, please!"

The wind catches all the words after that and carries them away from me on a breeze.

44

TARIK

TARIK BIDS PATRA TO STAY AT THE TOP OF THE stairs at the entrance of the Lyceum. She sprawls out along one of the wider steps and flattens on her side to take in the warmth of the sun. She aims to look at ease, he can tell, but a pair of crows nearby has caught her attention and her tail flicks with the irritation of not going after them.

He smiles, leaving her behind with her conundrum. Having visited Cy the Healer enough to know his way around the Lyceum, he doesn't wait for assistance before climbing the stairwell that leads to the Healer's grand hallway. He arrives in the large auditorium, which is normally used for teaching, on the third floor; now the room is lined with cots from wall to wall, a patient in each one, and Healers on the move in every direction. The scene has a certain sense of controlled chaos, and it turns Tarik's mouth down in a scowl.

The Quiet Plague is spreading too rapidly for them to keep up.

From among the Healers, Tarik is able to see Cy—the shortest and youngest tends to stand out—and he weaves his way between the beds to reach him. Cy gives him a brief nod of greeting before stirring a small pot of putrid-smelling liquid on a table next to his current patient. "I've something to show you, Tarik," he says, retrieving a needle from a cloth-lined tray on the bed.

"What is that horrible smell?" Tarik says, wafting his hand in front of his face in an attempt to escape it.

Cy laughs. "That, my friend, is the solution to all of our problems." He nods to the bowl of watery liquid, steam swirling up from the contents—an obvious mixture of glowing spectorium and something else. Carefully, he takes a spoonful of the substance and pours it into a metal tube with a needle poking from the end. He takes a seat on the bedside of the patient, a small, bony-shouldered girl whose blank stare hints of impending death. Why did her parents not seek help sooner? The day Sepora left, he'd made a decree about the plague. He'd made the Lyceum available to all citizens of Theoria. She could be in good health right now, if she'd arrived as soon as she'd shown symptoms.

Cy glances back at him. "She's a repeat case," he says. "They tend to digress much faster once they've been treated with spectorium." He straightens her arm and, after rubbing a small leaf over the inside crook of it, he injects the needle. The girl does not react to the penetration or to the withdrawal of the needle. She does not blink, does not even appear to be breathing as far as Tarik can tell.

"What did you give her?" Tarik says, sitting on the edge of the bed at her feet.

"Spectorium, the usual liquefying herbs, water. And . . . nefarite."

"*Nefarite*? This is what you needed the swords for?"

Cy nods. "It works, you'll see. And for the record, her parents consented to the treatment. They wanted me to try anything, and so I did."

"Has it worked before?"

"It has worked on six out of six treated patients."

"Six out of six." Tarik scratches at the light beard he'd allowed himself to grow these past few days. Or rather, the beard he'd been too busy to shave off. Preparing for war is a tedious job. At least, he's made it tedious. With Sepora gone, he'll do whatever it takes to keep his mind occupied with other things, even if it means keeping his commanders and advisers up all hours of the night and day and sitting in on the Lingot council to make sure all is as it should be. He'll even bother Cy at the Lyceum, so as not to think about *her*. "Why? Why does it work?"

Cy shrugs. "It acts as an amplifier. We both know that when used for good, it amplifies the ability to do good. When used for bad, it weakens the ability to do bad. I thought to myself, what greater good could there be than saving a life? So then, I found a way to mix spectorium and melted nefarite, altered their cooling temperatures, and began to test it on patients who consented. The results have been quite miraculous."

As if in response to his words, the girl in the bed begins to gasp for air, coughing and gulping for it as if she'd been drowning before. Blinking several times, she leans on her elbows at first, then hoists herself up to sit fully. "Where's my mother?" she croaks.

Cy gives her a brilliant smile. "I'll have her fetched immediately. We had to send her away; very little room in here, you see."

"I want my mother," the girl insists, this time her voice gaining some strength. With each second, her eyes become more alert, and she takes in the view around her. "I don't want to be here."

Tarik feels paralyzed in place. How could the injection have worked that quickly? Could it be possible? Could Cy have really found the cure this time?

"You may go home within the hour," Cy is telling her. "But you must promise me to drink plenty of water and get plenty of rest for the next few days."

She nods obediently, almost in reverence of the young boy. Tarik wonders how far apart they really are in age. "Yes, Healer Cy. I promise."

The boy Healer looks to Tarik then, pride gleaming in his eyes. "What think you of that, Tarik?"

"Incredible," Tarik says, barely able to manage a whisper. "How long will the effects last?"

Cy's brows knit together. "My hope is that it will be an indefinite cure. Only time will tell, though. We should know within months, I suppose. That's when the spectorium will have completely worn off on its own. That's when the nefarite will have its opportunity to shine, so to speak."

Within months. Could the Quiet Plague really be defeated in merely a handful of cycles of the moon? Cy believes it to be true.

So why don't I?

45

SEPORA

I SEE THE SERUBELAN CARAVAN AHEAD OF US just before the first catapult lets loose. I'd recognize the glow of cratorium anywhere. I have only enough time to flatten myself against Dody and wait for impact. It doesn't come; an explosion lights the sky beside us, sending Dody swirling precariously to the left. I gasp, maneuvering quickly to recover, attempting to lift us higher and out of their range, but a second explosion catches Dody in his back wing, and we begin a dangerous descent. They must think I am Theorian—a Theorian who has stolen one of their Serpens.

I let my hair loose from the linen I'd wrapped about my head for protection from the sun, to show that I am not Theorian, that I am Serubelan, one of their own. Or perhaps they already know who I am, and what I have done. Perhaps that is why they are shooting me from the sky.

And what is a Serubelan caravan doing in The Dismals yet again? Or, perhaps, still? Though "caravan" is not the word for the hundreds of tents and soldiers on the ground. No, this is an army. My stomach drops, even as Dody attempts to soar higher. This is a war party.

Dody's injured wing prevents us from avoiding the third blast, which strikes his chin and erupts into flames. Blood splatters on my face, my arms, my clothes. He falls limp beneath me, and I know at once that he is dead. We begin our inevitable plummet to The Dismals and I clutch onto him, wrapping my arms and legs about him as I was trained to do in case of a crash, hoping his body will cushion mine when we hit the desert sand and hating myself for thinking of such a thing when he has just died in my service.

I let out a pathetic wail as we close in on the desert floor, and I do not stop screaming until we hit—and everything disappears from my vision.

I'M NOT SURE IF GENERAL HALYON ERECTED THIS makeshift tent to shield me from the sun or to shield me from the ogling stares of his men. Even now, as we wait for my father, he will not look me in the eye, just shifts uncomfortably from one foot to the other and pretends to adjust the strap holding his sword in place. He is a large man with a warrior's body, though aged with wear and tear, but a fierce sight to behold nonetheless. As a child, I was fearful of the man and avoided him whenever possible, but now he seems to be more nervous about my presence than I am of his. Perhaps he heard the rumors about what I did to Father, that I forged a sword and wielded it against him. Surely a man such as Halyon is not afraid of a waif like me brandishing a sword at his nose when he could easily slay me where I sit. What a silly notion.

A lump knots in my throat. Perhaps he is upset with me some-how that he shot down and killed his own Serpen—the Serpen *I* rode to escape Theoria. Perhaps he thought I should have surrendered before that happened. And I would have certainly, if I had been paying better attention to what sprawled before us instead of focusing on the kingdom I was leaving behind. On the king I had abandoned.

But, perhaps Halyon should have given me the chance before lobbing cratorium into the sky against us. The idea of him mourning Dody is unlikely, however, since I am the only Serubelan who seems to dote on my Serpen and treat her as a pet. A great commander such as Halyon would never stoop to grief over a mere beast. Not even a beast as special and loyal as Dody.

Then it occurs to me: Halyon is so shifty because he's uncomfortable with my state of dress—or the lack thereof. I've grown so used to the scanty attire of the Theorians that I'm not even embarrassed by how far my clothing falls short according to Serubelan standards—even though part of the landing had torn a rip in my skirt extending quite a bit up my right thigh. I recall the memory of traipsing around the desert in servants' attire on my initial way to Anyar, sweaty and with heavy breath, and how relieved my body had felt—after the initial shock had waned, of course—upon discovering that Rolan and Chut had changed me into the attire that would ultimately sell me into the king's harem.

A small smile curls on my lips when I think of what Father's expression will be when he sees me. Will he be thankful that I'm alive? Will he tell me how devastated he was when he thought me dead? I shake my head with the unlikeliness of that. Father will be surprised, naturally, but that will not last long. He will see where I've been. He will ask what I've done. He will demand an explanation.

As if I'd thought him into our midst, the tent flap is thrown back and Father enters. Compared with Halyon, my father is a short man, thin in flesh and hair, the gray intermixed in the natural white atop his head. I'm unsure why, but I'm pleased that he appears to have grown more wrinkles in my time away from him. They all but frame his scowl now as he scrutinizes me as though he's never seen me before. I watch as his expression changes from disbelief to anger, to confusion, and finally settles on relief. Relief is not what I was expecting.

"Halyon, you are dismissed," he says without looking at his commander. Halyon does as he's told, exiting the tent without sparing me a glance.

I am now alone with my father. The last time this happened, I'd made a decision that would lead him to imprison me. And then I had fled.

"Saints of Serubel, is it really you, Magar? Can you really be here in front of me?" he says, his voice cracking just a bit.

No, not what I expected at all. I expected yelling. I expected his temper to reach new heights at the way I'm dressed. I expected wrath. "I . . . it is me, Father."

He devours the distance between us in quick, lengthy strides and just when I think he will strike me, he pulls me to him, embracing me sharply. "I thought I'd lost you. I thought Serubel had lost you. Our champion has returned to us! Tell me, child, who took you? Was it the Falcon King?"

Our *champion*?

He thinks someone *took* me?

Of course he does. Now that he finds me alive and well, he assumes I was taken. And, of course, he's not overcome with such touching emotion because his daughter has returned. He's overwhelmed with such relief because the last Forger has returned to him. To Serubel. His champion, to conquer the Theorians and their Falcon King.

I shake my head into his chest. "You mistake me, Father," I tell him, pulling away and taking a step back. "I was merely passing through."

"Passing through?" His arms drop to his sides. "How do you mean?"

"I was just leaving Theoria, on my way to Pelusia. I'd had the notion to visit elsewhere."

The words strike him as though a physical blow and he winces. Then his face tightens, and his hands fist. "Pelusia. Visit?" He spits the word at me. "I see." I want to take a step back, to retreat under the back wall of the tent and run away. But Father has brought an army with him, an army that would subdue me at his command. And Father is beginning to realize what happened.

I show him the spectorium pooling in my palm, illuminating the dark tent around us. His eyes are closed to near slits and his nostrils flare with rage. Slowly, he rolls up his sleeves.

"Do not take another step closer," I tell him.

He laughs, a laugh without whimsy. "Now you mistake me, child," he says, amused. "I merely meant to relieve myself of this stifling Theorian heat."

"All the same, stay back."

"Are you not glad to see me, Magar? Are you not glad to be home?" His voice drips with false innocence.

"We are in the Theorian desert, Father. This is not home. This is an army marching to its death."

He smiles. "You are fortunate that we intercepted you, then, daughter. You can now be witness to the battle that will conquer Theoria and bring its kingdom under our rule."

It is my turn to laugh. "You've a mind to conquer Theoria? With merely a few hundred men and a small supply of cratorium?"

"Cratorium?"

"Oh yes. That's what the Theorians are calling it. Didn't you know? Theoria knows just exactly what happens when you mix spectorium and venom dust. They have a supply of their own, you see, a supply of cratorium. More than that, they have the means to protect themselves from your attack, and a union with the Hemutians to use their army." I hope I do not show how deeply these particular words cut through me. "Yes, indeed, Father, you are marching to your death. If I were you, I would turn back immediately." Perhaps I've revealed too much to him. But revealing his disadvantages may change his mind on the matter. Perhaps counting his many disadvantages will prevent a war.

And perhaps I am not useless after all.

His eyes grow flinty. "And how is it that they came to know of such things?"

I take a deep breath. "Because I have been helping them."

46

TARIK

THE DOOR TO TARIK'S BEDCHAMBER BURSTS open, and Sethos strides in, fully armed.

Tarik is already sitting up in bed, open scrolls scattered among the linens where Patra does not take up the immediate space about him. He arches a brow at his brother. "Is this to be another lecture about visiting Cy at the Lyceum instead of you?" It is a tease, Tarik knows; now that Sepora has gone, Sethos does not show nearly as much interest in a midday visit at the Lyceum.

But Sethos ignores the bait. "An army of Serubelans has been spotted in the close Dismals, Tarik," he says. "Our riders say they number in the high hundreds. Surely they did not expect to defeat us with a handful of farmers?"

Tarik frowns. "Farmers armed with explosives, brother." And so far only half of Theoria's structures have been coated with the nefarite. The Baseborn and Middling Quarters are still completely vulnerable, something which bothers him to the core.

They are not fully prepared for war with the Serubelans. Not by far.

"Morg requests your presence in your day chambers," Sethos says. "The Serubelans flew a Seer Serpen close to us, just out of range of our archers. It carried a garment in its mouth, which it dropped and which we retrieved. Morg says you will know what it means."

"What kind of garment is it?"

"One of our own."

"What do you mean 'one of our own'? They could have obtained that garment through trade or purchase or even stolen it. What am I to glean from a Theorian garment?"

"It is the garment of a royal servant, brother," Sethos says grimly. "And there is a scroll with it that you will want to see."

RASHIDI AND MORG ARE ALREADY WAITING FOR them when Tarik and Sethos arrive at the day chambers. The blue dress lies on his table, and Tarik snatches it up immediately. It is Sepora's. It was the dress she wore the day she left Theoria on the back of Dody. It was the dress she wore the day he first kissed her, atop the great pyramid.

"They have Sepora," he says, more to himself than to the others present.

Morg stands and bows. "My king, they've also sent a message and . . . what appears to be a gift."

Tarik tears his eyes from the garment draped on the table to the offering Morg holds out for him. It's a figurine of fresh white spectorium, and it looks remarkably like Patra. New spectorium. Something even Serubel should be out of. *Have they found another Forger, then?*

"And the message?" Tarik says.

Morg hands that over as well. Tarik unrolls the scroll and immediately recognizes Sepora's handwriting and broken Theorian. He received enough correspondence from her during her stay in the harem so that he could choose hers from among a stack of parchments.

Greetings, Great Falcon King.

It is the wish of King Eron of Serubel to meet with you at a time and place of your choosing to discuss terms of peace and goodwill. Please send a response at your earliest convenience. His Majesty will guarantee the safety of any messenger.

Highest Regards,
Sepora

Tarik tosses the scroll on his desk and leans against it for support. There is no deception in the letter, but that doesn't mean it isn't a trap. Sepora could have written it truly believing that Eron wants peace. If that is the case, Tarik may not detect any duplicity. Did she flee Theoria with the intention of speaking with Eron all along? After all, she has been adamant against a war between the kingdoms from the beginning. She said before that she knew the king well and it had been the truth; does she have enough sway with him to convince him to pursue peace?

There are so many questions and so many risks. But the chance of a resolution between the kingdoms is too great a temptation not to at least hear out the king.

"Send three hundred soldiers to Kyra in case they mean to distract us with this visit while harvesting the Scaldling venom," he tells Morg. "Double the guards at the walls and have archers at the ready.

Send King Eron a messenger. He may break his fast with us in the morning, but he'll bring no more than a small personal guard with him. And the Mistress Sepora must accompany him."

"Highness, what if she was a spy for him all along?" Rashidi says. "What if this is a ploy to—"

"You underestimate me, Rashidi. I would have discerned if she was a spy. She happened upon us quite accidentally, of that I'm sure."

Rashidi lowers his eyes. "Of course, Highness. My apologies."

"You are right to be suspicious, my friend. We all must keep our wits about us. If peace is not his true desire, we must determine what is."

47

SEPORA

SUNLIGHT POURS INTO MY SLEEPING TENT AS Father himself opens the flap. "It is time, Sepora. I trust you're ready? You've Forged as we spoke of, child?"

I nod. I Forged early this morning and buried the evidence in a hole I dug inside my tent. Father wants me fully prepared, energized, my *wits about me*; for what I'm not sure. He is the king. He will be doing the negotiating.

As it were, I've been dressed and ready for several hours; my stuffy Serubelan attire nearly smothers me in the Theorian heat. I'd grown used to the scant clothing of this place and now I appreciate the necessity of it. But this soldier's attire? These pants and long-sleeved shirt embroidered with gold and red Serubelan colors, cinched at the waist with a length of rope—the only belt they could find? It borders on stifling now.

I've only been away for days, but the idea of returning to Theoria, of seeing Tarik again, wreaks mayhem on my insides, and I've nothing to do but ponder everything that has happened.

There is Father's new willingness to pursue peace instead of war, his willingness to speak with Tarik and negotiate a treaty. He's even spoken of opening up trade between Theoria and Serubel, of offering them fresh spectorium for their Quiet Plague. And what kind of person would I be to deny them that? I'd be preventing war and helping to ease the ravages of illness. It would be true peace. Surely Mother would approve of that.

He threw a banquet welcoming me home and honored my presence with a toast to peace. Indeed, Father is almost giddy with his new plans, as though a child with a new plaything.

Which makes me distrust him all the more. Never before have I so wished to be a Lingot.

But what more I can give for the sake of harmony, I do not know.

"We mustn't keep the Falcon King waiting, Sepora," Father is saying, pulling me by the wrist toward the entrance of my tent. This, and of course the secret Forgers of the freed slaves, are the only things I left out of my declaration to my father; that Tarik is kind and just, and not prone to violence or impatience. It would do my father well to think just the opposite, since nothing but fear seems to motivate him to do good. Let him think that Tarik would just as soon crush Serubel beneath his sandaled feet than to make peace with it. Let him wonder if Tarik will accept his offers of spectorium and open trade, or if he'll take what he wants, just as Father fears he will. Just as Tarik has the power to do.

Let my father think Tarik is just as greedy and power hungry as he is.

I also withheld the fact that Tarik is a Lingot. If I mistrust my father, Tarik must also; but he has the ability to discern his true intentions where I do not. I cannot take that advantage away from him now, not when it matters the most.

As we make our way to our Serpens, I spy Nuna, and my heart

swells. Father must have sent for her. I've missed my precious, ferocious-looking Defender. She greets me now by leaning her head into me for a caress, an action that earns me a disapproving look from Father. Still, he doesn't chastise me. I mount her and follow him as we glide smoothly into the sky. His indulgence makes me shiver. There was a time when I would have faltered under his glare. That time has far passed. But there is a gleam in his eye that speaks of false patience; I've seen that gleam before. It preceded many beatings, when he spoke of how I had fallen short of his expectations and of how long-suffering he was to deal with me so gently, when really, I should have been flogged.

Together, we fall in behind several soldier riders, with General Halyon at the head, mounted on a new Serpen, in case Tarik makes the unlikely move of attacking us in the air. I've learned that no matter if traveling by foot or by Serpen, the vast desert goes by slowly. Our tents disappear and the wall of Anyar makes a thin line on the horizon. The River Nefari flows as an unsubstantial thread to our right. Despite how I squint, I cannot see the shadows of any Parani lurking under the surface.

I wonder what Tarik is doing at this moment. What he is thinking, what he expects from me. If he'll even acknowledge my presence. But then again, his correspondence required my presence. Perhaps by now, he has discerned my deception. Perhaps by now, the Falcon King hates me for what I've withheld from him.

Soon we lower to the ground, just skimming over the wall protecting Anyar, and Halyon leads us in the direction of the palace. We maneuver through the Theorian sky as with familiarity; Halyon must have consulted his map a dozen times before we left.

Below, the people of the Bazaar stare up at us in wonder, gathering in crowds to watch us, a spectacle in the sky. From there, the palace comes into view, and it looks much grander from above. The care taken in the architecture of even the highest points is worthy of awe, an awe I had been too busy to enjoy before.

My nerves are on the edge of withering. I do not want to see Tarik again; yet, the very thought of him quickens my heartbeat as though I'd been running along the rope bridges back home or climbing the steep stairs of the great pyramid.

It stands to reason that if we indeed do make peace today, I may see much more of him than I ever had before fleeing Serubel. No doubt he'll bring his new wife for diplomatic visits out of his precious sense of duty. No doubt I'll be expected to entertain them as though nothing ever happened between us. No doubt I'll cry myself to sleep in my bedchamber after each dinner.

It seems I cannot have Tarik, yet I cannot escape him. I know what he meant when he said it was impossible to keep me, yet impossible to let me go. I've lived those words every day since I left. They are the words I think of when taking in a meal, when falling asleep, when waking to the morning sun. They are the words I dream. One moment I'm in his arms, and the next I'm taking flight away from him on the back of Dody while he calls after me to stop.

I square my shoulders. I will put that behind me. What happened between us cannot matter now. What we were is not what we are.

I am a princess of Serubel again. And I am here on terms of peace.

48

TARIK

THE KING OF SERUBEL SEEMS MORE AT EASE BREAK-
fasting in the grand dining room than Tarik would like. He is
exactly as Sepora had described to him before; his words are slip-
pery and full of false sincerity, yet they carry a forced respect that
is not counterfeit. He is afraid of the consequences of war with
Theoria.

Yet Sepora says nothing. She drinks from her goblet and pushes
food around her plate, never making eye contact with him. He owes
her much, he knows; she is the reason he is having this discussion
with the king of Serubel at all. She is the reason there may not be a
need for war in the first place.

And she is the reason he can concentrate on very little King Eron
has to say. Do the Serubelans always make a habit of wearing so
much clothing, which covers up all the delicious curves he'd taken for
granted all these months?

"My daughter tells me you've found a delightful new element.
Nefarite, is it?" the king is saying.

Tarik cuts his eyes to Eron. "Your daughter? Have you more than one?" Or had the rumors that the Princess Magar had fallen to her death been false? It could be that the second- or perhaps third-hand information he received on the matter had been faulty. He remembers his conversation about the princess, that perhaps she had been too dense to present to company. That had rung false in his ears. Perhaps all the mystery surrounding Magar had been contrived.

Eron laughs. "More than one? Saints of Serubel forbid! One is quite enough, thank you."

"Forgive me," Tarik says. "I was under the assumption that your daughter had passed away."

Tarik is not unaware that Sepora takes a large and very undainty gulp from her goblet.

"Why, you do not know, then? Surely that is not possible."

"What is not possible?" Sethos says, his plate of food untouched in front of him. He'd been brooding this entire time, and of course he would perk up at the mention of a woman.

Eron looks sincerely astonished. "Magar is my daughter. The Princess Magar Sepora. Yes, we did think she fell to her death, but as it turns out, she had the adolescent inclination to run away. Magar merely fled, and I must say, I'm glad she did so, now that we have a chance to speak so openly with each other."

Magar Sepora. Impossible. Yet, Tarik finds nothing misleading in the words. Sepora is indeed the princess of Serubel. He takes a sip from his own chalice, and then another, as pieces from their past together fall into place.

She'd said that the Princess Magar was a Forger and that they'd been close. There had been truth in her words. Underneath his skin, his anger catches fire and threatens to issue forth from him. Sethos cuts him a warning look, but why should he withhold his words? Has not enough damage been done from withholding words?

She could have Forged spectorium at any moment for him, given Cy a fresh supply to work with when combating the Quiet Plague. *She* could have prevented him from dismantling his father's final resting place, the last pyramid built of spectorium. Now his father rests in a dead pyramid, unfit for the great Warrior King.

It is *her* fault, all of it. She did not trust him enough to Forge. Clearly, she never believed in him, the way he had believed in her. He had acted a fool, had chosen to overlook her unwillingness to aid him, all in the name of love. He had been blinded. Even now, he wants so desperately to overlook all she has done—or not done, as it were.

Because he loves her. Yes, he's sure of it, as sure as he is that the sun will set over the Bazaar and that the moon will rise in its place. Against his will, he loves her.

At Tarik's continued silence, Rashidi clears his throat. "Well," Rashidi says, "this does come as a surprise to us all. Mistress—that is, *Princess*—Sepora did not mention that she was Serubelan royalty during her stay with us. But I suppose we can let bygones be bygones, don't you think, Highness?"

No, he wants to tell Rashidi. *They cannot.* But this meeting has nothing to do with his relationship with Sepora. This meeting is imperative to prevent a war. Imperative to prevent death among his people. This meeting is greater than he is at the moment. He must deal with his personal feelings later. He must put them aside and act as a king.

"Tell me," Tarik says, placing his hands on either side of his plate. "What can we do to open up trade between us again? We are in dire need of spectorium at the moment, as we have a plague ravaging our people, and spectorium is an important part of the cure for it. No doubt you've heard of it." Tarik is not sure which appears to please

Eron more: the prospect of Theoria having a plague or the fact that they need spectorium to cure it.

Beside him, Rashidi gives him a disapproving look for disclosing such a weakness, but Tarik suspects that if he shows a small amount of vulnerability to King Eron, the king will feel he's being generous in striking a deal—and will be more willing to do so.

Eron wipes at the corner of his mouth with his napkin and sets it back in his lap. He regards Tarik for several long moments before he says, "Our kingdoms have been at odds long enough, young Falcon King. It is my intent to end the animosity between us, here and now."

Tarik mulls the words over and over in his head, taking care to hide his reaction to them. "And how do you propose to do that?"

Eron smiles. "You will unite us by taking my daughter as your wife."

49

SEPORA

WIFE?

It takes all my effort not to choke on the fig I'd only just put in my mouth. I work to chew it into bites small enough to swallow and sip frantically at my water until the pieces slither down my throat, catching along the way so that I'm forced to cough. My cheeks burn hot as I feel all eyes on me. A servant behind me pours more water into my chalice but I wave him off.

Wife. This was supposed to be a meeting for peace and unity, an exchange of words, not an exchange of people. How dare Father put me in this position. After all I've done to save him, his kingdom, his rulership!

"That's an interesting proposal," Rashidi says neutrally. "But I'm afraid we've already negotiated a marriage with the princess of Hemut."

"Yes, Magar has informed me of this," Father says. "But I think you'll find a union between our kingdoms much more advantageous. Think of it, before you turn me away. You'll have a constant supply of spectorium, right at your fingertips. This Quiet Plague of yours will all but slip away from whence it came. We'll have a combined and virtually endless supply of Scaldling venom—or rather, cratorium, I believe you call it?—to use in case of war with other kingdoms. Together, we could be the most powerful force in all the Five."

Ambitious yet nebulous intentions, I can tell. Father may not be lying, but rather hides meaning in his words. He selects his phrases with a careful, fluid manner, as a soldier who would direct his blows with swiftness and precision. If I notice this, then Tarik surely will. And he will discern the truth from the deception. Which is why I did not warn Father of the Falcon King's Favor.

For his part, Tarik stares at me, and I at him, but neither of us will be the first to bend, to show an emotion regarding Father's inappropriate proposal of marriage. This is not the union with Tarik I had wanted. I had no idea Father would offer me up as a sacrifice, as collateral for a partnership, but of course he would. I should have anticipated his game. I should have known he would have a game to begin with. All his indulgences, the dinner banquet on my behalf, the patience he'd shown to what he'd considered impertinence. He'd been planning this all along. And he'd wanted to make sure I was in an agreeable mood when the time presented itself.

Tarik rests his gaze on Father. "Your offer is very generous, King Eron. Suppose I do accept this gift from you. The princess would be required to reside here in the palace. She would be my wife in every sense of the word. If she Forges, she will do it here."

If she Forges. And so the matter of business has begun. Who was I to think I actually mattered as a person to Tarik? He was going to marry another woman for the sake of his kingdom; to him, this would merely be an exchange, or rather an improvement, because of my ability to Forge. It is clear that is his utmost concern.

And it hurts worse than I care to admit.

Father nods. "I would agree to that, if, of course, distribution of the spectorium is split evenly between the kingdoms. And the nefarite?"

"If a union such as this were agreed upon, the nefarite would be made readily available to you, of course," Tarik is saying. "There would be the matter of supplying your own men to harvest it, though."

"Forgive me, Highness," Rashidi says, his face fallen pallid. After all, this turn of events threatens all the hard work he'd done in Hemut. "But we speak as though this is an actual possibility. Do not forget, we've an arrangement with the kingdom of Hemut. Theoria is only as good as its word. Tradition dictates that we stand by it."

Tarik takes a generous draught from his chalice. Setting it down, he looks at his adviser. "You're mistaken, my friend. Theoria is as good as its *strength*—as is any kingdom. And strength is what we will be securing in this arrangement."

"Highness—"

"The matter is settled," Tarik says sharply. "The princess and I will marry immediately. We will send word to Hemut along with the most lavish gifts to soothe the sting of rejection."

"And if they cannot be placated?" Rashidi says, glancing at me with a look of desperation. If he expects me to say something, he will be sadly disappointed. My ability to speak ended with the word *wife*.

Tarik smiles a smile that imparts a sort of cruelty I've never seen from him. "Perhaps the Princess Tulle will be content to marry my brother. He is a Theorian prince, after all."

Sethos bristles beside me. He'd made his dislike of Tulle very clear in front of me in Tarik's day chambers before departing for the Lyceum one day. I'd been surprised, as Tulle is reportedly the most beautiful woman in the five kingdoms—one of Sethos's weaknesses, if such a thing existed. But apparently the two of them had a squabble as children and he has not cared for her since.

"I'll not suffer through a marriage with that ostentatious halfwit, thank you," Sethos says.

Tarik pounds his fist on the table, something I've never seen before. Has everyone in this room gone mad? "You'll do as I command." This is not the Tarik I cared for. This is not Tarik at all.

"Excellent idea," Father says, slapping the table with a laugh. "Is it settled, then?"

"Yes," Tarik says, "I believe it is."

But Rashidi cringes—as do I. Hemut will not stand for this, I am sure of it. Sethos shakes his head; I can see that he is mentally washing his hands of his own brother. This does not bode well. Tarik needs Sethos and Sethos needs Tarik. He cannot dissolve the bond between himself and his older brother over this. I cannot allow that. I must speak to Sethos in private. We have both been wronged here; surely he will listen to me.

And that is when I decide that these two kings will not bully their way through the lives of all the rest of us. For I will marry the Falcon King and become his wife. I will do what it takes to stop the war between these two kingdoms, no matter the cost.

But I will not Forge for either of them.

50

TARIK

TARIK FINDS SEPORA IN THE MAKESHIFT STABLE built for her Defender Serpen Nuna while much grander accommodations are under way. For a time, he watches her as she pets the great beast and coos her affection into its ear. With this Serpen, she is gentle and kind. With Tarik, she has been venomous these past days.

He did not come here for an argument. Indeed, he wants to make peace with his future bride. But as she so clearly ignores his presence now, he thinks perhaps she needs reminding that *she* is the one who betrayed *him*. The one who had the cure for the Quiet Plague quite literally at her fingertips and yet she did not Forge an ounce of spectorium for that cause. If it had not been for Cy the Healer, the situation could have been much worse.

Had she stayed, would she have been able to watch people die? Would she still have kept her secret so close to her heart? And were she here in Theoria at the time, would she have allowed him to dismantle his father's pyramid? He dares not ask, for no matter what her answer, he will hear only the truth. And some truths he cannot bear the weight of. Only recently did he learn this about himself.

"Say your peace then leave me be," Sepora says finally without looking at him.

"I would have your full attention, Princess."

"Believe me when I say that you do."

He sighs, leaning against the wooden threshold. Sunlight spills in from behind him, casting a long shadow across Sepora and her Serpen. "I've come to inquire if your new quarters are satisfactory." She had been moved into the set of chambers reserved for the queen of Theoria, so she could become accustomed to the space that would be her own. The servants who had helped to settle her in said that she merely stated the rooms were "adequate." The entire east wing is dedicated to the queen and richly appointed more than any other set of chambers, including his own—"adequate" had been an insult to her attendants. One that he'd had to handle delicately, a balance between not reproving the future queen nor reproving the attendants for their sensitivity.

"They are adequate," she says.

"I'd hoped you'd find them luxurious. My mother took great delight in arranging them before she died."

At this, she turns to face him, her mouth drawn into a frown. "I did not know your mother had designed the chambers. She saw to every comfort imaginable. They are quite lovely. Thank you."

He detects remorse in her words; the last thing he wants is her pity. "Are you finding your servants agreeable?"

"Yes."

"You've not spoken much at dinner these past three nights."

"I've not been required to."

"Have I not been engaging enough to lure you into conversation?" He means to tease, but she gives him a dire look.

"I think we both know just how *engaging* you've been."

She is still sore with him about his intention to fulfill his obligation to marry Princess Tulle. And he's well aware that the manner in which their own marriage was arranged was quite distasteful. Perhaps one day, he'll make it up to her. Perhaps one day, they'll not be at such odds. But until then, until things are resolved between them, he must tread carefully with his future queen. For her sake, and for his. He thought he knew her nature. He thought he knew *her*. But there were many things Sepora was able to hide from him. He must take care that it doesn't happen again.

He takes a step forward. Nuna stirs, apparently uneasy with the chill of the atmosphere between them. "You did not make any objections to our union when it was being arranged. I assumed you were in agreement." He assumed nothing of the sort. Plainly she was shocked to silence. And sometimes silence is louder than words.

"Of course I wouldn't make any objections. You know I have always wanted peace between our kingdoms."

This hurts him more than he thought possible because there is no deception in her words. Of course the union had been advantageous from a ruler's perspective, and yes, he knew she'd wanted peace, but pride of the pyramids, he'd wanted *her*. More than anything else. And her father had made it so simple to have her. But he should have known, nothing with Sepora could be simple. Nothing with Sepora could be easy. She'd proven that time and again.

She agreed to marry him to keep the peace. To prevent what appeared to be inevitable war. She agreed to marry him out of duty. How very fitting his punishment. That he would marry another out of duty and expect Sepora to understand, and now *she* will marry *him* out of mere duty and expect him to understand. To accept that he will be in love with his wife, yet she will face him each and every day with the coldness of obligation and responsibility.

He'll not have it.

With little more than three strides, he consumes the distance between them. She seems startled at first, but then her eyelids seem to grow heavy and he does not miss when she glances at his lips. A blush sweeps across her cheeks and she steps back, but he will not relent; he eases forward. *This all could not have been for nothing. Surely losing her and gaining her is not the same thing.*

"Your father speaks riddles at me," he says. "He tells the truth with words and hides lies behind them. Tell me what you know."

She glares at him, her jaw clenched. "If you knew he was lying, why have you not said anything? Does he even mean for us to marry?" Her tone and manner suggest she asks these questions out of an honest need to know. That she suspected her father of lying as well. So then, she is not her father's accomplice in whatever his plans may be.

A sense of relief overwhelms him. He'd been afraid of just how much she could deceive him. That is, of just how much he'd been prepared to overlook. But what he came here for is answers. And with her questions, she has given him many.

"He does." Which is precisely why he hasn't called Eron on his deceptions. He will marry Sepora and deal with the king later. Rashidi is not in favor of this strategy. But Rashidi is not hopelessly in love with the princess of Serubel.

"Then what lies does he tell?"

"He means to have peace for now. There is deception in the word 'peace' but truth in the words 'for now.' I believe he has ill intentions after we marry."

"Why wait for him to act? Why not stop him now? He'll find out you're a Lingot soon. He'll learn to dance around the truth just as . . ."

"Just as you did?"

She lowers her gaze. "Your Favor is an unfair advantage. Sometimes deception is necessary."

"You didn't trust me."

"I'm glad for it. You made your motives clear. Truly, you have an impeccable sense of duty, Highness. It is much to be admired."

"I might say the same of you."

"Why, thank you, Highness."

He grinds his teeth. "I've tired of this absolute politeness between us," he whispers.

"Would you rather I be rude?" But her bluster falls flat. She won't quite meet his eyes.

"I would rather you be mine."

Her brows knit together, and she bites her lip. She does not want to have this conversation, he can tell. But he'll not let her out of it, either. Their wedding is just weeks away; this must be resolved. Something other than niceties must be exchanged between them, even if it is only understanding for now. She must know that she will be his, in more than just words. In more than just vows. Duty can rot in The Dismals for all he cares at this moment; he will no longer settle for a marriage of convenience. He will no longer settle for less than all of her.

Perhaps she never intends to return to him; perhaps she thinks things will never be as they were between them. But can she truly live with that? For the rest of her life, can she submit to mere polite exchanges and grace him with her presence only when etiquette requires it?

"I am yours, Highness," she says, bowing deeply, insincerity reeking from the action. "I'm completely at your disposal."

"Make me believe it."

"You're a Lingot," she says. "You know what I say is true."

"What you say is what duty requires of you. But what do *you* say, Sepora? If you were not the princess of Serubel, if I were not the Falcon King. If you could walk away from this without any sort of consequence. Would you walk away?"

Pride of the pyramids, but why would he ask such a direct question even as his heart squeezes at the answer on the tip of her tongue? But he has to know. He must know. Because everything he's about to do, every action he's about to take hinges on her answer. On her *real* answer.

He uses his finger to push her chin up, to look at those silver eyes of hers. They are on fire with things unspoken, with emotions swelling just below the surface of her collected poise. "Sepora, would you walk away?" he demands.

"Yes."

A truth.

And a lie.

ACKNOWLEDGMENTS

I think I'm not alone in saying that the acknowledgments are the most difficult part of the book to write, and not because I can't think of anyone to thank, but because of the sizable village of people who deserve my gratitude and special appreciations. If you are not mentioned here, it is not because I'm ungrateful; it is because sometimes my gray matter lets me down, even when it's time to recall important things, like you.

To begin, I'd like to say that *Nemesis* was written during a dark time in my life. I lost loved ones, endured medical issues, and even lost my love for writing. I wouldn't have regained that love if it weren't for my good friends Jessica Brody, Emmy Laybourne, and Leigh Bardugo. You know what you did, ladies. And I love you for it.

Also, I wouldn't have opened another Word document ever again if it weren't for my sisters, Lisa and Teri, whose endless encouragement would not be set aside, even while our family suffered through so much loss. I want the world to know that my sisters are fearless;

they will cry with you, laugh with you, and laugh *at* you, even at inappropriate times. For this, I cherish every moment with them.

There are people who come into your life that you know will change it forever. On January 27, 2011, I received a call from an agent, Lucy Carson, and I knew, just KNEW, that she would be one of those people. She's strict, she takes no BS, and she demands only my best. But she's kind, generous, and quick to laugh, and for all these things, Lucy, I thank you. Without you, there would be no book, no career, no success, no hope of a Sasquatch romance. Thank you!

Not to be outdone, though, I could not have made it to where I am now without my beloved editor, Liz Szabla. Liz, your patience and insights and ideas and sheer talent have been invaluable to me. I don't know how you balance keeping my writing in place with giving me such creative license; truly it's a gift you have. When I get notes from you, I feel so blessed, like I'm exactly where I should be.

Acknowledgments wouldn't be complete without including the outstanding publicity team at Macmillan Children's. Their ingenuity, thoroughness, and absolute enthusiasm for their work set them apart in every way. Thank you for hearing out my crazy ideas, and for taking the lead and showing me by example how successful a good marketing plan can be.

For Anna Booth and Rich Deas, this cover is amazing. I don't know what kind of sorcery you use to keep coming up with stunning covers, but there isn't a book yet that hasn't caused me to lose my breath when seeing my cover for the first time. Thank you.

To my critique partners, Heather Rebel and Kaylyn Witt, you are awesome and you pretty much know it. And now I've put it in writing, so you can hold it against me when I'm defending myself against your notes.

And last, but not ever (NEVER!) least, a huge group hug to all my fans and readers and book bloggers and supporters. Without you, there would be no acknowledgments. Without you, my world as I know it wouldn't exist. Thank you.

All My Best,
Anna

GOFISH

ANNA BANKS

Where do you write your books?

I have a personal home office where most of it gets done, but sometimes when a scene or plot point bothers me and I need new perspective, I'll either go to a bookstore or Starbucks to write. And if the situation gets really bad, then I'll rearrange my office so that I'm sitting in an entirely different attitude altogether. For instance, right now my desk overlooks the front yard, but I'm thinking about moving it to a corner to just overlook the rest of the room. A small change like that can give you fresh perspective.

Also, admittedly, I have been known to take my laptop and write in the bathtub. I'll bring a pillow and blanket to the garden tub and get in, especially when I'm under a tight deadline, because it's far easier to get settled in than it is to get out of a bathtub! So I make it difficult for myself to stop writing. It'd better be important if I'm going to wrestle myself out.

Do you ever get writer's block? What do you do to get back on track?

I don't call it writer's block per se. I call it writer's constipation, and here's why: If you push hard enough, at least a little will come out. And when you're pushing, push for at least 100 words. If you can press 100 words to the paper, you've accomplished something, and should reward yourself by reading a book. Reading is the best laxative, because it gets your creative juices flowing and flexes the writing muscle in a way watching television or YouTube can't. You're forced to notice sentence structure and voice when you're reading someone else's work, and you're forced to admit that you could do better yourself. By the time you get done with one chapter of reading, I bet you're ready to write again.

I also find that if you're stuck on a certain plot point, talk it out with your critique partners. You don't have to wait for another critique session to bounce something off them. You're actually doing them a favor by forcing them to think creatively out of nowhere, by flexing their writerly muscles as well. It's a win-win.

What would you do if you ever stopped writing?

This is a common question with an unusual answer, because most people might mean it as "What will you do when you retire from writing?" But have you ever heard of someone truly retiring from writing? I only ever hear of writers and authors passing away, never retiring. Because I think our minds are just inherently set up to create.

However, if circumstances did not permit me to write, I have a special love for dachshunds, so I would probably open a nonprofit, no-kill animal shelter or rescue organization for them. I could easily make that my next life course. But even if I stopped writing my own works, I would probably offer critiquing services for aspiring writers to help pay for my animal shelter. That would be ultimately combining two things I love dearly.

What is your favorite word?

Right now, my favorite word is *harvest* and not in the traditional sense. I like using it with snarky threats, such as, "If you don't shut up, I will harvest your tongue from your face and feed it to my dachshund." Or, "If he cheated on me, I would harvest his testicles and pickle them in a jar on my nightstand." Or, "Perhaps you could harvest the rest of your scattered brain from the air in your head and concentrate on the matter at hand." It's really easy to impress someone when you use the word *harvest* on them in an everyday sentence.

I also subscribe to the dictionary word of the day and try to use each word out of context in a sentence that day and see if anyone notices. No one usually does. And so it's my own personal amusement.

What's the best advice you've ever received about writing?

Writers write. That's it. That's what writers do. Not that we don't market and socialize and edit and critique. But THE most important thing we do is write. Because without writing, there would be nothing to promote. There would be nothing to socialize around. There would be nothing to critique.

I went through this phase once where I had so many great ideas. I kept sending my agent idea after idea, and she loved them. And one day she said, "Okay, which one are you going to write?" And that's when it hit me. None of them spoke to me enough to actually sit down in my office chair and start writing. They were just concepts. You see, anyone can come up with a concept. How many times have you met someone who's said, "I have a great idea for a book!" But how many times has that person actually sat their rear in the chair day after day after day and written said book?

Writers write.

Which brings me to the next great piece of advice: Write what you *want* to write. Don't write for trends, or what's hot right now. Write the story that will not leave you alone at night.

Write the story that wakes you up in the morning, that you think about as you commute to work, that makes you skip the toilet paper aisle at the grocery store because you had an epiphany for a plot point for it. That's what you need to write, because your best writing will come of it.

So, write. And write what you want.

If you were a superhero, what would your superpower be?

In the past, I would have written something badass or funny. But I'm taking this question seriously this time because of the state of the world we're living in. If I had a superpower, it would be to mind hop, and to just extend a calm sense of peace to everyone who is on the verge of doing something violent or saying something that might harm others. Not change their minds or their opinions, because they have a right to those. I'd just want to remove their hurt and implant empowerment, and, above all, love.

What book is on your nightstand now?

Well, I've got a Kindle full of romances and an iPad full of audiobooks, but the physical books on my nightstand right now are *Fangirl* by Rainbow Rowell, *The Lovely Reckless* by Kami Garcia, and *Nowhere but Here* by Katie McGarry. I've been swaying contemporary lately, as I'm gearing up to write one myself. ☺

What was your favorite book when you were a kid? Do you have a favorite book now?

My fave as a kid was *Anne of Green Gables*. My school had a bookmark-decorating contest, and I decorated mine with an under-the-sea theme (ironic?) that said "EVERYONE READS," and it won. The prize was that I could choose any book in the library, and I chose *Anne of Green Gables*. I read that book so many times. I always loved the swoon between Anne and Gilbert.

Now, my favorite book is *Graceling* by Kristin Cashore. I love the world-building, the character development, the romance, everything. I'm a total fangirl over her.

How did you celebrate publishing your first book?

When my first advance check came in for *Of Poseidon*, the very first thing I did was buy a new computer and desk and laptop, because I was determined to make writing my career and not just a one-hitter-quitter type of deal. So I looked at it as an investment into many more books to come. I am still, to this minute, typing on that same computer I bought all those years ago. ☺

The funny thing about my first book deal was that my mom thought the whole thing was a scam, even when that first advance check came in. She told me not to spend the money, because they would want it back soon. Sadly, she passed away just months before the book actually published and she could see it on the shelves. So each time I sell a new book, I buy her a new arrangement for her grave.

HAVING FORMED AN UNEASY TRUCE, WILL PRINCESS SEPORA
AND KING TARIK LEARN TO TRUST EACH OTHER IN TIME TO SAVE
THEIR KINGDOMS, THEIR RELATIONSHIP, AND EVEN THEIR LIVES?

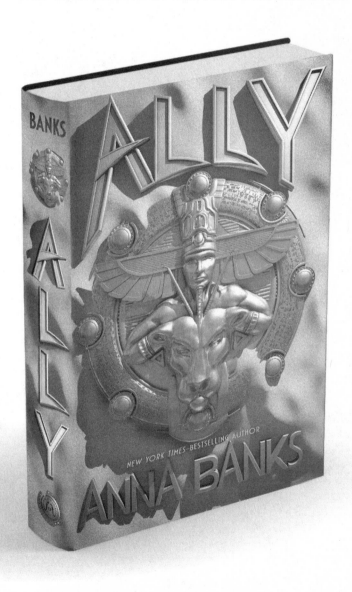

KEEP READING FOR AN EXCERPT.

1

S E P O R A

THE TIP OF SETHOS'S SWORD ALMOST CATCHES the bridge of my nose. As I sweep back, I use the inside of my foot to kick dirt in his face for daring to come so close to me. These are, after all, only practice sessions, and if he's going to test me this way, I'm most certainly going to return the favor. He glides to his left, an effortless movement, avoiding not only the sand, but the cloud of dust left in its wake.

I'm left infuriated and thrilled all at once.

I can't imagine there could be anyone faster than Sethos, Tarik's younger brother. I haven't seen many of the Master Majai train, as the king's highly skilled army of warriors spend their days at the Lyceum when not on duty, but of these Favored Ones I *have* watched from the balcony overlooking this courtyard, none are faster than Sethos, who only just turned sixteen. Even his shadow cannot keep up with his movements. I wonder whether his father, the Warrior King Knosi, was as nimble on his feet.

Sethos laughs. "Your antics might work—on a lesser warrior. But I'm afraid you'll have to do better than that, Princess, if you're going to overtake me."

We both know I'll never overtake him, no matter how much we practice. And we both know these lessons are not strictly for my instruction. Our sessions together bring us both relief from the delusions we used to call lives. There was a time once when we were both free to make our own decisions, free to marry whom we chose—or, at least, the illusion of that choice—and free to leave the palace walls.

Freedom now is like the hinge of a door rusted in place from lack of use.

Sethos's and Tarik's relationship has become strained. Where there used to be easy banter between them, it comes with sharper barbs and insincerity. Where there used to be shared opinions, Sethos takes the opposite side of Tarik, no matter the subject. It is difficult to watch sometimes, the deterioration of the affection these brothers once had for each other.

I shake my head, lowering my sword. Catching one's breath in the stifling Theorian heat seems almost as impossible as merely shaving Sethos with my sword. I want to graze him so badly, to at least nick him, anything to get that smug look wiped from his face. But other Majai cannot, and so when I get close, I know he is just toying with me. "Trust me when I say I'm doing my best," I tell him.

He makes a *tsk*ing sound with his tongue. I've come to abhor that sound, so mocking and condescending. "You know you're not. You know you could—"

"Do not say it," I hiss, lifting my sword again. I'm growing tired of this, the same conversation we have each session. He's bent on seeing me Forge, bent on teaching me to use my ability to protect myself. He insists that if I could produce spectorium fast enough, I could use it to scald my opponent. I suppose he's right. But even if I wanted to Forge, I couldn't. Not here in the open. I know it. Sethos knows it.

Our two impervious kings, Tarik and my father, have decided that my Forging should be kept a secret from the kingdoms. That my power, as the only Forger of spectorium, puts me in danger. And that my well-being is of the utmost importance.

Indeed. Tarik's sense of duty makes my well-being his concern. But Father? His intentions strike the opposite direction entirely. Every day, he grows impatient of my "well-being," threatening to chain me in the dungeon (the palace in Anyar, the heart of Theoria, has no such dungeon) until I Forge spectorium for him. He has thrown outrageous fits in our moments of privacy, demanding that I Forge, and when we are in the company of the Falcon King, he finds many diplomatic ways to suggest the same to Tarik. But for some reason, Tarik is not willing—not yet, at least—to force my hand. The Falcon King must think I will acquiesce, that I will give in and eventually supply him with the spectorium needed for the plague.

He is wrong.

I will no longer supply any of the five kingdoms with spectorium. Not Theoria for its plague nor Tarik's leverage, not Serubel for its economy nor Father's ambitions. The ice kingdom of Hemut will have to make do without the element, as will Wachuk and Pelusia, which I'm thankful have shown no interest in it in the past. The age of spectorium has ended.

I will no longer be used as a pawn in a game of power. And I will no longer trust anyone to decide what is and is not for my well-being.

Which, sadly, must include Sethos. How am I to know whether Sethos is secretly siding with Tarik, planning to bring him the fresh spectorium I Forge during our training sessions? Sethos, though one of my favorite people at the moment, is conniving and cunning enough to pull off such an act of betrayal. Perhaps that is why he constantly pesters me to Forge—Tarik has put him up to it. Though, the thought is truly unlikely. Sethos barely speaks to Tarik anymore, and while I'm not a Lingot as Tarik is, having the ability to discern the truth from a lie, I'm not a fool, either. It is plain that Sethos considers his older brother a tyrant—and the fact that Tarik has ordered him to wed the Princess Tulle of Hemut is irrefutable proof of that accusation. It came down as a royal order, one that the entire kingdom of Theoria knows about and one that Sethos cannot forgive his brother. No, Sethos is not trying to betray me. Not for Tarik.

Truth told, our practices together are the only time Sethos resembles himself anymore. Something happens to him after we finish—after we are sapped of energy and of sweat, after we've returned to our lot in life. When he arrives for the evening meal in the palace—another one of Tarik's requirements—he is sullen and quiet and bereft of charm.

He is no longer Sethos.

I know that it is his imminent marriage to Tulle that has him so depleted of his usual charm and so filled to the brim with ill temper. I cannot fault him there, for a marriage without love is what we are both facing, and the prospect of it makes most of my food lose its taste. But Sethos's circumstances are unique in that he actually despises his betrothed, whereas I have resolved to simply remain aloof. Any love Tarik and I once felt for each other has been twisted into something that resembles manners and diplomacy.

With Sethos, manners and diplomacy have never come easily.

"Why do you loathe Princess Tulle?" I immediately regret the question, which was blurted as an afterthought. I watch the moment he closes himself off to me. Our lesson is all but over now; I can see it in his eyes. Disappointment makes my sword even heavier.

He gives me an odd smirk when he says, "Don't worry, Princess. Tulle harbors no love for me, either. You're fortunate to be able to marry for love."

All at once, my face is full of warmth, a flush I know cannot be concealed. I should not have this reaction to Tarik, not after everything he's done. There was a time when I would have married him for love. But our time for loving each other has passed. And so has my willingness to marry him.

Yet Sethos grins wickedly. "You and my brother assume I'm blind, then? Did you know that you do not steal glances of each other no fewer than a dozen times at the evening meal alone?"

I lift my chin. I'd been working on that, not looking at Tarik. Not giving attention to his presence at all. And I've been failing, apparently. "I'm merely striving to be attentive. Perhaps you could set aside a portion of your busy day to reflect upon good manners." It is a blow, suggesting that Sethos is busy. He has been assigned to the security of the palace, and according to him, the place runs by itself. The only distraction he finds is when he feels of the mood to round up a group of guards, portraying himself as an intruder and tasking them with finding him, how he got in, and what he was after. This only serves to irritate him in the end; his ego does not allow him to be captured, and so the guards must resign themselves to another session resulting in failure with a Master Majai berating them incessantly. It is not good for anyone involved.

"Attentive?" Sethos is saying. "Your execution of 'attentiveness' is flawless, Princess. Coincidentally, so is my brother's."

I slide my sword into its sheath strapped across my back, as is the Theorian way. "If you are so proficient about judging everyone's apparent feelings, how is it that you could not secure the affection of Tulle?"

Sethos spits on the ground beside him. "Why are you so bent on seeing me tethered to someone as vile as Tulle? What have I ever done to you?"

"Aside from purchasing me for your brother's harem? Nothing. Why are you so bent on avoiding this discussion?" If I cannot beat him with a sword, I shall best him with words.

Or, perhaps not.

He closes the distance between us quickly, grabbing my arms before I can squirm—before I can even think of squirming. "Run away with me, Sepora. Run away with me tonight."

I try to step away, try to wriggle out of his grasp, but to no avail. His hands are large and my arms are small, and he has his shins and groin protected with platelets of copper. So much for learning to defend myself.

"We could settle ourselves in Wachuk. Make a life together there," he practically yells. "Say yes, and I'll see to it that you can bring Nuna, your glorious Defender Serpen. I'll never make you Forge. Not a drop."

I feel my eyes grow wide, darting frantically about the courtyard partly for help and partly to make sure no one is hearing this madness. "Sethos, has the heat gotten to you?" I hiss. "Let me go!"

"We'll make beautiful babies," he bellows, pulling me closer. I swear his shouting would wake the dead entombed in the pyramids on the other side of Anyar. "I want a girl with eyes just like yours."

Babies! If I kicked hard enough, surely the copper couldn't protect—

"If you ever wish to sire children at all, you'll unhand her directly," a familiar voice calls from behind. We both face Tarik, whose fury cannot be hidden by the golden body paint forced upon him by royal obligation.

Sethos releases me and laughs heartily. It's no wonder he was yelling. From his vantage point, he knew the moment Tarik arrived. Scoundrel.

"I'm going to kill you," I decide as I say it, reaching for the sword at my back.

But Sethos is already walking away and is, decidedly, not concerned. "You really must sport with my brother more often, Princess. As you can see, it's great fun," he says over his shoulder. When he passes Tarik, he doesn't deign to acknowledge him. But Tarik wouldn't have noticed anyway. He's staring at me now, as if I'm the one who'd planned to raise heathen children with his heathen brother in a heathen kingdom.

I cross my arms. "What are you doing here?" I nod to the bronze sundial situated in front of the courtyard wall, though I can't readily tell what it reads. "My lesson is not over."

Tarik raises a brow, making it a point to eye my sheathed sword. "Your tutor seems to think it is."

"You're early," I insist, nearly stomping my foot. The one liberty I do have is that I may practice self-defense with Sethos daily in the courtyard, though Tarik is not elated about extending this courtesy. Still, he does, and so I take full advantage of escaping the goings-on of the palace and my new place in it. When my lessons are cut short, I make it a point to be difficult.

"Your mother is early as well," he drawls. He is good at keeping his emotions to himself of late. His expressions, his body language. The Master Lingot Saen taught me how to learn like a Lingot to watch for these things, that there is more to what a person says than their words. But Tarik shows me nothing. If he is excited to meet my mother, or if he dreads it, I couldn't know. "Queen Hanlyn arrived moments ago by Serpen in the far courtyard. I thought you'd like to visit with her before the evening meal."

Queen Hanlyn. My mother. She wasn't scheduled to arrive until tomorrow; she'll be joining my father to attend the royal engagement procession, as is the custom in Theoria. In the procession, Tarik and I will lead by chariot what I'm told is a rather ostentatious exhibition of the throne's wealth and integrity, bestowing gifts on all of the citizens and, in effect, sealing my fate with Tarik. The thought of it brings shivers to me despite the heat. Or perhaps it is the look Tarik gives me now, one filled with curiosity—and something else I can't quite name.

Against my will, I hold his gaze. To back down now would be too telling.

To calm the sensations swirling in my gut, I try to focus not on his face, but on his words. It will be the first time I've seen my mother since she sent me on the journey to Theoria months ago. Her short visit to Theoria will reveal whether I have failed, and I'm more than curious to see whether she holds praise or wrath for me, with the outcome such as it is. Surely sacrificing myself in marriage will count for something. And it will be a relief to burden Mother with the task of keeping Father at bay where my Forging is concerned. She alone can handle him best, even at his worst, and if she cannot, she can at least manage to distract him long enough from his endeavors until she *can* handle him. But before we discuss the matter of my father, we must discuss the matter of Tarik.

That the great Falcon King is a Lingot, able to discern the truth from a lie.

And that as such, he *cannot* be handled.

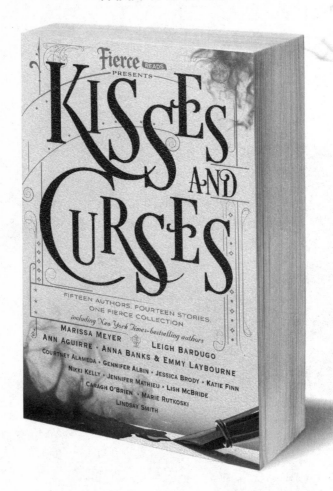